PRAISE FOR AARON N. HALL

THE WEVLIAN CHRONICLES

"Clean epic fantasy at its finest!"
—Kris, *The Fictional Escapist*

"A thrill ride of swords, kings, and prophecy. A story you won't want to miss."
—Alyssa Erin, *Everything But The Book Podcast*

"Readers will easily satisfy all of their mystical kingdom, godly dragon and usurped king cravings in this paperback tale."
—Mara Braddy, *Dixie Sun News*

THE HAMMERFIST SERIES

"I really enjoyed this super hero comedy from Aaron Hall. Hopefully he writes more stories in this engaging and unique fictional universe."
—Bryan Asher, author of *The Fear of Moncroix*

I'M SORRY, HERE'S A PLASMA RIFLE

"Cleverly weaving themes and lessons about humanity into stories of adventure and fantasy, *Plasma Rifle* becomes more than the sum of its parts."
—*The Fantastic Books Podcast*

"A delightful collection of stories that had me laughing, crying, and wanting to make a raspberry cheese danish."
—Tea & Tropes Podcast

LOVE LETTERS TO A HOUSE ON FIRE

"Hall's collection of short stories and poetry is filled with humor and heart."
—Cambria Williams, author of The Befallen

"I could not put this book down. The stories ranged from funny to serious to really thought provoking."
—TimWritesToday

THE LEGEND OF

Aaron N. Hall

This is a work of fiction. All characters, organizations, and events portrayed in this novel are either products of the author's imagination or are used fictitiously.

Copyright © 2024 Aaron Ned Hall. All rights reserved.

Published by IronFire Media LLC

ISBN-13: 979-8-9910978-1-9 (paperback)
ISBN-13: 979-8-9910978-0-2 (ebook)

Cover illustration by C. Alexander Larson

Map illustration by Joseph Spangler

This book is dedicated to four people:
Dad, Adam, Zach, and Brando.

The Territory of Uh

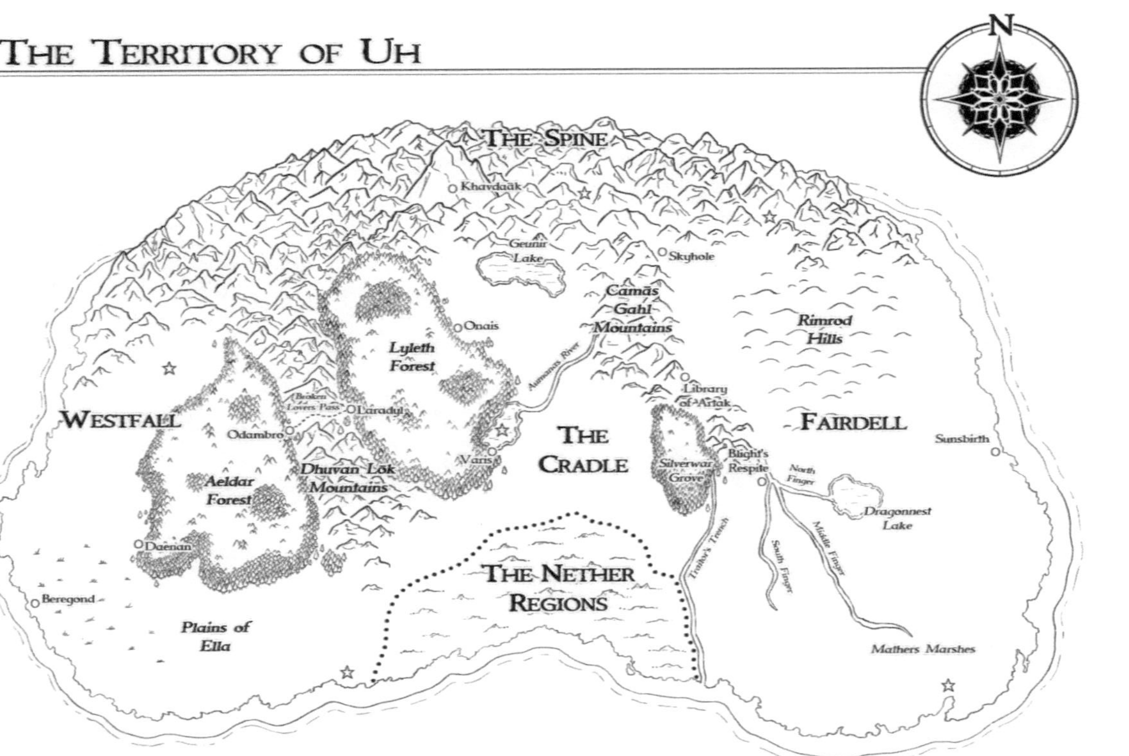

☆ - Temple of the Goddess

1

Fanfare, banners, and rousing cheers. Among it all, DJ let out a thick sigh.

He dragged his boots across the red carpet as scores of townspeople flanked him on either side, whistling and throwing confetti. A battalion of brass players filled the sky with triumphant song. A regal red cape fluttered around DJ's heels. He stared at the ground while he walked and tried to keep his hands out of his pockets.

Although everyone cheered, no one paid him much attention.

Before he reached the front of the crowd, he stole a glance to his left. A handsome, well-dressed man with flowing blond hair, sapphire eyes, and a perfect smile wore a matching red cape to DJ's. People around him patted his back and shook his hand and congratulated him. The man stole a glance at DJ, winked, and gave a subtle thumbs up. DJ returned the gesture with a sheepish grin.

After a few more steps, DJ reached the end of the red carpet. Above him, seated on a lifted dais, was Master Maeser. His thin silver hair fell to his shoulders, and when he stood from the throne, his round belly jiggled under his royal purple garbs. When he steadied himself, he lifted his hands. The crowd hushed.

"Hear ye, one and all!" Master Maeser said. "Tonight, we gather in the plaza of Beregond to honor Dashing Junior, son of the legendary, heroic, enviable, and beloved hero, Sir Dashing Senior!"

A swell of cheers from the crowd. DJ sighed again.

"Ever since his retirement nearly sixteen years ago," Master Maeser continued, "Sir Dashing Senior has provided his wisdom, strength, and service to the good people of this city. For which we are ever grateful."

More cheers.

"And since he has already been knighted once, we have chosen to knight his son as a way of honoring him a *second* time!"

A polite smattering of applause, followed by an errant cough. DJ tried not to shrivel at the lack of enthusiasm.

"Dashing Junior," Master Maeser said, "step forward!"

With drooping shoulders, DJ stepped up to the dais and knelt. His messy black hair dangled past his face, and his emerald eyes stayed focused on Master Maeser's polished boots. The flat of Master Maeser's blade dropped onto his shoulder. It would have felt like a tap to any other knight, but against DJ's wispy fifteen-year-old body, it was almost like a slap.

"From this day forth," Master Maeser said, "you shall no longer be known as Dashing Junior. On behalf of your father's heroism and continued service, you shall be known as *Sir Dashing Junior!* Arise!"

Half-spirited cheers, followed by whispers and snickers. DJ frowned at them as he stood up. Master Maeser slipped the sword into a scabbard and extended it.

"You know how to use one of these?" he asked, only loud enough for DJ to hear.

DJ looked away. "Uh—sort of, Master Maeser."

"Great. It's all yours, kid." He shoved the sword into DJ's hands, clapped him on the shoulder, turned him around, then pointed to his father. "Three cheers for Sir Dashing!"

The town erupted again. "*Hip hip, hooray! Hip hip, hooray! Hip hip, hooray!*"

Through the cheers, not a single eye was on DJ. All the residents of Beregond were focused on Sir Dashing Senior, the beautiful blond-haired man on the front row. The townspeople lifted him on their shoulders, his knightly red cape falling onto their faces. The knight laughed along to their hips and hoorays.

Forcing a grin, DJ reached inside his cape and lashed his new sword around his waist. "Congratulations, Dad," he mumbled.

"Let the feast begin!" Master Maeser proclaimed.

An army of servants hauled tables, benches, food, and barrels into the plaza. The area became a bustling hive of celebrating townspeople finding their places at tables or dancing on the cobblestone streets. Minstrels filled the air with music that mingled with laughs, clinking dishes, drinking songs, and shuffling feet. The smells of roasted pork, seasoned vegetables, and grainy ale wafted through the air. They made DJ salivate.

By the throne dais, a special table was prepared for Master Maeser, Sir Dashing, and DJ. Barmaids filled up plates for the honored guests, starting with Master Maeser and Sir Dashing. Master Maeser wasted no time diving into a turkey leg, grease dribbling from his mouth with every bite.

Sir Dashing nudged DJ with his elbow. "Congratulations!" he said brightly, leaning in. "You must be feeling pretty special about now, eh?"

No. Not even a little. "It's nice. Thanks, Dad."

"You know, I wasn't much younger than you when I was knighted," Sir Dashing mused. "I think I was twelve… thirteen? Goddess, it's been so long, I can hardly remember… Ah, thank you, my dear!"

A barmaid set a plate loaded with steaming meat and vegetables in front of Sir Dashing. She batted her eyes. He winked at her. Then she blushed and sauntered away. DJ rolled his eyes. Sir Dashing was about to start on his meal when a commoner called from a nearby table.

"Sir Dashing!" the man said. "Come! Tell us one of your stories!"

Sir Dashing's eyes lit up. He put his hand on DJ's shoulder. "I'll be right back! This will hardly take a moment!"

He took his plate and vaulted over the table with the grace of a dancer. DJ watched as commoners gathered around Sir Dashing to hear another tale of slaying monsters or rescuing maidens. DJ drummed his fingers on his new sword while he waited for a barmaid to serve him a plate.

As he studied the blade, he realized that along the cross guard, his name was engraved. But *Sir Dashing* was finely etched and *Junior* was crudely engraved, as if someone forgot to add *Junior* until it was too late. He scowled and put it away.

Minutes went by and Sir Dashing was still unraveling tales at the nearby table. More people had gathered to listen. Meanwhile, DJ's stomach growled and the space before him remained empty. He tried to catch a barmaid's attention several times, but they either ignored him or didn't hear. He stole a glance at Master Maeser just in time to watch him bite into a particularly plump tomato. The tomato popped like a zit and red juice dribbled down his fat chin.

DJ grimaced and looked back out to the crowd. Even at his knighting ceremony, it was like any other day. Everyone was enraptured with their own groups of friends or with the tales of his father. As far as they were concerned, DJ didn't exist. The newest Knight of Beregond wasn't worth a glance.

When DJ felt his stomach gurgle again, he spotted a table full of food down among the commoners. He scowled and pushed out his chair. He stomped toward serving table and squeezed himself between two oblivious townspeople. He loaded an empty plate with potatoes and mutton when he heard two boys jabbering nearby.

"He's so wimpy and small!"

"It's amazing he's Sir Dashing's son."

"Doesn't have a drop of his father's blood, if you ask me."

"He better enjoy tonight—there's no way he'd be knighted otherwise!"

Both boys laughed. DJ frowned deeper. The words weren't anything new. *Nothing like his father. Can barely lift a sword. Skinny, scared little DJ.* The words swirled until they formed a knot in DJ's chest. He gathered a morsel of courage and grabbed a potato to throw it, but the courage disappeared and he set it back down. With a huff, he weaved through the crowd toward the clock tower in the middle of the plaza.

The door to the clock tower was locked, but DJ found the key between a crack in the bricks. He slipped inside and climbed the stairs. There, on the top level, three giant clock faces stared out on the city. In front of each clock face, a narrow catwalk circled around the tower.

He went to the west clock—the one facing the sea. Beneath him, the city of Beregond sprawled out for miles, with stone buildings packed like pebbles inside a wall marking its vast perimeter. There were ships out at sea, sliding along the sunset-orange water like feathers on a pond. DJ watched them as he ate his dinner. His feet dangled forward and back off the catwalk's edge.

Footsteps approached from behind. DJ didn't flinch or look—he recognized the owner by the footfalls. The owner sat next to him with her feet dangling as well, then she blew a raspberry. "Some party. Look what I got."

DJ turned to find two things. The first was Riley. Brown hair fell down the sides of her narrow face and freckles peppered the bridge of her nose. Her thin lips formed an impish grin. The second thing DJ noticed with the full bottle of wine she clutched in her fist.

He smiled. "Something tells me you didn't take that with

permission."

"My best friend got knighted today." She smirked deviously. "You can bust me out if they throw me in the dungeon. Cheers."

She *popped* the bottle open and the two of them watched the cork fall upon the crowd. It disappeared among the celebration. Riley took a long swig of the wine and passed it to DJ.

"To the greatest knight in all of Uh!" she mused, "Sir DJ of Beregond, the Underwhelming!"

"Ha ha ha," DJ mocked as he took the wine and drank. He shook his head. "You know, I've got to be the only person in the history of Uh that got knighted on behalf of someone who's *already* been knighted before."

"Yeah, everyone's obsessed with your dad." Riley shrugged. "I saw the whole thing with the barmaids. I was about to punch them in the nose and serve you myself when I saw you leave. I knew you'd end up here, so I was kind of glad." She smiled. "Our spot is way better than that stuffy crowd down there anyway. Everyone smells like alcohol and manure."

It was the way she looked at him and smiled. It didn't happen often, but when the light hit her face just right, illuminating her fair skin and chestnut eyes, it made DJ's heart sigh. He always wondered why more boys weren't trying for Riley's affection. Maybe they were afraid of being put in a headlock or receiving a bloody nose. Having six older brothers doesn't help, either.

"What?" she asked.

DJ shook out of his stupor. "Nothing. Hey, they gave me a

cool sword, though."

"Oooh, let's see it! What the… they added the *Junior* after the fact. I'm sorry, Deej, that's so stupid."

DJ let out another heavy breath as he rubbed his red cape between his fingers. "What's the point of being knighted if no one respects you like one?"

"Don't take it personal. This city is full of idiots."

"It sucks having a famous dad," DJ continued to think out loud. "Everyone expects me to be just like him, but look at me." He gestured to himself. "Not exactly dragon slaying material."

"I dunno about that," Riley smirked again. "You could lull a dragon to sleep with your boring personality, then sneak up and go for the kill!" She jabbed his chest with her finger.

DJ tried not to smile and pushed away her finger. "You're the worst. Come on, you know what I mean."

"Maybe fighting monsters isn't your thing—" Riley leaned back. "—but there's got to be something knightly you could do. Your dad has basically just sat on city council meetings for sixteen years."

"He's also *Sir Dashing*." DJ twinkled his fingers as he said it. "His adventures are still talked about. I swear he's saved every village in Uh at least once. What could I even do?"

"Beats me." Riley shrugged. "But listen, if it takes you out of this city, you have to take me with you. I'm not going to learn to be a ranger by baking bread with my father every day. If I'm going to learn to hunt and track, I need to get out of Beregond."

DJ smiled. "Riley, if I were to go on any kind of quest,

you'd be the first person I'd bring. Besides, your face is scary enough to ward off anything that might hurt us."

Her nose scrunched as she suppressed a laugh, then she punched DJ's shoulder. As both of their giggles settled, Riley draped her arm around his shoulders and leaned her head against him.

"I'm sorry tonight sucks, Deej," she said softly. "But for what it's worth, you're a knight to me."

DJ tried to smile. "Thanks, Ri."

*

The next morning, DJ drifted down to the kitchen. His bare feet clapped along the polished marble floor, surrounded by walls of chestnut wood. Statues and paintings hung every-where, along with trinkets and gifts his father had received from his wonder years. Sir Dashing purchased this mansion in Beregond's upper district twenty years ago with the hoard he got from slaying two dragons simultaneously. It seemed on brand for him, so DJ never questioned it.

The kitchen featured stone countertops and two large ice boxes. There were also shelves upon shelves of perishable foods. From a shelf, DJ took a bag of oat clusters and found a jug of goat's milk in an ice box. He took both to the dining room, where he sat at the end of a long table and poured both contents into a bowl. The oat cluster crunched pleasantly in his mouth. Above him, eight dragon heads were mounted on the wall, snarling inanimate breaths.

A knock came to the door. DJ frowned. He left his bowl

of oats and milk and crossed the floor. When he opened the door, at least a dozen beautiful women were crammed shoulder-to-shoulder, giggling like excited schoolgirls. They all craned their necks to get a peek inside the house.

DJ's eyebrows furrowed. "Can I help you?"

The woman at the front hardly looked at him. "Is this Sir Dashing's house? We heard he lives here! Are you his boy servant? Could you get him for us?"

DJ slammed the door, locked it, and went back to his breakfast.

Minutes later, Sir Dashing came sauntering down the stairs, looking pleased as punch and well-rested. He stretched his long, strong arms and shook his head, letting his golden locks fall to his shoulders. His wide chest peeked out through two popped buttons on his nightshirt, revealing a manicured tuft of chest hair.

"Oh, what a night!" he said. He caught DJ's eyes. "Ho there, Son!"

DJ waved lazily.

Sir Dashing pulled a seat next to DJ and grabbed his son's shoulder. "Where did you go last night? By the time I returned to our table, you were gone!"

"Riley and I hung out instead."

"I know she's your friend, but it was your *knighting* ceremony! It's customary to sit at the honorary table! The barmaids serve you and the minstrels sing songs for you... It's special!"

"Dad," DJ gave him a look. "Let's be honest, it was *your* knighting ceremony. Your second one. No one in this city cares whether or not I exist." He paused. "What did you do to first get knighted, anyway?"

Sir Dashing pushed his fingers through his perfect hair. "Goddess, what did I do? I must have been twelve, thirteen? There was a dragon plaguing a village outside of the Aeldar Forest. That one." He pointed to one of the heads mounted above. "Then there was the troll blocking Broken Lovers Pass —stopped commerce for weeks. You don't want to mount those, though. Unsightly. I don't remember which came first."

"What knightly things could I do?" DJ asked.

Sir Dashing fell quiet. He scratched the grain in the dining table then said, "DJ, you're already knighted. You were given your cape and sword last night."

"But I haven't *earned* it, Dad. People still tell jokes behind my back. How could I actually earn my title?"

Sir Dashing folded his arms and shook his head. "I'm not quite sure, Son. To be terribly frank, being knighted involves a great deal of heroics, danger… blood and steel!" He shook his fist theatrically. "You're just… not built for that, as it is. But who knows? Maybe if you start pumping iron with your old man, we could build that little body of yours!"

DJ deflated. "You're sure there's nothing?"

Sir Dashing got up from the table. "Perhaps a service quest of some sort? But even then, traveling across Uh is a dangerous thing. Who's to say that you won't encounter a giant or dragon or troll? You'd be crushed!" He let the moment hang, then he snapped his fingers. "Say, why don't you visit the Stewards at the monastery? Stewards of the Goddess have a long history of assisting knights on heroic quests. Perhaps they'd have some insight for you."

DJ flexed his lower lip and nodded. "All right. Thanks, Dad."

"Hey." Sir Dashing winked and pointed at DJ. "You're a knight to me! And I'm one of the best. A hall-of-famer."

"You're also my dad, so you're biased."

"Regardless! I'm going to go do my thousand push-ups for the day. Let me know what the Stewards say, kiddo!"

DJ got dressed and left the mansion, making his way for the monastery. The city of Beregond was crisp and chill this early in the spring—the last of the snow had only melted weeks ago. He walked through the plaza where everyone celebrated last night. As he went, no one gave him any congratulations or hellos. DJ did catch the attention of some girls that frowned disgustedly as they noticed him. His cheeks turned scarlet and he turned away.

The monastery was a modest plot of land marked by a stone fence that ran its perimeter. A single gate opened to a courtyard that included a fountain and a well-tended garden. Stewards of the Goddess, all dressed in identical brown robes cinched at the waist, worked around said garden. When they noticed their visitor, they politely smiled and waved. DJ returned the gesture.

At least the Stewards are always nice, he thought.

Looking around, DJ caught the eye of the nearest Steward and approached him. "Excuse me, priest?"

"Oh, I am not a priest!" the Steward replied rather loudly. "Although the Goddess smiles brightly upon me, I have not yet earned the title of priest! I am but a friar! Friar Steve is my name!"

As DJ got closer, he got a better look at Steve and tried not to stare. The man was shorter than average, with no chin, a lazy eye, and an aggressive bald spot. He carried a basket of vegetables and walked toward the nearby chapel.

"Uh—nice to meet you, Steve," DJ said. "I don't know if you heard, but my knighting ceremony was yesterday."

"Congratulations, young knight!" Steve hollered. "We Stewards do not engage in such revelry to keep us focused on our worship! But I must commend you for your heroics!"

Sheesh, does this guy yell everything he says?

"Thanks, but that's kind of the thing. I'm a little short on heroics. Do you have a leader I could talk to, or…?"

"Father Tuckett!" Steve smiled and jolted so hard that he nearly dropped his basket. "I will take you to him! Follow me, young knight!"

DJ thanked him and trailed close behind. He noticed that as he followed Steve, other Stewards tended to give Steve strange looks… as if they were trying to avoid him but be gentle about it. DJ didn't blame them. Steve already felt like a lot, and DJ had only known him for a minute.

Inside the chapel, a Steward played an organ, filling the hall with reverent music. There were pews arranged in neat rows facing the front. Multiple priests, priestesses, and friars sat in those pews, heads bowed in prayer. At the front of the chapel, a podium stood in front of a statue depicting a triangle pointed upward and a radiant sun shining behind it.

Steve took DJ to the front pew, where a man with a long beard and gray hair sat with his hands pressed together. His breathing was deep and restful. A blue sash hung around his neck and gave him an air of authority. He remained calm and still, deep in prayer.

Steve gestured to him and his mouth blasted. "Father Tuckett! Young knight here to see you!"

Everyone gasped and jolted. Even the organ player fumbled with a chord. Father Tuckett clutched his chest and tried to breathe as he suppressed his ire. DJ got the impression that Friar Steve made this a common thing.

"Thank you, Friar Steve," Father Tuckett said. "You are... welcome to go." He swallowed. "Hello, young knight. I don't believe we've met."

"Sir Dashing Junior. Most people call me DJ. Or ignore me completely."

Father Tuckett's eyes brightened. "Ah, the son of Sir Dashing! How lovely to make your acquaintance! Shall we walk? Tell me how the Stewards of the Goddess may serve you today."

By the time the two of them left the chapel, Steve was nowhere to be found. DJ turned to Father Tuckett and asked, "What's the deal with Friar Steve? Does he yell *all* the time?"

"He can't help himself," Father Tuckett replied delicately. "From what he remembers, he fell on his head many times as a child, which gave him his rather loud condition. That all happened before he came wandering into our grounds. His parents left him behind when they departed the city. Never came back for him, either. Tragic, really. We took him in and taught him the ways of the Steward, and he adopted them quickly. He dreams of becoming a priest, our dear Steven, but he keeps failing the examinations. Goddess give him patience." He grinned gently. "Forgive me, I'm rambling. What's on your mind, young knight?"

"So, I just got knighted yesterday."

"I heard there was a celebration. Congratulations."

"Thanks. But I didn't really do anything to *earn* it. They just knighted me because they couldn't knight my dad twice."

"Your father *is* quite the specimen."

DJ sighed. "I know."

"He's strong, tall, handsome—"

"I know."

"—charming, brave, reliable—"

"I *know.*"

"—resourceful, witty, a voracious lover—"

"I *know!* But I need something to actually become worthy of my title. Until I do, no one is going to take me seriously. But I'm not built to fight monsters or rescue maidens, so I need something different." He paused. "Wait, how do you know that my dad is a voracious lo—"

"Sir DJ, there was a time not long ago that Stewards of the Goddess accompanied knights on sacred quests." Father Tuckett walked with his hands behind his back. "Have you considered such a journey?"

"Kind of, but my father advised me against it. Said I'd still run the risk of getting into fights with trolls or whatever."

"Perhaps, but if you're accompanied by a *party*, that assuages the danger." Father Tuckett stopped and faced him. "By yourself, yes, I would not advise it. You are small and frail and don't cross me as terribly brave." DJ glowered, but Father

Tuckett didn't notice. "But with a small party of experienced adventurers, it could be a tremendous opportunity."

DJ nodded. A party. A group of adventurers. That sounded good. Sir Dashing had to be connected with loads of people that could take DJ on a quest.

"So," DJ asked, "just wander around territory with a bunch of adventurers for a while? That's it?"

"Not exactly. You'll need a mission—a divine purpose." Father Tuckett's eye glimmered. "Come."

DJ followed Father Tuckett into the dining hall where most of the Stewards ate. At a long wooden table, Stewards dined on bowls of porridge with the occasional tart or apple. At one end of the table, DJ noticed Steve eating by himself, but he didn't appear lonely. As a matter of fact, Steve seemed to be attempting a speed record on porridge consumption. All the other Stewards kept their distance to avoid the messy collateral.

"Here," Father Tuckett pointed. "Look."

On one of the walls, a giant map of Uh stretched a dozen feet long. The map of the bean-shaped territory was detailed with every forest, mountain range, lake, city, and region. DJ saw the city of Beregond on the far west side—the Jewel of Westfall. In the middle of the territory was the Cradle, with its forests and lakes. East of that was Fairdell, an expanse of marshes and hills that took up the eastern third of the territory. Along the south part of the territory was the Nether Regions, rumored to be uninhabitable to non-orcs. And all along the northern edge of Uh, the Spine stretched with its lengths of tall, harrowing mountains.

Along the map, six stars were dotted in various locations.

"These stars represent Temples of the Goddess," Father Tuckett said. "And each Temple contains a sacred Artifact of the Goddess—a piece of her garb that she shed after she created the territory eons ago. There are six Artifacts in total: the Robes, the Sandals, the Bracers, the Helm, the Amulet… and the Brassiere."

"So I should go visit one of the Temples?" DJ said, eyes brightening. He pointed to two of the stars in Westfall. "What about those? They're pretty close."

Father Tuckett nodded slowly. "You could, but if you truly want to be respected as a knight, I'd recommend *that* one." He pointed to the star on the eastern edge of the Spine, thousands of miles from Beregond. "That is the Temple of the Amulet. If you venture for the Amulet of Uh, to handle it and see it for yourself, that should take you through every region of the territory. *That* is a quest worthy of knighthood."

A smile spread across DJ's face. The pieces were coming together. A quest for the Amulet, visiting every region in Uh —it had all the ingredients of a knightly quest. But his smile faded.

"Wait," he said. "Isn't every Temple guarded by something, though? I've heard stories about would-be knights getting killed by creatures guarding Temples of the Goddess."

"Most Temples are guarded, yes. Like the Temple of the Brassiere." Father Tuckett pointed to the star near the middle of the Spine. "Don't *ever* venture to the Temple of the Brassiere! No man entering the Temple of the Brassiere has ever returned! Not even your father would dare!" He gathered himself and pointed to the previous star. "The Temple of the Amulet is perfect for your needs. That Temple isn't guarded—you can simply walk in. There used to be a creature that asked a riddle, but a knight might have killed it or it's been on holiday for a couple hundred years.

"Anyway, I would recommend assembling a party of adventurers—three to five, including yourself—and make your way to the Temple of the Amulet. Visit every region of the territory on your way: Westfall, the Cradle, the Nether Regions, Fairdell, and the Spine. When you return, the people of Beregond will see you for the knight you are. I'm sure of it."

The grin returned to DJ's face. Everything was lining up. With a party of adventurers to protect him, DJ could go there and back in six to eight months. Besides, experienced adventurers would know the safest ways around the territory, so they could avoid anything big and mean that wanted to treat them like a snack.

DJ couldn't hide his excitement. "Thanks, Father Tuckett. This is great news."

"The pleasure is mine, young knight. Say hello to your father for me."

DJ shook his hand before he sped out of the dining hall. He left the monastery and kept running down the cobblestone street, mind buzzing. He didn't stop until he reached a bakery in the lower district of Beregond.

He threw open the door with a crash, and everyone inside stared. DJ ignored them and advanced to the front counter. His face was red and sweaty from running, but it couldn't mask his delight. He slapped both hands on the counter and his eyes flashed.

"I'm going on a quest for the Amulet of the Goddess," DJ said. "And *you* are coming with me."

Behind the counter, Riley's hair was up in a bun and her apron was coated with flour. When DJ said the words, a smile spread across her face. She said, "Can't wait."

2

"Yeah, I could have handled that better," DJ said.

Riley shook her head. "I don't think it would have made a difference."

Up in the clock tower, both of them let their legs dangle over the catwalk as they faced the sea. DJ lay on his back, his head in his hands as he stared up at the clock hands. Riley picked out hardened crumbs of dough stuck under her fingernails.

"What did your dad say?" Riley asked.

DJ shrugged. "He was hesitant but eventually agreed to it. He told me I'll need at least two people in my party: a healer and a strongarm. The healer should know restoration magic, not just medicine, so they can throw a healing spell in a pinch. And the strongarm should be someone who's seen a lot of combat. Scary. Intimidating. And it's best if they have a lot of travel experience, too."

Riley flicked away some dough crumbs. "I'm so mad that I

can't go with you. Dad lectured me for an hour when we got home from the bakery that day." She put her fists on her hips and mocked his voice. "'It's not safe for a girl out there! You want to be kidnapped and sold to a whorehouse? Stop with this ranger funny business. We need you here!'" She blew a raspberry. "With my six brothers to help? Yeah, right."

"I'm gonna miss you so much," DJ said. "The journey to the Temple of the Amulet could take months. I'll send you ravenpost at every town we visit."

"You better." Riley looked at him with eyes full of envy and admiration then went back to her nails. "So have you found a healer and a strongarm?"

DJ laid back down. "About that…"

He went on to recount the conversation he had days ago that led to his second monastery visit. Sir Dashing had told him that every Steward of Uh is trained in restoration magic, and some of them have travel experience from transferring to different monasteries. When DJ asked Father Tuckett about any potential volunteers, the answer flew off his lips.

"*Friar Steve!*" the priest blurted. "Yes, I'm sure Friar Steve would love to accompany you on your journey!"

They stood together in the mess hall. When the Stewards overheard the prospect of Steve's departure for an extended period, their faces brimmed with anticipation. Steve himself was sitting at a table, spearing potatoes with a fork when he heard his name across the room.

DJ tried not to grimace and lowered his voice. "Steve? Really?"

"Oh, yes," Father Tuckett nodded enthusiastically. "Steve

is a wonderful Steward. And this may be his opportunity to finally prove himself worthy of becoming a priest! A journey across Uh with a young knight? Marvelous! He's a competent cook, understands medicine… I'm sure he'll be a wonderful addition to your party! You should take him along." Father Tuckett leaned in and whispered. "*Please* take him along."

DJ didn't look at Steve—he didn't want the loud friar to see the displeasure riddled across his face. But the prospect of spending every day with a loud and clumsy friar sounded like a trial in and of itself.

"You're sure there's no one else?" DJ asked.

Father Tuckett shook his head. "Everyone else is busy. It has to be him. Yep."

DJ scratched his neck and imagined what traveling with Steve would look like. All the yelling would probably give him headaches. Maybe he could wait until another Steward was available. But when might that be? Weeks, months? It wasn't possible if he wanted to go to the Temple and back before winter. It had to be Steve. He let out a defeated sigh. "Well, all right. Guess I better go talk to him."

He approached Steve's table. He sat down across from the friar and laced his hands together. Steve stared back at him with big eyes, a potato skin dangling from his lips.

"Hey, Friar Steve. You remember me, right?"

A loud *gulp* and suddenly Steve's foghorn was available. "Of course I do! Young knight! The honor is mine once again!"

"Do you know any healing spells?" DJ asked. "I'm looking to go on a quest across the territory to the Temple of the

Amulet, and I'll need a healer to come along. Father Tuckett said—"

"I know many healing spells!" Steve yipped excitedly. "I once healed Friar Tomlin's broken leg when I bumped him off the roof! I'm well-versed in healing techniques, both novice and intermediate!"

"Nothing advanced, though?"

"I continue to learn!"

DJ thought and nodded. "Okay, so—"

"*Observe!*"

Steve slapped his hand on the table, and with a mighty *thud,* planted his fork through it like a flag. He let out a howl that was loud even for his standards. Everybody turned and gasped. DJ watched with wide eyes and dangling jaw. Steve yanked the fork from his flesh, and blood blossomed around the puncture.

Goddess Almighty! DJ swore without speaking.

Steve slapped his other hand over the wound, closed his eyes, and muttered a phrase in a language DJ didn't recognize. The palm of his healing hand glowed white. And after about twenty seconds, he lifted it.

The puncture was completely restored, good as new.

Lastly, he wiped his bloody fork on his robe and went back to his potatoes, all while wearing a satisfied grin.

When DJ told Riley the story, she burst out laughing. "Wow," she said when she finally settled down. "He definitely sounds like a few bricks short of a payload, but a healer is a healer, right?"

"Yeah. Now I just need to find some muscle to make sure

I don't get killed."

"Good luck. A goblin will probably eat you before you reach the Aeldar Forest."

They smirked at each other. DJ threw a punch at her shoulder, but Riley twisted out of it and laughed at him.

They stayed at the clock tower until it got dark. Word got around Beregond that DJ was looking for a party to quest with, and that led to a broad assortment of sellswords trying for a bite of Sir Dashing's wealth. For the next two weeks, DJ experienced a carousel of mangy, bloodthirsty adventurers visiting his home to interview for the position.

That also led to the gossip. None of it was said to DJ's face, of course. But DJ would hear it when he would pass people in the streets—commoners taking bets on how long he would live or if someone would capture him and hold him ransom. DJ kept silent and swore that he would make them eat their words. Eventually.

And the sellswords kept coming. Sir Dashing made it a point to attend each interview. He pushed DJ to lead most of the time, but Sir Dashing also found it difficult to stop from asking the *real* questions only a true adventurer would know.

Many candidates were highly qualified, but Sir Dashing reminded DJ that he needed to quest with someone he genuinely liked. Joint goals are the bread of a party, but camaraderie is the butter. If he was going to be on the road for several months with someone, he had to *like* them. And so far, not a single candidate had qualities DJ liked—all of them were either too cocky, brash, stupid, or slippery.

That was until a knock came to the door during supper

one evening. The sound was strong but measured. DJ and Sir Dashing exchanged looks, then Sir Dashing got up and answered it. DJ couldn't see the visitor, but he did notice Sir Dashing's face turn way up—so whoever it was, they were very tall.

"Hello," Sir Dashing said. "Here for the strongarm position?"

"Indeed, I am," a deep voice came. "I understand that it's late, though. I can visit another time if it's more convenient for you."

DJ perked up at the notion. *If it's more convenient?* This strongarm sounded strangely courteous for a hardened adventurer.

Sir Dashing gave DJ a look as if to say what-do-you-think. DJ shrugged as if to say why-not-it'll-only-take-a-few-minutes. So, Sir Dashing invited the applicant inside.

The applicant was a seven-foot orc with dark green skin, wide shoulders, a thick girth, prominent tusks, and a considerable stack of books under his arm. He was dressed mostly in furs, and he lugged a thick battle ax over his shoulder. He set the ax gently down by the doorframe as if he was worried about scratching the floor.

Sir Dashing extended his hand. "I'm sorry, I don't believe I got your name."

"Francis." The orc extended his hand and shook. "Thank you for letting me in your home on such short notice."

"Francis. Strange name for an orc." Sir Dashing studied him up and down. "What clan are you from?"

"I have no clan."

Sir Dashing blinked. "Every orc has a clan."

"Not this one, I'm afraid."

"I see," Sir Dashing said. "Please, sit down. This is my son, DJ."

"Of course," Francis extended his hand and DJ shook it. The hand was massive but surprisingly soft. "Congratulations on your recent knighting. I heard it was quite the celebration."

Sir Dashing tilted his head. "Heard? You didn't attend?"

The orc smiled bashfully then cleared his throat. "I prefer to stay home and read most days. Loud parties aren't my preferred pastime. I hope you'll forgive me, young knight."

"It's okay," DJ shrugged and meant it.

Francis pulled out a chair and sat down. It groaned under his weight, so he adjusted slightly to ease off the pressure.

"So, Francis the Orc." Sir Dashing sat down and pushed his plate aside. "Tell us of your travels and battles. A lot of broken bones and shattered shields behind you?"

Francis nodded subtly. "I have more than sufficient experience traveling. I'm from the Nether Regions, as most orcs are. My sojourn to Beregond took me through much of The Cradle and Westfall. As for battles..." He gestured to himself. "It's well-known that orcs come from long lines of brawlers that pass down their love of war. I've seen my share of combat."

Sir Dashing stroked his chin and nodded. He opened his mouth to speak again, but stopped himself and turned to DJ. "Son, what questions do you have?"

DJ pointed. "Have you read all those books?"

Francis smiled and stroked the top book as if it were a pet.

"These? Oh no, not yet. I acquired these from a merchant and I intend to bring them to the shop. I help manage Klepper's Keep—the bookshop down in the lower district. These will be added to our inventory."

"An orc that runs a bookshop?" DJ said. He couldn't keep the amusement out of his voice.

"Brawn and brains, young knight." Francis winked.

DJ beamed.

"Francis," Sir Dashing continued, "what about—"

"You're hired," DJ interrupted.

"Now hold on, DJ," Sir Dashing said, "we haven't even discussed price—"

"I'll do it for a thousand gold," Francis said.

Both Dashings went silent. That price was tiny compared to the offers they heard from other sellswords. They both shared a look of confusion, then Sir Dashing narrowed his eyes and examined the orc.

"Only one thousand?" he asked. "Why?"

"From what I understand," Francis said, "your quest is a pilgrimage to the Temple of the Amulet, correct?"

DJ nodded.

"There is a library on the way there," Francis continued. "The Library of Artak. It's nestled on the eastern side of the Camās Gahl Mountains. I've wanted to visit that library since I was a boy, but never made the journey. If you promise that we stop at the Library of Artak along the way to our destination, I'll lend my services for the entirety of the journey. You have my word."

DJ beamed again. This orc was willing to guard across the

territory in exchange for a sack of gold and a *library visit.* DJ had never been terribly religious, but in this moment, he felt like blessing the Goddess's name. Francis was perfect. The party was coming together.

Sir Dashing folded his arms and leaned back. "Well, DJ, do you have any further questions?"

DJ shook his head, still enamored with his latest find.

"Then it appears my son has already made his decision." Sir Dashing extended his hand. "Francis, thank you for visiting us this night. I know my son will be in good hands."

"The pleasure is all mine," Francis said. "Thank you for this opportunity, young knight. I swear to protect and guide you. The Library of Artak has been a great dream of mine, so I'll forever be grateful for this journey."

DJ stood up. "Okay! Yeah! Thanks!"

Francis bowed, then he saw himself out the door, remembering to take his battle ax with him. Sir Dashing and DJ returned to their supper, and DJ couldn't keep the grin off his face. He had a healer and a strongarm—his party was complete. But another question grew in DJ's mind, which caused his smile to falter.

"Dad," he said, "we did *just* meet that orc. How do we know we can trust him?"

Sir Dashing gave a sly grin. "You can always trust someone who runs a bookshop."

*

The day had come.

DJ tightened his knightly sword around his waist and counted the items in his pack one more time: a week's rations, a bedroll, some rope, a fire sparker, a mess kit, a canteen, and a generous sack of gold. He was also garbed in top-of-the-line adventure wear. DJ swore it would be fine to buy secondhand goods at the general store, but Sir Dashing insisted on custom-fitted gear that would last him the journey. DJ felt incredibly self-conscious as the tailor measured his every angle. He tried not to blush as shoppers watched him and pointed.

Friar Steve stood beside him, his thumbs in his pack straps and gazing all around Beregond while he had the chance. Then his uneven eyes fell on the looming eastern gates and he stopped. He took a deep breath and let it out.

DJ noticed this. "Been a while since you've been outside the city?"

"Oh yes!" Steve replied. "Many years! I was but a boy!"

"Excited?"

"Indeed! Perhaps this pilgrimage shall finally earn me the rank of priest! If it does, I shall thank the Goddess until my dying day!"

"I hope it works out for you, Steve." DJ shielded his eyes and measured the time by the sun's position. "Francis should be here soon. When he shows up, we'll be ready." He paused. "Dad, you doing okay?"

Sir Dashing had been standing with shifting feet and clasped hands, glancing all around. Passing people hailed him and wished him a good day, but he returned their enthusiasm with distraction.

"Me? Oh yes, fine, fine." He cleared his throat. "You know,

DJ, there is still time to reconsider. You don't *have* to go. No one is forcing you."

"Dad, I need to do this for *me*." DJ approached Sir Dashing and lowered his voice. "I'll miss you, too, but I have to do this. What about you? You were twelve when you had your first quest."

"That's different," Sir Dashing mumbled.

"I'll be fine," DJ assured. "I'll have Francis and Steve to look after me. We'll stay out of trouble, and I'll send you ravenpost along the way."

"The great Goddess above will grant us safety on this pilgrimage!" Steve was suddenly beside DJ. "Her Amulet awaits us!"

"Thank you, Friar Steve," Sir Dashing said. "If you don't mind, I'd like a moment with my son." Steve stepped back a few paces. Sir Dashing put his arm around DJ and leaned in. The following words were delicate and slow. "Just so you know, your mother still lives in Varis. It's the capitol of the Cradle—a beautiful lakeside city at the edge of the Lyleth Forest. I'm sure you'd be able to find her there, she's very well-known."

DJ pushed off his father's arm. "Not interested."

"Perhaps it would be good for you two to talk."

"There's nothing to talk about."

Sir Dashing didn't reply.

A short moment later, Francis arrived. His own adventure pack was slung over his shoulder, along with his battle ax. Steve's eyes grew to dinner plates as he saw the massive orc. Francis was over a foot taller than him, but he gave the friar a warm smile.

"You must be Steven," Francis said as he extended his hand. "I'm Francis. I suppose we'll be traveling together for the next several months. Pleasure to make your acquaintance."

Steve didn't say anything. He just stared with childlike wonder. Francis retracted his hand and suppressed a small chuckle.

"This looks like all of us," DJ sighed.

He let his eyes trace the stone buildings of Beregond one last time. People moved all about, carrying on in their usual activities. None of them seemed to notice or care that Beregond's newest knight was leaving on his first quest. DJ wondered why he expected anything different.

The last thing he noticed was the clock tower. From this angle, he couldn't see the westward clock face. His heart lurched. How many months would he be without Riley? The only one who cared that he existed besides his own father? The thought caused a lump to gather in his throat. They had gotten their final hugs the night before because she had to work at the bakery during DJ's departure.

"Be safe, okay?" she had sniffled into his ear. "Send ravenpost everywhere you go."

"I will," DJ replied, holding her tightly. "And when I come home, I'll be a tried and tested knight. It'll be like I never left. You'll see."

DJ tore his gaze away from the clock tower and tried to swallow the lump away.

Sir Dashing let out a deep breath. "Well, this is it!" With a large step, he scooped DJ into a bear hug so tight DJ thought he would break. But Sir Dashing caught himself. He released DJ, extended his hand, and shook it firmly. "I wish you triumph and success on your journey, fellow knight," he said with an official tone.

DJ half-smiled. "Thanks, dad. I'll send ravenpost once we reach Daenan." A pause as he turned to his new companions. "No time like the present, right? Let's go."

The three of them hiked up their packs and made for the gate. They didn't make it five steps before DJ heard a familiar voice behind him.

"*DJ! Wait!*"

He turned around to see Riley sprinting with a wide, toothy grin stretched between her ears. She wore traveling boots with a pack slung behind her, barreling toward DJ at top speed. DJ's heart lit up and Riley jumped into his arms. When they stopped hugging, Riley brushed the hair out of her eyes.

"Riley!" DJ said. "I thought you were working tod—"

"My dad changed his mind!" she said excitedly. "He said I can go! 'Just be careful and stay close to the bookshop orc.' I'm going to become a *ranger!*"

DJ couldn't have smiled brighter. "You're serious?"

Riley nodded.

"All right then!" DJ said. "One and all, to the Temple of the Amulet!"

Before them, the gates opened, and they left the city of Beregond behind. DJ looked over his shoulder. Just before the gates closed, he saw Sir Dashing smiling and waving. But his smile betrayed his eyes, which were unmistakably sad.

3

DJ's first foe wasn't bandits or monsters. It was blisters.

Even with his fancy new travel boots, walking miles and miles wreaked havoc on his city-conditioned feet. Francis had to teach him how to bandage his feet to let them heal properly and ease the pain. Riley and Steve weren't much better off. Francis was very patient as they made several rest breaks on the second day.

"Couldn't Steve just do a healing spell to fix these?" DJ said during one break.

Francis shook his head. "Not if you want your feet to become properly conditioned. Don't worry, they'll go away soon. It's all part of the experience."

Riley piped up as she poked one of her blisters. "Hey, Francis, DJ says you don't have a clan. Is that true?"

Francis tensed at the question. "Yes, you heard correctly."

"Why?" Riley's face turned mischievous. "You didn't kill a clan leader, did you? Are you secretly in hiding?"

Riley, you don't just ask that! DJ reproved silently.

Francis gave a thoughtful pause. "Perhaps someday I'll tell you. But not today." Francis was firm with that last sentence. Riley opened her mouth to speak again, but after looking him up and down, she closed it.

Steve pushed some half-chewed bread into one cheek and exclaimed, "Whatever you may have done, orc-friend, you shall find forgiveness and peace in the Goddess! That I promise you!"

Francis half-smiled. "The Goddess may forgive, Steven, but orcs rarely do."

Now DJ was dying to know what happened to Francis, but he wasn't about to pursue it. Maybe Francis would open up in the coming weeks. They would have a lot of time to get to know each other, after all.

Before and behind them, there were grassy plains carved with a dirt road traveling up and down every little hill. A soft wind moved along the earth, nipping DJ's ears and making the grass sway. Puffy white clouds drifted overhead like slow carriages moving through the sky. The party passed merchant wagons and knots of explorers every so often. Suspicious characters were few, but DJ found himself sliding behind Francis whenever they crossed a questionable stranger. Thankfully, most passersby avoided eye contact with the seven-foot orc.

They had just crested a grassy hill when they came upon a wooden stand erected on the side of the road. The sign above it read "Wizard Waffles," and it was staffed by a single man with a phony beard that dangled from hooks around his ears.

He twiddled his thumbs on the table, and a dopey grin adorned his face. On the wooden stand, a waffle press sat next to a considerable stack of waffles, accompanied with delicious fixings like blueberries, strawberries, butter, and cream.

DJ stole a look to Francis to measure his reaction. The orc was equally perplexed.

"Greetings, travelers!" the supposed waffle wizard said. "Or should I say… pilgrims?"

"That is correct!" Steve responded brightly.

"You sell… waffles by the road?" Francis asked.

"Right you are, my big green friend!" the wizard replied. "But these are no ordinary waffles! They are waffles made with love from your magically inclined friend." He gave a re-hearsed laugh. "And as such, they are imbued with magical properties like none other that you shall find in the territory!"

Riley studied the stack of fluffy yellow confections. "But they're just normal waffles."

"Just normal waffles!" the wizard repeated as if it were a joke. "Normal waffles, she says! Tell me, what waffles do *you* know that will stop mortal bleeding? Mend torn flesh? Re-store a broken bone?"

"Oh!" DJ said, pointing. "So these are like healing potions, but waffles!"

The wizard winked and said, "Observe!"

Without taking his eyes off DJ, he reached under the ta-ble, pulled out a small crossbow, and fired a bolt into Francis's shoulder. Everyone jumped as the shaft tore into Francis, sticking out of his shoulder like a small pylon.

"*Hundred Hells!*" Francis swore. He ripped the bolt out.

Blood seeped from the wound. His knuckles cracked as they formed fists and his green face mixed with crimson.

The wizard was unbothered by Francis's anger. He dangled a waffle in front of Francis's face, complete with cream and blueberries. "Go on! Eat!"

Francis snatched the waffle and stuffed it into his mouth. Before he even swallowed, the hole mended. Blood stopped leaking onto his tunic. He twisted his arm a little, then he poked the spot where his wound used to be. Good as new. The red drained from his face and he gave a satisfied grunt.

"For just the four of you," the wizard continued, "I'm offering a special deal—just ten gold apiece! Take them with you! Save them for when you need them!"

"But won't they get smushed in our packs?" Riley asked.

The wizard took another fully loaded waffle, shoved it in a small box, shook it around, and pulled it out. It emerged just the way it was before—pristine, no mess.

Riley bought two with the party's gold, much to Francis's chagrin. The wizard gave them generous bows and thank-yous, then the crew continued on. When they reached the bottom of the hill, DJ looked back to get another glance at the wizard. But the wizard and his waffle stand had disappeared.

DJ smiled, hummed to himself thoughtfully, and continued on.

*

Days went by. DJ had trouble adjusting to his bedroll. It

was nothing like the feather bed back in Beregond. The fur interior was itchy against his bare skin, so he found himself sleeping fully clothed more often than not.

Francis also insisted that each member of the crew have a turn taking watch each night. On DJ's first shift, he never let go of his sword and clamped his jaw to keep his teeth from chattering. Twice he awoke the camp to warn them of a potential threat, but each time, it turned out to be nothing. A fox instead of a wolf. A jackrabbit instead of a snake. Francis and Steve were a bit more forgiving, but Riley threw a stick at DJ after the second false alarm.

During the day, Francis made sure to teach combat techniques to every member of the team. He retaught DJ how to stand and hold his sword. Going through the basics made DJ remember why he stopped practicing with the blade ages ago —he genuinely hated it. Even his knightly shortsword felt too heavy and unwieldy. Francis was patient with him, but DJ struggled finding patience with himself, especially since his father had defeated hordes of foes single-handedly by the time he was DJ's age.

Francis even insisted on teaching Steve some combat basics. Initially, Steve was hesitant as a peaceful Steward of the Goddess, but after some gentle coercing, Francis managed to get him on his feet. The friar's weapon of choice? His cast iron frying pan. Riley and DJ sat on the grass and tried not to laugh as they watched him swing and jab with his favorite cookware.

To Riley's disappointment, archery was one of the few things Francis wasn't well-versed in. But Francis taught her and the others about berries and herbs they could forage along the way—still important knowledge for a ranger. From that point on, Riley appointed herself as the group's chief forager. They couldn't walk by a single edible plant without Riley stopping to pluck it.

When they were halfway between the cities of Beregond and Daenan, shouting came from far off the road. Everyone perked up.

"*Help! Someone, help!*" the voice called in the distance.

Steve—a Steward always eager to serve—nearly rushed toward the sound, but Francis caught his robe.

"Caution, friar," the orc said. "Be wary of traps. We investigate together."

DJ put his hand on his sword and moved toward the noise, following behind Francis. They went away from the road and over a short hill until they found a grown man hogtied and stripped down to his underclothes under a lone tree. Dried blood was caked on his lip and chin. When the man heard them approaching, he looked up and his eyes filled with relief.

"Oh, thank the Goddess!" he moaned. "A couple of bandits stole my things and left me for dead hours ago! I was worried no one would hear me!"

DJ looked around, his hand still on his weapon. As far as he could tell, no one else was around—no ambush. He relaxed a little when Francis bent down to cut the man's ropes. The man stretched out on the grass and sat up, rubbing his raw ankles and wrists.

He was surprisingly handsome. Strong chin. Broad shoulders. Soft black hair flowed down either side of his face in a neat part. Riley's eyes sparkled and she dove into her pack. "Here, you must be hungry." She handed him an apple.

"Thank you, sweet girl," he said as he took a bite. Riley blushed. DJ scowled. The man swallowed and forced himself to his feet. "I suppose that's what I get for traveling alone. Which direction you are going?"

"Will you give us your name first?" Francis said.

"Vennick," the man said. "Vennick of Laradyl. I was on my way to visit my sister in Beregond when I was attacked."

"Greetings, Vennick," Francis said. "We left Beregond four days ago. Our journey takes us eastward, through the Aeldar Forest."

"I see," Vennick thought. "Well, if you could find it in your heart, I would greatly prefer not to travel alone for the next four days. Especially in naught by my underclothes." He forced a smile. "If you'd be so kind, I would be honored to join your party until you reach Daenan. I won't be a burden."

The party was silent for a moment, then Francis said, "Excuse us." They moved a few paces away and huddled. "I want everyone's thoughts. Young knight?"

DJ shrugged and rubbed his arm. "I mean… I dunno. He's got nothing on him but his underwear. He looks harmless."

"I agree," Riley said. "We can't just leave him here."

"Agreed!" Steve yelped. "We must serve and—!"

After shushing Steve, Francis said, "Very well then, but let us remain wary. All we know about him is what he's told us, which may or may not be truthful. We never allow him to take watch at night—one of us must always keep an eye on him. And when we reach Daenan, we go our separate ways. Agreed?"

Everyone gave the affirmative, then they turned back to Vennick.

"All right, Vennick," Francis said. "You may join us. Can you walk?"

"Thank you! *Thank you!*" Vennick gave a generous bow. "Yes, I feel well enough to walk! May the Goddess bless your names! I'm sorry that I don't have much to offer—the bandits took my bow and knives, but I know plenty about tracking and hunting—"

"Are you a *ranger?*" Riley's eyes grew.

Vennick smiled. "Of sorts. I have the skills of a ranger. But I suppose it depends on who you ask." He winked.

Riley turned pink again. DJ looked away.

From that point on, Riley spent every possible moment with Vennick. She grilled him on questions about ranger experiences, and Vennick was more than happy to unravel heroic tales of hunting for starving families and guiding naive travelers through treacherous woods. Silently, DJ wondered how such a versed ranger could get robbed by a couple of bandits.

Vennick did prove to be pleasant company, however. He was quick with a joke and helped Steve with some of the cooking. He even pointed out certain herbs and roots that could mix with their food rations. As a thank you, Steve gave Vennick a spare robe to wear over his underclothes until they reached Daenan. Vennick's handsome face was positively radiant as he slipped on the robe. Steve applauded his approval.

That night, Vennick slept soundly by the fire. DJ was already awake when it was his turn to take watch. He scowled at Vennick as his body rose and fell with every peaceful breath. When DJ took over Francis's watch, he asked the orc, "What do you think of Vennick? Can we trust him?"

"He's growing on me," Francis whispered. "Riley and Steven sure have taken to him. But I'll trust him more when we reach Daenan. Be vigilant, young knight. Keep your weapon close."

But the sun came up with no surprises. They broke camp after a brief breakfast. Vennick bemoaned his missing bow, robbing them of the opportunity to hunt rabbits for stew. Riley was the first to console him, and DJ tried not to grumble about it.

By mid-day, the Aeldar Forest was visible in the far distance. The first leg of their journey would be complete. And much to DJ's delight, they would finally be rid of Vennick. Steve and Riley walked on either side of him as he unraveled more tales of hunting and guiding. DJ took some of his frustration out during combat practice with Francis. The orc commended him on his newfound ferocity. Vennick sat chewing on a blade of grass, watching DJ closely. DJ pretended not to notice.

Night fell. Steve took his watch, then DJ. He forced himself out of his bedroll, rubbed his eyes, then sat a little way from the fire. He kept his hand on his sword, looking out on the dark plains and occasionally glancing at his friends.

He listened for footsteps and watched for glowing wolf eyes in the dark. Up above, stars like little diamonds hung in an ink-black sky. He wondered what his dad was doing back in Beregond—probably sound asleep in his large feather bed. Inwardly, he was grateful that his new travel companions were so kind, unlike the kids back home. And they would be rid of Vennick soon, so that made him feel even better.

"Great job fighting today."

DJ gasped sharply and turned about. Not only was Vennick awake, but he had crept up next to DJ while he was lost in thought. The newcomer's stealth made DJ tighten his grip on his sword. "Thanks," he muttered.

Vennick frowned as he sat down. "You don't trust me."

"I barely know you."

Vennick sighed. "I don't blame you. 'Be wary, stay vigilant.' It's safer to distrust strangers on the road. When you put up walls, it's harder to get hurt. And people are so quick to betray when they have something to gain. It's a shame." He paused. "Is it true that you're the son of Sir Dashing? *The* Sir Dashing?"

DJ didn't respond.

"He's a tremendous man." Vennick leaned back and looked up at the stars. "I heard he once slew two dragons *at the same time*. No wonder his reputation is known throughout the territory. And for what it's worth," he turned to DJ, "I see that same spark in you. I've only known you for two days, Sir DJ, but I can tell there's something special about you."

DJ eased the grip on his sword. "Really?"

Vennick's smile turned impish. "No."

In a flash, Vennick scooped up a rock and smashed it against DJ's head. DJ struggled to remain conscious but failed.

He didn't even feel himself slump onto the grass.

Muffled sounds. Darkness. Head swimming. Pain. Shouting.

"DJ! *DJ,* can you hear me?" Francis's panicked voice sounded dull and distant.

DJ's vision grew back. His entire body felt weighted to the ground. He blinked hard and saw Steve standing over him. The friar's hands were over his head and he muttered words in the magic language. It must have been a healing spell, because DJ's vision and limbs regained their strength with unnatural speed. He even felt pieces of skull shifting back in his head. When he realized what had happened, he tried to get to his feet.

"Where's Vennick?" DJ said. "He smashed my head with a rock! Where—ugh…" DJ held his face and staggered.

Steve forced his hands to stay above DJ's head until the spell finished, then the friar backed off. Not far away, Francis stood with his arms folded, glaring into the fire.

"Gone," the orc growled. "I heard the noise and woke to see him fleeing into the darkness. You were laying on the ground here, your head bloody and smashed. I woke the others immediately."

"*Vennick!*" Riley stood at the edge of camp, shouting into the night. Her hands were balled into fists. "*Come fight me, you bastard!*"

His shattered skull was healed, but DJ still felt unsteady. He slapped his hands around his body, feeling for his possessions. Everything was on his person. That was, everything except one. The realization hit him like a lightning bolt.

"Where's my *sword?*"

No one answered. Vennick must have taken his sword the moment he knocked DJ out. Over by DJ's bedroll, his adventure pack had disappeared, too. Vennick must have snatched it while he ran into the night. DJ's stomach dropped. All of the party's gold was in that pack. And that sword was one-of-a-kind—his knight sword, given to him during his knighting ceremony. He would only get one of them.

When everyone realized the implications of Vennick's theft, a dark cloud of dread grew over them. The fury in DJ's chest rose up until it made his eyes burn. He turned away from the others so they wouldn't see his tears grow.

"So we have no gold now," Francis said. "And your rations are gone."

DJ trembled with fury and shame.

"I'm sorry, young knight," the orc continued. He rubbed his face and thought. "This complicates things. I was hoping we could stay in an inn when we reach Daenan, but now we'll need to find jobs in the city to earn some extra coin. But we'll be all right. We'll share our rations and—"

"He attacked during *my* watch because he knew I was the weakest," DJ mumbled angrily. He finally turned to let the others see his face, his eyes glowing red against the fire. "I bet he planned this all along. If I was more like my dad—"

"*DJ,*" Francis said forcefully. "That kind of talk will not serve us. In time, this shall be a small thing. But for now, get some sleep." He put a hand on DJ's shoulder. "We'll have more hardship ahead, but we'll face it together. I'll watch for the rest of the evening."

DJ let those words rattle around in his mind as he forced himself to his bedroll. He cursed himself over and over. He hadn't even been out for an entire week, and he had already been bludgeoned and robbed like a pitiful merchant. This never would have happened to his father. The kids back in Beregond were right. *Wimpy, helpless little DJ.* The thought made DJ's eyes sting harder.

"Hey, DJ."

The whisper came from Riley's bedroll not far away. DJ didn't reply, but he kept listening.

She said, "I'm sorry about your sword."

DJ sniffled, rolled over, and tried to sleep.

4

They trudged into Daenan with growling stomachs and boots dragging. Sharing rations turned out to be a tighter strain than they thought. Foraging wasn't enough, and they found themselves counting roots for each meal. Riley swore they would have more meat once she learned to hunt, but everyone only half-listened to her through their hunger.

The small city of Daenan was the lip of the Aeldar Forest, wrapped with tall, spiky tree trunks forming an outer wall. Guards patrolled on catwalks built into the wall's interior. Their armor was made of a mix of leather and steel, with animal furs wrapped around their helms. Two guards kept the city's entrance and frowned at the starving crew as they stumbled into town.

Before them was a city densely populated with cabins, inns, and taverns, all constructed from the coniferous trees grown in the forest. The city was cooler than the plains due to the thick forest surrounding it. And DJ drank in the smell of pine, amazed that anything could smell so naturally fresh.

Locals bustled around in every direction, carrying pails of water or logs for building or chickens for plucking. DJ saw a goose dangling from a butcher's hand and started salivating. He swallowed and wiped spit from the corner of his lip.

"Pardon me," Francis turned to a nearby guard. "We're without money and food. Do you know of anyone in town who is hiring temporary work?"

"Erm—" A guard looked up at Francis nervously. "Sellsword? Ain't heard of no bounties lately."

"We're not sellswords. Just travelers."

"Oh. I heard Sandy Brambleton is looking for some folk to run an errand."

Riley's eyes went wide. "Sandy Brambleton? *The* Sandy Brambleton?"

"Who's Sandy Brambleton?" DJ asked.

The guard pointed and Francis thanked him. Riley reared on DJ, her face riddled with incredulity. "*Who* is Sandy Brambleton? He's only the best author in the entire territory! You've never heard of *Stormhunter*? *Heart of the Emperor*?"

DJ shrugged.

Riley turned to Francis. "Come on, Francis. You know books. You've heard of Sandy Brambleton, right?"

Francis nodded and rubbed his neck. "I'm familiar with his work. Read a couple of volumes. I admire his world building and I can't deny his spirited fan base, but I find his prose a tad uninspired."

Riley waved her hand. "Don't listen to him. Sandy Brambleton is amazing. I'll let you borrow my copy of *Stormhunter* when we get back to Beregond."

Beregond. Just the mention of home made DJ sigh. And it formed a knot of anger in his chest. He could hear his peers now, trading jokes about his assault in the first week of his journey. Then he thought about how worried Sir Dashing would be—and how he would rush to rescue DJ like a distressed maiden if he found out. DJ clenched his teeth and kicked a dirt clod as he walked by.

It was in his resentment that DJ realized Steve had been surprisingly quiet since they arrived in town. He turned to see the friar absolutely enamored with his surroundings. Sniffing loudly, savoring the smells, turning all around as he walked. The turning made his pots and pans jingle.

DJ blinked at him. "Do you remember Daenan, Steve?"

"Hardly!" the friar yelped. "I had forgotten the forest! Isn't it wonderful? Basking in the creations of our great Goddess? The territory that bears her name is beautiful and varied!"

Steve isn't much better off than me, DJ thought. *And he's making the best of things.* For some reason, the thought made him half-smile, and the anger in his chest loosened just a hair.

"You just wait, Steven," Francis smirked. "Once we delve deeper into the forest, you'll see wildlife, sparkling clear pools of water, trees as wide as a house. After we take Broken Lovers Pass through the Dhuvan Lōk Mountains, we'll reach the city of Laradyl in the western region of the Cradle. Many elves live there, and they've made the city beautiful."

"Do you know where we're going?" Riley interjected, holding her complaining stomach.

Francis pointed. "The guard said to keep down the main

road until we see a mansion on the left side. Said we wouldn't miss it."

And the guard was right. As the eastern gate came into view, they noticed a mansion to the left overshadowing the other homes nearby. They followed the path to a lush estate surrounded by an iron fence. The mansion rose three stories tall, with vaulted roofs and a courtyard filled with trees and statues. Above the iron gate, a dragon's head was molded from steel and mounted above an arch.

Riley's eyes sparkled as she gawked at it. DJ smiled.

A gatekeeper stationed in a small booth rested with his head in his hand. With his other hand, he flipped the pages of a book. As the party approached, he looked up then went back to his book.

"Do you have an appointment?" he asked lazily.

Francis nudged DJ to the front. At first he was annoyed, then DJ had to remind himself that this was *his* quest. He cleared his throat. "No, uh, but we heard Mister Brambleton has some potential work for trav—"

"If you want to be considered, you have to set an appointment," the gatekeeper said, not looking up. He flipped another page and waved dismissively. "Plan better next time. Goodbye."

The crew collectively deflated, then Riley, fueled by her empty stomach, marched toward the booth. She put her hands on its little window and stared daggers at the gatekeeper.

"*Will you ride with me this night, Son of Light?*" she said. "*Will you stand with me on this path to ruin, to glory? Will your children and their children sing songs of this red day? This dark day? Stand with me! Raise your blade, Son of Light! Call to the Blackest Night and deny it your surrender! This day, we stand for the Emperor, and for all of Kels, and for all who Shine!"*

The gatekeeper actually looked up. He studied Riley as if she were an interesting bug. He closed his book and folded his arms over the cover. His eyes narrowed and a fraction of a smile appeared. "That is the first time anyone has ever quoted Kanger's War Cry at me."

DJ and Francis traded looks. Steve watched and picked his nose.

"Fine," the gatekeeper said. "Because you amused me, I'll show you in. But I can't guarantee that he'll be available. He has quite the schedule."

"May the Emperor rain his blessings upon your house." Riley put her fist to her chest and bowed.

The gatekeeper rolled his eyes and the gate squeaked open.

DJ caught up to Riley and nudged her. "Is that from a Sandy Brambleton book?"

"I told you, I *love* Sandy Brambleton." Riley grinned.

"You're a nerd."

Riley punched him. DJ blushed.

They traveled through the lush courtyard—turning all about to examine the statues of people who had to be Sandy Brambleton characters with radiant weapons, armor, and robes. Then they arrived at the front door. The gatekeeper gave a rhythmic knock and the door opened. He motioned everyone to follow inside.

As soon as the party entered, their jaws fell. The interior of Sandy Brambleton's mansion was a fortress of mahogany and leather. Custom swords hung on display. Oil paintings adorned the walls. Marble busts stood on pedestals. And among it all—books. Books everywhere. Most of them were on shelves, but some special copies remained displayed in glass cases. DJ recognized some of the titles that Riley mentioned earlier.

Riley turned all about with eyes full of stars. Every corner and cranny seemed to hold some new treasure for her. But there was no time to ogle. The gatekeeper ushered them through the house, passing one luxurious room after another. Sounds of rustling paper and scratching grew with every step.

"Mister Brambleton," the gatekeeper called. "Three travelers and one zealous fan are here to see you about the special job. Do you have a moment?"

A voice returned with, "Great, yes, send them in!"

The gatekeeper motioned for them forward then excused himself. The party traced the papery sounds until they found Sandy Brambleton in the flesh.

For someone who lived in such a mighty fortress, his demeanor was surprisingly approachable. He had a soft, boyish face adorned by circular spectacles, and a tweed jacket covered his wide shoulders. He stood at a table, his arm moving with the precision of a swordsman. But his weapon of choice was a quill and ink. Two assistants rhythmically slid books to him, giving Sandy Brambleton just enough time to sign each one before they snapped it shut and gave him another. They moved with practiced rhythm, building on a stack that already had hundreds of books.

"Is that," Riley's face beamed, "the special leather-bound edition of *Light of the Star Path*?"

"Well spotted!" Sandy smiled as his arm kept moving. "I'm Sandy, by the way. Nice to meet you all."

"Oh, I know who you are," Riley stammered.

"I didn't!" Friar Steve piped up. "Neither did DJ!"

DJ shushed him.

"It sounds like you're all aware that I could use some help," Sandy said as his arm continued to go. "And you look like a trustworthy bunch. There's gold involved if you can complete it."

"What's the job, Mister Brambleton?" Francis said.

"It's the local witch, Ursula," Sandy said. "She put a curse on me months ago. Didn't say what it was at first, but I've felt its effects since then. I've started writing big books. *Really* big books." Sandy threw up his free hand in exasperation. "I can't help myself from writing *really big books* now! My publisher is worried that they're so big, no one will buy them. But I can't write anything smaller! That's where you come in. I just need you to go to Ursula's house and convince her to break the curse."

No fighting, DJ thought. *Sounds like my kind of side quest.*

"Where is this witch?" Francis asked. "Is she a peaceful one?"

"She lives less than half a day's journey outside of town," Sandy said. "As for peaceful, eh… depends on who you ask. I think she's odd, but I've never considered her dangerous. I did see her turn a child into a toad once, though. Don't know if he ever got turned back."

DJ gulped and his face turned cold.

"I'll happily pay you five hundred gold," Sandy said. "And I'll give you some rations for the journey as well. I keep some of the best bread, cheese, and dried meat in the city. Isn't that right, Damniel?"

One of Sandy's assistants, a bored-looking man with a beard and wide-brimmed hat, nodded. "We should have plenty left, regardless of our supply that was recently pilfered."

DJ was beginning to imagine himself as a toad, and his appetite and missing pack suddenly felt unimportant. Surely they could find some other work in town that would be less risky. But before he could say anything, Riley piped up with full enthusiasm. "We'll do it!"

"Excellent!" Sandy replied. "Damniel, would you share some of those rations with our guests? Thank you. Once again, nice to meet you all! I look forward to being free of this curse."

Damniel escorted the party out of the room. But before Riley left, she turned around, put her first to her heart, and bowed. "*May the Emperor rain his blessings upon your house!*"

Sandy's eyes twinkled. "*And may your path ever be bright.*"

Riley squealed and scampered away.

Damniel loaded everyone with portions of bread, cheese, and dried meat. The party waited until they were off Sandy

Brambleton's property before they tore into it. Sandy had excellent taste—the food was a Goddess-send compared to the roots and berries they had been eating recently. But they knew they had to make it last another day, so they didn't gorge themselves. It was too late to visit Ursula the witch before dark, so they hiked a ways into the forest and set up camp for the night.

For once, DJ enjoyed staying awake to keep watch. The nighttime forest sounds were enchanting—unlike anything he had ever heard. Crickets chirping. Owls hooting. The rustle of trees shivering in the wind. The very air seemed to sparkle. He was almost disappointed when Riley awoke and took over.

That morning, the party broke camp before starting out for Ursula's house. After just a couple of hours through the forest, they reached a trail off the main road marked by three large mushrooms that were almost big enough to sit on.

"This is it," Francis said. "Damniel said the witch's home is nearly a quarter mile down this path."

Sure enough, after that quarter mile, they found it. It wasn't a normal house, though. It was a hut that had been carved from the interior of an astonishingly large tree. Its branches shot out in every direction to create a coniferous canopy, and on the side of the trunk, a door was sandwiched between two circular windows. In front of the entrance, a doormat laid on the ground with the words *BUZZ OFF* printed on it.

Francis went up to knock, but he stopped himself. He looked over his shoulder, addressing DJ. "This is your quest, young knight. I'll knock if you command me, but only if it's your command."

DJ felt everyone's eyes on him. Truthfully, he didn't want to knock on that door. The witch on the other side could very possibly turn him into an amphibian. But everyone's expectant eyes created a silent pressure, telling him to scrape up some courage, rise up to his knightly title, and knock.

The toad thing, though. That kept him hanging back.

"Go ahead, Francis," DJ said.

Francis nodded and knocked. There was a muffled scampering from inside the tree, then a sliding peephole opened on the door. A pair of bulging eyes filled it.

"Wuddaya want?" a raspy voice said.

5

Francis didn't answer. Instead, he looked over his shoulder at DJ—a silent indication that DJ was the leader. DJ felt the witch's bulging eyes fix on him. He swallowed, looked around, and cleared his throat.

"Are you—*ahem*—Ursula the witch?" DJ asked.

"Who's askin'?"

Francis took over in the diplomacy department. "We're just a few travelers sent on an errand from Sandy Brambleton. We only seek a brief conversation."

"Oh, the writer?" Ursula's tone changed immediately. "All right, come in then! I thought you were the tax collectors again. Persistent buggers, those ones."

The peephole slammed shut and the door pulled open to reveal a stereotypical storybook witch. Large eyes, a long, hooked nose (complete with wart), a hunched back, and two craggy rows of grinning teeth. Ursula stepped aside and motioned them in. Tentatively, the group entered, DJ last of all.

The inside was just as adorable as the outside. Furniture crafted of wood and animal furs were all around, mostly occupied by black cats. Plants were aplenty, splashing the living space with green. Sunlight streamed in through the round windows. Something delicious floated through the air, too. It was coming from a large, bubbling cauldron in the center of the room.

"I hope you don't mind," Ursula said. "I've almost finished with the cauldron for the day. Should be done in a few minutes."

"A potion?" Steve yelped.

"Even better!" Ursula said as she stood on a stool and stirred the contents. "Soup! Cheddar and broccoli!" She brought the spoon to her lips and had a taste, then she smacked her lips. "Just enough salt. You hungry?"

Together, they all sat around the room with bowls of soup while Ursula jabbered about all the hot gossip in Daenan. A tavern keeper was cheating on his wife with a butcher's wife, but the butcher's wife was secretly seeing the mayor's assistant, and the mayor's assistant had a little brat that never learned his manners, so Ursula turned him into a toad. She cackled with delight but assured everyone that she turned the kid back. That assuaged DJ's fear, but only a little.

Meanwhile, they sipped on their soup and black cats investigated them. Riley petted a cat that had made itself at home on her lap. Francis had cats all over him—he tried to keep very still as they rested on his head, shoulders, lap, and feet. Steve pulled up his robes and cinched them around his face so they covered his nose. DJ wondered if he was allergic.

"...so that's when I said, 'No spell can fix *that!*" Ursula cackled. Her laughs settled down and she wiped her eyes. "I'm rambling. I was rambling, wasn't I? Well, spit it out then. What does the author want?"

"Go ahead, young knight," Francis said casually as he sipped some soup.

DJ felt the pressure of everyone's eyes again. He cleared his throat. "Ursula, Sandy Brambleton is, um, really worried about the curse you put on him months ago. He's started writing really big books and his publisher is afraid that they're too big to sell. He'd really like it if you broke the curse. I'm sure he feels really bad if he made you mad. So, if you could, uh, break that… it would… be good."

Ursula watched DJ intently. Her bulging eyes turned to tiny slits. DJ gulped, wondering if his time as a toad had finally come.

"This is a grave thing you ask of me, boy," Ursula said.

DJ's heart rate picked up. The tension in the room became thick.

"I cursed that man for a good reason," she said. "It is not easily undone. And I'm not sure you have what it takes to lift it."

DJ clamped his jaw. What kind of price does this curse require? Would it be dangerous? He was starting to consider that a curse of writing big books really wasn't *that* bad. Maybe Sandy Brambleton would just have to live with it. DJ and his friends could find some other job in town to make some coin and replace their stolen things. It couldn't be that hard.

DJ was already thinking up his apology to Sandy Brambleton when Francis spoke up. "What is this price?"

Ursula snapped her fingers twice. From under the kitchen table, a box sprouted legs and bounded all the way across the floor until it reached DJ. Then its little legs bent down and it jumped into his lap, making him spill his soup. DJ let out a startled yelp and the box's legs disappeared.

"In order to break the curse," Ursula said seriously, "you must reach into the box and retrieve the Talisman of Uk'trok. Don't look at it, but you must hold it. If you look upon it, your mind will descend into madness. It must only be viewed by those cursed, see? The Talisman has the power to break curses, but if you're not cursed and you gaze upon it, madness will ensnare you."

DJ trembled in his seat. He set aside what was left of his soup and looked upon the box with wide eyes. "So, I have to hold onto it with my bare hand until we reach Daenan? Then we have Sandy Brambleton look at it, and his curse will be broken?"

Ursula nodded with white-hot eyes.

"Is there—*ahem*—anything else in the box?"

Ursula shook her head.

DJ looked around the room once more. Everyone silently urged him to open it. Even the cats stared at him. *This is what knights do, DJ. Show some backbone.* Gathering bravado and swearing to prove himself to everyone back home, DJ kept his gaze focused upward as he opened the box and reached inside.

But he didn't feel a hard Talisman. Instead, he felt a mass of stringy wetness. His face twisted in confusion. "What the?"

He wrapped his hand around the slippery knot and held it up.

There was no Talisman in the box. Just a giant wad of wet spaghetti.

Ursula cackled louder than ever, holding her stomach as she rocked to and fro. The cats scattered. Ursula kicked her feet and wiped her eyes and slapped her knee and pointed at DJ. "You should have seen your face! You were ready to run out that door, weren't you? Such a scaredy-cat! *Bahahaha!*"

DJ's cheeks burned as he shoved the wet spaghetti back into the box and set it on the floor. A black cat came up to investigate and started nibbling the end of a noodle.

"Wait a second," Riley protested. "What about the Talisman? What about breaking Sandy Brambleton's curse?"

"There is no Talisman!" Ursula proclaimed brightly. "It was a joke! A hoax! A fib! Just like the curse I put on that author!"

"Hold on," Riley said loudly. "Sandy Brambleton *isn't* cursed?"

Ursula shook her head. "Only cursed with an undying need to tell stories, but that's not my fault! No, I didn't like how one of his stories ended, so I made a little show of cursing him at a book signing. I was only joking! I could never do anything to that nice man!" She cackled again and wiped her eye. "Oh dear, this is too good! I can't wait to tell the girls!"

"But wait," Riley said, "if you didn't curse him, why has he been writing such big books?"

"He probably just likes it." Ursula shrugged and stifled another laugh. "If it makes you feel better, you can tell him the curse is lifted. *Skibbity bibbity bop!*" She waved her hand in the air. "There you go." Satisfied, she had another spoonful of soup and smacked her lips. "Hm. Could've used more salt, I think."

Everyone finished their soup and Ursula sent them away. The witch chuckled one last time as DJ walked out the door. In his heart, DJ was embarrassed that he let himself get so scared of a witch that only liked to eat soup and pull pranks.

On the road back to Daenan, all of them guessed what Sandy Brambleton would say when they broke the news of his phony curse. Steve, in his friarly honesty, said they should tell Sandy Brambleton the whole story. But DJ wondered if Sandy Brambleton would still pay them if there was no curse after all. No one seemed to have an answer to that.

They reached Daenan before the setting sun could fill the trees with oranges and reds. Guards nodded at them as they entered through the eastern gate. Sandy Brambleton's estate wasn't far away.

"That was quick," the gatekeeper said when the party approached. He opened the creaky gate and led them into the mansion again.

When they found Sandy Brambleton, he was comfortably reading in a large leather armchair. His face brightened and he stood up. "Well?" he said. "How did it go? Did she break it? I don't feel much different."

Everyone stayed silent, waiting for DJ to speak. The young knight took a small step forward.

"Um… yep!" he said. "We talked to her, and she agreed to break the curse. You're free now." Feeling his conscience protest, he let out a hefty sigh. "Mister Brambleton, you were never cursed. Ursula said the curse was a joke. It wasn't real."

Sandy Brambleton blinked. After a moment's hesitation, he asked, "So... I've been writing really big books just... because?"

DJ shrugged. "I guess so."

After a big breath, the author took off his glasses and rubbed his forehead. "Well, my editor isn't going to love hearing that. But I suppose a deal is a deal, isn't it? You still traveled all the way out to Ursula's house, so I suppose I owe you five hundred gold." He reached for a sack on a nearby table. "Here you go. Side quest complete."

DJ caught the gold in both hands, but it didn't feel as rewarding as he hoped. "Mister Brambleton," he said, "I appreciate this, but I feel weird taking—"

"No," Sandy held up a hand. "You earned it. Besides, if you don't mind me saying it, you look like you could use the gold more than I." He smiled and pointed at Riley. "And for *you!* I have a gift." Sandy reached for another parcel on the table— one of the books he was signing the day before. "One of the first signed copies of *Light of the Star Path.* It's yours."

Riley squealed and jumped up and down. She calmed herself just enough to take the book with both hands and thank the decorated author. Sandy thanked them one last time and said the party was welcome to visit the next time they were in Daenan. As the party left the estate, the gatekeeper didn't look up from his book as they walked away.

As they walked through town, Steve commended DJ on his honesty. Francis echoed the sentiment—something about truth being a quality of a true knight. Riley was barely listening—she kept her face buried in her new book. She let DJ hold it for a brief time. The book was roughly the size and weight of a cinder block.

They made their errands quick. They stopped by a blacksmith and picked up a secondhand shortsword to replace DJ's stolen one. They also picked up a hunting knife for Riley so Francis could teach her how to skin animals. They bought more rations at a general store, and DJ got a new adventure pack with all the essentials. In the end, they were left with roughly two hundred gold. Francis admonished the others to be frugal in case an emergency came up.

"So I can't buy a bow?" Riley whined.

Francis shook his head. "We'll need this gold for food and rooms. Be patient, and perhaps a bow will find its way to you."

"Can I use one gold to send some ravenpost?" DJ asked.

Francis shrugged. "I don't see the problem with that. Riley, why don't you go with him? I'll order us rooms and supper at the inn over there. I believe we all deserve beds tonight."

DJ took Riley to the nearest ravenpost tower. It stood like a tall, fifty-foot wooden finger—far above the other buildings in Daenan. That finger was pocked with windows just large enough for ravens to fly through. Inside, it was filled with crisscrossing rafters that made excellent roosting spots for hundreds of ravens. DJ and Riley's ears were assaulted by a chorus of *caws*, and their noses couldn't escape the aggressive stench of bird droppings.

Right inside the entrance, a front desk attendant focused their attention on DJ. They would have appeared like a typical human if it wasn't for their small antlers and unusually bright green eyes.

A druid! DJ thought. *Of course they would work the ravenpost towers—they can talk to animals.*

They must have been about to close, because the druid at the desk gave DJ a foul look. Another druid from deeper in the tower wore a poncho dreadfully stained in raven droppings. They gave DJ a foul look, too.

"I'm sorry," DJ grimaced. "I'll make it quick. It's going to Beregond."

DJ handed them a gold piece and they snatched it away in exchange for a quill and parchment. Using druidspeak, they summoned a raven. A beautiful black bird swooped down and landed on the desk. It blinked and watched DJ write. Riley tried to pet it, but it *cawed* at her angrily.

Dad,

Just arrived in Daenan yesterday. Met Sandy Brambleton. Riley was so excited. Also met an old witch that fed us some soup and didn't turn us into toads.

Going to stay the night at an inn and leave for Odambro tomorrow. Things are going great.

-DJ

He felt a little guilty not mentioning Vennick or his stolen sword, but he knew that if he made a fuss, Sir Dashing would fly out to the rescue and DJ's quest would be over. And there was no way he was returning home like that. He would never live it down.

He folded up the letter, wrote *To: Sir Dashing, Beregond*

on the side, and handed it to the druid. They sealed it shut with the wax seal of Daenan Ravenpost Tower and spoke to the bird in druidspeak. The bird *cawed* then clutched the letter in its beak and soared out the nearest window.

DJ turned to Riley. "Do you want to write your dad while we're here? Francis won't miss another gold piece."

Riley shook her head tightly. "No. It's fine."

DJ frowned curiously. "Okay then." From what he knew of Riley's dad, he was far too protective of his only daughter not to care. But DJ decided not to press it.

They met Steve and Francis at the inn and enjoyed a hearty meal of meat and boiled vegetables. It was a modest dish, but compared to a week of travel food, it might as well have been a feast. When they retired to their rooms, DJ locked the door and lay on the bed, hugging his adventure pack. The mattress was musty and old, but it beat sleeping on the ground any day.

Within seconds, DJ's eyes grew heavy and he drifted to sleep, dreaming of books, soup, and friendly witches.

6

They took their time leaving Daenan. The inn's breakfast was just as satisfying as the supper—flaky cheese pastries with sausages and fresh cow's milk. The orc and succubus who owned the inn were peddling a strange drink they called "coffee." Francis paid a gold piece for a cup, but after a sip, he puckered his lips and shook his head. Too bitter.

They were on the road traveling east within the hour. Trees flanked them for miles, sandwiching the dirt road that carved through the forest. The sounds of chirping birds and singing insects echoed all around. Shattered sunlight spilled through the cracks in the branches.

As they went, they stepped over dried pine needles that made a thin cushion along the road. They also kept their eyes peeled for unsavory characters. Riley gathered edible mushrooms off the road but always checked nearby bushes for bandits first. DJ walked with his hand on his sword, peering around nervously and praying that no one would leap out.

Francis read *Light of the Star Path* and looked up every few steps. Steve hummed a tone-deaf jingle to himself, blissfully unworried.

Riley perked up when she noticed something. "*Guys! Guys, look!*"

Against a tree, a small hunting bow and quiver leaned, completely abandoned.

"Hold these," Riley said as she shoved an armful of mushrooms into DJ.

"Riley, hold on," DJ protested. "Maybe the owner will be back soon. Don't get too excited."

"I agree with young knight, Miss Riley," Francis said.

"Stealing is a crime against the Goddess!" Steve yipped.

"Come on guys, I'm not going to *steal* it," Riley said, approaching the weapon. "I just want to look at it for a sec…"

As soon as she touched it, a woven net *fwipped* out and ensnared her. Riley screamed as her body disappeared into the treetops.

"*Riley!*" DJ dropped the mushrooms.

Something swooped down and *thumped* into the middle of the road. It was a gnome riding a direcat like a man rides a horse. The gnome had a pointy gray beard, a bright red hat, leather armor, and a mischievous grin. Even the gray-and-black direcat seemed to smirk. The gnome carried net full of squirming Riley over his back.

"*Oho!*" the gnome gloated. "I sure *bow* how to make a good trap, don't I, Mittens?"

The direcat mewed approvingly.

Riley struggled and shouted, "*Let go of me, you pint-*

sized piece of—"

"Manners, you!" the gnome barked and elbowed her.

Francis drew his ax. Steve hunkered down with his frying pan. But DJ couldn't bring himself to draw his sword. This was his first battle, and that realization sent a wave of fear through him. A gulp pushed down his throat and his hands grew clammy. Instead of rising, he melted halfway behind Francis for cover. Would he end up with a smashed head again? Was it worth the risk? He told himself that Steve and Francis could handle this.

Francis shouted the order, "Release her now or face our wrath, gnome!"

The gnome laughed. "Face your wrath? Oh my! If only your chubby legs were fast enough to catch us. *Mittens, away!*"

He kicked the stirrups and the direcat took off, headed for Daenan. Francis lunged for the kidnappers, leaving DJ exposed, but the direcat was too quick. The gnome cackled as he and the direcat evaded Francis's grasp.

DJ's heart sank. *Riley is getting kidnapped. And all I did was hide behind Francis. I'm not a knight. I'm a coward. I—*

Just as DJ was despairing, Steve threw his hands about and said something in the magic language. In the middle of the road, just ahead of the galloping direcat, a translucent blue Barrier materialized in the air. The gnome and direcat smashed into it like a brick wall and landed in dizzy disarray. Riley fumbled from their grasp and slid across the dirt.

Francis shoved DJ forward. In his stumble, DJ gathered a shred of courage and sprinted for the gnome. By the time the gnome staggered to his feet and clutched his head, DJ tackled him and wrestled him to the ground. It was easy since the gnome was half his size.

Not far behind, Francis snatched Mittens by the scruff of the neck and dangled it in the air like a house cat. The more Mittens came to, the more it struggled and swiped against Francis, but the orc held it at arm's length. Finally, the direcat gave up and let out a threatening hiss. Francis didn't budge.

"Excellent work, Steven!" Francis said. "That was some quick thinking!"

"Praise the Goddess for this victory!" Steve yelped as he waved his frying pan in the air.

The gnome struggled and pushed against DJ, but it was no use. DJ looked down with eyes full of fire, adrenaline pumping through his veins.

"Got you, you little twerp!" he spat. "What was your plan, huh? Sell her to a brothel somewhere? I ought to strangle you right now!"

"A *brothel?*" The gnome's face turned red. "You *dare* challenge the honor of Sir Percival Buttons! I was hired to retrieve the girl, fair and square!"

"Hired?" DJ repeated. "What the heck are you talking about? She's out here with permission!"

"Then why did *her father* pay me two thousand gold to bring her back to Beregond?"

Silence fell upon the group. DJ kept the gnome down, but he turned toward Riley. She had just cut herself loose with her new hunting knife. After she squirmed out of the net, she turned pink and shriveled.

"So… um…" she said. "I might have a little confession."

"Are you *serious,* Riley?" DJ shouted.

"Hey!" she hollered back. "You knew he would never let me go! And you knew how much I needed to get out of the city!"

DJ was so upset he couldn't bring himself to speak. He just crouched there, keeping the gnome pinned down and mouthing things like an idiot. Finally, Francis towered over the two of them, still carrying Mittens with one hand.

"You've been bested this day, gnome," he said. "If you truly are a warrior of honor, take your direcat and go."

Francis dropped Mittens. It hissed at him as it curled around Buttons. DJ released the gnome, red-faced and furious. Pouting, Buttons mounted the direcat and scowled.

"I am Sir Percival Buttons, a gnome of noble blood," he muttered. "Do not wrongfully assume that I shall abandon my mission. I will retrieve the girl. Perhaps not this day, but another."

Francis frowned. "She is not to be harmed?"

"No."

"Good," DJ muttered.

"Then be gone, noble gnome," Francis's tone was respectful, but firm. "Fight another day. We'll be ready."

Buttons *yawed* and Mittens took off eastward. As they disappeared into the woods, DJ paced back and forth, his hands on his hips. He stared at the ground, breathing heavily.

Riley looked over at the previous tree and perked up. "Hey! He forgot the bow!"

"Spoils of battle," Francis murmured.

Riley hurried over and picked it up. Her elation turned to disappointment. "It's small. But I guess it'll do until I can get a human-sized one. Maybe we'll find someone who can teach me." She turned back to the group to find everyone glowering at her. Her arms slumped her eyebrows furrowed. "Look, I said I was sorry!"

"No, you didn't!" Steve observed.

"Hey, if I knew my *dad* was going to hire some fun-sized sellsword, I would have thought twice, okay?"

"You've complicated our quest heavily, Miss Riley," Francis admonished. "It's bad enough that young knight had his things stolen. Now we'll have that gnome looking for us all across the territory. He's sworn not to harm you, but he didn't say anything about *us*."

Riley rolled her eyes. Then she noticed how quiet DJ had been. "What, nothing from Sir DJ the Brooding?"

"You lied to me, Riley," DJ murmured with his arms folded. "I never thought you'd do that."

That quieted her. She hugged her elbows and didn't say anything more. DJ thought he caught a glimmer of a tear forming, but she turned away before it became obvious.

For the rest of the day, Riley marched in silence. She didn't take out her new bow even once. Meals of sauteed wild mushrooms were eaten with little chatter. Night fell, and the forest engulfed them with sounds of nocturnal life.

Riley's watch was first, then DJ's. When her watch was done, she wordlessly tapped his bedroll then retreated to her own. DJ rubbed his eyes and took her spot, keeping his sword in hand. It didn't take him long to notice a little note pinned under a rock nearby. It had his initials on the front and was folded in half. He brushed the dirt off it, opened it, and tried to read it against the firelight.

I'm sorry. I won't lie again.

DJ crumpled the note and stuffed it into his pocket. He tiptoed over to Riley's bedroll and tapped her shoulder. She sat up, and DJ held her. The two hugged for a long while.

"I'm still glad you're here with me," DJ whispered.

She held him little tighter when he said that.

Then he went back to his watch and Riley fell asleep.

*

The next morning, Steve and Francis were surprised to find Riley and DJ back to their usual selves. They ate breakfast together, trading little jabs and quips like they always did.

Riley finally practiced with her bow when Francis stopped with the others to spar with sticks. The bow and arrows were too small for her arms, which led to a lot of frustration. Every time she lined up a shot, the bow felt restrained and uncomfortable. And when she released an arrow, it would shoot wildly off course. Then she would spend several minutes searching the forest floor for them. Several got lost.

Days went by with no sign of Sir Percival Buttons or Mittens the direcat. What they did find was traveling merchants selling wares at unreasonable prices. And no bandits, surprisingly. DJ wondered if the mere sight of a seven-foot orc with a battle ax deterred any lurking threats. Inwardly, he thanked himself for choosing his company.

One evening as they were setting camp, Steve had gathered a sufficient pile of wood but trekked deeper into the woods to find more branches. Riley was bathing in a stream nearby, and the others stayed well away to lend her some privacy.

Francis read Riley's copy of *Light of the Star Path* while DJ gazed at the sleepy logs ready to be lit. The young knight thought of Steve's fire-starting technique. The friar didn't use a traditional fire sparker—he used some sort of magic.

"What's that spell Steve does every night?" DJ thought aloud.

"An Everspark cantrip," Francis responded as he flipped a page. "I know of it. Supposed to be fairly simple if you're magically inclined. Not a magical bone in my body, though."

DJ thought back to the hand gesture Steve would do and the word he would say. Out of curiosity, DJ focused on fire and drew from some magical well in his body—if there was one. He swished his finger in a backwards S, then said the word, "*Scintyll.*"

He felt it—a stirring of energy that started from the edges of his body and traveled to his hand. A spark spat out of his fingertip. It was just enough. The kindling caught and a cozy campfire grew at his feet.

A smile stretched across DJ's face. "Ha, look! Nothing to it!"

But when he looked at Francis, the orc was wide-eyed and slack-jawed. DJ shrunk, wondering if he had done something wrong. Francis put a thumb in his book and closed it, then he watched the growing ember. The red flicker glistened in his astonished eyes.

"Sir DJ," Francis marveled. "Is that the first time you've attempted a cantrip?"

DJ answered slowly. "Yeah. But like you said, it's an easy one."

"I said it was a *simple* one for the *magically inclined*," Francis said. "For a novice mage, even a simple cantrip like that can take days of practice." He paused. "You've never attempted magic before?"

DJ leaned back on his hands. "No way. Magic has never really been my thing."

"Why not?" Francis couldn't keep the surprise out of his voice.

"Because!" DJ said. "Mages are nerds and socially awkward weirdos that spend their time drooling over tomes and scrolls. It's like my dad always said: all magic, no maidens. I mean, just look at Friar Steve." DJ's last sentence was hushed.

Francis narrowed his eyes. "Need I remind you that Riley would be halfway to Beregond if it wasn't for Steven days ago?" He put the book aside so he could focus all his attention on DJ. "Young knight, no disrespect to your father, but that sort of talk is perpetuated by chest-beating neanderthals who *can't* perform magic. I've never seen someone complete any kind of spell on their first try. You have a *gift*."

DJ was quiet. He knew of some aspiring mages back home, and they were the kind of boys he tried to avoid. Not that they were dangerous, but they were squirrely and awkward. DJ was already so unpopular that he knew their company would only cement his position as a weirdo.

"Here," Francis said as he dug around in his pack. "I knew this might prove useful."

Francis handed DJ a slender, leather-bound volume filled with dry, yellow pages. Its title was printed in tiny gold letters: *Basic Techniques for the Novice Mage.* DJ tried not to scrunch his nose at it. He flipped it open to find descriptions and illustrations of many magic techniques—destruction, healing, even a little bit of alchemy.

"Read it every day," Francis encouraged. "Become familiar with it. If you pick up the techniques in that book as quickly as that Everspark cantrip, you'll be amazed at what you can do."

DJ weighed his words, replying slowly. "Thanks, Francis, but I'm not really interested in studying magic. Besides, Steve is already a mage. I think as Sir Dashing's son, I should probably put my effort into more knightly skills, like swordplay and stuff. I know you understand."

DJ tried to hand the book back, but Francis didn't take it.

"What I understand," the orc said, "is that you have a serious talent for something and you're afraid to explore it because you're a fifteen-year-old boy who desperately cares what other people think. And what *you* need to understand is that although you are Sir Dashing's son, you are also your own person with your own destiny, and that is something that is all your own." He half-smiled. "The book is yours. Give it a try. It might give you new confidence to handle yourself in battle."

Francis went back to *Light of the Star Path*, and DJ was

left dangling his new gift in the air. He knew Francis didn't mean it, but the last bit about confidence in battle was a knife in his chest. Francis had never brought up DJ's cowardice during Riley's kidnapping, and DJ hoped he never would. But there it was, and more annoyingly, it was mingled with wisdom.

DJ stuffed the book into his pack and tried not to pout.

The next day, Francis told Steve about DJ's little talent. DJ shriveled with embarrassment, but Friar Steve was positively elated. He held DJ's tunic with both hands and swore with bulging eyes said he would teach DJ everything he knew. DJ tried not to grimace as he politely declined the offer.

"I dunno," Riley said when she overheard the conversation. "I've never heard of a mage knight before. Sounds rare. That makes it kind of cool, right?"

When she said it, it was during one of *those* moments. The light hit her face just right. Her chestnut eyes glowed. Her nose freckles became pronounced. DJ swallowed and tried to still his beating heart.

And at that moment, he decided to be more open-minded to magic.

During his watch that night, DJ sat with his hand on his sword, staring into the fire. The sword that he had never used. The sword that he was *nervous* to use. His attention was pulled to his pack and the magic book inside it. Francis's sage admonition was still fresh, but DJ imagined the taunts of the kids back home. *"DJ is a mage! Is it any surprise? All magic, no maidens! Haha!"*

But Riley thought it was cool. So maybe…

DJ scowled and tore his eyes away. But even then, curiosity was a slippery little creature. His eyes were pulled back to it. The pressure became too strong. Finally, he set down his sword and fished into his pack. He made sure to move quietly at the risk of waking the others. He didn't know why he was sneaking—everyone knew he had that magic book. Maybe it was the imagined voices of his peers.

Regardless, against the crackling firelight, DJ read from its pages.

He thought about skipping the introductory section explaining the mechanisms of magic. After all, who cares about how magic works? Only nerds who live in their nerd universes care about that mystical brainy stuff. But he knew that if he understood the system, it would help him master the techniques faster.

"Since the Goddess Uh created the territory with a song and dance," DJ read to himself, *"our understanding of magic stems from the connection between movement and language. Magic language, known as magetongue, coupled with specific movements, are known to successfully execute spells and cantrips. Like a dancer or singer would practice a leap or phrase, so must the mage memorize and repeat techniques to master various magicks."* Huh, that's it? Words and movement? Seemed easy enough.

"We do not yet understand why some individuals are magically inclined and others are not. Studies indicate that magical inclination is not bound to any race, although there are some exceptions. Bloodline may play a part, but the findings are still inconclusive." He thought of his dad. Then he

thought of his mother. The thought of her made his eyebrows bend, so he pushed it aside and read on. "*We encourage the novice mage to begin their practice slow. Expending magical energy can still take a physical toll similar to any sparring or dueling match, and overexertion can cause nausea, fatigue, blurred eyesight, headaches, and in extreme cases, uncon- sciousness or death. Please follow the recommended outline for beginning techniques.*"

DJ ignored that admonition and flipped through the pages until he found one that looked interesting. What he saw was a demonstration of a man flicking one arm aside then thrusting his fist forward, resulting in a burst of fire.

"Flamefist," DJ said.

He memorized the word and movements, then he closed the book and crept away. He didn't venture too far—just far enough to find an open clearing by the stream. The water bab- bled softly as it mixed with the sounds of croaking frogs and hooting owls. The pine needles muffled the sound of his feet. He tried to point himself in a direction where he wouldn't catch anything, then he breathed deeply to steady himself.

He focused on fire, visualizing it, feeling it in his memory. Then, for his second time, he drew from that magical well in- side. He swung his arm, punched, and said, "*Mynus-ignys!*"

With a *pop*, the energy gathered through his body and shot from his fist, blasting a six-foot row of fire through the darkness. The clearing flashed with red light. Birds scattered in the distance. The force staggered him—he should have planted his feet better.

DJ stumbled and fell onto his rear. His head throbbed and

his vision blurred. He clutched his aching head, pressing his palms into his temples. After a minute of slow, deliberate breathing, his vision returned, his headache subsided, and he got to his feet.

DJ turned his hands around, studying them. These were weapons now. The sword slung at his hip was obsolete. A smile stretched across his face.

"Sir DJ," he thought aloud, "the *Mage.*"

As he said the words, embarrassment coursed through him. But there was also… *excitement.*

7

The party was thankful they entered Odambro in better condition than they entered Daenan. It was another city surrounded by a wall of forest-grown timber. But inside, the city was a lovely mix of wood and stone buildings—likely from resting on the western foot of the Dhuvan Lōk Mountains. Conifers sprouted throughout the city, popping up between buildings and roads.

It was late evening when they reached town, so they found the first modestly priced inn that offered baths for a small up-charge. DJ reveled in the feeling of scraping grime off with soap and warm water. He would miss trudging through the beautiful Aeldar Forest, but it was almost as nice to watch brown bathwater circle down the drain, leaving his body clean and refreshed.

Francis gave his recommended plan the next morning over breakfast.

"Broken Lovers Pass will take six to eight days to cross,"

he said. "We were lucky not to encounter any ne'er-do-wells in the forest—sans Percival Buttons—but I can almost guarantee we'll deal with some measure of trouble down the Pass. It's an incredibly popular spot for bandits and thieves since it's the only path between the two forests."

"Yipee," Riley mumbled with a spoonful of porridge.

"I'm just trying to be the voice of reality," Francis said. "It'll be best for us to pay for guarded passage or team up with another party until we reach Laradyl. Preferably someone big and strong."

"Like you?" Steve yelped, porridge dripping down his chin.

Francis smirked. "Yes, Steven, like me."

They agreed to spend the day visiting taverns and inns to investigate safe passage to Laradyl. Guarded passage was too expensive even with the cheapest guide—five hundred gold per person. Since that was out of the question, they asked about other parties traveling the same way. A local recommended an inn close to the eastern gate called the Burnt Apple. The inn had a public signup sheet for parties looking to travel through the Pass together. The four of them found the inn and scanned the list, looking for a group that stood out.

"What about these guys?" DJ pointed. "The Hammerstone Oathbreakers. They sound pretty tough."

"Party of four, too," Francis rubbed his chin. "That would make our group fairly sizable."

"I bet they're all dwarves with big hammers." Riley's eyes flashed.

They talked to the barkeep and told him they were interested in traveling with the Hammerstone Oathbreakers. The barkeep told them he'd pass on word, then he asked for the name of DJ's group. Everyone looked at each other, puzzled.

Then Steve piped up. "The Pilgrims of the Goddess!"

Sure, why not? The Pilgrims of the Goddess. The barkeep wrote it down.

They wouldn't depart until the next day, so the party enjoyed the city of Odambro while they could. They went to a performance of some popular local minstrels and enjoyed some treats called Odambro Braids that were twisted bread sticks sprinkled with sugar and cinnamon. The Braids reminded them that they had uneaten wizard waffles in Riley's pack. Riley checked on them, and they were as fresh as ever—they hadn't even gone cold.

Steve visited the Odambro monastery to offer prayers of safety. During that time, Francis and DJ ventured to a bookstore nearby, and DJ happened upon a volume called *Intermediate Magic Made Easy.* He hid it under his arm and bought it for three gold pieces before Francis could notice. Riley went to buy a human-sized bow, but the cheapest one was out of their budget even if she pawned her gnome-sized one.

The following day, they went to the eastern gate to meet the Hammerstone Oathbreakers. But they didn't see anyone that resembled weathered dwarves. It was just a handful of normal townspeople talking in tight knots.

"Anyone see the Hammerstone Oathbreakers?" DJ asked.

The party shook their heads. Then they heard a voice.

"Oho! Did someone call for the Hammerstone Oathbreakers?"

Four flamboyant men bounded toward the party with theatrical grace. Everyone in the party tried to hide their disappointment. The Hammerstone Oathbreakers weren't anywhere close to intimidating adventurers. The group that stood before them wore brightly colored outfits, tights, dainty gloves, and swishy hats. And they had dancing shoes instead of traveling boots.

"You are the... Hammerstone Oathbreakers?" Francis said.

"That's right!" one of them said.

"The one—"

"—the only—"

"—the Uh-famous—"

"*Hammerstone Oathbreakers!*"

Jazz hands from all of them. They all spoke as a synchronized entity, finishing each other's sentences. The Pilgrims of the Goddess didn't know what to say. Everyone looked to DJ for a response. Feeling the pressure to say something, DJ sighed and stepped forward.

"Listen," he said, "I'm going to be really honest. You guys aren't what we expected."

One of them laughed. "Yes, we have a reputation for exceeding expectations."

Another of them leaned forward. "That's what the barmaid told me last night!"

All of them laughed. Riley slapped her hand over her face. Steve kept smiling, missing the joke by a mile.

"No, you don't understand," DJ continued. "No offense, but this is Broken Lovers Pass we're going through. We were looking for hardened adventurers to join us, not… whatever you are."

"Bards," one of them said.

Riley pointed. "If you're bards, where are your instruments?"

One of the Oathbreakers grinned, as if hoping for the question. "Instruments? Who needs *instruments?*"

It started one at a time. One of the Oathbreakers made drum beats with his mouth—little *booms* and *pats.* Then another one joined in with low *dooms dooms.* The third one jumped in with higher *doom dooms.* Finally, the fourth one stepped forward and crooned into verse:

> *My lovely Bonnie is a funny girl*
> *With a bright blue dress that she loves to twirl.*
> *The village tells me that I've got the finest lass*
> *With her big soft lips and her tight, round—*

Friar Steve bounced in place and clapped along while everyone cringed hard enough to turn inside-out. DJ's stomach sank.

Goddess Almighty, he thought. *They're a cappella bards.*

After what felt like too long, the Oathbreakers finished their song with their customary jazz hands. Steve applauded while the Oathbreakers took a bow. With bated breath, they awaited DJ's reaction.

"Yeah… I don't know guys." DJ scratched his chin. "I don't think this is going to work out."

"Okay, okay." One of the Oathbreakers stepped forward

and held his hat in both hands. "You're the *third* party to back out this week. We understand that we're not the most intimidating bunch"—Francis snorted—"but we're beginning to lose hope that we'll ever make it to Laradyl. We're desperate. If you can find it in your heart, we'll do whatever we can to make the journey easier."

DJ pursed his lips and thought. He retreated back to the group. "What do you think? I feel bad about leaving them here."

"I don't," Riley said firmly. "I'd rather get stabbed than hear that again."

"I like them!" Steve piped.

Francis folded his arms. "Small groups of bandits may ignore us depending on our size. But these four will need a change of wardrobe and weapons to look like seasoned travelers. Then we *may* be all right bringing them along."

DJ met back with the Oathbreakers to tell them the conditions, and the Oathbreakers heartily accepted. Within an hour, the Oathbreakers returned in traveler's clothes, each armed with something big and sharp—or at least, things that *looked* big and sharp. When Francis inspected them, he found all their swords and axes completely dull—stage weapons, meant for performances. Francis buried his face in his hand and swore quietly.

But like that, they were off to Laradyl.

*

The Dhuvan Lōk Mountains proved to be a harrowing

mess of rock, trees, and rubble. All around the travelers, the mountains rose toward the sky in jagged peaks covered in conifers and thin grass. The path was carved through a mountainside just wide enough for two carriages to come and go, twisting and bending around each slope. As the joint parties marched eastward, DJ looked all around.

It was nothing like the peaceful rustling of the Aeldar Forest. Deep in the mountains, it was mostly silence. Trees clung to the slopes in defiance of their conditions. The air was noticeably chilly and thin. He brushed his arms as his skin sprouted in goosebumps.

As night fell on the first day, the two parties struggled to find an adequate camping spot. They couldn't camp on the road, but the mountains were so steep and the road was so wide that there was hardly anywhere else. So that night, they slept single file on the edge of the road with no fire.

DJ chose not to practice magic during his watch on the road, but he hadn't forgotten that night in the forest. Just the memory of Flamefist lighting the darkness brought an embarrassing thrill to his chest. He had attempted the spell a few more times since, and each time, his head hurt a little less.

During his watch, he tried to read from his magic books in the dull moonlight. He found techniques for healing, manipulating water, and even turning his body hard as iron. When someone would stir in their bedroll, he would tuck the books away and only reveal them when they settled.

Day after day, the Hammerstone Oathbreakers treated the venture like a jolly vacation. DJ, Riley, and Francis tried to find elegant ways to ignore them while the Oathbreakers sang songs and Steve clapped along. No song was an improvement on the one they sang back in Odambro.

The mountains stretched on. Other groups of travelers came and went. Merchant caravans guarded by mercenaries gave them stern looks as they passed. DJ frowned. They could have afforded guarded passage with Sir Dashing's money, but this was DJ's first quest. The hardship had to be real, or the people back in Beregond would say that he was spoiled. He marched a little harder as he thought of them.

"Three days," Francis finally said. "We're nearly halfway there. And no sign of trouble, either."

As if on cue, they appeared.

From out of the trees, the bandits bounded onto the road —over a dozen of them. All of them were girdled in wolf fur, with wolf heads fashioned on their heads like helms. Their bodies were mostly naked except for the pelts covering their privates and the war paint covering their extremities.

Their weapons were raised in the air—cruel, cragged things stripped from previous owners. Some of them were still covered with dried blood.

DJ froze. He knew his hand should go for his sword, but his body and mind seized. This was his second battle. His first *real* one. This wasn't a gnome and his cat. This was a group of crazed mountain dwellers with violence in their eyes.

Francis flipped around to face the team. "The Moon-shadow Clan! Show them no mercy, friends, for they will give you none!"

To the Oathbreakers' credit, they ripped their stage weapons from their bodies and roared. Riley nocked an arrow with shaking hands in her tiny bow, poised to shoot. DJ's hands hovered somewhere between the air and his sword, unsure of whether to cast magic or draw his weapon. But there was no time to think. The clash had begun.

Francis set the tone by stealing forward and launching a giant fist into a Clansman's chest. The man flew backward, slamming into a rock face. Whether he was dead or unconscious, no one knew. But Francis wasted no time. He drew his ax and fell it on another Clansman's skull with a meaty *crunch.*

The blood began to fall. The sight of red made DJ's eyes bulge. He fought the bile from creeping up his throat as his face turned white.

Riley launched two arrows with no success—the bow was simply too small to master. One Clansman spotted her and made a mad dash for her. Riley tried to nock another arrow to defend herself, but her hands were shaking too hard. She went for her hunting knife. But the Clansman was already on her, billowing like a banshee, blade raised and poised to strike.

"Fulgyr-fylum!"

Bang! A bolt of blue lightning shot from out of view, boring a black hole in the center of the Clansman. Their eyes rolled back and they toppled to the earth. Riley stood clutching her bow, trembling. Just a few yards away, Friar Steve stood with his feet planted, index finger smoking, pointed at the remains of the Clansman.

DJ's jaw hung.

"Goddess give me strength!" The friar's prayer reached the heavens.

Steve performed a fluid movement and cast his hand toward Riley and DJ. "*Ferrum-kyro!*" he cried. Both of them simultaneously felt their skin harden. An Ironflesh spell—one DJ had read about earlier.

Seeing the threat, four Clansmen descended upon the friar—four on one. DJ's heart sank. But in another motion like a graceful dance, Steve spun around and thrust his hands outward, his fingers fanned out. "*Undatio-ignys!*" he shouted. From his fingers shot plumes of fire a dozen feet long. It engulfed the four Clansmen. They howled with anguish as the flames devoured their skin.

Fire Fan. DJ noted the intermediate spell with wide eyes.

The burning Clansman bodies stumbled along the road as the smell of burnt flesh filled the air. Steve staggered, clutching his head.

Meanwhile, all of the Oathbreakers had climbed atop a large Clansman, swinging from his arms. The Oathbreakers punched and kicked with childlike strength. The Clansman threw one of them off and stabbed another's thigh. The injured Oathbreaker howled and fell to the ground, clutching his leg. When the Oathbreakers saw Francis advancing, they all let go and scrambled away. The large Clansman and Francis traded blows, dodging each other's ax and knife. Francis finally scored a mortal blow against the behemoth, lodging the ax deep in his shoulder.

Most of the Clansmen retreated, but one focused on DJ and sprinted. DJ stiffened. His hands were still hovering above his sword, unsure of whether to draw it. He knew magic—he had practiced the words and movements. But was it too soon? Was he ready? Was there even time to wonder?

There wasn't. The Clansman lifted their weapon to strike.

DJ flicked his arm and punched. "*Mynus-ignys!*"

With a *pop*, fire shot from his fist. It engulfed the Clansman. Their garbs caught fire, mixed with the already-strong scent of burning bodies. They dropped their weapon, screeched with agony and rolled along the ground. But the flame had taken them, and the only escape was death.

The rest of the Moonshadow Clan fled. The Hammerstone Oathbreakers held their weapons in the air, cheering. Broken Lovers Pass seemed to sigh as the mountain's quiet swallowed them once again.

DJ's knees were weak. His eyes stayed on the black, charred mass that used to be a person. The Clansman had attacked him, and DJ fought back. And DJ won. He actually won. But what was this feeling? DJ had heard the tales of knights besting others in battle—a feeling that DJ's peers told him he'd never experience. It was so romanticized, branded as heroics, lauded like something available to a select few.

They never talked about the emptiness that followed. DJ felt like a part of himself was killed along with that Clansman. He knew he was only defending himself, but part of him played the scene over in his mind, wondering if he could have diffused the situation somehow. Did that Clansman have a family they would never return to? Are they desperate and starving? Do they—

"Sir DJ. Are you well?"

DJ had been so lost in his thoughts that he hadn't noticed Francis approaching. He glanced at Francis out of the corner of his eye. He swallowed in a dry throat and muttered, "I don't know."

Francis looked away. "And you, Miss Riley?"

"Yeah," Riley's voice croaked as if awakened from sleep. "Yeah, I think so."

"The way I was brought up," Francis said as he cleaned his ax, "I was taught that your first kill was something to celebrate, like marrying your love or welcoming a child." He shook his head and let out a tired breath. "I never saw the glory in it. Regardless, you both fought bravely today." He gave DJ a particular look. "Your magic saved you. Remember that."

DJ swallowed again and nodded stiffly. It was then that he noticed Francis's battle scars. In the scuffle, he had been cut badly across the arm and he walked with a limp.

Regaining herself, Riley reached into her pack. "Francis, here." She pulled out one of the wizard waffles.

Francis took it and thanked Riley. He ate it, and within seconds, the bleeding stopped. But he still walked with a little limp.

"Oh my Goddess, oh my Goddess, oh my Goddess—"

The Oathbreakers hunched over their fallen comrade who had suffered a stabbed thigh. The downed Oathbreaker clutched his leg, but the blood was flowing heavily. His skin was pale.

"Remember me, fair brethren!" he spoke theatrically. "If this be the end of me, I shall live on through your song!"

"Please no!" one replied.

"Say it ain't so!" another said.

Riley rolled her eyes. "Oh, brother. Eat this." She dropped a fully-loaded wizard waffle on the man's chest and walked away.

He ate it. The bleeding stopped. And he joyfully hopped onto his feet. But he was still lightheaded from the blood loss, so he nearly fell to the ground again. His brothers in song helped him stay vertical as they cheered and celebrated his recovery, mingled with song, as you would imagine.

Francis looted the bodies, looking for anything valuable. For the most part, he just found a few gold pieces, dirty weapons, and ragged clothing. To Riley's chagrin, none of them carried a full-sized bow.

But ahead of Francis, Steve went one by one, saying prayers over the fallen bodies. He didn't speak any words but mouthed them while making circular gestures with his hand. Every time he approached a body, he knelt down and gave the same prayer. And when he was done, Francis would take any valuables and roll them off the road.

The last one that got rolled off the road was DJ's kill. DJ watched as Francis took a few gold pieces from the body, stood up, and pushed the body down the mountain with his foot. DJ shivered slightly. Then the orc turned to face him. "Shall we continue, young knight?"

DJ took a deep breath and cleared his throat. "Yeah. Let's go."

So they did. Several minutes went by in silence. DJ looked over his shoulder to see Friar Steve following him not far behind. The friar didn't give his jovial wave or goofy smile. He just kept his eyes on his boots and walked. DJ realized that

Steve killed multiple Clansman to protect him and Riley just minutes ago. Maybe he was feeling similar things. He slowed his pace so he could walk side by side with the friar.

"Hey, Steve."

The friar nodded his reply.

"What was that prayer that you were giving over every Clansman?"

Friar Steve responded in a tone that, for him, was quiet and collected. For anyone else, it was speaking at normal volume. He said, "I gave them each two prayers. One for forgiveness, and one for a peaceful sojourn to the Seven Heavens or Hundred Hells. Whichever the Goddess sees fit."

"Do you think they have any chance making it to the Seven Heavens? Being murderers and thieves?"

"That is not for us to judge."

DJ thought about that for a moment, then said, "I've never had to kill anyone before today."

"Nor have I."

"I hate this feeling. Do you think the Goddess will forgive us? We were just defending ourselves, right?"

The friar paused. DJ was half-sure that he was silently praying. Finally, Steve shook his head. "The Goddess understands the intent of our hearts."

"I never want to kill anyone ever again," DJ muttered as he relived the moment in his head. "Thanks for saving Riley and me."

"I swore an oath to protect you. It is my duty and my honor."

DJ took a long look at the friar. With his hunched back,

chinless face, and lazy eye, he wasn't much to look at. But there was something that radiated deeper within this friar. DJ wondered why he never noticed it before.

"You're a blessing, Steve," DJ said. "People don't appreciate you as much as they should."

For the first time in a while, Steve smiled.

8

When they crested their final peak and saw the Cradle stretched out before them, DJ's eyes filled with wonder. Far to the north, the Hollow Mountain stood impossibly tall, housing the dwarven city of Khavdaāk, the capital of the Spine. But below that, the Cradle stretched for hundreds of miles. Pushed against the Camās Gahl Mountains was the Lyleth Forest, a lush green blanket across the valley floor. And just behind it was glimmering hint of Varis Lake, which meant the shining city of Varis.

Varis.

The thought of the lakeside city put a fist of resentment in DJ's stomach. Sir Dashing's recommendation to visit his mother came flooding back. But why? Why would he want to see her? She obviously didn't want to see *him.*

DJ tore his thoughts away from his mother and pointed at Khavdaāk. "Francis, are we going to visit Khavdaāk? I've heard stories about the city inside the mountain."

"I've heard them myself," Francis said. "A splendid, cavernous metropolis carved by ancient dwarves from the mountain's interior. But that would divert us from our journey. If you want marvel at dwarven architecture, you'll see it at the Library of Artak. Like Khavdaāk, the Library is carved from a mountain's belly."

DJ pictured it and smiled, but he smiled more over Francis's visible excitement.

They traveled down the last mountain before arriving at the stone gates of Laradyl. The elvish influence was immediately apparent. The cream-colored stone wall surrounding the city was accented with motifs and curved lines to give it an air of elegance. The giant wooden gates also looked brand new, free from any chips or splinters. They remained open to welcome the city's westward visitors.

In the city, each building was a boxy mix of wood and stone, similar to Odambro but a noticeable step finer. Wooden beams were carved into beautiful curves as if they had naturally grown that way. Not a spec of rubbish was on the streets. And the elvish population was noticeably dense. The party couldn't walk ten paces without seeing a beautiful face, pointed ears, and striking features.

The Hammerstone Oathbreakers thought they had become great friends with the Pilgrims, but Steve was the only one who gave them a warm goodbye. The four performers skipped merrily away while Steve lamented the songs he would no longer hear.

The Laradyl ravenpost tower was just inside the gates. When DJ saw the tall structure, he felt a wash of guilt for not writing to his father back in Odambro. He took a gold piece and went inside while Francis and the others waited.

To his delight, there was a letter waiting for him.

"DJ of Beregond?" DJ asked.

The druid at the front counter handed him a folded-up letter. "Came for you three days ago," they added.

DJ broke the seal and unfolded the letter.

Ho there, Son!

I was happy to get your letter when you visited Daenan. Did you visit Odambro, or pass it by? I wrote this letter to Laradyl just in case. I hope you're safe and your party is being kind to you.

The city council has insisted of building a statue of me in the city plaza. It's embarrassing. We're planning for this fall's Harvest Festival and they even want to put on a play reenacting one of my escapades. I've been asked to approve the script. They just can't give an old man a break.

The house is quieter without you. Be well, dear son! May the Goddess grant you safety!

-Sir Dashing

DJ purchased some parchment and a quill and started scribbling.

Hi, Dad.

Sorry I forgot to write in Odambro. I'm fine. We just crossed Broken Lovers Pass with some a cappella bards that Friar Steve fell in love with.

I loved the Aeldar Forest. It's so beautiful and serene. If the Lyleth Forest is anything like it, I'm going to want to move here!

He hesitated before writing the next part but swallowed and put the quill back to the parchment.

By the way, I'm starting to experiment with magic. Turns out I have a knack for it. Francis gave me a book on it, and I even learned a spell that saved me from a tight spot. There aren't many mage knights, so maybe it makes me unique.

Thanks for thinking of me. The next city is Varis, so I won't forget to write you then.

-DJ

He handed the letter back to the druid, who gave it to a raven. DJ walked out of the ravenpost tower with his head down, thinking. He could picture his dad's face when he learned that DJ was becoming a mage. Maybe he would keep it a secret—how typical would it be that the disappointing son of Sir Dashing would become a *mage?* DJ imagined the whispers and snickers of the townsfolk and frowned.

The party was standing in the middle of Laradyl's main concourse when DJ rejoined them.

"I forgot how lovely Laradyl can be," Francis muttered.

"Yeah," DJ said, hiking up his pack. "Elves have to make things as showy and perfect as themselves."

A voice called, "Hello again, dear travelers!"

When they turned to find the source, all four of them

were rocked with surprise. It was the wizard waffles merchant, with his same goofy grin, fake beard, and pointed hat. His wooden waffle stand rested at the edge of the street. DJ could have sworn it wasn't there a moment ago, but regardless, there it was. He and Riley ran toward it.

"I hope my vitalizing cuisine has served you well!" The wizard's statement was more of a question.

"It did!" Riley said. "How did you get here with your waffle stand?"

The wizard shrugged playfully. "I have my means."

"We're going to need more," DJ said.

"You already know the price! Ten gold a piece!"

While DJ fished around in his pack for the gold, Francis asked, "How are we doing on coin?"

"Pretty low," DJ murmured. "We've got less than a hundred gold. We might need to find a job while we're here." He focused on the wizard. "How long have you been here?"

The wizard loaded four waffles with cream. "Long enough."

"Know anyone in Laradyl looking for help?"

The wizard served the waffles and tapped his chin. Then he snapped his fingers. "*Ah!* I heard of a big chap over at the Squealing Boar who's gotten himself into a ripe old pickle! Could use a hand from some generous adventurers like you."

"What does he look like?" Francis said.

The wizard chortled. "Oh, you'll know him when you see him. The Squealing Boar is down the road and around the corner. He might still be there if you're lucky." He slapped his hands on the table. "Welp, pleasure doing business with you!

Ta-ta then!"

The party packed their waffles away and proceeded down the road. But as they walked, DJ backpedaled, keeping his view fixed on the waffle stand. The wizard watched him out of the corner of his eye, then he gave DJ a subtle wink and a tug of his beard. A townsperson walked by DJ, and in that fraction of a second, the waffle stand disappeared. DJ laughed and turned around.

The Squealing Boar had to be the diviest dive bar in all of Laradyl—the only building with broken windows, chipping paint, and a faded sign. The party pushed open the splintery door and fell victim to the smells of cheap alcohol, body odor, and simmering stew. Steve coughed and waved his hand in front of his nose. An ugly barkeep watched them as he cleaned a mug with a dirty rag.

Riley scanned the crowd of ruffians. "So where do you think this—*Good Goddess!*"

It had to be him. Sitting in a corner was an enormous, red-skinned man dressed in furs. He had to be about nine feet tall because was holding a pint of beer like it a was thimble between his fingers. A dozen empty pints were strewn across his table, along with a war hammer at his feet. He wore a regal captain's hat complete with a peacock feather. And around his collar hung a necklace decorated with a large number of severed ears.

A giant? DJ wondered. *No, he's got to be a half-giant—a full giant couldn't fit in this building. I thought they only lived in the mountains!*

He gulped. Riley prodded him forward, but DJ planted

his feet.

"No way, not me," he said, shrinking. "Francis, you talk to him. We'll follow."

Francis cleared his throat, hiked up his pack, and marched. When they approached the half-giant, Francis turned on his orcish intimidation. "Someone told us you might have a job."

The half-giant set down the pint and gave Francis a look. His voice was gravelly and deep. "Depends if you can keep a secret."

"As long as it does not offend the Goddess above!" Steve yelped.

Both DJ and Riley shushed him.

"Ease your conscience, ugly human, there will be no crime." The half-giant smirked. "But first, you must prove that you are worthy of the task."

"Name your test," Francis said.

The half-giant held up a gold coin then placed it on the table. He covered it with an empty pint then flanked it with empty pints on either side.

"Follow the coin," the half-giant said. "You get one guess. If you're wrong, no job. Who of you will do it?"

Francis was about to speak, but Riley's hand shot up. DJ's brow furrowed in surprise. The half-giant leaned in expectantly.

"The little girl, then," he said. "Come. Sit. I hope your eyes are stronger than your shoulders."

DJ was amazed at how unbothered Riley appeared as she sat down. She put her elbows on her knees and leaned forward, her chest pressed against the table. She stared unblinkingly at the pints as the half-giant moved them all around with his forefingers.

After a dizzying moment, the half-giant stopped the pints and leaned back, folding his arms. With little hesitation, Riley pointed. "The middle one."

The half-giant lifted the pint. No gold. The entire party deflated.

"Shame," he said. "And to think you could have made eight hundred gold."

"Wait," Riley said. "The left one."

The half-giant lifted it. No gold.

"So it's gotta be in the right cup," Riley said.

The half-giant lifted it, and… no gold. The group gave incredulous looks. The half-giant replied with a satisfied sneer.

"The half-giant is a mage!" Steve yelped.

Riley relaxed and gave a smirk of her own. "He's not magic. He just thinks he's clever."

From under the table, she flipped a gold coin onto the table's surface. It sang and spun and shimmered until it came to a halt in front of the half-giant.

The half-giant narrowed his eyes. He scooped up the coin to inspect it, then, finding it to be the true article, clutched it in his great red hand let out a satisfied chuckle.

"I noticed the crack in the table," Riley said smugly. "I caught it so it wouldn't fall in your lap."

The half-giant grinned widely and slammed his fist on the table. The empty pints rattled. "I like this one! Tell me your name, clever girl!"

"Riley of Beregond," she extended her hand.

"I am Duane of Nowhere. But everyone calls me Pebble." The half-giant shook her hand. "You lead this crew?"

"They're a package deal," Riley said.

"Very good. Gather around, Package Deal. You have earned the job, and you must know the weight of its secrecy."

Everyone pulled in stools around the table. Pebble hunched down as much as his massive body would let him. He spoke in a low tone.

"Thieves hit the Rhinestone Palace—a jewelry shop not far from the town square. The owner, Barbas, is a friend. He promised me one thousand gold if I could retrieve his stolen jewels."

"Do you know who took them?" Francis asked.

"Goblins," Pebble replied. "They made sure to leave their mark—wanted to let Barbas know who did it. It's a clan that lives just north of the city. I'd retrieve the jewels myself but there could be dozens of them. My strength gets me far, but even I cannot strongarm dozens of goblins alone."

"We're trying to avoid violence where possible," Francis said.

"Me too," Pebble said. "Which is why I gave you the test. I need someone clever." He pointed at Riley. "Goblins love riddles. And they're willing to put wagers on riddles. I'm sure if we wagered the jewels as a prize, they would accept."

"What if we can't solve their riddle?" DJ ventured to ask.

Pebble kicked the massive war hammer laying by his foot.

DJ thought back to Broken Lovers Pass and a shiver slid down his spine.

"So you're trusting us?" Francis said. "A group of

strangers?"

"I knew as soon as you came in that I could trust you." He pointed at Francis. "Strength." Then to Steve. "Honor." Then to Riley. "Cunning." Then to DJ. "I'm… still deciding with you."

DJ frowned.

"And you're fine to split the earnings five ways?" Francis asked.

Pebble nodded. "The jewels are more important than the reward. You see…" He leaned in closer and looked around, voice barely a whisper. "I made a pendant to propose to my partner. It was stolen along with the other jewels."

Riley brightened and she gasped. "*Cuuuute!*"

"*Sssshhh!*" Pebble waved his hand at her. "It has to be a surprise! Everyone in town knows Brooks! They'll start acting different around him and he'll catch on then the surprise will be *ruined.*" Pebble sighed. "He has the eyes of a hawk and the ears of a fox."

Riley looked to the crew for approval. She got it. Then she gripped Pebble's hand with both of her own. "We'll do it. Let's get that pendant back so you can propose to Brooks."

Pebble smiled at the lot of them. "Do you have a place to stay for the night?" They said they didn't. "Then you shall stay with us. I will tell Brooks that you're friends from my adventuring days. Off we go."

As they left the Squealing Boar, DJ found the grit to ask one itching question. "So, uh, what's with the, um…?" He gestured all around his neck.

Pebble lifted his necklace of ears. "This?" An evil grin

formed across his lips. "Do I really have to explain?"

DJ shook his head and didn't speak again.

Before long, they arrived at a tall stone building with a sign that read "Brooks's Bakery." Interestingly, the building was made almost entirely from stone—unlike the wood and stone hybrids all around town. But that didn't make the quality any less fine. The edges and corners could have been carved from the Goddess herself, with steep diagonal lines that gave an air of strength and majesty.

Francis nudged DJ and pointed. "Dwarven architecture," he whispered.

They didn't enter through the front door. Instead, they made their way around the side and climbed an exterior staircase that ascended to an upper floor. As they did, bakery smells wafted to their noses through vents on the building's walls. DJ's mouth watered as he smelled fresh bread, pastries, and pies.

Pebble unlocked a door and they all entered. The flat was astonishingly cozy for someone as brutish as Pebble. Couches with velvet upholstery, a garrison of healthy plants, wide rugs with varying patterns made the space pop with life.

And a dwarf was kneading dough on the kitchen counter.

"Oh! You brought guests!" he said. He hopped off a stool and nearly disappeared. The top of his head—bald, for the most part—bounced up and down as he walked around. When he emerged, DJ noticed the dwarf had a black beard separated into neat braids, and every finger had a ring glinting with colorful jewels.

Pebble beamed at him. "Everyone, this is Brooks. Brooks,

these are some friends from past adventures. They're visiting Laradyl and need a place to stay."

"Oh, well you're welcome to stay in the guest room." Brooks rubbed his hands on his apron. "The bed might only big enough for the green fellow, but there should be space enough your bedrolls if you're willing to get cozy."

Get cozy. DJ resisted the urge to glance at Riley.

"Thank you for sharing your home with us," Riley shook the dwarf's hands.

There must have been something in Riley's tone, because Brooks immediately stiffened and nodded suspiciously. He narrowed his eyes at Pebble, probing. The half-giant bristled.

"They're, uh," the half-giant stammered, "going to help me with Barbas's jewelry bounty. We'll venture out to the goblin cave tomorrow morning."

Brooks freed his hands from Riley. "Oh, *I* see! Always trying to bring back your adventuring days when all they gave you was a body full of scars and lower back pain!" He pointed all over Pebble. "Why are you so set on recovering those jewels anyway? Let the authorities handle it."

Taken aback, Pebble searched for an excuse. "Barbas is my friend. Friends help one another."

Brooks put his hands on his hips and searched Pebble's face. Pebble gulped. DJ tried not to laugh as he watched the two. Brooks clearly wore the pants in the relationship, which was hilarious considering Pebble was five times his size.

"Fine then," Brooks marched around the counter and hopped back on his stool. "But if you come home bleeding, so help me!" He snatched up a rolling pin and pointed it like a sword. "You made me a *promise*, Duane! You said you were done with this life when you moved in!"

"We'll be there and back within hours!" Pebble whined. "It's more like an errand!"

"Regardless!" Brooks said. "You get those jewels and you come back home without a scratch!" He smiled for his guests. "Dinner will be ready in an hour. You're welcome to relax here or come back then. Our home is your home."

Since they had just arrived, the party decided to step out. They snickered to each other over the exchange in Pebble's flat as they went about the city. They visited an armory, and Riley fawned over the bows she could buy after they recovered the jewels. At the local monastery, Steve offered more prayers of safety. As usual, Francis and DJ found a bookstore. DJ tried to be inconspicuous as he searched for magic books. Unfortunately, none of the titles were interesting.

When Francis approached the front desk with a poetry book in hand, the elf at the register gave him a sour look. "Doesn't *your* kind frown upon such literature?" they said.

"*My* kind frowns upon most literature," Francis replied. Then his face got barbaric. "What they *do* celebrate is destroying the belongings of those who wrong us." He made a show of glancing all around the bookshelves.

The elf stiffened, took the payment, and wished Francis a lovely evening. DJ snorted a laugh as they walked out.

"What did you get?" DJ asked.

"Some poetry from Gilbert the Fair." Francis smiled.

"Are his poems good?"

"All of them are."

"Read me one."

Francis licked his thumb and flipped through the pages. He landed on one and read it aloud:

Love was once my only care—
a medal to be earned.
Finding love in solitude—
my sweetest lesson learned.

"Hm." DJ grinned. "I like it."

"You have good taste, young knight."

Francis reached out and tousled DJ's hair. DJ smoothed it out and kept grinning.

Evening fell and the local lamp lighters lit the streets. Dinner with Pebble and Brooks was delightful—warm buttered bread with boiled vegetables seasoned with rosemary and thyme. The couple also shared some of their wine, although Steve politely declined as a sober Steward. When dinner was over, the party excused themselves to the guest room.

Brooks was right—the bed was only big enough for Francis. He graciously invited someone else to take it, but everyone told him he could have it. Through the night, Francis breathed quietly. Steve snored loudly. And after a few hours passed, DJ awoke to gentle nudging. It was Riley kneeling over him.

"Hey," she whispered. "Is it cold in here to you?"

Blearily, DJ blinked and looked up at her. She was shivering. He rubbed his eyes and yawned. "I guess… maybe a little bit?"

"I've gotten too used to sleeping by campfires," Riley said.

"Come on. Scooch."

That got DJ's attention. Riley's expression didn't change—she was serious. Turning a little pink, DJ whispered, "Um… sure. Okay."

Carefully, Riley squeezed into DJ's bedroll, pressing herself against him. DJ's heart raced—he hoped she couldn't feel it. A dozen questions shot through his head. *Is she trying to make a move? Does she kind of like me? What do I do with my arm? Are we supposed to cuddle, or—?*

"Oh my Goddess, this is *so* much better." Riley turned away from him and her shivering settled down. "This is perfect. Thanks, Deej. G'nite."

DJ blinked and put his back against hers. "Good night." After a few deep breaths, he was back asleep.

9

Six-year-old DJ sat at the edge of the bed with his feet dangling over the side. His legs were still too short to reach the floor. In his hands, he turned a plush toy dog around, feeling its button eyes and puffy body. Downstairs, the ruckus of screaming, excited children finally died down. And with it, the muffled sound of Sir Dashing's footsteps grew louder as he ascended the stairs and approached DJ's door.

DJ sniffed and wiped his nose. Sir Dashing knocked gently and entered.

"Ho there, Son," he said softly. "I sent the other children away. Are you well?"

DJ shrugged. Sir Dashing came over and sat next to him. The mattress sagged with his grown-up weight.

"Were the other children being unkind to you again?" Sir Dashing said. "That Riley girl seemed nice. You two seemed to hit it off!"

"I guess," DJ mumbled.

Sir Dashing's face became grim. "It's your mother, isn't it?"

DJ nodded, his throat tightened, and his bottom lip trembled. Sir Dashing hoisted DJ onto his lap and cradled him, holding DJ's head beneath his chin. DJ sank into it. Sir Dashing rocked back and forth while DJ's sniffles grew.

"I'm sorry, my son," Sir Dashing said. "I'm sure you're disappointed."

"She never comes," DJ's voice shook. "Why? You told her, didn't you?"

"I did," Sir Dashing stroked DJ's black hair. "Your mother is… very busy. The situation is hard to explain. You'll understand more when you're older."

DJ didn't reply. He was afraid that if he spoke, his voice would shake harder and the tears would come. And no one wants to cry on their birthday.

"I know I'm not your mother," Sir Dashing said, "but I promise that I'll never leave you behind. You have my word as a knight and your father."

DJ swallowed and sniffled.

*

When DJ awoke, diffused light seeped through the floral curtains covering the window. The smell of freshly baked bread wafted to his nose. He could hear his friends eating and chatting outside the guest room. DJ realized he was the last one to wake. He groggily sat up and shook the sleep from his eyes.

A scowl pressed his face. That dream again—that memory

of his sixth birthday party. It made his hands flex and his stomach burn, but he pushed the thought away. He was nothing to his mother, so he would make sure she was nothing to him, too.

He stowed away his bedroll and left the guest room. In the common space, Pebble, Brooks, and the others sat in a circle eating toast and jam made from a fresh loaf Brooks had baked. The smell made DJ's empty stomach grumble.

Pebble spoke with his mouth full, spraying crumbs everywhere. "Are you ready to claim our bounty, small knight?"

DJ tried not to frown at 'small knight,' but to Pebble, everyone was probably small. He just nodded.

Riley handed him a large slice of bread with jam already on it—she wanted to make sure he wasn't left out. DJ was silently grateful, especially after the dream he just had. Everyone gave their empty dishes to Brooks, who took them to the counter. Then Brooks filled a sack with treats and handed it to Pebble. The gift came with an admonition: "Like I said, Duane, not a scratch! Be back before dark. Love you."

"Love you, too," Pebble mumbled as he took it.

Brooks hugged him around the thigh and Pebble patted his head.

The team filed out the door. Laradyl was still waking in the blue morning light. A chill nipped at DJ's arms and made goosebumps sprout. He finished his bread and jam and licked his fingers. Very few people were out as they crossed the sleepy streets of Laradyl—it was mostly lumber workers starting their shifts at the nearby mills.

They left town through the northern gate, passing some

droopy-eyed guards. After less than an hour, though, Pebble veered off the road and took them northward into the forest. DJ and Steve stayed close to Francis. Riley, however, was more than happy to walk side by side with the half-giant. As she did, Pebble unraveled stories from his past exploits.

"Five thousand gold!" Pebble exclaimed. "*Five thousand!*"

Riley laughed. "*That's* how much they paid you for it?"

"Mmhm," Pebble grinned. "That clan caused much trouble in Sunsbirth. When I brought the leader's head on a plate, the governor was happy to pay. You should have seen his assistant! He *fainted* like a frightened goat!" Pebble roared with laughter.

Steve gulped and DJ patted his back. But Riley laughed and shook her head. "So you traveled across Uh hunting bounties for years?"

Pebble put his hands on his head casually. "That's sellsword life."

"Any ranger skills?"

"Yes. Why?"

Riley lifted her chin proudly. "I'm going to become a ranger. When we take the jewels back and I get my share, I'm buying a bow my proper size."

Pebble dropped his hands. "*Buy?* Why buy?" He looked around. "Do you have a cord? Small rope?"

"Actually, yeah. Right here in my pack."

"Good." His eyes darted around the forest until he found a strong sapling. He pointed. "Hickory."

He put his hand to Riley's chin, measuring the height, then he revealed a large knife and cut the sapling down. As they walked, he carved the sapling like a human would a large stick. Before long, the sapling was in the crude shape of a bow. Pebble bent it with his leg, told Riley how to lash the cord at both ends, and when she did, she had a fully functioning, human-sized hunting bow.

"There," Pebble said. "Spend money on arrows."

Riley gave the makeshift bow a couple of dry pulls before hanging it on her shoulder. Then she threw her arms around Pebble's waist. The half-giant gave a bashful smile—it was hard to tell if he was blushing under his red skin. Then he slowed to a stop and pointed with a serious look.

It was the goblin's cave. It yawned up from the ground in a great mass of gray rock. Spikes stuck around the perimeter to ward off potential intruders… but you could still walk around them. The cave's mouth had been completely boarded into a solid wall with a single goblin-sized door. On its exterior, the door was marked with torches and armed guards on either side.

The goblin guards saw the party approaching and stood at attention, weapons in hand. They wore no armor—just some pelts covering their privates. They visibly trembled when they saw Pebble and Francis.

The half-giant turned to his companions. "Remember, riddle first, battle later. Clever Riley, you take the lead. If danger comes…" he motioned to the hammer resting on his shoulder.

DJ's heart thumped and he flexed his fingers. He reviewed spells in his head, just in case. They approached the cave, and the two goblins pointed with their spears.

"This is the cave of the Mean Green Fiends!" the left one

said with a raspy gurgle. "What business have you here?"

Riley put her hands on her hips. "The jewels you stole from the Rhinestone Palace in Laradyl."

The right goblin cackled with a voice just as raspy as the first. "Hehe! What about them?"

"We're here to take them back."

"Fat chance!" Left said. He pointed his spear again.

Riley smirked. "How about for… a riddle?"

The goblins brightened up like they were children who had been offered ice cream. They turned to one another, nodding profusely.

"Riddles, yes! *Riddles, yes!*" Right cleared his throat.

"Riddles?" Francis frowned. "As in plural?"

"Of course!" Left said. "You think we'd give all those jewels for just one riddle?" He straightened his back and unpointed his spear. "You must pass *three* riddles. Follow the signs to the goblin king's citadel. You'll get the riddles along the way. We wish you luck, but you'll be no match for our goblin wit!" It cackled.

The goblins opened the door and ushered the party through. Everyone ducked in, but Pebble had to crawl on his belly to get inside. The cave proved to be much roomier than the outside let on. The cave sloped down with enough headroom for everyone to walk comfortably, even Pebble. The path was marked with flickering torches and goblins going about their dailies. They all stared with wide eyes as five outsiders marched through.

Sure enough, wooden signs marked *Sitadell* (spelled incorrectly) pointed deeper into the cave. And the cave had little to no charm. Decorations—a term generously used in this case—consisted of poorly cleaned animal parts like bones, skulls, and furs. Goblin-sized bedrolls were laid out in the open, with a couple of campfires cooking stew in cauldrons. Whatever was cooking smelled like dried fish and wet dog. DJ pinched his nose to keep himself from coughing.

They found the first door where four goblins stared with large eyes and trembling knees as the five Big People approached.

Riley puffed out her chest. "We're here for the jewels. Give us a riddle."

The goblins beamed with delight at the mention of a riddle. They huddled and chattered among themselves then shoved one goblin to the front. The unwilling volunteer cleared his throat and tried to sound tough. "And, *ahem,* what will you give us if you fail?"

Riley frowned. "What do you want?"

The goblins huddled again, whispered, then pointed at Pebble's swishy hat. The half-giant growled. Frightened, the group huddled a third time, and adjusted their offer. "You leave!" one of them said.

"Fine," Riley said. "Let's hear that riddle."

The first goblin smiled and rubbed his hands together. "What… has four legs and barks?"

The party was silent. After a brief pause, Riley said, "A dog?"

The goblin's smile dropped. "You've already heard that one?"

DJ pressed his lips together, but his laugh came out like a

snort. Steve loudly observed how easy that was. The three goblins were so busy bopping the first goblin's head with their little fists that they didn't mind the party opening the door to the next room.

In the second room, conditions were better than the first. There were crude, mismatched beds pushed against walls with some bedrolls still strewn around the floor. The goblins here seemed stronger and taller than most of the goblins in the first room.

It's got to be a class thing, DJ thought. *The peasants are the first to go if there's danger.*

They found the second door, guarded by another gaggle of goblins. The goblins asked for collateral, and again accepted the Big People's departure if they lost. One goblin stepped to the front, grinning with horrible teeth.

The goblin asked, "What has four walls, a roof, a kitchen, living area, and potentially a half-bath conveniently placed for hosting guests?"

"A house?" Riley said.

The goblins pouted, pulling their ears and stamping their feet. When they got their composure, they glared with pint-sized fury in Riley's direction.

"Blasted human! Listen close," one said. "The goblin king awaits you behind these doors. And he'll give you the *last* riddle! Don't expect this one to be so easy, no sir-ree! It'll be a real zinger for sure!"

They pushed the door open and squeezed through. Inside was a room uncharacteristically ornate compared to the rest of the cave. All around the walls were fine paintings, sculptures, and even a gold toilet seat. Although it was the same size as the other rooms, it was only inhabited by a single goblin, wearing purple robes and a big, pointy hat while sitting on a throne. He had a scepter in one hand, and in the other hand, a tiny brass bell.

By the goblin king's feet, a wooden chest was filled with jewels. Pebble's eyes flashed.

"Welcome, adventurers!" the goblin king's voice crackled. "I see you were clever enough to outwit my subjects."

It didn't take much, DJ thought.

"I'm ready for your final riddle, goblin king," Riley said confidently. "When I solve it, we'll take back those jewels you stole."

"*If* you solve it," the goblin king sneered wickedly. "You have not asked me what I require if you fail!"

"You want us to leave? Like all your subjects did?"

"No! I want *you!*" The goblin king pointed with his scepter. "Each and every one of you. You see, if you guess in-correctly, I'll ring this bell"—he held it up—"and my citadel will fill with our finest goblin warriors. They will kill you, gut you, and put your innards in a stew." He licked his lips. "We haven't tasted half-giant or orc in some time."

DJ shuddered. That horrible smell they experienced in the cave's first room—was that a stew made from…? He had heard of goblins eating people before, but he always assumed it was a joke. His blood turned cold and he reviewed spells in his head again, praying he wouldn't have to use them.

Riley swallowed, hiding her fear. "Fine then. Give us your riddle."

The goblin king grinned horribly. He said, "Three monkeys sit on a branch. Two face forward, one faces back. There are three hours before sunset, and the monkeys still haven't eaten supper. Twelve branches are between them and the forest floor. Will they have time to eat before nightfall?"

The party fell deathly still. DJ's heart thumped in his throat. Riley twisted her face. Everyone watched her with clammy, twitching hands, ready to shoot for their weapons. Riley asked for the goblin king to repeat the riddle. He did. That led to more silence and more thought.

Riley opened and closed her mouth twice. But finally, she said, "That riddle has no solution. It's just double talk. You're making it up so you can keep the jewels and eat us."

Everyone tensed. Riley's response was a bold one, but if she was right, they would walk away without a fight. If she was wrong, however, they would have a battle on their hands. Everyone's hands hovered by their weapons. DJ clamped his jaw to keep his teeth from chattering.

The goblin king squinted and clutched the bell tighter. "Is that your final answer?"

"Yes," Riley said. "And no matter what I say, you're going to ring that bell."

The goblin king sneered then lifted the bell.

Like a dart, Pebble snatched his hunting knife and hurled it across the room. The steel gleamed in the firelight as it found its mark between the goblin king's eyes. It cleaved his skull in half. A sopping *crack* bounced off the walls, and the goblin king's arms flopped to his sides. The bell landed silently in his lap.

Steve let out a startled yelp, but Francis clapped his hand over his mouth to silence him. DJ's face turned white and Riley stared at the slain goblin king. But, as casually as a spring morning, Pebble stepped forward and tore the knife from the goblin king's face. Then he cleaned the blade with the goblin king's robe.

Riley found her voice. "*Hundred Hells, Pebble!* We said no violence!"

"Did *you* want to turn into a stew?" Pebble said. "You know he was mischief."

DJ didn't take his eyes off the goblin king's severed face. He took deep breaths, swallowing the bile that crept up his throat. He said, "I think Pebble's right."

Francis's voice was stern. "But now they'll know we killed their king."

Pebble wasn't listening. He carved off one of the goblin king's ears and added it to his necklace. Then he sifted through the chest of jewels before extracting one glimmering, dangling item. "Ah, here it is. Thank the Moon."

He held up the pendant so it could catch the firelight. DJ frowned when he got a better look at it. The pendant was the most crudely designed thing he had ever seen—like a child had made it. The ruby in the middle was off center and the necklace was soldered unevenly so the pendant hung crooked.

Riley scrunched her nose at it. "You're proposing with *that?*"

Pebble scowled defensively. "It's dwarven custom to propose with jewelry you crafted. Do I look dwarvish to you? I have big fingers!"

"We'll have time to discuss this *later*," Francis urged. "Right now, we need a plan."

While they had been standing around, DJ had been assembling a plan in his head. It wasn't great, but it was something. He raised his hand. "Hey, um, what if Pebble took the goblin king and put him in his bed over there? Covered him up like he was sleeping. Then we could tell the goblins that we won the jewels fair and square, and the king decided to take a nap. With any luck, we'll be gone before they notice he's dead."

Everyone stared for a moment. Then Francis said, "Sir DJ, I'm sorry, but that's not a terribly good plan."

DJ blushed and he threw his hands up. "Well, does anyone else have any bright ideas? I think no matter what we do, there's no way we can leave here without looking a little suspicious. All thanks to loverboy over here."

"I won't apologize," Pebble folded his arms. "I saved our lives. Plain and simple."

"*Plain and simple,*" Riley mocked.

"*Later!*" Francis hissed. "We need to move *now*. Fine. We'll try DJ's plan. Everybody, remain calm and do what he said. Steven, give us a prayer for success—silently. With a bit of luck, we'll survive to see Laradyl."

While Steve prayed, Pebble tossed the goblin king onto his bed and threw a blanket over him. Then the half-giant picked up the jewels. Everyone took steadying breaths before putting on relaxed expressions and emerging from the king's citadel.

The upper-class goblins all blinked with surprise as they

watched the party march out with the chest. One of the goblins said, "You… won back the jewels?"

"Yep!" DJ said a little too quickly. "Sure did! Easy riddle. Don't bother the king, though. He's sleepy."

The goblins traded confused glances and scratched their heads. The party increased their pace as they made for the second door.

"Anyway, it was nice to meet you all!" DJ called. "Have a great day! I like your cave!"

"Don't oversell it," Francis whispered.

One goblin peered into the king's citadel just as the party entered the first room. They slammed the door behind them and power-walked to the main entrance. Every pair of goblin eyes watched them as the jewels jingled in Pebble's arms.

The party had just reached the main entrance when they heard the shouts from deep in the cave.

"*The king is dead! The king is dead!*"

Pebble hoisted his hammer. "Time to go!"

Crash! Pebble smashed a hole in the wall so large that the party poured through without ducking down. They flew past the guards, ran around the spiky perimeter, and sprinted into the forest. Their legs pumped and breaths came in great gulps. Steve had to hike up his robes like a dress to keep pace.

DJ stole a glance over his shoulder. A flood of goblins poured out of the cave, chattering and wild, hungry for revenge. And despite their small legs, they were *fast*. They gained on the escaping party with every second.

"Why didn't you tell us goblins could run so fast?" DJ hollered at Pebble.

"Less talking, more escaping!" Riley shouted.

It was no use. The party was losing steam, and the goblins were advancing. From dozens of yards back, their voices became clearer.

"*Stop them! After them!*"

Pebble bared his teeth. "Enough of this!" He planted his feet and slid to a halt, brandishing his hammer and huffing like a boar. "Get behind me!"

The party slid and stopped, arming themselves. Riley nocked a gnome-sized arrow in a human-sized bow. DJ steadied himself and held up his hands, ready to cast Flamefist. Steve did the same, swinging his frying pan like a sword. And Francis gripped his ax with both hands.

The goblins circled them, forming a tight ring. But they didn't converge. They kept a wide birth, surrounding the party, jumping up and down, whooping, throwing their hands in the air.

They weren't angry. They were *celebrating*.

Francis was the first to relax. "What the…? None of them are armed."

He was right. Not a single goblin carried a spear, bow, or blade. One by one, the party relaxed. A lone goblin stepped out from the crowd. The goblin dropped to his knees, prostrated himself and bowed as if greeting royalty. DJ and his friends traded puzzled glances.

"Thank you, kind travelers!" the goblin said. "Thank you, thank you, thank you! We can never repay your kindness!"

The party traded looks, dumbfounded. Pebble said, "But we—I killed your king."

The goblins cheered at the mention of it. The leading goblin raised his hands and the crowd fell silent.

"Indeed, you did!" he said. "King Grignak, in all of his cruelty, malice, and barbarism… is *no more!*"

More cheers filled the forest. DJ couldn't clear the confusion from his face.

"He said he was going to kill you and put you in a stew, didn't he?" the goblin said. "*Blech!* We don't even like eating people! It's disgusting!"

"And all of the pillaging and plundering he made us do!" another goblin spoke up. "We didn't want to! It perpetuates hurtful stereotypes!"

"So, hold on," DJ waved his hand. "You're glad we killed your king? And you're fine with us taking the jewels back?"

All the goblins gave their affirmative.

"If he was so terrible," Pebble frowned, "why did you not end him yourselves?"

Some goblins turned bashful. "We… were working on that. But you took care of it, and that's even better!" They gave each other thumbs up and high fives.

"So… are we free to go?" Francis asked.

The leading goblin nodded. "With our deepest gratitude! This new freedom will allow our clan to pick a new leader— one that's democratically elected! After all, a leader should be established by the consent of the governed, not by the forceful hand of authoritarianism!"

Francis tightened his lower lip and nodded. "Well spoken."

"Goddess be praised!" Steve cheered.

The goblins echoed his celebration. The leading goblin continued. "What are your names, heroes? Sir DJ, Riley, Francis, Steve, and Pebble, you will forever be known as true friends of the Mean Green Fiends."

"No!" another goblin piped up. "The *Nice* Green *Friends!*"

Applause of agreement from the goblins.

"Take care, heroes!" the lead goblin said. "We're off to write our constitution! May peace guide your path!"

And just as loudly as they arrived, they trampled back to their cave. The forest grew quiet, and the party was left standing in a circle, guarding a chest full of jewels, mouths agape. Not sure what else to do, they shared an awkward laugh and continued southward to Laradyl.

They arrived before nightfall. The jewels were returned to an exhilarated Barbas, who happily paid them the thousand gold. Pebble tucked the pendant away in his pack, and from that point, he walked stiffly and spoke very little.

Riley touched his arm. "Hey. Feeling nervous?"

"What? Me?" Pebble jerked. "No! No. I've wrestled bears. Slain trolls. A proposal is nothing." But even as he said the *proposal*, he lurched as if a weight dropped in his stomach.

Riley rubbed his arm. "Brooks is gonna love it."

By the time they made it back to the apartment, Brooks was making dinner. The smell of fresh bread filled the home. Before they could even dive in, Brooks dragged his stool over to Pebble, hopped on, then patted down his partner, searching any area he could reach.

"Hey!" the half-giant protested. "What are—stop—*excuse you!*"

Brooks turned to Steve. "Did you have to heal him? Did he get hurt? As a Steward of the Goddess, I know you can't lie."

Steve grinned and shook his head. "Pebble never once was harmed!"

"Good," Brooks said. Then he pointed. "What's in the pack? There's more than just two hundred gold in there."

DJ furrowed his brows in surprise. *He can tell that?*

Pebble stiffened and stammered. "Uh—it's nothing. Let's talk later."

Brooks put his fists on his short hips. "Show me, Duane."

"I—"

"*Now.*"

Swallowing, Pebble reached into the pack and pulled out the pendant. It was astonishingly plain compared to everything else in the room.

"A pendant?" Brooks crinkled his nose. "It looks like you made it yoursel—" And as soon as he said the words, he knew. The dwarf's eyes grew to saucers and his hands covered his face.

Pebble grimaced and eyed his guests. "I... wanted to do this another time." He got down on both knees and held the pendant in his great red hands. He cleared his throat, but his voice was so tiny it was nearly silent. "Brooks, will you marry me?"

The dwarf nodded stiffly, fighting back tears. Brooks took the pendant, hung it around his neck, then threw his arms around his partner. They held each other for a long while.

"I'm sorry it's not pretty," Pebble mumbled.

"It's the most beautiful thing I've ever seen," Brooks blubbered.

Riley squealed with delight and clapped her hands. Steve praised the Goddess. DJ grinned. Francis didn't say anything, and that's when DJ turned to get a look at him.

The orc wore a smile, but the rest of his body spoke of something much deeper—a profound sadness. Mist gathered in his amber eyes and his shoulders slumped as if pressed by a long-felt weight. DJ opened his mouth to say something but thought better of it. Maybe Francis would discuss it when he was ready.

10⊕

The party stayed with Pebble and Brooks for another day before leaving Laradyl. Riley took her earnings to a local blacksmith and purchased a set of human-sized arrows along with a quiver. When she put the quiver and bow over her back, DJ told her she looked like a bona fide ranger. That made Riley beam.

Pebble took her to a range in town and taught her proper hunting technique. Riley spent the next few hours firing arrows until her fingers became raw. All the while, Francis stayed with them, sipping tea and reading his new poetry book at a nearby table.

Steve went to the monastery to visit with the local Stewards and offer prayers. DJ stayed at Pebble and Brooks's apartment to rest. Or at least that's what he told the others. He sat on the couch with his first magic book spread over his lap. The pages were opened to the section on cantrips.

Learning cantrips came as a recommendation from Friar

Steve: "Spells are bites, but cantrips are nibbles!" Most of them were safe enough to practice indoors. DJ lit a candle a dozen times with Everspark. He also turned a quill into a glowing light with Luminate. Then he broke that quill and repaired it twice with Mend. All the while, his head never hurt.

DJ wanted to see Laradyl as a tourist, too, so he caught up with Francis and Riley after the archery range. They visited the shops along Laradyl's main concourse and DJ nearly bought a toy that made bubbles when you flicked it just right. Riley had her eye on a ranger cloak but couldn't afford it after her arrows. Francis followed along and watched them like an amused older brother.

That evening, Pebble and Brooks served everyone their last Laradyl supper before bed. They all stayed up late into the night, laughing and swapping stories, then went to sleep with full bellies. The next morning, the adventurers gave their reluctant goodbyes. They got affectionate hugs from Pebble and Brooks before they left the city.

DJ found the Lyleth Forest to be even brighter and livelier than the Aeldar Forest. Hickory and aspen trees sprouted everywhere. Elk and foxes were common. Riley stalked a jackrabbit for a brief time and managed to skewer it with an arrow. She burst with excitement and Francis had to calm her down before he taught her how to skin and dress it. Steve made a stew from the rabbit meat, some carrots, potatoes, and spices he bought in the city. Riley turned the rabbit pelt into a shoulder wrap for her quiver.

A few days later, a deer crossed the road and Riley lined up a shot, but the game bounded away before the arrow could fly. The party was just as eager to see Riley get her first big game kill, so they followed her into the forest. But hours passed, and the deer disappeared. Riley was visibly disappointed, but she did, however, bag another jackrabbit as a consolation prize.

Their traversal led them to a clearing with a glistening clear pond nearby. It seemed comfortable enough, so they decided to establish camp there for the day. Feeling the grime cling to his body, DJ told everyone he would go wash.

As DJ disrobed and dipped into the water, he was surprised at how warm it was—not like the icy cold streams of the Aeldar Forest. He scrubbed the dirt from his skin and ran fingers through his hair, then he remembered a spell he had read in his intermediate spell book.

Ice Spike. The book told him that he had to have access to water—the ice wouldn't just materialize in the air, unlike spells that used fire or lightning. Well, there was plenty of water here, and he was all alone to practice.

He dug his feet into the muddy pond floor. The motion was fluid with his arms and torso. He twisted to his left, slid his left hand back through the air, and made a smooth snapping motion with his right hand. "*Glaci-talum!*"

An ice spike the length of his hand materialized from the water and shot up from the pond's surface. It crested like a child's throw and splashed back into the pond, gliding along the surface.

DJ's head swelled with pain and his eyes watered. He pushed on his temples between his palms. "*Ugh...* that one's gonna take some work."

Snap! A branch broke at the other end of the pond. DJ heard it rustle and crash as it hit the forest floor. He froze and slid deeper into the water. He squinted and looked toward the sound's source, but the forest replied with stillness. Nothing moved.

DJ blinked. "Don't love that," he whispered to himself.

Whoosh! Another sound from up in the trees—leaves shook as if something large bounded from one branch to another.

DJ sank lower into the water. Even quieter, he said, "Don't love that either."

His heart rose into his throat. With methodical slowness, he tiptoed out of the pond. When he reached his clothes, he dried off and dressed as quickly as he could, then he sprinted back to camp.

He arrived to find Francis sharpening his ax by the fire and Riley shooting arrows into a tree stump. They both watched curiously as DJ bounded into camp. DJ hunched over and put his hands on his knees as he panted.

"Your bath looks like it was less than relaxing," Francis observed.

"Something was in the trees," DJ said seriously. "I heard a branch fall, then there was a bunch of rustling. We should probably get out of here."

Riley nocked an arrow and scanned the treetops, but nothing moved. Francis stood with ax his in hand, likewise searching the branches.

DJ looked around. "Where's Steve?"

"Getting more firewood," Francis said. "Come to think of

it, he should have been back by now. He never takes this long."

"Should we go look for him?" Riley asked.

Francis nodded. "Given your recent premonition, it's best that we leave this place. Keep together as we search, though. Weapons out."

They armed themselves and broke camp with haste, creeping through the woods while shouting for Steve. They never received an answer. As their boots moved along the soil, their eyes darted to the forest floor, the treetops, and everything in between. But as far as they could tell, they were the only ones making noise.

A loud *thump* sounded behind them. Riley screamed. Francis roared. DJ tried to flip around and cast a spell, but a black bag was shoved over his head. Expert hands lashed his wrists together while he squirmed and shouted. It was the same with Francis and Riley. DJ felt himself lifted off his feet and carried away.

It was hard to tell how far he was carried. All the way, the three adventurers protested and threatened. The thought of Francis being subdued and carried unwillingly made DJ shiver with dread. Whoever took them hostage must be *strong*.

DJ heard what sounded like wooden gates opening. Then there was the gentle plodding of footsteps all around. And he heard the voices of strangers pipe up.

"New brothers and sisters!"

"What a glorious day it is!"

DJ felt himself be turned upward and pressed into a chair, his bound wrists still behind him. Someone yanked the black sack off his head, and he had to blink against the light. He was still outside—in the middle of a village, oddly enough. It was a conglomerate of modest wooden cabins with a large building at one end—a tiered wooden structure that had to be a place of worship built by inexperienced hands. A long set of stairs led to its entrance, and above the entrance, painted in crooked letters, it said *Temple of Phillip.*

To DJ's right, Francis and Riley got the sacks pulled off their heads. To DJ's left, he found Steve, along with a stranger he didn't recognize. It was an elf with handsome, sharp features, but his face was riddled with confusion and violence. He gave DJ a look, hoping for an explanation, but DJ couldn't offer one.

"I am reunited with my friends!" Steve yipped. "Goddess be praised!"

In front of them stood a woman with shoulder-length blonde hair and bright brown eyes. Her round face and petite frame gave her the appearance of a charming schoolteacher. She, along with dozens of other villagers, wore matching black robes cinched at the waist. On every pair of robes, an insignia was printed on the chest: a steaming bowl of noodles with chopsticks poking out.

And where were all the villagers? Surrounding DJ and his friends. They formed a circle around the woman and her captives—none of the prisoners could leave without breaking through them.

DJ felt all of their eyes on him, and he turned pale.

"Welcome, and congratulations!" the kind-looking woman said as she raised her hands. "You are all the newest inductees to the House of Phillip! What a glorious day it is!"

"*Glorious indeed!*" the whole village echoed and raised their hands.

"What in the Hundred Hells?" Riley muttered as her eyes moved about.

"Yes, this is our village, and you are our newest members!" the woman said. "It's clear that Phillip has led you here this day! And for that, we have much cause to rejoice! What a glorious day it is!"

"*Glorious indeed!*" the village echoed again.

"No one was *led* anywhere!" Francis barked. "We were abducted! This treatment is barbaric! Who is 'Phillip?' We demand to speak to him at once!"

The woman gave a knowing laugh and shook her head. "Oh, my large green friend. I am Phillip! They are Phillip! We are all Phillip! Our names from the world have no use here, along with our old possessions, family, and friends! We have separated ourselves from the world to achieve a higher existence, with Phillip as our guiding star. He is us, and we are him. And now, you will join us as our new Phillips! What a glorious day it is!"

"*Glorious indeed!*"

"This is madness," the mysterious elf said.

Steve's eyes widened and his face turned pale. "But I worship the Goddess Uh! I cannot forsake her!"

The woman put her hands on her knees and spoke like Steve was a child. "Oh, but you must, you strange, ugly man! Here, you will find the *truth*. Here, you will be taught from the Book of Phillip and help us prepare for the Great Cleansing. This is a great blessing to be here—to accept the truth and usher in a greater world. What a glorious d—"

"Wait, wait, *Great Cleansing?*" Riley said. "What's that supposed to mean?"

The woman's eyes flashed. "Why, it's when Phillip will grant us the power to expand his House across the territory! This world is rife with *ignorance*, and *evil,* and *sin.*" Speaking those words actually made her frown. "But here, Phillip has guided us to create a community of love and peace. When the time is right, we shall spread it across the territory! All will join us! And if any oppose us, they will drown in rivers of their own blood. We will be Phillip's hands in exacting righteous vengeance upon them. It is as the Book of Phillip foretold."

DJ shivered as he pictured the horror. Steve's face turned white. The others traded looks of incredulity. The elvish stranger leaped up from his chair, his hands still bound behind him. He glared at the leading Phillip with sharp eyes.

"This is a sick, violent cult!" he shouted. "And I shall have no part in this! Farewell!"

He crouched down and barreled with full speed to the edge of the circle, thinking he could break through the Phillips. But two Phillips grabbed him by the shoulders and yanked him back in. The elf kicked and squirmed as they dragged him back to his chair.

The lead Phillip shook her head and sighed. "Oh no, this just won't do. I'm afraid we'll have to use the No-No Juice. Phillip?"

"Yes, Grand Phillip?"

"Bring the No-No Juice, please."

As two Phillips restrained the struggling elf, a third Phillip handed a small bottle of blue liquid to the Grand Phillip.

"Thank you, Phillip," she said.

"You're most welcome, Grand Phillip!"

Two Phillips tilted the elf's head back and pried his jaw open with forceful hands. With sad eyes, Grand Phillip unstopped the bottle and carefully poured the liquid down the elf's throat. The elf coughed and sputtered, trying to resist, but it was no use.

The effect was immediate. The elf screamed with holy agony. His legs tensed and shivered. His gurgling cries rang through the trees as his skin melted off his bones like sludge.

Riley shrieked. Everyone else turned still. The Phillips let go—there was no need to hold on to a melting mess. Smoke wafted off the body and the smell burned everyone's nose hairs. A puddle of molten flesh formed at the foot of an elvish skeleton, cascading in gross clumps through its clothes and down its chair.

DJ's throat was too tight to scream—he thought he might pass out. Steve actually did, and a nearby Phillip straightened his unconscious body in his chair.

Grand Phillip sighed. "So sad to be a potential Phillip falter. His heart was impure." She put on a smile as she addressed DJ and the others. "We Phillips understand that this is a lot to take in. But don't worry! We have everything you could ever want here! Food, shelter, friendship, pickleball courts… so yes, count yourself blessed as our newest Phillips!

And please." She pointed to the melted elf. "Do not try to escape. What a glorious day it is!"

"*Glorious indeed!*"

DJ tried to swallow, but he couldn't stop staring at the goopy mess. There had to be a way out of here, but whatever that was, they would need to be *very* careful, or their quest for the Amulet would end in gooey failure.

11

The first thing the Phillips did was destroy all of the party's possessions. They built a large fire, threw the party's packs in, then celebrated the destruction like it was a grand victory. Riley's first edition *Light of the Star Path*, DJ's spell books, their gold, their wizard waffles—all gone. The Phillips didn't even bother to look through their stuff; they just threw it on the fire and danced.

They did, however, keep the weapons. Those would be needed for the Great Cleansing.

The next thing they did was give DJ and the others matching robes and copies of the Book of Phillip. The robes were clearly made from a low-quality wool that made DJ's skin itch. He wondered how everyone wasn't breaking out in hives. The Book of Phillip was small enough to fit in a robe pocket. It had a matching black cover and the cult insignia. Steve pinched the corner of his book and dangled it in front of him like it was filthy. His eyes stung and his lip trembled.

Lastly, the Phillips split apart the group. Everyone was given two Phillips to escort them on a village tour, and they split into opposite directions so the party would be separated.

"Wait a second," DJ said as he was led away. "Why can't I go with my friends? Why are you keeping us away?"

"No one is truly apart in the House of Phillip!" a sister Phillip said. "But you need to be introduced to the other Phillip brothers and sisters! Spending too much time with your old friends will keep you from becoming one with us. What a glorious day it is!"

"How long are you going to keep me from them?" DJ asked. He looked over his shoulder just in time to catch Riley's eye. She waved at him miserably.

"As long as it takes!" a brother Phillip said as if it would be fun.

So the Phillips showed him around. Everywhere they went, people greeted DJ as "New Phillip" and DJ hated it every time. He was shown his barrack, where he would sleep in a large room filled with bunk beds for other Phillips. He was shown the mess hall where the Phillips ate. He was taken to the gardens, the well, the pickleball courts, and the training grounds.

They really pulled out all the stops for the training grounds. There was a fully outlined sparring area with straw dummies, bows, swords, axes, clubs, nunchucks, even cannons. Currently, a crowd of Phillips gathered to watch two Phillips spar. The two swung and jabbed with wooden weapons until one Phillip was downed with a broken leg and bloody lip. The crowd clapped, but no one stepped in to help the injured

Phillip.

DJ frowned at the spectacle. "Shouldn't someone help him? Don't you have healers or something?"

"This is how we are made strong for the Great Cleansing," one of the escorts said. "And magic? We could *never*. Magic is an abomination that nearly makes us equal to gods. It's blasphemous." She stopped and stared at DJ. "You're not a *mage*, are you?"

They destroyed my pack without looking in it, DJ thought. *They didn't see my spell books.* He shook his head vigorously. "Me? Nope. No way. All magic, no maidens. That's what I always say."

Both Phillips sighed. "What a blessing," one of them said.

As they walked away, DJ noticed a large shed next to the combat area. It had a large painting of an explosion on the door. He motioned to it. "What's that?"

One of the Phillips gazed upon him with wondrous eyes. "If Grand Phillip finds you worthy, in due time, you'll be trained to destroy the sinners with the Holy Boom Powder. Melee combat will only get us so far in the Great Cleansing —we'll need something *much* bigger to destroy the heathens."

Holy. Boom. Powder. DJ repeated the words in his mind and shuddered. These people didn't seem to have the slightest problem with mass murdering people in the name of their god. So much for a culture of peace and harmony.

The last stop of the tour was the Temple—the large building DJ saw earlier. They climbed the steps and entered through the double doors. DJ was expecting it to be ornate, but the interior was mostly bare. It would have been completely empty if it wasn't for a white statue of the most average-looking man DJ had ever seen. Average build. Average height. A face devoid of any interesting features. But in one hand, he held a bowl of noodles. His other hand was lifted in a friendly wave.

Grand Phillip was waiting next to the statue with candles lit at the its base. Francis, Steve, and Riley were gathered in a circle by their escorts. Their escorts held each of their shoulders firmly to keep them from escaping.

Steve's face was wet with tears. The sight made DJ's stomach burn and his hands turn into fists.

"Welcome, newest Phillips!" Grand Phillip said. "It is now time to take upon yourself the name of Phillip! Your new home is here, and we know that you'll find happiness and joy. This is truly an occasion for celebration! What a glorious day it is!"

"*Glorious indeed!*"

Steve sniffed loudly and his bottom lip shook. New tears formed and dribbled down his chinless face. Grand Phillip's shoulders drooped and her face sweetened with concern. She stepped forward and took his hand. Steve didn't acknowledge her.

"I know it's difficult to leave the world behind, to turn from your false god and come toward the light." She held his hand with both of her own. "But I promise you, New Phillip, that you will find love here like you've never felt before. No one will judge you for your hideous appearance or loud voice. You are equal with us."

Steve said nothing, but DJ noticed his eyebrow twitch. Grand Phillip squeezed his hand and stepped back. "Now, let us begin with the swearing ceremony!"

"We're not going to take your stupid oath," Riley said.

The Grand Phillip's chin turned toward her with menacing slowness, but she kept smiling. Her brown eyes flashed. "I truly hope you don't mean that. Because if that were true…"

The escorts tightened their grip on the captives, and each escort withdrew a bottle of blue No-No Juice from their robes. DJ trembled as they dangled the bottle just inches from his face.

"…we would have to make a mess in the Temple of Phillip," Grand Phillip said. "And that would be most tragic. Okay? Okay! Now, put your hand on your copy of the Book of Phillip and raise your right hand."

Hesitantly, everyone followed. Steve last of all. Every movement to him was pure torture. DJ thought he saw the friar mouthing a prayer of forgiveness. The sight made DJ want to jump at these fanatics, but he couldn't risk a mouthful of No-No Juice.

"Repeat after me," Grand Phillip said. She raised her hand. "I forsake the ways of the world to join the House of Phillip. I take upon his name and become one with him. I shall destroy all those who oppose him in the Great Cleansing. And I will always use the signup sheet for the pickleball court."

DJ and the others repeated every word. The last bit about the pickleball court felt a little unnecessary, but he wasn't about to point it out. When they were done, his escorts loosened their grip and he felt like he could breathe again.

"Congratulations! You did it!" Grand Phillip said brightly. "Hugs! Welcome to the family!" She went one by one, giving each member a hug, which wasn't returned. Steve last of all. His frame quaked. His tear-streaked face was red.

DJ wanted nothing more than to embrace Steve and reassure him that everything would be okay, but the threat of nearby Phillips kept him still. He and his friends were New Phillips now, so every other Phillip would be watching them to make sure they didn't escape. Whatever escape plan they made had to be in complete secrecy, or they would become a melted mess like the elf from earlier.

DJ knew there was no way he or the others would live out their days here, so he resolved to make a plan.

When the swearing ceremony ended, Steve fled the Temple. DJ and the others tried to follow him and comfort him, but the friar was too fast. By the time they made it out the main doors, Steve had disappeared into the barrack and a group of Phillips forcefully insisted that the New Phillips accompany them to dinner. It was all smiles. Overbearing, commanding smiles.

Once they entered the mess hall and got their food—noodles and broth—the Phillips separated the three of them to different tables. DJ tried to arch his neck and get a look at Francis or Riley, but every time he did, one of the Phillips would move to block his view. After the third attempt, DJ huffed and turned to his meal.

"You'll love it here!" one Phillip said. "Never have I felt such happiness and purpose!"

"There is much wisdom to be found in the Book of Phillip!" another one said. "Have you read your copy yet?"

DJ pushed the noodles around his bowl. "I literally just got here."

"Behold! This passage is my favorite."

The Phillip pushed the book by DJ's hand, and DJ glanced at it. His feelings went from annoyed to confused. He grabbed the book to get a closer look. It was nothing like the Ancient Text that Stewards of the Goddess read from. Instead of verses and chapters, it was bulleted lists of ingredients and instructions. DJ flipped through the pages. More of the same.

"What the?" he said incredulously. "Guys, this isn't scripture! This is just a recipe book! And it's all noodles!"

One of the Phillips smiled and rolled his eyes. "Oh, New Phillip, look with your spiritual eyes! The broth is symbolic of the heart, and the noodles are the soul." He laughed then took his book back. "You'll see the truth in time. I'm sure of it."

DJ was already few slurps into his noodles, and he had to admit they made him feel pretty good. Strangely good, honestly. Like fireflies were floating in his belly and brain. His body relaxed and he ate until the noodles disappeared, then he licked the broth out of the bowl. He had never licked the broth out of a bowl before, and it wasn't that the noodles were *that* good, but something about them just… compelled him. When he finished, he set the bowl down and smacked his lips.

It's not so bad here, he thought. *Maybe we need to give it a chance.*

DJ shook his head. What was he thinking? This place definitely did *not* deserve a chance. But something about this bowl of noodles made his head funny. And even as the slippery thoughts wore down, they never seemed to go entirely away. They lingered like a low, quiet hum, barely audible in the back of his mind.

Through the rest of the day, the Phillips were careful not to let the new recruits spend time together unless they were chaperoned. They were probably worried that the New Phillips would devise a plan to escape, which was exactly what DJ and the others wanted to do. But the close presence of every Phillip crippled any hopes of making that happen.

That night, DJ lay in his bunk trying to formulate fragments of an escape plan, but he knew he'd have to know the village better. Look for weak points. Find opportunities to exploit. And while he did, he would have to look innocent. Otherwise he'd turn into a smokey puddle.

So he did just that. For the next couple of days, DJ wandered the village with every opportunity he could scrape up. Then at night, he would lay awake piecing it all together in his head. He couldn't write anything down for fear of materials being discovered. Everything had to be locked in the vault of his mind. And that made everything more complicated.

Meanwhile, Steve became elusive. It was so unlike him. Each day, DJ and the others looked around the village for him, but their efforts were in vain. Whenever they did find Steve, he would be sitting alone, eyes closed, dissociating. DJ, Riley, and Francis tried to comfort him—provide some veiled nuggets of wisdom and hope. But the friar never opened his eyes or acknowledged them. It didn't help that other Phillips were always listening nearby.

DJ managed to write notes on a few scraps of parchment for Riley and Francis. They said, *I'm making a plan. Leave it to me. Destroy this paper.* Then he slipped them into Riley and Francis's copies of the Book of Phillip. As far as the nearby Phillips were concerned, DJ was just showing them a passage he liked.

As more days passed, that low hum in the back of DJ's mind grew. The fireflies in his mind lingered longer after every meal. He tried skipping meals to lessen their hold on his mind, but there was always a group of Phillips to grab him by the arms and drag him to the mess hall. They made sure he got at least three bowls of noodles a day, without fail.

DJ hoped beyond hope that he wasn't losing himself here. But everything about the village became brighter and warmer with the passage of time. He held white-knuckle to the image of the melted elf in the chair. That had to keep him grounded.

Over a week had gone by and DJ had only formed pieces of a plan. It involved setting the Temple on fire with Flame-fist, then high tailing it out of the village while the Phillips tried to quell the flames. But that didn't solve the locked gates and the forest agents that would abduct them again. The humming in the back of his mind made it harder to think about leaving. He held on to the image of the melted elf, re-playing it in his mind, but even then, it was getting fuzzy.

"It is your turn to spar, New Phillip!"

DJ jolted to attention. "Huh?"

He had been lost in thought as he stood at the edge of the

sparring ring. He had managed to avoid the responsibility of training for the Great Cleansing up until this point, but now it seemed that his luck had run out.

"Yes!" one Phillip said. "We have not seen you battle yet, New Phillip! Take a weapon and stand against one of us!"

The rest of the Phillips cheered as if it were karaoke night. But DJ hadn't forgotten the broken leg from the Phillip he saw days ago. A shiver of dread slithered down his back. He gulped and put his hands in his robe pockets.

"Uh, sorry Phillips, I'm not feeling well today so I'll have to sit this one—"

"Nonsense!"

Two Phillips shoved him into the ring and a challenger entered from the other side. It was none other than Grand Phillip herself. Her blonde hair was tied in a ponytail and her brown eyes flashed. She chose a staff and brandished it as she met DJ in the middle of the ring. "We absolutely *must* watch you spar, New Phillip!" she said. "Choose a weapon! May Phillip smile upon our battle!"

DJ stammered for a moment, hoping to say something clever to escape the situation, but drew nothing. Slowly, uncomfortably, he dragged his feet to the rack of practice weapons. He grabbed a wooden shortsword and met Grand Phillip in the middle of the ring.

A swallow pushed down his throat. *No magic,* he thought. *Hope all of Francis's lessons paid off.*

"I wish you the best, New Phillip!" Grand Phillip said. "But I am highly prepared for the Great Cleansing! I will not hold back!"

DJ smiled feebly. "Wouldn't expect it."

The crowd watched with wide smiles and fixed eyes. They counted down, and as they did, DJ's heart crept higher in his chest.

"Three, two, one, *fight!*"

Grand Phillip lunged. DJ knocked the blow away. Phillip gave three more decisive swipes as she peddled forward. DJ backpedaled in kind, dodging and blocking each blow. A surprised staccato jumped from his lips. He was actually holding his own! But a fourth slash came dangerously close—DJ dodged it by collapsing to his knees as the staff passed just an inch over his head. The strike surely would have cracked his skull.

DJ slashed but Phillip bent away from it. She spun around and swung her staff, which DJ narrowly dodged by throwing himself backward. DJ's butt hit the ground. He rolled out of the way just as Grand Phillip swung her staff in a vertical strike. The Phillips around the ring applauded. DJ gulped in heavy breaths and gazed up at Grand Phillip with heat.

Is she actually trying to kill me? The thought terrified him, but something else burned inside him. *No way. I'm not going to be worked over by a ditzy cult leader in the middle of the forest. I've got that Sir Dashing blood in there somewhere.*

DJ leaped to his feet and brandished his sword, baring his teeth like a tiger. The sight didn't phase Grand Phillip. If anything, it only excited her.

"Wonderful!" she said. "I'll love to see this passion during the Great Cleansing!"

DJ shouted and lifted his weapon. Grand Phillip swung her staff in an angle he didn't expect. A bolt of panic shot through him. He twisted his sword to block it, but it wasn't enough. The staff slammed into DJ's arm, smashing the bones in his forearm and badly bruising his shoulder.

DJ cried out and fell to his knees, grimacing through the pain. He wished more than anything that Steve could come over and fix him up with Healing Hand, but magic was taboo here, and Steve was impossible to find anyway. So DJ just knelt and writhed, staring at his mangled forearm.

"Grand Phillip is the victor!" someone called.

Everyone clapped. Grand Phillip gave generous bows all around. DJ clamped his teeth so hard he thought they could break.

"Sorry, New Phillip!" Grand Phillip said. "Someone take him to the Boo Boo House. Don't worry, New Phillip, you'll be right as rain before you know it. Today, you learned that you are full of potential. What a glorious day it is!"

"*Glorious indeed!*" everyone echoed.

12

The Boo Boo House was a small hut with a few beds where people were treated for injuries. One Phillip staffed it, providing various potions and primitive medicine. She reset DJ's forearm, wrapped it in a splint, and put some kind of cream on his shoulder. Then she tied his arm in a sling and fed him a potion of some sort. DJ wondered if it was more broth, because it made the fireflies dance in his body again.

The potion made him think of how grateful he was to be in a safe place like this, with such loving, caring people. All the smiling faces. All identical names and clothing. Everyone was equal here. How glorious.

Goddess, DJ thought. *It's getting worse.*

The melted elf. The melted elf. The melted elf.

Riley and Francis visited, with other Phillips following on their heels. Both of DJ's friends lamented over his broken arm, a slight dash of fear laced across their faces.

"Yeah," DJ said. "It's going to keep me from doing a lot of

things. A lot of things that matter a lot to me."

He didn't have to say it, but Riley and Francis knew what he meant. Magic depended on movement and language, and many spells couldn't be performed without both arms. So as it stood, DJ couldn't use magic. And if DJ couldn't use magic, he couldn't carry out his formulating escape plan. Who knows how long it would take his arm to heal without magic? Weeks? Months? By then, he knew his mind would be lost to this place. Francis and Riley both left with their heads hung down.

Surprisingly, Steve came to visit DJ not long after. DJ sat up in bed at the sight of his elusive friend. But Steve wasn't as mopey as he had been in previous days. He walked with a pep in his step and his arms swung widely. His jubilant manner contrasted to the dark circles hanging under his eyes—he looked like he hadn't slept in days. DJ watched him with bent eyebrows.

"Hello!" Steve said as he reached DJ's bed.

"Steve! Uh—Phillip!" DJ stammered. "Thanks for visiting me. Really bad luck with the arm. It's going to *keep me* from *doing a lot*." DJ tried to be deliberate with his words. He knew how dense Steve could be.

Steve blinked innocently. "When shall they release you?"

"Tomorrow."

"Wonderful!" Steve shouted. "Very grand indeed! Then I shall withhold my gift until then! We shall all be blessed!"

Where was the moping? Where was the sullen, distant, detached Steve? DJ twisted his face and cleared his throat. "A gift? Hey, uh, Phillip, are you okay? You seem different."

"Never better!" Steve said. "I have been blessed with clarity and purpose! A bright new future awaits us!"

DJ's heart sank. *Oh no. They got him.* His throat got tight and he tried to stay composed. "I'm glad you think that, Ste— Phillip. Thanks for coming to visit."

Steve bowed so low that his face nearly touched the bed, then he turned on his heels and left the Boo Boo House. As the door closed behind him, DJ clenched his jaw and punched the mattress with his good arm, silently mourning the loss of his friend.

*

DJ still had to wear a sling and splint after he was released, but at least that got him out of sparring practice. He walked by the ring and met the gaze of Grand Phillip. She grinned brightly and waved at him. DJ forced a smile and a wave, then he muttered some very rude things under his breath.

Riley and Francis sat with DJ during every meal, along with a few other Phillips. DJ could tell that the noodles and broth were wearing them down too. Whenever they ate, they got the same dopey smiles on their faces, and those smiles lingered for several minutes after each meal. DJ wondered how long the image of the melted elf would help before the fireflies in his brain completely took over.

"Hey," DJ said after supper. "Did *our friend* mention anything to you guys about a gift?"

Riley and Francis traded glances then shook their heads.

Riley asked, "Did he say something to you? How did you find him?"

"He showed up at the Boo Boo House yesterday after you two left. He said he had a gift for me and that he had been blessed with clarity. I think he's… fully acclimated now."

Riley's bottom lip trembled. Francis's shoulders drooped and his gaze fell to the ground.

A setting sun threw red light over the forest. Most of the Phillips were getting ready to retire to their bunks for the night. But just as the crowd was thinning out, they heard a familiar voice over by the Temple.

"*House of Phillip!*" Steve shouted. "Gather and hear me! I have an announcement of grave importance!"

There he was, standing at the foot of the Temple with his arms outstretched. Steve looked out on the village with a huge smile. Curiously, Phillips whispered to one another and began to gather in the center of the village, facing the Temple. DJ, Riley, and Francis pushed to the front of the crowd, anxiously awaiting whatever Steve had to say.

Steve noticed them. "Yes! My friends! Please join me!"

Cautiously, DJ and the others joined Steve on the first step of the Temple. DJ leaned toward Steve and whispered. "Steve, what are you doing? Is this the gift you were talking about?"

Steve didn't answer. Instead, he faced the crowd of Phillips that stood before him. No one was left in the barracks, combat ring, or even the pickleball court. Everyone in the village stood facing one of their newest Phillips. Steve had their unbridled attention.

"This announcement is of great importance!" Steve hollered. "We have been part of your village for many days! You have adopted us into the House of Phillip! You have given us your Book and fed us your noodles! And I am proud to say that this day, through me…" He paused for dramatic effect. "The mighty Goddess rains her fiery vengeance upon you!"

KABOOM!

The Temple of Phillip burst into a fireball of destruction. The ground trembled. Splintered, burning wood chunks hurled through the air, raining across the village. Phillips screamed and cowered. They watched the sky for falling bits of woody shrapnel. All the while, DJ's ears rang, and he raised one arm to shield himself.

Steve's arms were still in the air. "May your thirst for death grant you the deepest pits of the Hundred Hells! May your false god Phillip cower at the awesome might of the Goddess Uh! As your Temple has been torn asunder, so shall your cursed dogma crumble! Farewell, House of Phillip, and may you know torment until your dying days!" He threw out his arms. "*Vytrium-tholys!*"

With those words, Steve encased every Phillip inside the largest Barrier spell DJ had ever seen. It was a giant blue dome one hundred feet in diameter, full of raging Phillips pounding their fists against its glassy edge like caged animals. Pandemonium ensued. Agony racked their senses. They wailed and pulled their hair, fell to their knees, clawing and scratching at the blue Barrier.

DJ watched the sight with a dangling jaw, still absorbing

everything that had happened. But Steve wore a smile. He turned to DJ and said, "Time to go! Weapons are here!"

Steve reached under the Temple steps. He withdrew Francis's ax, DJ's sword, Riley's bow, and his very own frying pan. Everyone watched him incredulously as they armed themselves. The Phillips screamed and cursed as chunks of debris bounced off the Barrier dome.

"Steve!" DJ said. "How—when did—?"

"No time for words, Sir DJ!" Steve hollered. "For now, we must make our escape! May the Goddess grant us safety!"

Steve led the way as they sprinted for the south gate. The tall wooden structure was sealed tightly, locked with a series of bolts and chains. When they got close enough, Steve planted his feet and jabbed a finger forward. "*Fulgyr-fylum!*"

A bolt of blue lightning blasted into the gate, blowing a hole through the timber almost big enough to crawl through. Francis went to work immediately, hacking the hole larger with his ax. DJ looked over his shoulder, terrified that the Barrier spell would drop soon. His fear was confirmed. He could see the blue shell flickering, so they only had seconds.

"Let's pick up the pace!" Riley shouted.

"Your criticism isn't constructive!" Francis said.

It would be a tight squeeze, but Francis hacked a large enough hole. Riley wiggled through first. Then Steve. It was tough to make it through with their robes catching on the broken wood. Francis struggled to get through with his massive shoulders and hefty gut. He finally plopped onto the other side just as the Barrier spell vanished. DJ looked over his shoulder and saw hundreds of cult members stampeding toward him.

He yelped and tried to climb through, but it was nearly impossible with one arm. DJ started to panic, but Francis thrust both his hands through the hole, grabbed DJ's shoulders and hoisted him through.

"*Ooowww!*" DJ complained.

Steve threw both hands toward the hole. "*Refyctio!*" The broken bits of wood flew back into the wall, sealing it up, good as new. Just a second later, Phillips flung their bodies against the gate. Muffled thumps and angry shouts came from the other side.

"We're nearly free!" Steve said. "Southward we go! Quickly! *Invisi-pallyum!*"

Everyone in the party vanished. Invisible. DJ slapped his hand all over his torso to make sure it was still there. Then he remembered reading about Evercloak in his spell book—it granted invisibility for a short period of time. Steve just cast it on all of them, which was a pretty hefty feat. Hopefully it would last long enough to put some distance between them and the village. Under the cover of darkness, they'd have an even better chance.

DJ heard the footsteps of his friends take off southward. He followed.

As they went, Steve unraveled his story. When they were forced to take the oath and join the House of Phillip, Steve said the words with his mouth, but in his heart, he vowed to exact justice on the murderous cult. So for days, he meditated —while hidden, if possible—to focus his magical energy. Then at night, he would cast Evercloak on himself to invisibly study the village and devise an escape plan.

It was after the first night that he knew what to do. He managed to break into the shed by the combat ring and turn barrels of Holy Boom Powder invisible while he moved them to the Temple. It took several nights of working until dawn before most of the barrels were moved. Then he tied a series of fuses long enough that he'd be able to give his speech to the village while the fuse burned and the Temple got ready to blow.

Of course, he knew he'd need a plan to get out of the village after the explosion, and he knew exactly what spells could be effective. He meditated for an entire day so he could perform a massive Barrier spell to trap the villagers, Shockthread to break the gate, Repair to fix it, and Evercloak to make him and his friends invisible.

"How are you not magically exhausted after all that?" DJ said.

"Oh, I can hardly see!" Steve returned. "My head feels ready to burst! But we must fly! Do not forget the forest people that took us!"

That's true. DJ hadn't forgotten the people in the trees that stalked, captured, and carried them to the village. With any luck, the spell would wear off once they were out of range. But if not, they would have a battle on their hands. DJ cursed his broken arm and clutched his sword.

Dark bodies flickered into view just ahead of DJ—his friends. They all did their best to sprint in their cult robes, but it was hard to get a full stride. When they fully appeared in the darkness, everyone was running out of breath, so they slid to a halt.

They tried to keep their panting quiet but took in measured breaths. They stayed still and listened to the forest. Steve squinted and kept his fingers splayed. Riley readied her bow and DJ drew his sword.

Silence. It lasted for a long while. DJ relaxed and retracted from his fighting stance.

Then a rustle above. Everyone looked up. Eight shapes dropped from the trees. They were dressed entirely in black, with nothing but a slit to reveal their eyes. Upon their chests, their garb had the same noodle insignia as the cult robes.

Everyone dodged out of the way and scrambled to their feet. All except DJ, however, who landed on his broken arm. Pain rocked through him and he writhed upon the ground.

Steve cast Shockthread. The bolt of lightning ripped through three cultists, dropping them with gaping, smoldering holes in their bodies. As the smell of scorched meat wafted through the air, Steve dropped to his hands and knees and vomited. The magic had finally proved too much.

Francis buried his ax in a cultist's stomach. Another cultist lunged and swiped at him with a dagger. Francis took the blow in the shoulder and winced as the blood seeped down his arm. Then he grabbed the cultist's head and smashed it against a tree. Skull fragments and brain matter oozed through Francis's fingers, and he threw the body away. It slumped across the ground next to its slain ally.

Riley shot an arrow into an advancing cultist. It found its mark in the foe's shoulder, and the cultist dropped to one knee as it growled. Then it snapped the bolt in half. With shaking hands, Riley nocked another arrow, but she noticed one of the cultists advancing on Steve while he retched on the soil. She let the arrow fly to protect him, but it missed. That's when the cultist focused on Riley instead.

Now she had two cultists advancing on her. She nocked a third arrow and clenched her teeth to keep them from chattering. DJ scrambled to get up with one good arm. In a sitting position, he fought through the pain and scooped up his sword. Then he hurled it like a boomerang toward one of the cultist's legs.

The strike was true, and the sword sliced through the cultist's hamstring. The cultist roared and collapsed, unable to move. The other cultist advancing on Riley stopped. It looked around. At that moment, Francis swung his ax into the last standing foe. With six cultists slain, one still standing, and one badly wounded, the battle turned to three against one-and-a-half.

The cultist paused, tensed, then turned on its heels and fled northward. That left the last cultist—the one with the severed hamstring—laying on the ground, bleeding into the dirt. Utterly defeated.

Steve regained himself, and he wiped the sick from his lips. Francis helped him to his feet, and DJ stood as well. Everyone stalked toward the remaining cultist, unsure of whether or not to land a killing blow. They didn't get the chance.

"*Heathens!*" the cultist shouted. "I will not die by your hand! All glory to Phillip!" It turned its knife backward and plunged it into its chest. It gasped, gurgled, twitched, and stilled. The cultist's eyes stared lifelessly into the night sky.

DJ shivered. Seven dead bodies littered all around. The smell of death was beginning to fester in the air. He found his bloodstained sword in the dirt and scooped it up. He was worried he would have to kill again tonight, but it wasn't the case. Thank the Goddess.

"Steven," Francis said. "You have truly outdone yourself. That was a magnificent escape."

Steve didn't have the energy to reply. He just gave a woozy thumbs up. He would have collapsed again if Riley hadn't held him up. She turned to DJ and said, "We should go."

"Definitely," DJ said. "Next stop, Varis."

As DJ said the words, though, he was filled with a different sense of dread.

13

They reached the northern shore of Varis Lake after a day of hiking south. Thankfully, Riley's bow and knowledge of traps ensured they didn't starve, but grumbling stomachs became frequent. When they reached Varis Lake, Riley and Francis made fishing spears out of branches. They would lure fish toward them with tiny bits of meat and skewer them when they got close. So fish became part of the menu, but meals were still scanty.

Steve couldn't use any magic for a while after pushing himself so hard, but the first thing he did was heal DJ's broken arm. DJ was infinitely grateful to remove his splint. His arm would still be tender and sensitive for days, though— that's how it is when you heal a broken bone with magic.

But as they put distance between themselves and the cult village, their hearts grew less worried and the forest shrouded them in wonder. They camped by the lake's edge night after night, hearing the gentle swishing of water lapping against the sand, frogs croaking, and crickets singing. From the forest, the shivering leaves and hooting owls would whisper from the darkness. And each breath of lakeside air was sweet in DJ's lungs. With each night watch, he reminded himself that he never had this back in Beregond. That made him smile a little.

At last, they saw Varis at the edge of the lake one evening before they settled for the night. They ate a rationed meal of fish, berries, and jackrabbit as they watched the distant lights dance along the darkening water. They fell asleep to the forest's usual symphony, and the following morning, they broke camp and reached the gates.

Varis was clearly a city brimming with style and function. The gates loomed wide and tall with an elegant arch made from cream-colored stone. The city walls reached nearly fifty feet high with plenty of soldiers stationed along the top. Even the walls looked immaculate, like they were washed and scrubbed daily from top to bottom.

A set of guards frowned at the derelict bunch as they entered the city. The travelers still had their cult robes and weapons, nothing else. And those robes had grown tattered and worn from sleeping in the dirt night after night.

But inside the gates, Varis was everything Sir Dashing had said it would be. Gleaming, beautiful structures were made of timber and white stone. Handsome locals were freshly washed and adorned in the latest fashions. They hustled to and fro like a hive of multi-colored bees. DJ saw street performers dancing for gold and barkers selling their wares. The smells of street confections made his stomach groan. It truly was the City at the World's Center.

It all should have filled DJ with wonder, but the knot in his chest only grew.

The locals stared and turned up their noses as the party walked by. Those unfortunate enough to walk close gagged and coughed at the smell.

Francis leaned toward DJ. "I'm sure we could all use baths."

DJ nodded stiffly. "Probably."

"Are you well, young knight? You've become sullen since approaching the city."

"I just want to replace our things and get out of here."

Francis was quiet, then he said, "It's your mother, isn't it?"

DJ gave him a look. "How do you know about that?"

"Miss Riley told me," Francis said. "It sounds like your mother hasn't been very present in your life. I'm sorry. But please, don't let thoughts of her spoil your experience. Varis is a tourist destination—the largest and liveliest city in the territory. Your chances of seeing her are practically nonexistent."

DJ clenched and released his jaw. "Fine."

The party reached the central plaza, an even thicker pond of street vendors, minstrels, and busy shoppers. Across the way, DJ noticed the ravenpost tower. This one was made of smooth white stone instead of wood. Ravens popped in and out of its many windows. "Be right back," he told the others.

He weaved through the crowd and entered the tower. It was cleaner than the other ones he had visited. The tower section was closed off behind a wall that kept the raven smell out. The front desk was wiped clean and the floor was swept.

The druid at the front counter scrunched his nose at DJ's

grubby robes. "Name?"

"DJ of Beregond."

The druid thumbed through a neatly organized box of letters. He pulled two out. "One arrived eight days ago. The other came yesterday."

DJ broke the Beregond seal on the first and unfolded it.

Ho there, Son!

Same old same old back home. I can't believe you've been gone almost two months now. Has anything interesting happened on your little quest? Or has it felt more like a holiday? I hope it's the latter and that your new friends are keeping you safe.

The maid was going to clean your room yesterday, but I insisted on doing it myself. You always kept your space so tidy. Your bed still smells like you.

Magic, eh? I always thought you'd take after the sword like your old man. But if that's what you like, that's all well and good. Just don't hurt yourself.

Write me when you arrive in Varis! I know you're not eager to see your mother, but let me know if you two meet. It may be good for you.

-Sir Dashing

DJ stuffed the first letter in his pocket and unsealed the second.

Ho there, again!

It's been nearly two weeks and I haven't gotten a raven

from you. Did you arrive in Varis? Are you well?

Please write back as soon as possible. I'm sure you're fine, but I'm your father. You understand.

-Sir Dashing

DJ's mouth twitched into a smile. So concerned. DJ was surprised at his father's response to his magic lessons, too. No discouragement, no imploring to reconsider, just *if that's what you like, that's all well and good.* A smile twitched across his lips again. He stowed the second letter in his pocket and patted it then turned to leave.

The druid frowned. "No return letter?"

DJ shrugged. "Dude, I'm broke."

The druid looked him up and down then rolled his eyes. "I should have assumed."

DJ left the ravenpost tower. He saw his friends gathered in a circle among the crowd. He rushed up to meet them, but in his haste, he failed to see a group of upper-class women cross his path. He collided with the woman in the middle.

"Oh, sorry, ma'am!" DJ stammered.

The woman's friends caught her shoulders to keep her steady. In that moment, DJ saw her. Jet black hair. Bright green eyes. Slender face. It was like looking in a mirror. The only difference was that she was dressed in the silk garbs of a noblewoman, and DJ wore the tarnished robes of a poor traveler.

The two of them stared, suspended in time. The color drained from the woman's face. Her eyes grew to dinner plates as if DJ was something from a nightmare.

DJ didn't know how he knew, but he did. His heart fell to his ankles. "It's *you*, isn't it?"

The woman's legs turned to jelly and her eyes rolled back. Her friends caught her before she hit the ground. They gasped and yipped like frightened birds, fanning her with their gloved hands.

DJ clenched his jaw. "Shit."

*

"So… this is your…?"

"Yes, Robbert. From long ago."

"Hm… I see."

DJ sat with his hands between his thighs at the end of a long mahogany table. A plate of food was made for him, but his appetite had disappeared a while ago. The amount of elegance surrounding him was raised to a nearly comical level. Furniture carved by artisans across the territory. Marble statues. Polished granite floors. Servants standing at attention at the room's corners.

At the opposite end of the table, his mother dined with a straight back, picking at her food rather than eating it. To her left was her husband, Robbert, with perfectly parted hair, square shoulders, and a dimple in his chin. He wore fine silks just like she did. And to her right, two small children—a boy and a girl—who stared at DJ with curious disdain.

"You know him?" the little boy asked. He pointed with a fat little finger. "Why is he poor?"

"Donicus," his mother replied. "We don't talk like that."

166

"Trust me, kid," DJ said, "I'm not happy about this either."

"You're the son of Sir Dashing?" Robbert asked, trying to dispel the tension. "*The* Sir Dashing?"

DJ chased his food around his plate. "The very same."

"He's a tremendous man. A living legend."

"Yeah, I know," DJ said. "He really knows how to rise to any occasion. Take on certain responsibilities when no one else will."

DJ stared daggers at his mother. She bristled and didn't look up, but she continued picking at her meager portions. Sensing the losing battle, Robbert cleared his throat.

"I see, well," he said, "I get the feeling that you two have some catching up to do. We'll leave you to it. Children?"

"But my supper will get cold!" the girl whined.

"Deirdre, the cook will make you something fresh when mother is done. Come along now."

With haste, Robbert and his spawn scampered out of the dining room. Their steps reverberated until a pair of double doors opened and slammed behind them. A stiff quiet settled. DJ's mother dabbed her lips with a napkin and set it on her plate.

For the first time, she mustered the courage to look at him. "What brings you to Varis?"

"I got knighted recently," DJ said flatly, "so I'm on a quest for the Amulet of the Goddess. Its Temple is on eastern end of the Spine. Varis is along the way, so this is one of our stops."

"Congratulations," she said. "Thank the Goddess you're not venturing for the Brassiere. No one who has entered that

Temple has ever lived to tell of it."

"That's what I hear," DJ said impatiently. "Not even Dad would try."

The mention of Sir Dashing had a reaction with DJ's mother. Her cheeks turned pink and she swallowed. "What... has he told you of me?"

"That your name is Melanie," DJ began. "You were really young when you two met. You're the daughter of a noble house in Varis. You 'weren't in a position to raise me' when I was born. That's why you sent me away. That's it. With all the women he's been with, it's amazing he remembers you."

Melanie's lips twitched into a smile. DJ realized his did the same sometimes. Now he hated it. She put her hands in her lap and began her story with a deep breath.

"It was nineteen when I met your father," Melanie said. "I had been entertaining a line of suitors, but no one I found appropriate for marriage yet. During that time, Sir Dashing defeated an entire outfit of bandits outside the city. My father held a congratulatory banquet for him, and that's when we met." She paused. "He always had a natural charisma. Strong. Charming. As a young woman, I was smitten immediately."

"Oh, tell me about it," DJ crooned sarcastically as he reached for some wine. "I've nearly fallen for him myself."

"When I found out I was pregnant, my father was mortified," Melanie said. "You must understand nobility in Varis. There are eight noble houses, and we are only allowed to marry and grow children with one another. Anything outside of that is scandal, even if it is someone as respected as Sir Dashing."

"So you've got some upper-class inbreeding going on. Lovely."

"I didn't leave my father's home for a year. Anyone who asked was told that I was bed-ridden with an illness. The truth was, he knew what my little mistake could do to our family. My lack of restraint would bring shame to our house. If people knew, it would have ruined our standing. So you grew inside me in secret."

Mistake. The word made DJ's fingers flex around his goblet.

"Then you were born," Melanie said. "It pained me to do it, but our servants carried you hundreds of miles to Beregond and delivered you to Sir Dashing. And being the noble, brave man he is, he agreed to raise you. And now you're here." She paused and took a cleansing breath. "I must beg your forgiveness."

DJ shrugged and swished his goblet. "Go ahead then. Beg."

Melanie frowned. "You must understand how difficult that decision was for me."

"Yeah, sounds hard," DJ swished the wine some more. "But nearly sixteen years have gone by, Melanie. Where have you been?"

Melanie shriveled slightly. "You still don't understand. A woman of my position—"

"*Sixteen! Years!*" DJ cried. "I'm nearly at the age of manhood! You mean to tell me in all those years you couldn't come visit or *at least* send some ravenpost? Not even once?"

Melanie's jaw tightened. "You're not being fair."

"I'll tell you what's not fair," DJ slammed the goblet on the table. "I grew up *without a mother* because you cared more about your reputation than raising me. I grew up thinking—no, *knowing*—that your position in society was more important than I was." A pause. "And what about Dad? He easily could have adventured for ten or twenty more years. Could have saved every village in Uh twice over. But he retired early for *me*. The most famous knight in Uh! Done in his prime! And what were you doing? Attending charity dinners and wearing designer dresses? Getting on with your life like I never existed? And somehow *I'm* not being fair?"

Silence crushed them. Melanie quelled a tremor in her lip. "I know what I did was wrong."

"Glad we agree on that."

"But what would you have me do now?"

"At this point? Nothing." DJ drank from his goblet. "You know what? Strike that. My friends and I need adventure packs and clothing. Ours were stolen. Being part of a noble family, I'm sure you could spare the coin, couldn't you?"

Melanie nodded. "It shall be done."

"Good."

Melanie turned to one of her servants. "Bring him some coin." They didn't speak until the servant returned with five bulging sacks of gold. "Looks to be about five thousand. Will that suffice?"

DJ ogled at the five sacks and tried to restrain his awe. A thousand each. It was so easy for her, and this was more money than he had seen on his entire journey. He snatched two sacks and pushed out his chair.

"This will be enough," he said. He stood up. "Are we done?"

Melanie nodded faintly. "All I ask is that—"

"Is that I don't reveal my identity as your son. Then it would be scandal all over again. So, in a way, this is hush money."

Melanie fell quiet. That was all the confirmation DJ needed. He forced out a laugh and shook his head.

"Looks like you never changed." He started for the door but stopped. "Melanie, there are only two people in my life that have ever made me feel like I'm worth anything. One is a girl named Riley. The other is my dad. He's not perfect—he's really distracted by his past heroics—but he's always been there for me. Tried to show me that I was okay when no one else did." A pause. "He's actually a really good dad."

His heart pricked when he said the words. The thought had never dawned on him until this moment. And with that thought, a dozen memories sped through his mind. The time Sir Dashing surprised him with a stuffed dog toy. The time Sir Dashing comforted him when DJ's bullies reduced him to tears. The time Sir Dashing pulled DJ out of a battle instruction class because he hated every moment of it.

Hundreds of miles away from home, DJ realized that Sir Dashing was a good father. He really was.

DJ's throat knotted, so he coughed it free. "Bye, Melanie. Good luck with your life."

She didn't say anything as he walked out the door.

DJ squinted against the sunlight. Down the courtyard path he went until he reached the main gates, passing perfectly manicured shrubbery and flowers. A servant opened the exit for him. Right outside the gate, Riley, Steve, and Francis sat against the fence, looking remarkably like beggars. As soon as DJ joined them, Riley popped up from her spot.

"How did it go? Are you okay?" She spotted the sacks. "*Whoa.* That's a lot of gol—"

DJ dropped the sacks and threw his arms around her. Riley was only surprised for a second, then melted into it. She held him and rocked him back and forth, stroking his hair, whispering to him. "It's okay, DJ. It's okay."

DJ tried to hold back the sobs, but they escaped in restrained bursts. Those little arms and brown hair were familiar. They never left him behind or went away, no matter how difficult. Riley was there. She was always there.

A shadow cast over them as Francis got up and encased them in his big green arms. Then Steve got to his feet and plastered himself across the group. Together, they cocooned DJ in a warm embrace. And in his chest, his heart settled.

Here, in the arms of his friends, he wasn't forgotten.

14

Hey, Dad.

We're safe in Varis now. Just met Melanie. It was a little tense. But I think you were right. It was good for me. I know she moved on without me, so in a way, I can move on without her, too.

Melanie gave us gold for supplies, so we're going to restock on everything and stay at a fancy inn tonight. A bath is going to be amazing after sleeping in the dirt for so long.

Also, thanks for always being there for me. Being out on this quest has made me learn a lot, including what an amazing dad you are. You didn't have to take care of me, but you did. Thanks.

Love you, Dad.

-DJ

DJ folded up the note and handed it to the druid before he walked out.

The first thing the group did after letting DJ write his ravenpost was check into an inn and take baths. They each got their own room as a one-time treat—luxurious suites equipped with their own king-sized beds, baths, and stocks of treats. Once everyone was bathed and filled for the afternoon, they met in the polished marble lobby and set out on the town.

The shopping district wasn't far from the main plaza—a long, wide street packed with busy shoppers and hawkers. The street's edges were so tightly packed with upper-class boutiques that it was hard to find an affordable general store. It took them half an hour before they found a reasonable shop that let them replace their clothes and adventure packs. At a nearby bookstore, Riley found a new copy of *Light of the Star Path* and DJ purchased a considerable tome of magic techniques covering beginning to advanced levels. He bought it without feeling embarrassed for the first time.

It was at the bookstore that Steve picked up a pamphlet that gave interesting facts about Varis. The most interesting was that a Temple of the Goddess resided at the very bottom of Varis Lake. Dwarven engineers had tried to create passage to it for centuries, but every attempt was soon destroyed by supernatural forces. The only way to reach it was through highly advanced magic or potions. Francis gave DJ a look. DJ smiled and averted his gaze.

Night descended on Varis and the city stirred with man-made light. Every street was illuminated with torches and small glass orbs that radiated when the sky grew dark. Steve's pamphlet said the light orbs were crafted by mages to glow when the sun went down. They needed to be magically recharged once per year.

Sounds like Varis is influenced by a lot of magic, DJ thought. *Maybe I could live here one day.* He thought of Melanie and frowned. *Actually, never mind.*

The inn food that evening was divine—the finest they had enjoyed in weeks. Roast duck, salted pork, seasoned greens, buttery sweet potatoes, smooth wine. They ate until their stomachs couldn't take any more, then they stumbled upstairs to their bedrooms and fell asleep wrapped in luxurious sheets.

DJ awoke the next morning to the sunrise tapping at his eyelids. He coasted in bed for nearly an hour then gave himself another bath just to enjoy the feeling. He dried himself off with a fluffy towel and put his new clothes on before he left his room and strolled to the next door—Riley's room.

He gave three generous knocks on the door. "Heard you snore like a troll last night!"

In response, nothing.

He frowned a little. Another loud knock on the door. "Riley, you up yet?"

Still nothing.

This time, he banged his fist on the door. "Riley, come on!"

Silence.

DJ jiggled the handle. Locked. Gathering his strength, he stepped back, took a deep breath, and crashed his foot through the door. It hurt a lot more than he expected, but it broke the lock.

Riley's room was in disarray. Bed sheets were strewn across the floor. The window dangled open. But her pack and bow were still untouched.

DJ thought he saw something small on her pillow, roughly the size of a coin. He stomped over to inspect it. He pinched it between his fingers and held it up.

A button. Like something from a vest or tunic.

The gnome. That stupid gnome and his stupid direcat. DJ clenched the button in his fist and hurled it across the room. He fled out of Riley's quarters and sped down the hall, knocking on Steve and Francis's rooms loudly.

"Steve! Francis! Wake up! Riley's gone!"

Frantic rustling from inside their rooms as his companions shook awake and got dressed. All three of them entered Riley's quarters. Steve looked all around in shock. Francis's shoulders squared with anger, and he paced the room with hulking steps.

"Sir Percival Buttons," the orc growled. "It has to be."

"No doubt," DJ said. "And now he's got her in *Varis.* This city is miles wide! How in the Hundred Hells are we supposed to find her here? For all we know he's already taken her west."

"Or," Francis countered, "the gnome will keep her here for a time, assuming we'll go west to intercept them."

"Do we talk to the authorities?" DJ said. "Are the guards in Varis worth anything?"

Francis shook his head. "An investigation could take weeks. That's assuming they never leave the city."

DJ kicked the discarded bed sheets and a fist grew in his chest. "So *stupid!* Why did we get separate rooms? We should have stayed together."

A thick quiet fell upon them. But Steve popped up as if suddenly struck by inspiration. "*Clairvoyance!*"

Francis and DJ gave him confused looks.

"Steven, what are you talking about?" Francis said.

"Clairvoyance!" Steve yapped. "It is an advanced spell that will help us find Miss Riley!" His face brightened. "It will need supplies, but if she is still in the city, she will be within the spell's range! But if they have already left…" He didn't finish.

"Supplies?" DJ asked. "What kind of supplies?"

"Ingredients!" Steve hollered. "For a potion! I will create the potion, drink it, and cast the spell! We must find an alchemist or apothecary! They will have ingredients!"

DJ's heart fluttered with hope. "There's got to be an apothecary nearby. It's Varis for crying out loud." He held Steve's face between his hands. "Steve, if this works, I could kiss you."

Steve turned a little pink. "Oh my!"

"Let's go," DJ said. "I'll throw Riley's stuff in my room."

So they did. They dashed down the stairs, fully geared. As they made a beeline through the lobby toward the main door, they slid to a halt in front of a bellhop—a smartly dressed goblin wearing a red uniform, bow tie, and glasses.

"We're looking for potion ingredients," DJ said hurriedly. "Where's the closest place?"

"You'll want Doctor Snipe's Apothescary," the goblin replied.

"Don't you mean Apothe*cary?*"

"No," the goblin answered flatly. "Take a left, follow it to the intersection, then turn right. It'll be the third shop on your right."

DJ thanked him and the party sped away. Varis locals stared distastefully at the strange group dashing through the streets. It took only two minutes for the adventurers to arrive at their destination.

A wooden sign dangled above a door with a snake slithering around a skull and crossbones. Above the design, the words *Doctor Snipe's Apothescary* were printed in sharp letters. Normally, DJ would have hesitated at such a spooky omen, but Riley was in need. That pushed him forward. He threw open the door.

Apothe*scary* was right. There was hardly any light in the stony store, making it feel more like a dungeon. The bones of humans and various animals hanging on the walls only strengthened the ambiance. And the *smell...* It was hard to place, but it was something between onion juice, troll sweat, and cat piss. It made DJ's eyes water. Francis frowned and Steve pulled his robes up over his nose.

"Welcome," a voice drawled nearby.

The service counter was just ahead of them. Behind it, a thin, pale-skinned man stood with greasy black hair dangling to his eyes. He wore a black robe and his face gave the impression he hadn't smiled in years.

"Hi," DJ said shortly. "We need ingredients for a Clairvoyance Potion. You must be... Doctor Snipe?"

"Indeed," Snipe said. His voice came out like a depressed, slow-moving animal. "A Clairvoyance Potion. You must be quite the mage."

"He is," DJ jabbed a thumb toward Steve. "I'm still learning. Do you have everything we need?"

"I have the finest selection of ingredients in Varis," Snipe droned on. "Dried bat wings, pickled newts, thousand-year lavender, troll toe jam… I have it all. But it all comes at a price."

"How much? Name it. We're kind of in a rush."

Doctor Snipe let out a petulant sigh before gliding around the shelves and picking off items. "For a Clairvoyance Potion, you'll need eight frog legs, the eye of a leercat, a cup of fairy water, a glob of dragon mucus… and a dash of cinnamon for flavor." He slammed all the ingredients on the counter. "Six hundred and thirty gold."

DJ's jaw nearly hit the floor. Inwardly, he cursed his pride for not taking more gold yesterday at Melanie's mansion. Steve deflated and Francis muttered his displeasure.

"We don't have that kind of gold," DJ said. "Is there something else we can do? Anything? Seriously, this is kind of an emergency."

The doctor's eyes softened as he studied DJ's features. It was like DJ's question never reached his ears. After an uncomfortable pause, DJ cleared his throat.

"Uh, hey doc," he said. "You okay?"

Snipe awoke from his daydream. "Please. Forgive me. It's just that you… remind me of someone."

DJ narrowed his eyes. "Who?"

"Miss Melanie of House Porter." Snipe said the name as if it were honey on his lips. "Your eyes are like hers—emeralds against a pale fog. She was my friend as a child. But as the years grew, so did my feelings for her. Such grace. Such beauty. I wrote a letter for her long ago, expressing my true feelings, but I was too timid to deliver it. But I will always cherish the time we spent together. *Always.*"

A gross taste grew in DJ's mouth as soon as Snipe mentioned her. He cleared his throat and said, "Listen man, she's been married for like, ten years. And she's… kind of awful. You should move on."

"*No!*" Snipe slapped his hand on the table. "You do not know my heart! You do not know what it means to love so truly, so deeply! But still, my letter remains undelivered. So did I ever truly love her? Oh, *Goddess!*" Snipe buried his face in his arms.

DJ tried not to grimace at the pitiful display. But then a thought crossed his mind. Hesitation only gripped him for a moment's fraction. "Listen, I sort of have a connection with Melanie. What if… you gave us these ingredients at half the price if we deliver your letter?" Feeling like he needed to add more, he said, "Gold comes and goes, but that weight off your chest will last forever."

Francis and Steve traded mildly surprised looks at DJ's offer. Doctor Snipe studied DJ a little more, thinking, considering. The doctor narrowed his eyes, thought some more, then gave a resolute nod.

"Yes," he conceded. "Yes, you're right."

He reached into his robe and pulled out a folded envelope sealed with black wax. It was yellow and crinkly from age and had a couple of stains on it that had to be various ales.

"Additionally," Snipe said. "Take this Proof of Delivery

with you. She must sign it so I know it's been delivered. Then bring it back to me. I know her signature well, so if you're lying"—he scowled—"I'll know. Do not disappoint me."

Sheesh, this guy is obsessed, DJ thought. Regardless, he took the Proof of Delivery and the three of them left the Apothescary. The morning sun was blinding compared to the Apothescary's dingy darkness. DJ shielded his eyes and made a beeline for the Porter estate.

"That man needs some serious help," Francis observed.

"*Riley* needs some serious help," DJ responded. "And we're one step closer to finding her."

Soon they were at the Porter mansion—grand, majestic, surrounded by a beautiful courtyard. DJ stomped up to the main entrance, which was guarded by two soldiers.

"Hey," he said, "I've got a letter delivery for Melanie. It needs her signature."

A guard frowned at him. "You were here yesterday. We were told to keep our eye out for you. You're not allowed in."

DJ's stomach fell. The guards tensed as they saw the friar and orc on either side of him. DJ tried to muster some gusto.

"Listen, this is *really important,*" he said. "This goes beyond whatever Melanie and I have. I need this letter delivered and a signature from her *right now.*"

Stoic silence from the guards. They stared down their noses at him. DJ thought of Riley tied up and hauled back to Beregond then thought of himself punching these two guards. It felt like a satisfying course of action, but he knew picking a fight with two city guards was un-knightly behavior.

"Thanks for your help, boys," DJ said snidely. "You're doing great. I hope they put medals right there and right there." He pointed at their chests, then saluted. "Keep up the good work!"

DJ stormed away, his friends following closely behind. He tried to formulate a plan in his head. Maybe they could sneak in? Or they could wait for Melanie to come out? But who knows how long that could take? By that time, Riley could be long—

Someone coughed nearby. Then again. They weren't natural coughs—they were coughs of someone trying to get another person's attention.

DJ looked around for the source. It was coming from inside the courtyard. It didn't take him long to spot Deirdre, his bratty little half-sister, eyeing him over the top of some shrubbery. Little blonde pigtails popped out the sides of her head. She cocked her head, motioning DJ to follow. Not sure what else to do, DJ obeyed. He walked in step with her until he turned a corner at the courtyard fence.

Deirdre poked her little face between a gap in the bars, examining him. From this spot in the fence, they were too far away to be heard by any of the guards. DJ got the impression that Deirdre had used this spot many times.

"You need to deliver that to my mom?" she asked.

"Yeah," DJ said cautiously. "But I also need her signature. It's important. It's a lot to explain, but I really need her to sign this Proof of Delivery."

Deirdre stayed quiet for a moment then turned her nose up. "I can forge her signature for you."

"You can?" DJ replied in disbelief.

"I do it all the time," Deirdre said. "Mother and father never let me do anything. So whenever I need a parent's signature to do something cool, I just…" She made a swishing motion with her fingers. "I can do that."

DJ squinted. "What do you want?"

"What's your offer?"

He looked over his shoulder at Francis and Steve. Neither of them had answers. DJ gave a quick inventory of himself, thinking of anything that a child like Deirdre might want. Then it struck him.

"I bet your mom would never let you have this." DJ unbuckled the utility knife from his belt. Nothing special, just a basic single-edged knife with an oak handle and iron blade, made for small tasks like cutting rope or skinning animals.

But it was enough. A weapon—a treasure from the world of adventure. Deirdre's eyes widened with desire, and she lunged for it. DJ pulled it back.

"Ah-ah-ah," he said. "Signature first."

Deirdre frowned. "How do I know you'll hold up your end?"

"I'm a Knight of Beregond. I'm honor-bound."

DJ extended her the Proof of Delivery and the letter. Deirdre snatched it and scrawled a quick signature, then she handed back the Proof. DJ gave her the knife. Her face radiated with delight as her finger traced the edge.

"Be careful with it," DJ admonished. "It's not a toy."

"What do you care?" Deirdre raised an eyebrow. "You're never going to see me again."

Well, you are kind of my sister, DJ thought. *So I guess I care a little bit.* "I just don't want you to get hurt. That's all." He paused. "Thanks for this."

He got up to leave, but before they could get too far, Deirdre said, "You're my brother, aren't you?"

DJ stopped. He looked over his shoulder at her. He almost confirmed it, but the reason he had clothes on his back now was because of a certain payment the day before. That kept his mouth shut.

"She probably paid you to stay quiet," Deirdre said. "You don't have to say anything. The look on your face is enough." She blinked. "You look just like her."

DJ squinted but gave a little smile. "You're a smart kid, you know that?"

"Yeah, I do." Deirdre smiled. "Good luck with whatever. Bye."

She disappeared into the courtyard and the others ventured back to the Apothescary. DJ couldn't help but smile. Who knew he would like his mischievous half-sister more than his own mother? It was nice to have at least one friendly face in Varis.

When they made it back to the Apothescary, DJ and the others held their breath while Doctor Snipe inspected the Proof of Delivery. They hoped beyond hope that Deirdre's forgery was a good one. The lonely old alchemist welled with tears when he saw it, so it must have been close enough.

The party took the ingredients back to Steve's room, where he used a small table as a makeshift alchemy station. They needed something important of Riley's for the potion to work, so Francis cut out a sliver of wood from her bow. As

Steve stirred, the potion let out puffs of gas that smelled like rotten eggs.

At last, Steve held the green, murky mixture up to his uneven eyes. "Behold! The Clairvoyance Potion!"

DJ pinched his nose as he spoke. "Steve, you're brave for drinking that."

"For Miss Riley, it must be done!" Steve hollered. He held the glass higher. "A toast to friendship and the Goddess above!"

He downed it. Seconds later, he doubled over like he had been punched in the stomach. Francis knelt down and put his hand on Steve's back. Steve twitched and shuddered and groaned. His back stretched out like a cat's—something was traveling from his stomach to his mouth.

It happened. Steve ripped a belch that made the whole room vibrate. DJ caught a whiff of his breath and coughed, fanning the smell away.

Steve jumped upright and patted his belly like nothing had happened. "Much better! Now then!" He planted his feet and swished his arms all about as he muttered a long phrase in magetongue. As he did, his hands and eyes glowed bright blue. He finished by squatting and clapping his hands together in front of his chest.

Francis and DJ waited. Then Steve straightened out, hiked up his pack, and pointed. "Away we go!"

The friar jogged out of the room and his friends followed. DJ tried to catch what Steve was looking at as they flew down the steps.

"Wait," he said, "how do you know where to go? Do you

see something?"

"A pink sparkle moves just before my path!" Steve yelped. "It always stays a few paces ahead! It will guide us!"

"Be ready for anything," Francis warned. "The gnome and his direcat could be expecting us."

DJ flexed his fingers, thinking of spells and cantrips. He also made sure his sword was strapped tightly to his waist.

They left the inn and traveled down the street. Steve's pots and pans jangled with every step. They must have run a mile before the sparkle led them to a shabby-looking building near the southeast gate of Varis. In this part of town, farther away from the lake's shore, things weren't as sparkly and beautiful. Uneven streets were made from mismatched stones and hasty mortar. Some buildings had boarded-up windows. Long gone were the clean folks with colorful garbs glistening in the sun. Here, there were knots of hardened, scarred, calloused adventurers carrying weathered weapons and bitten armor.

DJ made eye contact with one as he passed. They bared their teeth and growled at him. He gulped.

"Be on your guard," Francis said lowly, clutching his ax.

Steve turned around and put his fingers to his lips before he pointed at a nearby building. The three of them crept up to it slowly, trying to be discreet but not look sneaky. As they drew closer, they heard voices inside.

"Forget it. I don't want to play."

Riley. DJ recognized her voice and his heart leaped.

"Come now, we'll be on the road together for weeks! You don't want to be tied the whole way, do you?"

There he was. That stupid accent that DJ couldn't place. It

was Buttons all right. That meant his direcat had to be closeby, too.

"Pick better games then!" Riley sounded more annoyed than distressed. "I don't want to play Three Witches and a Frog. It's for little kids."

The party could tell the sound was coming from the building's basement. An open window let the sound drift onto the street. The three of them walked around at a safe distance in case Buttons was watching the windows.

"It's a game of strategy and cunning!" Buttons insisted. "Hardly a game for children, I would say!" The direcat let out a meow. "Yes, Mittens, I agree!"

The party found a staircase leading down to a basement door. They armed themselves—sword, ax, and frying pan. When they crept to the bottom of the stairs, DJ reached for the handle.

"Young knight," Francis whispered, "don't be hasty."

"What kind of plan could we even make?" DJ hissed. "We just rush in and catch him unawares!"

"I don't believe that's—"

DJ wasn't listening. He flung the door open. "*Found you, you little twerp!*" he shouted as he busted in.

He didn't see it. A large drawing on the ground—a circle marked with shapes and runes. As soon as DJ stepped on it, it burst with a fiery pulse that flung him across the room. He slammed against a wall and fell to the ground, coughing and gasping for breath. His ears rang and his sword clambered next to him.

Through blurry vision, he didn't see much. Francis

stormed into the room, roaring. The direcat leaped for him, scratching and clawing his arms. Francis pulled the cat off and flung it against a wall. Mittens hit the wall with a *thud*, falling into a mess of boxes, but scrambled to get back on its paws.

Riley ducked for cover. Buttons darted from his post with surprising agility. Steve threw a series of cantrips at the gnome but kept missing. The gnome raised a dagger and lunged for him. But with a twist and an errant swing, Steve batted him away with his frying pan. A satisfying *clang* filled the room as Buttons rolled across the floor.

DJ's vision was returning, but his leg seared with pain. He tried to stand, but any movement sent bolts of agony to his ankle. As soon as he saw it, he knew it was broken. Stepped on a magical rune. He cursed himself for his stupidity.

Francis threw Mittens off him again. The orc was covered in deep cuts from sharp claws. As the direcat righted itself, it noticed DJ. Easier prey. Mittens snarled, baring its fangs. Fear washed over DJ and he struggled for his sword. His hand wrapped around the hilt just as the direcat leaped for him.

A blind swipe—a successful one. DJ's blade ripped across Mittens's belly. The direcat startled backward, let out weak meow, then fell onto its side, eyes growing glassy.

"*Mittens!*" Buttons cried.

The fight stopped immediately. Francis and Steve huffed and puffed as they stood covered in scrapes. Riley got to her feet. And just a yard away, DJ watched as Sir Percival Buttons slid to his knees, watching his direcat rapidly lose blood.

"It's okay, it's okay," the gnome consoled. "You're going to be all right." He fumbled for a vial on his belt—a bright red liquid. He uncorked it and held up Mitten's mouth as he poured it in. The direcat resisted but swallowed. The bleeding slowed and the gnome put pressure on it.

Sir Percival Buttons spoke through his teeth. "You have won again this day. Take her and leave."

No one moved. They just stared.

"*Leave!*" Buttons commanded.

Francis bent down and scooped up DJ like a child. DJ gritted his teeth and clutched his bloodstained sword. Riley and Steve scurried close behind. They closed the door as they climbed up the stairs to ground level.

Rain clouds gathered in the sky, turning everything gray. Slowly, a soft trickle of cold water fell to the cobblestones, making tiny rivers at their feet. The people of Varis retreated to nearby shelter. Steve struggled to keep his hands over DJ's leg and mumble Healing Hand. DJ's leg mended. It was no longer broken, but he knew it would be tender for days, just like his arm. Francis let him down, and DJ limped along with them.

"I hate that gnome and his stupid cat," DJ glanced at his sword, which was still stained with blood. "He kidnapped *you,* and here I am feeling sorry for *him.*"

Riley stared at the ground as she spoke. "*I* feel sorry for him."

Everyone turned to her, waiting for an explanation. She kept her eyes on the wet cobblestones.

"He made some mistakes back home," she said. "They won't let him back to his village until he does a noble deed. This is his noble deed—taking me back to my father." She paused. "The gold doesn't matter to him. He's trying to do the right thing. And I get it. He just wants to go home."

Francis clenched his jaw and his eyes grew dark. DJ's heart pricked again. He glowered and tried to force the feeling down. He didn't want to feel guilty about defeating another knight. But as he thought about it, he realized Buttons's mission was even more noble than his own, and that made a storm cloud gather in his chest.

He let the rain fall, clearing the blood from his sword.

15

The party couldn't afford to stay at the fancy inn for an-other night, so they rented a single room at a cheaper one. It was cramped, but they all felt more comfortable about it after Percival Buttons's abduction. Rain pelted on the creaky win-dow and the roof had a slight leak—Steve placed one of his pots beneath it so the water wouldn't pool on the floor. No one spoke much. They all fell asleep on the creaky floor, listen-ing to the rhythmic raindrops dripping into Steve's pot.

The following morning, they gathered their things and made their way for Varis's southeast exit, which wasn't nearly as grand as the western exit. The sight that lay ahead wasn't bad, though: an expanse of grassy plains split by a dirt road occasionally interrupted by a farm or hostel. This road pointed south toward the Nether Regions.

"Will it be weird to go back to the Nether Regions, Fran-cis?" DJ asked.

The orc nodded without any light. "Almost certainly."

An uncomfortable silence. DJ said, "Is that because you don't have a clan?"

Francis nodded again.

"Are you… ready to talk about it?"

Francis didn't answer right away. Instead, his face pressed with thought. After a long moment, the silence became too much for DJ. He said, "Listen, if you don't want to go to the Nether Regions, we can go farther east toward Silverwar Grove. Cross Traitor's Trench a little farther north. I really don't mind if we miss the Nether Regions. It's not a big deal."

"It *is* a big deal," Francis gazed hard at DJ. "For you to be fully respected as a knight, you must visit every region in Uh. I made an oath to help you do that, and that is why we're passing through the Nether Regions." He gave a big, cleansing breath. "With any luck, we won't run into my old acquaintances. Last I remember, they were farther west."

DJ chose to drop the conversation, but Riley's curiosity pushed her forward. She pranced up to Francis and patted his arm. "Are you sure you don't want to talk about it? We've been through a lot together. You can trust us."

Francis opened and closed his mouth twice. Everyone could tell he was on the verge of sharing something, but the words got caught each time. Finally, he forced a smile for Riley.

"If it doesn't come up in the Nether Regions," he said, "I'll tell you everything when we reach Blight's Respite. Is that fair?"

Riley nodded and squeezed his hand. The orc gave her an affectionate hug around her shoulders.

Within the hour, they crested a hill to find an old woman standing in the middle of the road. She was an odd-looking one—wispy gray hair fell from her scalp and her entire body was plagued with wrinkles and liver spots. She pressed a walking stick into the ground and watched the party with bright gray eyes.

"Greetings, travelers!" she said. "I am the Highway Hag, and you have approached my crossing!"

DJ raised an eyebrow. "*Your* crossing?"

"Yes!" she said. "You cannot pass until you've played my game!" She stifled a cackle. "Have no fear, it is simple enough."

Everyone traded irritated looks. DJ spoke first. "Are you serious?"

"I am."

"But we could just walk around you."

"I suppose you could, but it wouldn't be any fun!"

DJ frowned and tried to keep a cautious distance as he walked around, but as soon as his foot passed her, it was magnetized to the dirt. No matter how hard he strained, his foot wouldn't budge. Unless he pulled it back to stand before the Hag. Then he was free. The Hag cackled as she watched him struggle.

DJ let out an irritated sigh and looked at his friends. "Does anyone want to play?"

"*You* must play!" the Hag said, pointing. "You are the leader of this motley crew, yes? *You* must play!"

"Go on, young knight," Francis sounded tired. "Let's get on with it."

"Fine," DJ said. "What's your game?"

The Hag's eyes flashed. "Truth… or dare?"

DJ nearly laughed. *Really? A maiden's slumber party game?* He knew he didn't want to pick dare, because a dare from an anonymous Hag could be any kind of outrageous thing. He didn't want to take the chance. Truth was the obvious choice.

"Truth," he said.

The Hag's gaze traveled from DJ, to Riley, and back again. She grinned with crooked teeth and pointed a bony finger. "You wanna kiss her, don't 'cha?"

DJ flushed cold and his face turned beet red. Riley laughed as if it were some great joke, but Francis and Steve said nothing. They had seen the signs. They saw the occasional stares and DJ's protectiveness. Now the truth had to come out or they couldn't continue.

"Come on then!" the Hag jeered. "Tell us the truth!"

Could I lie? DJ floundered. *Could she tell?* He tried to swallow in a dry throat. Riley laughed a second time, but less spirited. A foreign truth was dawning on her, and her voice betrayed her discomfort. DJ knew the longer he waited to answer, the more awkward it would get.

His heart pounded. His palms grew clammy. Throwing away his pride, he swallowed and said, "Yes."

Deafening quiet slammed the party. But the Hag gave a delighted cackle.

"*Ha!* I knew it!" she said. She tottered to the side. "Right! Off you go then!"

DJ blushed so hard he nearly got dizzy. He hiked up his

pack and walked on, not looking behind him. No one said anything. The tension followed them like a rain cloud. DJ wondered what Riley must look like. Did she have a pep in her step like this was a delightful revelation? Or did she frown disgustedly and stare at her boots? He wanted to know, but not badly enough to turn around and look.

For the next two days, DJ avoided interacting with Riley from sheer embarrassment. He would steal away and practice magic as much as he could. When they set up camp and established watches at night, he passed his watch to Steve or Francis so he wouldn't have to confront her.

One night, DJ tapped on Francis's shoulder and made for his bedroll, but Francis caught him. DJ flipped around. The orc gripped his ankle and his amber eyes were filled with sharpness.

"You need to talk to her," he whispered.

"Right now? She's asleep!" DJ whispered back.

"Soon."

"Francis, let go of me."

"She is your dearest friend and you've barely said a word to her in days. The more you let this fester, the worse it will become."

DJ yanked away his ankle and narrowed his eyes. "Maybe I'll wait until Blight's Respite to open up. How about that?"

Francis bared his teeth and growled. A sliver of fear ran down DJ's back, but he knew Francis would never actually hurt him. He said, "I will, just... what do I even *say?*"

Francis left his bedroll and picked up his ax. "Whatever's in here." He pointed at DJ's heart. "She loves you, young knight. Even if it's only as a friend. She'll listen."

Only as a friend. That's what DJ was afraid of. He tried desperately to keep his voice from wobbling as he spoke. "What if she doesn't like me back in that way? What if it ruins everything? She's the only friend I have."

Francis thought about it for a moment. He said, "I don't believe it will. Be brave, Sir DJ. The mightiest battles are often fought within." He patted DJ's head then left to keep watch.

That morning, Riley was gone by the time DJ awoke. Cool blue light covered the plains and DJ struggled to leave his bedroll. He braved the chill to rekindle the fire, and as he warmed himself by it, Riley approached with faint steps along the grass. She dangled four jackrabbits in one hand and a dusty sack in the other. Francis and Steve stirred as she approached.

"The traps worked amazing," Riley said. "And I managed to find some fernweed in the grass. The roots are edible, so we can add them to our breakfast." She dropped her bounty by the fire.

Swallowing, clearing his throat, DJ lifted his voice. "You're getting really good at that."

Riley looked at DJ. She gave a little smile. "Thanks. Do you… want to help me dress the rabbits?"

DJ nodded. "Yeah, but I gave my utility knife to Deirdre back in Varis. Francis, can I borrow yours? Thanks."

Together, DJ and Riley dressed the rabbits and cleaned the pelts. Conversation started slow, but before long, they were back to talking as they always did. Francis watched them out of the corner of his eye. Steve cooked the rabbits and roots and spices, resulting in a satisfying breakfast.

For the next few days, DJ and Riley acted like the Highway Hag never happened. DJ didn't bring up his untimely confession, and Riley never asked about it. Maybe she was willing to let it go and ignore it. But that also made a knot of concern in DJ's chest—how did she truly feel about it?

The wall of the Nether Regions came into view—an expanse of solid timbers carved into spikes. There were thousands of them standing edge-to-edge across miles of land. DJ marveled at the sight. The design was primitive, and it must have taken decades to complete. He wanted to ask Francis how long it had stood for, but as they traveled closer to it, Francis only became more tense. His eyebrows furrowed and his hands clenched.

The road led directly to a gate forged out of similar timbers. Two orcs stood sentinel on the opposite side of the wall, watching the road. DJ surmised that there must be a catwalk on the inside of the wall, at least near the gates.

One orc called out, "Who seeks consent to explore the Nether Regions?"

DJ almost answered, but Francis stepped forward. "We do. We seek passage to the eastern bridge to cross Traitor's Trench."

"What clan do you claim, orc-brother?" one of the guards called.

Francis replied with visible discomfort. "I have no clan."

This made the guards pause. Then one of them spoke to the other. "Wait."

The guards climbed down from their posts. Francis gulped

and cracked his knuckles. The gate opened and the orcs marched out to meet them. Both of them were dressed in animal furs and leather armor. Tattoos marked their arms, necks, and legs. As they approached, DJ noticed that Francis was still taller than both of them. The Nether Region orcs, however, were much more chiseled and sinewy.

One of the orcs leaned forward, examining Francis's face. Francis stood his ground. Then the guard's voice filled with wonder. "*Frok?* It's you, isn't it?"

"Frok?" DJ wondered out loud.

"His name is Francis!" Steve piped up.

"It wasn't always," Francis muttered.

DJ's jaw fell. Riley and Steve were the same. The guard orcs frowned deeply, their cheeks like stone.

"You got fat," one orc grumbled. "And you gave yourself a *human* name?"

"What difference does that make to you now?" Francis said sternly.

The second orc puffed out his chest. "We have orders if you returned."

"I'm not returning," Francis reassured. "We're merely passing through. We won't make ourselves at home."

"But you will pass through the village on the eastern road," one orc said. "We moved two years ago. There was a great battle with the Fangtooths. We took their land."

Francis let out a heavy sigh.

"Gasha ordered us to bring you to her if you returned," the other orc said.

For the first time, Francis's face grew soft. "Gasha? She

leads the clan now? That means…"

Both orcs nodded.

Francis's tone fell. "I see."

What in the Hundred Hells is going on? DJ knew his face spoke his thoughts.

"Gog will guide you," one orc said. "The clan is five days away. Do not speak, and move quickly. Gasha will decide your fate at the village. Go."

One of the guards led them through the gate, and that's when DJ got his first glimpse of the Nether Regions. He immediately understood why most people avoided it. Trees were far apart and appeared to be mostly dead. Not even grass or brush grew between them. As far as he could see, it was an expanse of barren, dry dirt. DJ wondered why anyone would choose to live here, even orcs.

For hours, they moved along a barely visible path with no chatter and quiet steps. The first night, they sheltered in a cave that had a wall and door built into its mouth. When they were secured inside, Gog told them the orcs marked these caves within a day's journey of each other so they could have safe places to hide during the night. DJ awoke to the sounds of something outside—guttural gurgles and huge paws trudging across the earth before it scratched at the outer wall. He trembled with wide eyes as he waited for the creature to give up and leave. He swore he felt the footfalls through the ground. Whatever it was had to be *massive.*

The five days of near silence were agonizing. Gog explained that they were meant to stay quiet to avoid attention of creatures, because many of them hunted by sound. The road they walked was specially carved to avoid the nests and colonies of these beasts, but that didn't mean one wouldn't wander off occasionally in search of prey. Frequently, he would command them with his hands to stop and lay low if he heard a suspicious sound. Most of the time it was false alarms, but once, DJ saw the back of a great monster move beyond a hilltop. Its back was covered in long spines and its mouth was big enough to bite his arm off. Its growl was a low rumble that traveled hundreds of yards away. A shivering Friar Steve had to hold his pots and pans to keep them from jingling.

All during their trip, DJ would check Francis's face to measure his emotions. Francis hardly spoke, even in the shelter of sealed caves. DJ got the impression that Francis was as nervous to reach their destination as DJ was to reach Varis. Maybe it was for similar reasons? Soon they would know after months of wondering.

After five days of silence and cave camping, they arrived at the village—another wide circle surrounded by a tall fence of timbers. A deep mote surrounded the fortress, lined with long spikes that could skewer a mammoth. A bridge dropped as the group approached, and the party crossed it.

Francis inhaled a shaky breath. DJ patted his back. It clearly didn't help.

"Welcome to the village of the Ironhands Clan," Gog said.

The village was constructed of huts made of wood and dried mud. A single well stood in the middle of the space. DJ heard the clanking of a blacksmith at work. And the village filled with the smell of burning *something* that was almost appetizing. It turned out to be a creature the size of a carriage with no eyes and a snarling jaw, frozen in death, surrounded by fire.

Noticing DJ's awe, Gog said, "Larkbeast. This catch will feed the village for days."

DJ also noticed that as they trudged through the village, orcs stared. When they spotted Francis, they turned to each other and whispered. Many of them scowled. Elderly orcs leaned on walking sticks and shook their heads. Clearly, Francis was a familiar face, and an unwelcome one at that. Francis pretended not to notice, but DJ could tell he felt the weight of those stares.

Gog led them to the largest hut in the village. Dangling above its door was a red banner with a fist crudely painted on it. Francis swallowed. The rest of the party watched him.

"This is where I leave you," Gog said. "Gasha is inside. Farewell, Frok and humans."

That was it. Gog marched out of the village and was gone.

Francis stared at the door for a long while. And everyone in the village stared at Francis. DJ could feel hundreds of amber eyes on him, and it made his hands clammy. What he was experiencing only had to be a fraction of what Francis felt, though.

Francis forced himself forward, breathed deep, and knocked on the door.

"Who approaches?" a voice came from inside.

"Frok," Francis's voice was hoarse. "Traveling east toward Traitor's Trench."

There was a brief pause, then the door flung open. A she-orc answered that was taller than DJ, but twice as thick. Strong arms stretched out of an iron chest piece that was branded with the same design as the banner above the door. Her black hair was tied into a long braid that reached the tips of her shoulder blades.

She slammed the door behind her and gazed up at Francis. Her face was hard for a moment, then it softened. She held Francis's head between her hands and stroked Francis's cheek with her thumb. A smile graced her green lips.

"At last," she said. "Welcome home, my love."

16

DJ felt his brain operating at full speed, trying to sort through the facts. *Francis isn't his real name? The village doesn't like him? But the village chief is happy to see him? What in the name of—*

Friar Steve said the words on every human's mind, loudly and deliberately, accentuating every syllable. "*I—am—very—confused!*"

The orcs hushed, awe-struck at the human who could speak like a war horn. Steve shrunk a little, suddenly feeling everyone's attention on him. Not far away, the village chief, Gasha, put her elbow on Francis's shoulder and smiled.

"You speak with your chest, human," she smiled. "Fear not, we will answer your questions. But for now, we must dine. Stay as long as you wish."

Francis furrowed his eyebrows at her. "I thought—"

"It is a new time, dearest Frok," she said. She held his face with both hands again. "It has been too long since I gazed upon your face."

Francis held Gasha's hand and gazed into her eyes.

DJ watched them, feeling something between shock and envy. Weeks ago, he would have traded snide glances with Riley at a moment like this, but after the Highway Hag incident... there was no way. Deep down, he ached for what Francis had.

Gasha patted Francis's cheek. "The larkbeast is almost done! Can you smell it?"

Francis sighed dreamily. "It's been too long since I tasted larkbeast. This shall be a meal to remember."

Gasha nodded to an orc, and they rang a bell. Like a calm flood, orcs spilled out of their huts to gather in the village center. They brought their own roughly carved bowls made of wood or stone. A couple of orcs handed spare bowls to the travelers, and everyone formed a neat line to the cooked beast.

DJ tensed as he inched closer to it. The larkbeast had no eyes and its head tilted to its side so its jaw hung open. DJ noticed that the tongue was cut out. Inwardly, he wondered if it was an orcish delicacy. When he saw someone give it to Gasha, that confirmed his suspicion.

In that moment, they also handed a bowl to Francis. They scowled at Francis then spat at his feet. Francis ignored the abuser. Gasha, however, bared her teeth, stood, and growled. The serving orc winced then bowed apologetically and went away.

When DJ reached the beast, an orc with a messy apron cut off a considerable slice and dropped it in DJ's bowl with a *slap*. As DJ left the line, he discreetly lifted the bowl to smell it. The larkbeast didn't smell awful—a lot like unseasoned chicken. He was about to ask someone for a fork when he noticed all the orcs tearing into the meat with their bare hands. Hesitantly, DJ pulled up a patch of dirt, sat with his legs crossed, and followed suit.

The larkbeast tasted just like it smelled—unseasoned chicken. Nothing compared to the cuisine of Varis, but it was better than boiled roots and half-moldy bread.

Riley plopped down next to him, followed by Steve. But as soon as Steve sat down, he was surrounded by four orcs. Riley and DJ watched apprehensively. The friar retreated within himself, eyes wide like a nervous puppy. The orcs leaned forward curiously.

"You speak loudly, human!" one said. "Louder than any human that has crossed our village!"

"Uh—thank you!" Steve hollered, not knowing what else to say.

"Your chest is strong," another orc said. "You must be a warrior of great deeds. Tell us how many foes you have slain!"

Steve counted on his fingers, remembering Broken Lovers Pass and the House of Phillip. "Eight? Perhaps nine?"

A third orc marveled. "Impressive for a human! Me?" He beat his chest. "Eighteen orcs on the field of battle. Clean kills, each one."

"How can they be clean when blood is so messy?" Steve asked.

The orcs stared, blinked, then burst out laughing. One of them grabbed Steve's shoulder and shook him. "The human has jokes! I like you, human! Give us your name!"

"I am Friar Steve!"

"Fryo-steeg is now a friend of the Ironhands Clan!" an orc said. "Let us drink to Fryo-steeg!"

Orcs passed around cups filled with ale, presumably. DJ received one, followed by Riley. Steve's fan club smacked their cups together in a toast then drank deeply. Steve—a sober Steward of the Goddess—merely sat among them looking somewhere between confused and flattered.

DJ brought the cup to his nose. Whatever it was, it didn't smell like much of anything. Feeling parched from the long walk, DJ knocked back the cup and took a deep gulp. The liquid scorched his throat and scraped the breath from his lungs. He coughed and sputtered as orcs watched and laughed, jeering about how the little human couldn't hold his liquor.

"What *is* this stuff?" DJ gasped.

An elderly orc appeared by his side and patted his back. "Orcish firewine. It is not best for young humans." He spoke to Steve's new entourage. "Orc-brothers, I desire to speak to the loud Steward and his clan."

The orcs bowed and left, assuring Fryo-steeg that they would return. The elderly orc that patted DJ on the back had to be a shaman of some sort. His tattoos were different from the other orcs, and he wore colorful beads around his neck made from polished rocks. His most prominent feature was a triangle made with white paint on his chest; it pointed upward.

Steve's face brightened. "A fellow Steward of the Goddess!"

"Greetings, Steward-brother," the orc reached out a wrinkled hand. "I am Torq. May the Goddess smile upon you."

"May the Goddess smile upon *you!*" Steve shook his hand.

"Hi, Torq," DJ leaned across Riley to speak. "We're all really confused."

"I am sure," Torq replied. "Tell me what troubles your mind."

Riley pushed DJ aside. "What happened to Franc—Frok? Why did he change his name? Why has everyone been so mean to him? But the village chief is happy he's back?"

"Ah," Torq said. "For that, we must start at the very beginning. Listen closely. Frok is the born leader of the Ironhands Clan. His father, Forgruff, was the village chief until his death two years ago. May he rest in might."

Village chief? DJ thought in awe. By the looks on Riley and Steve's faces, he knew they were as surprised as he was.

"In the beginning," Torq continued, "the Goddess Uh gave orcs dominion over the barren places. We have survived through strength. You listened to your new friends boast of their victories in battle. It is in our blood. It is who we are. We fight, and we survive. It is the orcish way.

"Frok was always the largest and strongest boy in the village, but he had no desire for battle, despite his noble blood. He preferred to read books or be alone, nay-saying our traditions of struggle and conquest. When he turned old enough to lead his first battle, he decided he would conquer through speaking and agreements. Many disagreed. They called it weak. But Frok did not listen. He met the other clan with our mightiest warriors, but without weapons, only words. The enemy clan saw their opportunity. They fell upon us and slayed many. Frok's plan failed. Many of our brothers and sisters perished."

If the three humans could have gotten any quieter, they did.

"Such shame it brought Chief Forgruff and our people," Torq continued. "But Gasha was Frok's truest friend, even through the shame. She did not mind that his head was in wrong places. They were always together—like a sword and shield. Frok and Gasha were destined to marry when they reached proper age. Chief Forgruff loved her like a daughter, and he approved."

DJ didn't look at Riley.

"But Frok did not learn from his blunder. He wanted to leave us for *college*." Torq said the word as if it were a swear. "He desired to get more book learning then return to marry Gasha and lead the clan. It caused the clan much anger. Would he be worse after years in a human city? Why must he leave at all? Does he not love the clan as his father did? Chief Forgruff decided it must end.

"On the day of Frok's departure, Chief Forgruff told him to never return. He was exiled from the Ironhands clan. 'You have forsaken our way of life, so you have forsaken your place here.' Those were his words."

Riley gasped. DJ's heart dropped.

"It has been eight years," Torq said. "Frok gave himself a new name—left behind his orc-born name. There was no other heir when Chief Forgruff was slain, so the mantle passed to Gasha, and she has led us. But we knew she wished for Frok to return. Now look."

Everyone turned to see Francis and Gasha whispering and giggling several paces away. It was like they were in their own little world, blissfully unaware of anyone else. Before long, they put down their bowls of larkbeast and wandered away. DJ thought he saw Gasha put her hand in Francis's.

"Let me get this straight," Riley said. "Francis's dad kicked him out of the clan because he doesn't like to *fight?*"

"He turned his back on tradition!" Torq said. "Favoring the book over the ax! An orc must *never* forsake battle! It is how we survive! The Goddess made us this way!"

"Apparently not all of you," DJ mumbled.

Torq let out a heavy sigh. "I knew humans would not understand." He stood up and bowed. "Farewell to you. May the Goddess give you peace on your journey." Then he left.

Steve's fan club began to gather again, bombarding him with questions and jokes. DJ nudged Riley as he watched Gasha and Francis disappear around a hut. "Where do you think they're going?"

Riley shrugged.

*

"So you own a shop of books now?" Gasha smirked. "I should not be surprised."

"I don't *own* it, but I help run it," Francis said. "It's truly a blessing. It was difficult to find a job after attending the College of Beregond, especially as an orc. Klepper gave me a chance, and I've been there ever since."

Gasha looked at him for a moment. "You talk like them,

too."

"What, humans?"

"Yes."

Francis nodded thoughtfully. "I suppose that's what comes from living among them for so long."

"And reading much."

"That too, yes."

The two of them wandered through the darkening village, their fingers laced together. Every other orc was still dining on larkbeast back at the village center, so they had the rest of the village to themselves. Gasha took the chance to give Francis a tour. She pointed out the village's apothecary, blacksmith, distillery, and garden. All the while, Francis watched Gasha's face in the moonlight, silently in awe of who she had become.

She caught his eyes. She pulled him close. Her voice lowered to a sweet rumble. "I've missed you greatly. I hoped this day would come. The village whispered. Many thought me a fool."

Francis brushed some hair out of her eyes. "I missed you too. Desperately. The young knight's quest brought us together. And I will always be grateful for that."

Gasha's eyes sparkled. Her hands moved from Francis's shoulders to his chest, slowly feeling with thick fingers. "You are still strong."

"And you've become stronger."

"But *your* bloodline is special," she said. "It would be shameful to let it end."

Heat swelled in Francis's chest. Gasha's eyes did the rest of the talking. The moment bent and strained until it snapped.

Francis burrowed his fingers in Gasha's hair and pressed his lips against hers. Gasha welcomed it. Her hands explored his chest and back.

Francis lifted Gasha and pinned her back against a nearby tree. They sank into each other's passion, drinking from a vessel filled with eight years of longing.

When it was over, they melted into each other's arms and their heartbeats settled. They held each other, laughing softly and kissing each other's burning skin. Francis stroked Gasha's hair.

"It will be a boy," Gasha said. "Strong and tall, like you."

"He'll have a strong mother," Francis replied.

Gasha's eyes met his again. There was something different in them now—a dash of sadness. She took his hand once more.

"Come," she said. "There is one more thing for you see."

Francis didn't have to ask what it was. Something inside him already knew. But he followed nonetheless. She led him to a large cabin. Around its base, flowers and trinkets were scattered—signs of remembrance. They lifted a flap that hung over the door and entered. Inside, Francis saw it.

Candles lit all about, illuminating the large cabin with a dull orange flicker. Various incense and spices made the cabin thick with a medley of scents. Urns were placed all around, marked with names and dates. He followed Gasha as she led him to a particular one. It didn't take long. She didn't touch it. She just stopped, put a hand on his shoulder, and pointed.

This urn looked to be the most recent. It was formed out of charcoal black clay, and it was large enough to reach a human's knee. Francis took a deep, steady breath and picked it up. The words were printed on the side.

Chief Forgruff
8A 937

Gasha rubbed Francis's back as he turned the urn in his hands. He didn't weep, which surprised him. But as he thought about it more, it wasn't that surprising. After all, his father had been dead to him—or he had been dead to his father—for over eight years.

"So this is him?" he muttered.

Gasha nodded. "Four arrows pierced him in our battle with the Fangtooths. It was his bravery, along with others, that earned us this land."

"That's how it's always been," Francis said. He let out a sigh and his shoulders drooped. "Why are you showing me this? It's you he loved, not me."

"He did love you, Frok." Gasha rubbed his shoulder. "But he was a Chief first. Father second."

"A father ashamed of his son." Francis set the urn down.

Gasha stood before Francis and held his face again. "But I am chief now. And I say you can stay."

Francis smiled sadly. "That wouldn't be wise. You already know the truth: I'm no longer welcome here."

"You are if I say you are," Gasha said fiercely.

Francis shook his head and pulled her hands down. "Your heart is fighting a battle your mind has already won. You saw how our—*your*—people treat me. They haven't forgotten what happened. There is no forgiveness in their hearts. They would hate you if you brought me back, and you know this."

Gasha started pacing back and forth, her hands on her hips. Her strong jaw flexed with thought. "They will learn. They will see the past is the past. They will learn to see forward."

"They won't."

"Then I will order them to give you respect."

"As She-Chief, you need all that respect for yourself," Francis said. "There hasn't been a She-Chief for hundreds of years. And I know many elders still see orc-sisters as hardly more than vessels for childbearing. Orders to bring back a banished orc would make your authority crumble and break. They would rise against you. It's better for you and everyone that I remain in exile."

Seeds of tears grew in Gasha's eyes. "Do you not want to return to me?"

Francis was on her in a heartbeat, holding her face. "For *eight years* I craved your touch. Ached to hear your voice. I slept for thousands of nights wishing I was here to keep you warm. I want to return to you so badly that everything inside me is *breaking*." His voice settled. "But I am *exiled*. And you are She-Chief. We can't simply go back to the way things were. Our—your—people would never allow it."

Gasha gulped away a hardening throat and gave one loud sniff. "What of your child that grows inside me? He will need his father."

"This is the Ironhands Clan," Francis said with a half-smile. "He will have a village full of fathers. I won't be a stranger to you and the child, and I will do all that I can to support you from afar. This I swear to you on the ashes of my father."

Gasha took a great, shaky breath, and when she let it out, it came with a trickle of a tear. She wiped it away quickly. "You were always the voice of wisdom. It angered me, and it still does."

Francis chuckled in his throat and kissed her forehead.

"When do you leave?" Gasha asked.

"Whenever the young knight decides," Francis answered. "I've vowed to be his protector as we venture to the Spine. We'll stay as long as we wishes."

"Then we shall show him hospitality like the Ironhands Clan never has before!" Gasha proclaimed. "You shall never leave!"

Francis smiled and held her tightly. "I will always love you, Gasha, She-Chief of the Ironhands Clan. Today has been a gift."

By the time they arrived in the village center, everyone had finished eating their larkbeast and the clan was practically drowning in firewine. They danced and sang songs, stumbling and hanging off each other. No one seemed to notice that Francis and Gasha returned—at least no one except DJ. He locked eyes with Francis and gave a little smile. Francis returned a smile, but it felt forced, like it was locking inside a profound sadness.

They stayed with the Ironhands Clan for three days. By then, DJ felt that they had had enough. But during that time, the Ironhands Clan gave DJ the best that they had to offer, almost to the point of smothering. They fully replenished the party's supplies for the trip to Blight's Respite. They made sure the party was always first to eat at every meal. They even offered to take DJ hunting with them—a great honor—but DJ had no desire to see a live larkbeast up close.

Francis spent every possible moment with Gasha. They even spent each night together, sleeping in her hut. Normally, DJ would feel nervous sleeping without a big intimidating orc nearby, but the whole village was full of big intimidating orcs that had to treat him like royalty, so the fear was diminished.

Riley spent her time trying to learn as much as she could from orcish hunters. She knew that orcs living in this environment had more to teach her about foraging and hunting than anyone else could. A few friendly she-orcs took her to gather mushrooms and edible plants and even challenged her to an archery contest. They outclassed her easily, but Riley took the defeat with grace and accepted their helpful tips.

And Steve could hardly get a moment's peace from his admirers. The four orcs they met during their first meal— Glib, Kork, Urg, and Gnoth—followed Fryo-steeg everywhere, insisting on playing games, eating meals, or challenging each other to contests of manhood. He was beat badly in a pull-up contest. His fan club could out-eat him at every meal. But Fryo-steeg was the first to headbutt a larkbeast skull so hard that it cracked. The four orcs positively lost their minds when that happened.

But at last, it was time to leave. The village saw them off. Gasha commanded a special ceremony to be performed marking DJ, Riley, and Steve official "Friends of the Ironhands

Clan." She went one by one marking a red square on their foreheads. When she painted Steve's forehead, his fan club barked and whooped in approval.

But she didn't mark Francis's forehead. Instead, they held a gaze that could have written thousands of sad stories. They held it for as long as they could before the clan grumbled.

For the next four days, they were led out of the Nether Regions in the same manner as their arrival. A guide silently led them to secured caves along the way until they reached the eastern drawbridge reaching over Traitor's Trench. Their footsteps clomped along the wooden bridge until they set foot in Fairdell. With that, the drawbridge went up, and they left the Nether Regions behind.

As soon as the *boom* of the drawbridge sounded, Francis let out a large sigh, as if a weight he had carried for eight years had been let go.

DJ turned to him. "You okay, Francis?"

Francis nodded half-spiritedly. "In the years since my exile, I've experienced every emotion. At first, I was angry—I felt abandoned by my people. But with time, reflection, and study, I began to feel peace again. I had to search deep inside to find forgiveness." Another sigh. "I know my home is no longer with the Ironhands Clan, but happiness is still within reach."

DJ was hesitant to say the next part, but he said it anyway. "You'll miss Gasha, won't you?"

"I always will," Francis admitted. "I missed her for eight years. Orcs mate for life. She'll always be my love. I shall do my best to love and support her from afar. That is how things must be."

DJ patted Francis's shoulder. "I'm glad you came on this journey with me, Francis."

Francis smiled down on DJ. "As am I, young knight. As am I." He tousled DJ's hair.

17

Riley's observation was loud. "How can a place called *Fairdell* suck so much?"

"Tell me about it," DJ grumbled. "Not very fair if you ask me."

In the distance, the southern end of the Camās Gahl Mountains rose to the sky. But in the expanse before it, plains of dark brown dirt and yellow grass stretched for miles. Tree stumps were everywhere. Healthy patches of green were rare —a drastic departure from the lush forests and rich plains they had experienced before the Nether Regions.

Francis shook his head. "Come now, it's not that bad. Fairdell has its own beauty."

"Francis, you're from the *Nether Regions*," Riley said. "Everything is beautiful compared to there."

DJ held his tongue and waited for Francis's response. The orc chose not to be offended but squinted and smirked at Riley.

"Give it a week or two," he said. "I've heard the Camās Gahl Mountains are tremendous. And on our journey to the Spine, we'll walk along their eastern edge."

DJ said, "And that's where we'll find the Library of Artak."

"That is correct," Francis's eyes flashed.

Steve pointed with his frying pan. "Behold! The Goddess has blessed us with water!"

As they crested a hill, a stagnant pond came to view just off the road. The sun would set in another hour, and this was one of the few bodies of water they had seen all day. The group agreed that this would be a decent place to set up camp.

Steve cleaned the pond water for consumption. He did it by sifting out the algae with a length of cloth and boiling the water before pouring it in everyone's canteens. It wouldn't taste great, but it would keep them hydrated and they wouldn't get sick.

As night fell, DJ took the first watch, and the faint sounds of Fairdell grew. Some frogs croaked at the pond's edge. Crickets sang as they hid in the prickly yellow grass. Cattails swayed by the water's edge. But DJ missed being surrounded by the sounds of the forest—the hooting owls, cool breeze, and chirping birds. He silently resolved to visit Daenan and the Aeldar Forest often once they returned to Beregond. Maybe Ursula or Sandy Brambleton would welcome his company again. He could bring Riley along, too.

Riley.

DJ shot a look over to the campfire. She was still asleep in her bedroll. A knot of dread grew in his chest as he thought of the Highway Hag incident. In an effort to push it from his mind, he focused on the water and went back to practicing Ice Spike. He drew from the pond water and used nearby cattails as targets. He would cast the spell over and over until his head hurt then take a break and keep trying. After an hour, dozens of cattails lay punctured by the water's edge, and the tolerance in his head was building up.

DJ heard footsteps approach but didn't turn around. He recognized the footfalls.

"Hey," Riley whispered. "It's time for my watch, right?"

"Is it? Okay. But watch this first." DJ made the proper motions. "*Glaci-talum!*"

A sharp finger of ice materialized from the water and shot toward a cattail. Direct hit. The punctured cattail drooped down to the ground.

Riley beamed. "Deej, that's amazing!"

"It took a lot of practice," DJ smiled. "But I can do it as long as there's a little water nearby."

Their eyes met, and one of those moments happened. Her face caught a lick of light from the campfire. Her eyes sparkled. DJ's heart sighed. And he realized that now was as good a time as ever. He remembered Francis's words: *The mightiest battles are often fought within.* He scraped up some courage and gave himself a cleansing breath.

"Hey, Ri."

Riley smiled inquisitively.

DJ cleared his throat. "We, uh, never talked about that thing with the Hag before the Nether Regions."

Her smile faded and her shoulders tensed. "Oh. Yeah. That

was weird."

"Yeah, it was." DJ paused. "What… do you think?"

"About what?"

"About what the Highway Hag got out of me," DJ said. "That I… kind of like you as more than just a friend."

It was hard to tell if Riley was blushing between the moonlight and the campfire. She hugged her elbows and turned away. "I don't know, DJ."

"Okay. Well… what does 'I don't know' mean? Is it like a maybe-I-don't-know, an I'm-leaning-toward-no-I-don't-know, or…?"

"It means *I don't know*," Riley said firmly. "We're hundreds of miles away from home. There's a gnome sworn to hunt me down. I'm not thinking about romance right now."

DJ nodded tightly and said, "Yeah. Yeah, that makes sense."

A hush fell. It made DJ uncomfortable. Feeling the need to speak, he said, "So… you just need time to think about it?"

"Yeah. But not now. After all of this is over."

That's a long time, DJ thought. "Okay," he said. "It's not gonna make the rest of this journey weird?"

Riley raised an eyebrow at him. "Only if you make it weird."

"I'm not gonna make it weird!"

"You made it pretty weird before the Nether Regions. You didn't talk to me for days."

DJ blushed. "I'm sorry. I didn't know what to do. I was afraid I had ruined everything."

Riley half-smiled and shook her head. "No, nothing is ruined." A beat. "Are you… going to be okay if I just want to be friends?"

DJ's heart fell and dread swelled in his chest again. He had never been rejected by a girl before—he had never been interested in any other girl. Being zero for one would hurt a lot. But it was *Riley.* Not having her around at all would be much worse than being rejected for something more. She was too important.

DJ nodded. "Yeah. I'd still want to be friends."

"Good."

Quiet settled between the two of them again, then Riley took a big breath to dispel it. "I should probably take my watch now. Cool magic, DJ. Good job."

DJ forced a smile. "Thanks. G'nite, Ri."

He marched to his bedroll and slipped inside. A weight lifted from him, but waves of uncertainty still lapped his heart. *She needs time to think about it? But she's not even going to start thinking about it until we're back home? That could be months!*

In his heart, he hoped she wasn't just trying to protect his feelings. But she promised she wouldn't lie again, so there was that.

*

More dirt and yellow grass in the following days. And tree stumps. And rare patches of green grass. There were enough ponds to make drinkable water along the way, but it was a pain to strain algae and boil water over and over. Steve never complained, though. He whistled while he did it.

At last, they saw Blight's Respite stretching across the Great River. It occupied the north and south banks of the Great River, and the massive bridge that joined both ends was wide and long enough to be populated with hundreds of buildings. DJ suddenly realized why they had walked by so much deforestation—the whole bridge was probably made from that timber.

The chilly river air grazed their skin as they hiked closer to the city. The walls around Blight's Respite weren't high—maybe twenty feet, constructed from timbers and stone. The guards keeping the entrance gave them curt nods.

In the city, they found muddy roads with rubbish strewn everywhere. Ragged, coughing townspeople with sallow faces glared at them. Animal droppings were left in the road. DJ grimaced. Compared to Blight's Respite, cities like Beregond and Varis were the Seven Heavens.

"Is all of Fairdell going to be like this?" Riley muttered to Francis.

"It's the reason your ancestors migrated west ages ago," Francis said. "Humans who live in Fairdell treat it as a point of pride—like they're the strong ones who chose to stay, despite the less-than-ideal conditions. That's why the river between the Cradle and Fairdell is called Traitor's Trench."

"Hello!" Steve greeted a Blight's Respite resident as they walked by. The resident gave Steve a foul look.

"Charming," Riley murmured. "How are we doing on coin?"

"Low as usual," DJ said. "The Apothescary nearly drained

us back in Varis. That's kind of the story of our journey, huh? Get broke, find a job, barely escape, earn some coin. Rinse and repeat."

"Sounds like lazy writing," Francis said.

"What?"

"Nothing."

"So we'll need another side quest," Riley sighed. "Hopefully there's something here that doesn't involve shoveling shit."

"Language!" Steve yelped.

A familiar voice sounded to their right. "Hello, friends! It has been far too long!"

The wizard waffle merchant. His bright garb and clean wooden stand stood out like a diamond in a manure pile. Knowing they were low on medicine, Riley and DJ hustled toward the stand.

"Welcome to the ill-tempered community of mud and depression known as Blight's Respite!" The wizard waved his hands theatrically. "Better watch your step and keep your belongings close! A waffle or two wouldn't hurt, either." He winked.

"We'll take two," DJ said. "We didn't even get to eat the last ones. They were destroyed by a violent noodle cult in the middle of the forest."

"A shame!" The wizard served up two fully loaded waffles with strawberries and cream. "Since you all have been such loyal customers, the third is free!" He pulled a third one from under the table, fully prepared like the other two.

"Thanks!" Riley said as she stuffed the waffles in her pack.

"Any leads on some work around here? You always seem to have the answers."

"Haha! I certainly do." He made a show of tapping his chin and gazing all around, then he snapped his fingers. "I know! I happen to be well acquainted with Kathryn the Kind."

"She sounds nice!" Steve yipped.

The wizard nodded. "She's the governor of Blight's Respite! A high-ranking official. She's in a bit of a pickle, last I heard. There's a festival fast approaching—The Kathryn the Kind Beat the Onyx Wing So Let's Celebrate and Get Drunk Festival. It commemorates the time that Kathryn the Kind beat the Onyx Wing, so everyone celebrates and gets drunk!"

Francis blinked. "Thank you for the clarification."

Riley put her hands on her hips. "So what does she need for the Kathryn the Kind Beat the Onyx Wing So Let's Celebrate and Get Drunk Festival? Does she need someone to make cotton candy or something?"

"Oh no!" the wizard said. "For the Kathryn the Kind Beat the Onyx Wing So Let's Celebrate and Get Drunk Festival, she'll likely need protection!"

DJ sighed. "Of course."

Francis raised an eyebrow. "The festival is named after her and she needs protection for it? Sounds like she's not terribly popular."

The wizard laughed. "Quite the contrary. As you can imagine, it's the Onyx Wing that wants to see her gone. She'll explain it all at the governor's manor! Tell her I sent you!"

"All right then," Francis said. "But… you never gave us your name."

"Because it doesn't matter." The wizard grinned and shrugged.

Riley narrowed her eyes. "What's your deal? You're an actual wizard, right? Why do you show up in random places selling magic waffles?"

The wizard smiled. "I really must be going. Pleasure doing business with you! Ta-ta!"

The entire party gave him looks as if to say all-right-then-keep-your-secrets, then they bid him farewell and walked northeast. After they ventured a little farther up the main concourse, DJ looked over his shoulder. Of course, by that time, the wizard and his stand were gone.

"The Onyx Wing," Francis repeated as they trudged through the mud. "I've heard of them. Thieves. Murderers. Rumors came down to the Nether Regions when I was a boy, but I didn't know if any of them are true."

"If they *are* true," Riley said, "maybe Kathryn the Kind is good news. Especially if people like the Onyx Wing don't like her. She's Kathryn *the Kind* after all."

Eventually their boots made it to the vast wooden bridge of Blight's Respite. The entire thing had to be half a mile wide and a mile long—a feat of engineering. DJ wondered if they had dwarven help or if the humans did it themselves.

The main road went straight through the bridge wide enough for six lanes of carriages. All the other bridge space was packed with shops, inns, and homes. These buildings looked nicer than the ones they saw on the southern edge of town. They weren't Varis-esque by any means, but comfortable and charming. Maybe they would make enough coin to stay at one tonight—and maybe they would even have baths.

DJ spotted the city ravenpost tower, stretching up to the sky. "I'll be back in a minute."

After weaving through some disgruntled locals, he entered the tower and asked the druid if there was any mail for him. The druid grumbled, belched, then dumped a box of letters on the counter. DJ frowned as he watched the druid sort through them. The druid found three letters and handed them over. DJ broke the seal of the first one.

Ho there, Son!

I must admit your last letter nearly brought a tear to this old man's eye. I'm very proud to be your father. I'm sorry meeting your mother wasn't pleasant. But it sounds like you got the closure you need, so that is good.

Did you visit the Nether Regions on your way to Fairdell? Did you eat larkbeast? I prayed to the Goddess each night that you wouldn't get eaten by anything.

Stay wary in Blight's Respite! It's a dreadful town! Avoid the Onyx Wing when possible and keep your sword close. Or do magic. Whichever is best for you now.

Be safe!

-Sir Dashing

The second letter said:

Ho there again, Son!

Hope you're doing well. It crossed my mind that I should have given you more advice in my last letter. Members of the Onyx Wing have black wing tattoos on their wrists or neck. Don't engage with them if you can help it, and certainly don't pick a fight with them. They run most of the city and they won't hesitate to cut you down.

Stay vigilant!
-Sir Dashing

And the third:

Son,
You're making me very concerned. Write back as quickly as possible.
-Dad

DJ smirked and paid the druid for a slice of parchment and a quill.

Hey, Dad,
I just arrived in Blight's Respite. Yeah, this place sucks. But there might be an opportunity to help the city governor so I'll let you know how that goes.

Larkbeast wasn't bad. We had much better food in Varis, though. We met Francis's old clan. It's a lot to explain in a letter, I'll tell you about it later.

Getting even better at magic. I hardly use my sword at all.

How's the Harvest Festival stuff coming along? Have they started building that statue of you yet?

I'll write you again when we reach the Library of Artak. Francis says there should be a village outside it with a raven-post tower.

Love you, Dad.

-DJ

DJ handed the letter to the druid and left. When he reached his friends, he said, "Even the ravenpost druid is grumpy here."

"Seems to be the way with this town," Francis said. "The good news is that the Library of Artak is less than a week's journey from here."

DJ smiled at him. "You're so excited."

"You haven't the faintest idea." Francis bore his tusks with glee.

"Hey," Riley said to a stranger. "Which way is the governor's manor?"

The haggard local rolled her eyes. "Follow the signs, stupid girl!"

Riley went pink with embarrassment as she noticed signs several feet away pointing the proper direction. Then she clamped her jaw. "Of course, how silly of me." She gave a regal bow. "My sincerest apologies, your highness!" Then she made a rude gesture with her hand. "Dirty eastern half-wit."

"Candy-ass trench hopper!" the local barked back.

Riley took a step forward, but DJ held her by the shoulders and wheeled her away before she could clap back. She scowled and said, "The sooner we leave this Goddess-forsaken dump, the better."

Steve looked all around then shook his head. "The Goddess does not smile upon Blight's Respite!"

18

They followed the signs that led them to a residential area. The homes on this street were uncharacteristically fine compared to the rest of the city. They had windows with clean shutters, roofs with metal shingles, and woodwork adorned with detailed motifs. Not to mention the even paint and colorful flowerboxes. Steve took a big whiff of some azaleas as the party walked by.

The governor's manor was the building at the end of the neighborhood, with its back to the edge of the bridge. It was considerably large, with lots of tall windows armed with thick iron bars. The property was surrounded by a tall iron fence that framed a courtyard. An array of plants and trees grew from raised boxes inside.

Dozens of guards stood watch around the fence. A couple of them near the gate watched the party approach.

"What do you want?" one of them growled.

"We were told Kathryn the Kind is looking to add to her

security detail for the Kathryn the Kind Beat the Onyx Wing So Let's Celebrate and Get Drunk Festival," DJ said. "A friend of hers sent us."

"What friend?" the second guard said.

"The wizard waffle merchant!" Steve replied.

The guards traded unbelieving stares.

Riley whispered in DJ's ear, "Maybe they don't know about him."

"Experience in security?" the second guard asked.

"*Do* we!" Riley stepped forward with her hands on her hips. "Listen tough guy, we've traveled to this mud hole all the way from *Beregond.* We've fought bandits, killed an evil goblin king, escaped a cult in the middle of the forest… your governor would be *lucky* to have us on her detail."

The first guard gave a tiny smirk. "All that, huh? You look like a breeze could blow you over."

Riley turned scarlet.

"We could let her size you up if you're willing to disarm yourselves and take a Truth Serum," the second guard said. "But that's the only way we can let you in."

Truth Serum? DJ was amazed that something like that could even exist. The whole party considered, then agreed.

"Good," the first guard said. "Follow them, and be prepared to hand over your weapons."

Some guards inside the courtyard unlocked the gates and brought the party inside. There were two guards for every party member. DJ and the others removed their weapons and handed them over—one guard was puzzled to receive Steve's frying pan. Then the guards swiftly marched the party to the front door, passing by the raised trees and shrubs that populated the courtyard. They gave a special knock, the door unlocked, and they entered.

Given the tight security, DJ was surprised to see how modest the governor's manor was. He expected a Sandy Brambleton-esque fortress of mahogany and leather, but it wasn't the case. The furniture was fine, but there wasn't much of it. Empty wall and floor space were common, occasionally marked with discoloration where long-time fixtures had been removed. The place had obviously been decadent in the past, but now it felt mostly empty. And frankly, it all could use a bit of dusting.

The guards led the party to a main room with a wide fireplace, a couch, two chairs, and a rug made from a large snow-bear pelt. The bear's white fur was a strict contrast against most of the home's dingy gray-and-purple interior.

More chairs were brought in. The party sat down. Guards surrounded them. Then one guard came in with a small vial of a liquid so purple it was almost black. He held it up as he spoke.

"This is Truth Serum," he said. "Each of you hold out your tongues. I'll only ask once."

You didn't ask at all, but okay, DJ thought bitterly. He stuck out his tongue.

The guard put a single drop of the Truth Serum on everyone's tongues. DJ's face twisted. It was like rancid apple cider —he wondered what ingredients made it up. The guard put his hands behind his back and stared daggers at the group. His words were deliberate and slow, impossible to misunderstand.

"Do any of you have intentions to harm Kathryn the Kind?"

"No." "No." "No." "No!"

DJ was amazed at how the word tumbled off his tongue, completely involuntary.

"Are any of you in league with those who would do harm to Kathryn the Kind?"

"No." "No." "No." "No!"

"Do you have any intentions to remove Kathryn the Kind from her position?"

"No." "No." "No." "No!"

The guard nodded. "Good." He turned to another guard. "Return their weapons. I'll bring her in."

The guards returned the weapons. DJ smacked his tongue against the roof of his mouth and slid Riley a look. "This stuff tastes awful, doesn't it?"

"Yes," the word jumped off Riley's lips.

DJ laughed, realizing his innocent question commanded an honest answer. Giggling, a mischievous grin spread across Riley's face.

"When was the last time you wet the bed?" she asked.

"Age seven," DJ blabbed the answer. His cheeks flushed red. "*Hey!* Not cool."

Riley laughed. Then she turned to Francis. "What's a secret you never told anyone?"

"My favorite book genre is sensual romance," Francis blurted. He turned on Riley with eyes more nervous than angry. "Er... please forget you heard that."

Having a grand time, Riley leaned toward Steve. "What's your biggest fear, Steve?"

"That I do righteous deeds for unrighteous reasons!" Steve said with wide eyes. "As a Steward of the Goddess I find a degree of joy in my service, but I occasionally question if I truly thirst for righteousness or if it is merely the fruits of selfishness! Do I serve to create a life of goodness of its own merit, or as an attempt to find belonging among my fellow Stewards? Is my service truly for others or for myself? I have lost much sleep over this!"

Everyone grew quiet. Even the guards shifted uncomfortably. Riley clammed up and her eyes fell to her boots.

DJ leaned over. "Are you glad you asked?"

"No." The word popped off her tongue.

Clomping footsteps entered the room. The party turned to see a strong, beautiful woman donning leather armor. Her burgundy hair was shaved on one side, cascading down her right shoulder. On the shaved side, three long scars raked her ear, jaw, and neck. DJ wondered if the scars and the snowbear rug were related. She looked at the crew with a satisfied smirk and folded arms.

"The waffle wizard sent you, huh?" she asked.

"Yes." "Yes." "Yes." "Yes!"

Her smirk grew. "Well, he hasn't led me astray yet. And don't worry, the Truth Serum will wear off in a few minutes. I'm Kathryn. Sit by the fire, it's more comfortable."

The group cautiously joined her. Francis took up most of the couch, but there was still room for Steve and Riley on either side. DJ sat in the armchair nearest to Kathryn.

"So our waffle-loving friend told you I could use some protection?" Kathryn asked.

Francis answered. "That's right, Lady Kathryn. Said the Onyx Wing isn't too fond of you."

"That's putting it lightly," Kathryn half-laughed. She turned to one of the guards. "Bring me a bottle of wine, would you, George?" Then she glanced at her visitors. "Hungry? Thirsty? I'm sure you want to wash down that Goddess-awful Truth Serum."

Everyone graciously accepted her offer, and two guards brought them a platter of cheese, bread, and wine. While everyone helped themselves, Kathryn pulled a utility knife from her boot and carved into an apple.

"Here's the short version of the story," she said. "I grew up on the South Bank of Blight's Respite. You've probably seen it—rough neighborhood, and it used to be even worse. I turned sixteen, and instead of getting married off to the highest bidder, I left town and became a ranger. Did that for about twelve years."

That had Riley's full attention. She watched Kathryn with sparkling eyes. DJ smiled at her.

"Meanwhile, the Onyx Wing ran this town like they did for decades," Kathryn continued, "muscling their way into everything, charging 'protection fees' to everyone. If you could pay, you got their *protection*, but if you didn't, well…" She paused. "Obviously the rich assholes on the Bridge District had no problem, but the rest of us struggled.

"I got some ravenpost when I was chasing a bounty near Daenan. My mother and father could no longer pay the protection fees, so the Onyx Wing beat my father within an inch of his life. I came home as fast as I could, but by the time I arrived, he was already dead."

Riley gasped. DJ's heart sank.

"That lit a fire in me," Kathryn said. "I was sick of the Onyx Wing and their corruption. And as a ranger—a damn good one—I knew I could do something about it. For months, I stalked their captains like prey. I learned everything about them. I found an evening when they were all gathered together, and…" She made a slicing motion with her hand. "Stuffed all their heads in a bag."

The color left DJ's face.

"That same night," Kathryn said, "I climbed a post in the middle of town, called out to the city that Blight's Respite was free, the leaders of the Onyx Wing were dead, and if any members stayed in the city, they would suffer the same fate. Then I dropped the heads in town square and disappeared— had to stay mysterious to keep the Onyx Wing afraid.

"I stayed hidden for days, and as far as I knew, most of the Onyx Wing fled. Then the whispers about me started. Blight's Respite had no one to lead it anymore, and from the sound of things, people wanted *me* in charge. It was funny because I never viewed myself as a politician. But as I thought about it… maybe that's what this city needed. So here I am, appointed by the voice of the people."

"You're the coolest person I've ever met," Riley interjected with wide eyes.

Kathryn suppressed a smile. "That was nearly three years ago. Since then, there have been a lot of messes to clean up.

The city's poor like me because I gave them the Onyx Wing's wealth. The city's rich hate me because I stripped away part of their power. And some members of the Onyx Wing stay in hiding." A small laugh. "Guess it wasn't really the short version, huh? Anyway, I received this recently."

She gestured to a nearby guard who handed her a note. Kathryn unfolded it and set it on the table. In black ink, it said, *Revenge is ours.* Beneath the writing, a stenciled painting of a black wing.

"The Kathryn the Kind Beat the Onyx Wing So Let's Celebrate and Get Drunk Festival is in three days," Kathryn said. "It'll mark three years since I killed the Onyx Wing leaders and dumped their heads in the middle of town. I think the Onyx Wing is going to attempt something during the festival, so I need all the help I can get." She leaned back and folded her arms. "I'm usually much pickier about my guard detail, but that wizard seems to like you four. I take that as a good sign."

"It'll be an honor to serve you," Riley bowed.

"I hate to bring it up at a time like this," Francis said, "but there is the question of compensation."

Kathryn leaned forward and rubbed her hands. "Here's the simple truth: I can't pay you handsomely, but I can promise you beds, food, and supplies for your upcoming journey. I can also see what coin I can scrape up, but I won't make lofty promises. I'm already spread thin hiring guards that I can trust, and even then, they make a lot less than they would have under the Onyx Wing." She smirked at one of her guards. "But you don't mind, do you, Lyle?"

One of the guards—presumably named Lyle—said, "Serving you is an honor in itself, Lady Kathryn."

"If that's not enough, I understand," Kathryn said. "There won't be any consequences if you choose to leave."

Everyone turned to DJ. He hated how everyone always looked at him whenever there's a major decision. But this whole quest was for him, wasn't it? He took a breath and considered it. Kathryn seemed honest enough, and the waffle wizard never steered them wrong. Maybe this was destiny. Or something close enough.

"If you guys are in," DJ said, "I am too."

Everyone agreed.

Kathryn smiled approvingly. "We've got a barbarian, two mages, and a… ranger?"

"Working on it," Riley beamed.

"Good," Kathryn said. "The guards will tell you everything you need to know. My life is in your hands now, so don't get me killed." She winked. "Welcome aboard the Blight's Respite Town Guard."

Kathryn shook all of their hands, and the party followed a guard down to the manor's basement. There, they found the manor's supply of food, a modest armory, and rooms full of bunks. The bunks were a bit cramped even for humans, so Francis knew he'd have to sleep on the floor. After their long walk into town, they chose to spend the evening eating, washing, and getting ready for bed.

The next morning, they awoke with the other guards before the sun had peeked over the river. They shared a modest breakfast of salted fish, vegetables, and bread. As they ate, a guard instructed them on what to look for when it came to the Onyx Wing.

The guard told them about the black wing tattoos on necks and wrists—DJ already knew about that one thanks to his dad. They were also admonished not to take bribes from or share information with any civilians. And they were told to watch for anyone who moved or talked suspiciously, which felt obvious enough.

Lastly, every volunteer was stamped with an insignia on the back of their wrist. It had two crossing arrows on a bridge —the crest of Blight's Respite. They were told showing this insignia would get them into guard facilities, including the governor's manor.

DJ and the others decided it would be wise to get a lay of the land. They explored up and down the Bridge District, spending plenty of time on the main concourse. Their feet clomped on the wooden bridge, weaving around locals who complained under their breath about out-of-towners.

On the concourse, vendors and performers had been set-ting up their spaces in preparation for the Festival. Lights and streamers were hung between posts. Stages were erected for minstrels and bards. Merchants built booths for games and prizes. And there was lots of food that filled the misty air with sweetness—DJ even noticed travelers from Westfall selling Odambro Braids. He salivated and smacked his lips then told himself he'd get one later.

Something about all the festival preparations resurrected a memory in DJ's mind. When he was a small child, Sir Dash-ing took him to the Beregond Harvest Festival where they saw dancers, minstrels, and jesters performing in the street. He remembered the lively music and jubilant crowd as he sat on Sir Dashing's shoulders, laughing and smiling and pointing all around. They even enjoyed frozen strawberries later that day as a treat. DJ smiled. He'd have to remind his father of that memory soon.

He and his friends traveled to the North Bank, which wasn't much different from the South Bank—dirty, muddy, and full of irritable locals. There were, however, more farms on the North Bank.

There wasn't much else to do since they had no money, so the party sparred with the local guards. The South Bank had a training ground complete with wooden dummies, practice weapons, and a first aid facility. It was scanty, but sufficient.

DJ was a little self-conscious about practicing magic around city guards—stereotypical meatheads famous for their brawn. When they saw him utter magetongue and conduct his magic movements, he heard a couple of them snickering quietly. He even caught the words, "All magic, no maidens." With a scowl, DJ lodged a foot-long Ice Spike in the chest of a wooden dummy. The guards kept quiet after that.

"Impressive!"

DJ turned toward the voice. It was Kathryn, strolling into the training facility with two guards and an assistant. She must have noticed the guards mocking DJ, because she gave them a sly look.

"Not bad, right?" she said, pointing to the Ice Spike. "Why can't *you* do that?"

The guards shuffled their feet uncomfortably.

Kathryn focused on DJ. "Know any other spells?"

"Oh yeah," DJ said, counting on his fingers. "Flamefist, Ironflesh, Healing Hand…"

"What about your friend? He any good?"

She gestured to Steve, who had just batted a wooden dummy across its face with a frying pan. DJ watched him wind up another swing and grinned. "He's a lot better than me, actually."

"Mages don't get the respect they deserve," Kathryn said. "A mage that's been on the road and seen some action? Worth more than their weight in gold. That's why I want you two close on Festival day. You'll be part of my closest guard detail. That all right?"

Feeling somewhere between awkward and honored, DJ swallowed and nodded. "Of course, Lady Kathryn."

Not far away, Riley was shooting arrows into a wooden dummy. Almost all of them hit their mark—a stationary target was easier. She stopped to look when Kathryn entered but put extra moxie in her pull when she knew the governor was watching.

Kathryn raised her voice. "How are you doing, ranger? Are your shots true?"

"Oh, I'm not a full ranger yet," Riley clutched her bow and blushed. "But I'm getting there! I've learned a lot!"

"Yet?" Kathryn raised an eyebrow. "Haven't you traveled all the way from Beregond, hunting, trapping, and foraging?"

"I mean… yeah."

"Then you're a ranger," Kathryn said. "An inexperienced one, but a ranger nonetheless."

Riley could have levitated.

Kathryn turned to DJ again. "What do you need from me? Something tells me you'll be important during the Festival. That wizard tends to arrive just when he's needed. I hope you understand the trust I have in you."

So this is why she's called Kathryn the Kind, DJ thought. "You've already given us what we need. We just hope the Kathryn the Kind Beat the Onyx Wing So Let's Celebrate and Get Drunk Festival comes and goes without issue."

"You and I both," Kathryn said. She paused. "That name is a mouthful, isn't it?"

"Yeah!" DJ said. "Who came up with that?"

Kathryn gave a half-smile and shrugged. "Don't blame me. I let the people make their own choices."

At that moment, a stray guard came sprinting to the training area. He slid to a halt before Kathryn, who watched him with furrowed eyebrows.

"Lady Kathryn," the guard said, panting heavily. "There is something you must see at the town square. Quickly."

Kathryn nodded. "Lead the way."

She and her entourage followed the guard out, hurrying northward toward the Bridge District. DJ and his friends only had to exchange a brief glance before they followed. After they ran through the mud and reached the town square, they saw it.

A crowd had gathered in the middle of the festival preparations. The throng was focused on a single post near the center of it all. From that post dangled a stuffed dummy of a woman with red hair shaved on the side. A rope was tied around the dummy's neck—a noose.

DJ and the others pushed themselves to the front of the crowd. Locals murmured around them. A guard took a ladder and severed the rope, handing the dummy to Kathryn. She turned it around in her hands, feeling the red yarn and stitched scars that mimicked her own features. Most prominently, there was a note stabbed into the dummy's chest. The words on the note were short:

We'll rise again. Then there was a stencil of a black wing.

Kathryn crumpled up the note and threw it aside. She looked around the crowd, realizing every gaze was fixed on her. For a moment, DJ thought he saw unease pass over her face, but she chased it away and replaced it with an amused sneer.

"Who knew the Onyx Wing still played with dollies?" she said. The crowd laughed nervously, to which she replied, "I don't fear these cowards, and neither should you. In two days, we'll celebrate without incident as we always have. Our guards are doing a tremendous job securing the city, and we're as safe as we've ever been. So if you lack confidence, have some of mine."

With a collective sigh, the people of Blight's Respite applauded. Kathryn dropped the dummy and marched through the crowd with meaningful steps. As she passed DJ, she put an arm around him and pulled him along. His friends followed. When they left the crowd and were sure no one could hear, Kathryn leaned in, speaking inches from DJ's ear.

"Be ready, mage," she said. "My life is in your hands."

She patted him on the back then retreated with a few of

her associates. As Francis, Riley, and Steve gathered around DJ, he gulped and shuddered.

245

19

The morning of the Kathryn the Kind Beat the Onyx Wing So Let's Celebrate and Get Drunk Festival, the guards awoke everyone long before the sun rose.

DJ rubbed the sleep from his eyes and armed himself. Kathryn wouldn't appear at the Festival until dusk, but the guards had their orders to patrol the festivities throughout the day. DJ and Steve were requested to stay at the governor's manor and watch Kathryn while Riley and Francis patrolled the Festival with the rest of the guards.

"Don't worry," Riley said. "Francis and I will stick together. No one will try anything on a seven-foot orc."

Francis held DJ's shoulder. "Be wary, young knight. Stay close to Steven."

They left the manor to patrol with the other guards. DJ and Steve stayed in the manor's common area. Kathryn leaned back in an armchair, resting her feet on a nearby table. Everything about her manner spoke relaxation, but her face betrayed her demeanor. There was worry etched in those features. DJ could see them across the room.

"Make yourselves comfortable," she said. "The festival's best ale is brought out at dusk, and that's when I'm supposed to have the special Drink to Freedom. It's easier to keep me alive in one room, right?" The question came with a weary smirk.

Guards kept their eyes on windows and doors. They played cards. They sharpened their weapons. Stories and chatter were sparse. Any attempt at levity was short-lived and feeble. Frequent glances were taken toward their leader, and she did her best to keep up the nonchalance. DJ knew she was thinking about the notes she had received. *Revenge is ours. We'll rise again.*

It didn't take long before Steve prodded DJ. "Sir DJ! We must meditate together!" The friar sat down, crossed his legs, closed his eyes, and breathed. DJ felt everyone's eyes on him, and normally that would make him self-conscious. But given the circumstances and Steve's experience, DJ knew it was foolish to resist. He crossed his legs and closed his eyes.

Time ticked slowly by. Itching impatience grew in him— as well as a rumbling stomach—so after a while, he got up to retrieve some rations. DJ finished a fist of bread and an apple, and all the while, Steve kept meditating.

This could be like the House of Phillip all over again, DJ thought with anticipation.

Hours passed. Steve never stopped. Guards came to the manor to report on the Festival. The day had started off with general unease, but as the Festival went on and the people drowned themselves in cheap liquor, their spirits turned high. And there were no signs of the Onyx Wing yet. Guards frequently checked visitors and locals for black wing tattoos, but there were none.

"Maybe they're just trying to scare you," one guard said.

"Or they're hiring someone else to do their dirty work," another guard replied.

"What say you, Lady Kathryn?" a third guard asked.

Kathryn twiddled her knife and said nothing for a time. She gazed at her reflection in the blade, then said, "The Onyx Wing came to power through cunning and force. So did I." She paused. "Does that make us the same?"

Everyone held their breath and traded nervous glances. The soldier named Lyle knelt by her side and frowned seriously. "You stand for freedom, not oppression, Lady Kathryn. You cut them down because someone needed to. You're a hero."

Kathryn gave another tired smirk. "Hope it always stays that way."

No one knew what to say to that.

The hours felt like days, but at long last, the sun turned orange and red in the windows. Lyle stooped down by Kathryn's chair. "My Lady, it's nearing time for the Drink to Freedom."

Kathryn put on her best smile. "The mead better be good this year. Ready, all?"

Finally, Steve opened his eyes. There was a steely focus in them DJ had rarely seen. The friar stood and everyone assembled by the door. Together, they surrounded Kathryn as they marched rhythmically through the courtyard and out the gate. As they traveled toward the town square, the dull noise of the crowd grew. The smells of sweet pastries drifted through the air, along with shimmering music. When they broke into the open, the noise transformed into a raucous cheer.

The entire concourse was illuminated with lines of tall torches flickering with light. Bards broke into a celebratory song. And as the city celebrated, DJ noticed that most of the townspeople had colored their hair red. Some of them even painted fake scars across their faces and wore ranger cloaks. He scrunched his nose at the lot of them and thought of how strange it was to worship a politician, even if it were someone like Kathryn the Kind.

Surrounded by over a dozen guards, Kathryn smiled and waved all around—most likely scanning for threats. DJ and Steve stayed on either side of her. DJ kept both hands splayed and ready for magic. All the while, the city vibrated with joyful noise.

In the middle of the concourse was a stage loaded with an astonishing number of mead barrels. One of Kathryn's close guards gave her a tankard. She carefully picked a barrel to draw from then stuck her tankard under its spout and filled it with rich, frothy drink.

Her guard detail created a tight circle around her. DJ and Steve stayed close, along with two other guards. DJ studied the crowd, watching for anyone suspicious. He saw Riley and Francis at the edge of the crowd. Riley waved. DJ grinned.

Kathryn held up the tankard and the city quieted.

"People of Blight's Respite," she said. "I hope you've enjoyed the third annual Kathryn the Kind Beat the Onyx Wing So Let's Celebrate and Get Drunk Festival!"

A swell of cheers and one errant, "*Marry me, Kathryn!*"

"There is still much work to do," Kathryn continued. "But together, we will keep building a happy and free Blight's Respite, far from the grasp of those greedy, murderous, *Onyx Wing bastards!*"

A louder swell of cheers. No marriage proposals.

She gestured to the barrels behind her. "Are you ready for the best mead in the city?"

The city roared.

"*Are you?*"

The city roared louder.

"Then let's get on with it!" She raised her tankard. "To freedom, to peace, and to the City Over the Water!"

Hesitating, she tipped her head back and drank.

That's when the strike happened.

Half of her guards turned with military speed. They shot arrows. They flung knives. A traitorous assault of projectiles aimed at Kathryn the Kind.

It was fast, but Steve was faster.

His arms moved like snapping cobras and his lips spoke magetongue with godlike precision. A dome of translucent blue materialized around Kathryn and the close guard detail. Knives bounded off. Arrows severed in two. The nearby guards ripped their weapons from their holsters. DJ crouched down, hands outstretched, heart pounding, ready.

Outside the protective dome, Blight's Respite burst into chaos.

Townspeople screamed and ran. Guards wrestled other guards to the ground. Riley and Francis jumped the traitorous guards nearest to them. Francis subdued one, but his shoulder was horribly gashed in the process. Riley failed with her prey —the guard trapped her in a headlock. In the struggle, Riley knocked his helm off, but she was still helpless in his grasp.

DJ's fingers twitched. Magetongue stayed on the tip of his teeth. He remained trapped inside the protective dome, unsure of what to do. Most of the traitors had been subdued, but others snatched innocent townspeople and pointed knives at them, holding them hostage.

But the traitor who captured Riley stumbled into the open, holding a sword to her throat, stomping all around.

"Silence!" he cried. "*Silence!*"

That voice. As the guard clutched a resisting Riley, DJ recognized him. The handsome face. The parted black hair. The strong chin.

Vennick. And the blade pressed against Riley's throat was DJ's own knight sword. He sneered horribly. "The Onyx Wing sends its regards."

Rage flared in DJ's chest. "Let her go!"

Vennick laid his eyes on him. That sneer became even worse. "Well, I'll be… the sniveling, pampered son of Sir Dashing. I thought I killed you months ago."

"Should've tried harder," DJ seethed.

"The night is still young," Vennick's voice slithered. "By the way, I thought of pawning this blade of yours, but I grew rather fond of it. It's finely made. Besides, the word *Junior* decreases its value."

Riley struggled against him. Vennick held tighter. DJ's hands trembled.

"Release her, you coward!" Kathryn put her hand on the sword by her waist. "Fight me yourself!"

"Ah, but you're in there, and I'm out here." Vennick motioned to the blue dome with his chin. "Creates a bit of a predicament, doesn't it? Not that I would fight you to begin with. I've heard you're quite the specimen." His eyes seared. "How about this: for every ten seconds you stay alive inside that dome, we kill one of your people? I'd be happy to start with this one. She was never terribly bright to begin with."

Whimpers from the other hostages. A bead of blood trickled down Riley's neck. DJ tried to formulate a plan, but he was still reeling with shock and anger.

"I'll make it easy for you," Vennick said. "I'll count down from ten. Ten."

Riley's eyes were wild. They locked on DJ.

"Nine."

DJ shot a look at Steve. The friar stood frozen with worry.

"Eight."

DJ turned to the guards behind him. Neither of them budged.

"Seven."

DJ bared his teeth and looked back at Riley.

"Six."

Riley stayed insanely focused on DJ. She puckered her lips.

"Five!"

Riley was sucking her cheeks in, like she was getting ready

to spit in the air.

"Four!"

Spit into the air. *Spit into the air.*

"*Three!*"

The sudden realization hit DJ like lightning. He nodded.

"*Two!*"

Riley spat out a wad of saliva. DJ planted his feet.

"*One!*"

DJ shot out his arms. "*Glaci-talum!*"

Before that wad of spit could hit the ground, it transformed into a pick of ice and shot into Vennick's eye.

The mercenary cried out. He loosened his grasp. Taking her opportunity, Riley twisted around, disarmed him, and slammed the sword's hilt into his temple. The handsome mercenary crumpled into an unconscious heap.

As a collective gasp flew through the town, the guards acted quickly. They subdued the murderous guards with fists, weapons, and tackles. The hostages were freed.

Riley stood in the middle of the crowd, clutching DJ's knight sword, breathing heavily. Feeling all of Blight's Respite watching her, she looked at Vennick and a swell of victory grew in her. She raised DJ's sword and planted her foot on Vennick's unconscious body. "Down with the Onyx Wing! *Blight's Respite remains free!*"

Deafening cheers.

As the guards tied up the surviving traitors and hauled them away, townspeople threw vegetables and half-eaten pastries at them. Riley hurriedly pulled a wizard waffle from her pack and threw it at Francis. The orc ate it and the wound on his shoulder stitched up. He struggled to stand—his green face was paler than usual and his arm was caked with blood.

DJ took a deep, heaving breath and turned to Steve. "I thought you were going to do something there—like, stick them all with Shockthread or something!"

Steve shook his head. "I could not risk the lives of the captives! But the Goddess spoke peace to me, saying there was another way! *You* were the other way! Goddess be praised!"

That pulled DJ's lips into a smile.

Riley approached him. "Hey. This is yours." She held out his sword.

DJ had to admit Vennick took good care of it. It was polished and sharpened—even his name on the cross guard was in pristine condition. But inwardly, he wondered what awful deeds were done with it. He tried not to think about it. Instead, he lashed his knight sword on the other side of his waist.

"I was worried you weren't going to catch my idea," Riley said.

"Almost didn't," DJ replied. "Totally saved your life, though."

"If you weren't so dim, you would have saved it sooner."

DJ broke into a smile. She hugged him, and he held her back.

For the rest of the night, DJ and Steve stayed close to Kathryn the Kind in case there were other threats. She had enough mead to turn pink in the cheeks. The rest of the town, however, got absolutely shitfaced. Strangers approached Steve and DJ to drunkenly offer drinks and thank them for protecting Kathryn, which made DJ feel a bit uncomfortable. He and Steve were only doing their jobs after all. But several locals swore that they would reward the mages somehow for their service. DJ didn't think much of it—drunken promises are hardly more than fleeting ideas. The people of Blight's Respite didn't retire until very late, staggering home like a host of undead. And by that time, DJ's body demanded sleep.

When they returned to the manor, they learned that the traitorous guards were never guards to begin with. They were mercenaries who killed guards the night before and stole their armor to blend in with the crowd. That's how they were able to walk around Blight's Respite so freely.

That morning, DJ and the others took their time waking up and helped themselves to modest portions of cheese and bread for breakfast. As they finished their meal, a guard approached them.

"Hey," the guard said. "Lady Kathryn wants to see you four."

The four adventurers made their way to common area. Kathryn was already fully dressed and waiting for them, lounging in her favorite chair. Her face brightened when she saw them.

"Morning," she said. "Hope you all slept well. I definitely did after last night. The waffle wizard was right, as usual. You were brought here for a reason."

Everyone sat with her, filling up the couch and armchairs. They noticed four trinkets laid across the table.

"You two saved my life," Kathryn said to DJ and Steve.

"And because of that, the town adores you. Some of these gifts come as donations from them."

Suddenly, DJ felt a little guilty for harboring salty feelings toward Blight's Respite. Seems like under their hard shell, the locals were a little soft after all. And it seems like they still keep their promises, even when they're rip-roaring drunk.

"Friar Steve," Kathryn said. "From the chef at the Purple Pony, this frying pan is enchanted to work without fire. You can cook anything in it without heat. And if you hit someone with it, it'll likely burn them."

Steve took it and turned it around, admiring it. His hands cautiously explored its surface, but it was cool to the touch. He bowed gratefully. "May the Goddess bless the people of Blight's Respite!"

"Sir DJ," Kathryn said. "To you, the local mage guild has donated these mage robes. Wearing them will increase your magical capacities."

The sparkling purple robe was like water in DJ's hands. It definitely wasn't woven from human hands, and DJ was sure it was worth a fortune. He bowed his head. "This is… awesome. Thank you."

Kathryn turned to Francis and Riley. "The town also heard about you two—how you're close friends with the two heroes. They didn't want you to feel left out." She pointed toward a book on the table. "Francis, the town library is donating its copy of *Withered Leafs*. It's hundreds of years old."

Francis's eyes grew to saucers as he took the book. His green hand traced the cover as if it were something holy. "The orc poet, Unlef! His works are rare finds." He held it to his chest. "I will cherish it until my dying day."

"And for *you*," Kathryn's eyes sparkled as she addressed Riley. "This is from me personally. It's called Windfeather. It was with me during parts of my journey across the territory. It's yours now."

A fine hunting bow. Riley's eyes positively sparkled. She traced its smooth, worn wood and taught string. She swallowed and said, "This is the best thing ever. Thank you."

"You can stay for as long as you like," Kathryn said. "You're heroes to this city. But I know you're eager to reach the Amulet of the Goddess, so I won't keep you. You have my thanks and the thanks of Blight's Respite."

The party thanked her again. Riley even gave her a hug, which she returned warmly. But they felt no need to needlessly linger. They took their time packing their things, but before long, they were on their way.

As they ventured north, people battled raging hangovers to hail them in the streets and shower them with praise. They called the travelers the Heroes of the First Drink. They handed the party bread and apples and gold pieces. One woman even offered to perform very un-Stewardly acts on Steve. But her euphemisms went right over the friar's head, much to his friends' amusement.

The Great River greeted them to the west as they left the city. The party followed its edge, feeling its cool breeze nip their bodies as it flowed southward.

The next stop was the Library of Artak. Francis couldn't have walked with larger strides. And he managed to do it with his face buried in *Withered Leafs.*

20

It felt lopsided walking with two swords slung around his hips. DJ hoped it made him look cool and intimidating, but he was sure his waddle didn't do him any favors. He had become noticeably stronger since leaving Beregond, but two swords felt like a hundred pounds after walking for miles and miles.

Their first night outside Blight's Respite, DJ practiced magic with the mage robes on. He felt the effect immediately. It was like his insides lapped with cool ocean waves—the magical well inside him grew bigger. And when he practiced magic, it felt effortless. Spells that would normally test his limits became an easy lift. He cast a flurry of Ice Spike, Flamefist, two Barriers, and Ice Spike again before his head started to throb. As he clutched his temples between his palms, he smiled.

Everyone's gifts came in handy. Steve would prepare eggs or bacon while walking like an invisible fire hovered under the pan. Riley talked about how much smoother Windfeather was to handle than her Pebble-made bow. And, of course, Francis read *Withered Leafs* cover-to-cover multiple times.

"He was one of the few orcs like me," he told DJ. "He lived five hundred years ago and was banished for his criticism of violence. His published works are difficult to find—many orcs burn them if they can."

"Will you read me a poem?" DJ asked.

Francis flipped through the volume. "It's written in orcs-peak, so it won't translate well to commonspeak, and it won't rhyme, but let me… ah, here's a good one."

The night is cold and wide
The meat is dry and cannot fill
I am alone not only in my body
But in my mind and spirit.

Goosebumps spread along DJ's arms. As Francis read the words, DJ knew the orc felt them.

After two days of travel, they met the Camās Gahl Mountains on their left—tall, awesome, sloping to the sky. At night, they loomed mightily, forming jagged lines where the stars ended. DJ worried about bears or mountain lions, but Francis assured him that as long as they kept the fire going, they wouldn't have to worry. Riley brought up trolls or giants, but Francis smiled and said those creatures dwelt much farther in the mountains.

The next morning, Steve made breakfast and the others broke camp. They walked without chatter for miles before they reached a familiar face standing at the crest of a hill.

Sir Percival Buttons.

The sight of the little beast halted them. Everyone armed themselves. The gnome stood with his hand on his sword in the middle of the road. No trap. No sleight of hand. Beside him, Mittens hunched on its paws, hissing and baring its fangs.

"Across the territory," the gnome muttered. "From the Aeldar Forest, to Varis, and now, at the foot of the Camās Gahl Mountains."

The party remained deathly quiet.

"I grow tired of these traps and games," Buttons spoke through his teeth. "I will take the girl to her father and restore my honor. I challenge you for her, here and now." He pointed at DJ with his little sword. "You struck Mittens, so it is you I challenge. And this I promise you: *you* will be the one to bleed."

A shiver swept through DJ. He wasn't wearing his mage robes, so he would only be able to fight at his basic capacity. But that wasn't the main worry. He knew he could torch the gnome if necessary—but the thought of reliving Broken Lovers Pass filled him with dread.

There had to be another way. He just had to think.

Francis stepped in front of him, clutching his ax. "There will be no battle. And you will not take Miss Riley."

"I will," Buttons growled. "Or you will bleed too."

"*Meow!*" Mittens agreed.

DJ's mind pulled out whatever volumes of information he had on Sir Percival Buttons. It was while he considered Buttons' mission that an idea struck him. And it would avoid spilling more blood.

"No, I accept," DJ said. He put his hand on Francis's arm to pull him back.

Francis protested. "Young knight, think about—"

"I have. Let me handle it."

"DJ," Riley said. "Don't fight him. I'm a ranger now. I can go home."

"Do you *want* to go home?" DJ asked.

Riley shrunk. "No… We're so close to the Amulet. But I'd rather go home than see you get hurt."

DJ smiled. "I'll be fine. Trust me."

Steve watched the young knight nervously. "Goddess give you safety, Sir DJ! My prayers shall be with you!"

Buttons squared up. DJ trudged up the hill, meeting him on equal ground. The two faced each other several paces away. DJ's friends moved off the road, shifting on their feet and biting their nails. Mittens hunched down beside Buttons, swishing its tail, ready to pounce.

DJ clamped his jaw to keep it from chattering. He swallowed and nodded to Francis. "Count us off."

The orc straightened his back and tried to stay calm. "Three. Two. One. *Fight!*"

Buttons dashed forward, weapon raised. Mittens dug in his paws and followed.

DJ dropped to one knee as fast as he could. "I yield!"

Both Buttons and Mittens slid to a stop before the gnome's steel could taste blood. Button's arms fumbled to his sides and an angry frown spread across his face. "What?

Coward! I want a duel! What trickery is this?"

"You had your duel." DJ put his other knee on the ground and gazed into Button's beady little eyes. "It commenced, and I yielded. It's over, and you are the victor. Now you deserve a gift as a token of your victory."

Buttons watched him in stunned silence, unsure of whether or not to be insulted.

"Listen," DJ's tone became serious. "Riley told me about your mission—about how you're trying to restore your honor and go home. And it made me realize I misjudged you. You *are* a noble gnome. And I think this gift will prove it to your people."

DJ put his hands on his waist and unlatched his newly reclaimed knight sword. All his friends watched with bated breath. Buttons just watched. DJ extended the sword in his hands, sheath, belt, and all.

"As a Knight of Beregond, I bestow on you my knightly weapon," DJ said. "On behalf of your bravery and dedication, and as a token of your victory over me this day. Show it to the people of your village so they know your honor has been restored. All I ask is that you return whatever sum was paid to Riley's father. We both win here, Sir Percival. What do you say?"

The gears turned in Button's mind. DJ watched silently, praying that the gnome wouldn't raise his weapon and strike him down while he had the chance. Buttons's attention turned from the knight sword to DJ's face over and over.

"If this is a trick," the gnome said. "I will hunt you until your dying day."

"It's no trick, Buttons. The blade is yours."

Buttons reached out with cautious hands and took the blade. He hefted it in his small hands, admiring the weight and craftsmanship. Out of the corner of his eye, DJ saw his friends staring with dangling mouths. DJ grinned.

"It is a fine weapon," Buttons mumbled.

"You know it's a high honor to be gifted a knight's weapon," DJ said.

"I'm aware." The gnome thought for a moment more, then gave a nod. "Yes. This shall suffice."

"Thank you," DJ bowed as a weight lifted off him. "Riley is my best friend. It was her wish to travel across Uh and become a ranger. I didn't want you to take that from her. But in the process, I hurt *your* best friend." DJ faced the direcat. "I'm sorry, Mittens. I hope you can forgive me."

Buttons slung the sword over his back. DJ thought it could function like a greatsword in the gnome's hands. Buttons extended his hand to shake. DJ shook it in a firm clasp. Then Buttons mounted Mittens and gave them all a nod.

"It appears that our business is at an end," he said. "Farewell, travelers. I wish you safety in your journey."

"Thank you," DJ said. "You'll always have a friend in Beregond, Buttons."

Buttons kicked Mitten's stirrups, the direcat meowed, and they galloped westward for the mountains.

As DJ watched the gnome and his direcat become small in the distance, Francis lumbered up and put his hand on DJ's shoulder. "Tremendous," he said. "You've diffused the ire of an enemy. You never cease to surprise me, young knight."

"Goddess be praised!" Steve said, waving his frying pan in the air. "You have achieved victory through peace!"

"Victory?" Riley smirked. "It was your first duel and you yielded the second it started. As it stands, your stats are terrible."

DJ squinted at her. Riley smiled with a twinkle in her eye. She said, "You *just* got that sword back. You're not gonna miss it?"

"Nah." DJ shook his head. "I'm a mage. I just carry a sword to look tough."

Riley suppressed a laugh. "That was brilliant, Deej. Thanks."

She gave him a tight hug then punched his shoulder. DJ blushed.

*

The party marched northward until they found the dwarven village of Artak pushed against the mountain's foot. Francis couldn't keep his pace reasonable once it came into view. His amber eyes shone with childlike wonder and his arms swung a little more when he walked. Everyone had to jog to keep up with him.

The village of Artak was too small to be a city but had all the fixings of a typical city—inns, taverns, stables, even a monastery. Each building was hewn from finely cut stone in the similar manner of Brooks's Bakery back in Laradyl. The rock was a rich iron gray, excavated from the nearby mountain's interior, and they utilized the steep sloping lines that felt sturdy and majestic.

DJ had never seen so many dwarves in one place. They took up nearly half of the village's population. He spotted one wearing a white robe with a matching white hat. The robe had a large insignia on the left breast—a set of doors with a book illustrated across them.

Francis nudged DJ and pointed. "A Wordkeeper of Artak! They took oaths to watch over the Library. They keep the books, clean facilities, help visitors… They make a covenant with the other Wordkeepers to serve in that capacity until they perish."

"Wow," DJ said, watching the Wordkeeper march through town. "Can anyone be a Wordkeeper?"

"No," Francis shook his head. "You must be a dwarf. Otherwise I would have applied years ago."

The party traveled along the dirt road until they reached a large intersection in the middle of the village. When they looked to their left, they saw it.

The Library of Artak stood with massive, yawning stone doors at the foot of the mountain. The doors were exactly like the ones DJ saw on the Wordkeeper's robes. Local guards stood at the Library's entrance, keeping watch.

Francis went straight for it. The rest of the group followed behind but struggled to keep up.

"Francis!" Riley called. "Shouldn't we stop and get something to eat? Or pawn some of our old weapons to pay for a room?"

Francis looked back at her like she was crazy. "Miss Riley, I've wanted to visit this library since I was a child! I cannot wait a moment longer!"

DJ ignored his grumbling stomach and followed Francis.

When they reached the doors, DJ was surprised to see that the guards didn't look anything like the Wordkeepers at all. Usually there was a smart uniformity among town guards, but these guards' armor was completely mismatched—as if they got dressed from a blacksmith's lost-and-found. There were four of them at the doors, armed with swords and spears. None of them were dwarves either, just dirty-faced humans.

Francis ignored their appearances and stopped before them. His smile stretched to both ears. "We seek entrance to the Library of Artak."

One of the guards sized up the group. "Four of you?"

"Yes."

"Two hundred gold."

Francis's smile dropped. He spoke through his tusks and couldn't keep confused heat out of his voice. "But... the Library is supposed to be free. That's how it's been for hundreds of years!"

"That was before the Nightwolves took over." The guard pointed a thumb into his chest. "The Wordkeepers graciously relented control of the Library when we came to town. So if you don't got the coin, you can take a hike."

Francis's green cheeks mixed with red. His fists balled at his sides and his massive frame trembled. "This is a sacred place of learning."

"And now it's *ours*," the guard said smugly. "Don't get any funny ideas." He tightened his grip on his spear. "There are four of us here but a dozen more inside. Even if you knock us down, the rest'll kill ya before you touch a single book. So pay up or get lost."

Francis stayed rooted in his spot, uncharacteristically lost for words. He opened and closed his mouth, but the anger that crashed through his body kept his brain from working.

Riley put her hand in his. "Francis, come on. We'll figure something out."

With some hesitation, Francis left the doors and turned back to the village. During the walk back, he stared ahead like his mind was elsewhere. His fists stayed balled up and the muscles in his jaw flexed.

DJ raised his eyes and said, "Francis, I'm really sorry. I know how much you were looking forward to seeing the Library."

Francis didn't speak.

"Maybe we can scrape up some coin?" DJ said. "Sell some of our stuff. Find a little hustle like we always—"

"I'm not paying *one coin* to a group of greedy bandits," Francis growled. "The Library of Artak is supposed to be *free*. The mission of the Wordkeepers is to bring light and knowledge to all who seek it. Not for profit. Not for personal gain. For the benefit of all, *free of charge*."

"The Goddess will provide!" Steve yelped. "She has so far!"

Francis looked like he wanted to argue, but he stopped himself. He squelched the anger thundering in his chest. "You're right, Steven. It's not the time to get hasty." He looked around his friends. "Let's sell our old weapons. Purchase a room and a hot meal. Once we're settled, we should speak to the Wordkeepers. They'll know more about this."

They did just that. Riley's old bow and Steve's old frying pan didn't fetch as much as they were hoping for. But that amount along with Riley's collection of jackrabbit pelts, roots, and mushrooms was just enough to afford them a modest room and some meals.

At the tavern, Francis finished his stew before anyone else and tried his best to hide his distress. His arms folded over his wide chest and his toe tapped under the table. The other tavern patrons watched Francis out of the corners of their eyes, wondering what this strange orc could be so upset about.

At last, they left the tavern and found the Wordkeepers' Temple near the western edge of the village. It was one of the larger structures in town, five stories high, made of the village's same iron-gray stone, complete with a belltower on top. All around it, a generous courtyard teemed with trees, shrubbery, and flowers. Two Wordkeepers stood at the courtyard's entrance, but they felt more like greeters than guards. They bowed to the group as they approached.

"Friends," Francis said as he bowed back. "Today I learned the terrible news about the Library."

Both Wordkeepers' faces drooped with sadness. One said, "The Nightwolves have controlled it for the better part of a year now."

"How did they overpower you?" Francis asked. "These bandits must have vast resources."

"They caught us unawares," the other Wordkeeper said. "We were unable to resist them. Now they hardly let us enter at all."

"There must be something we can do," Francis said.

"We've been very fortunate on our journey thus far. Perhaps we can drive them out."

Both Wordkeepers' eyes got wide and they shook their heads. One said, "Please, don't! They hold nothing sacred—lives nor books! They've threatened to destroy it all if we resist!"

Francis's voice died down and he stole a glance westward, as if the guards could hear him from hundreds of yards away. "Do you know how the bandits are stationed inside the library? Or have a map of the library that we could reference?"

"*Please don't!*" the second Wordkeeper said, gripping Francis's tunic. "We must insist! It's not worth the knowledge that could be lost!"

This quieted Francis. He calmly released the Wordkeeper's hands. "I see. Peace be with you, then, Wordkeepers."

The crew turned and solemnly marched back toward the inn, leaving behind two very distressed Wordkeepers. As they traveled along the main road, DJ leaned toward Francis. "Seriously, let's find some odd jobs around town and save up enough to visit the Library. We came all this way, Francis. You can't just—"

"We'll enter the Library, young knight," Francis said. He stopped abruptly in the road. Everyone in the group hung onto his next words. "Are you willing liberate it with me? Our plans have proven effective so far, Sir DJ. Perhaps fate—the Goddess, what have you—is on our side."

Suddenly, DJ felt very small with Francis's intense amber eyes focused on him. As the leader, DJ knew that they would go where he instructed, but the Wordkeepers' admonition was firm. Yet, this was Francis's wish—the reason he joined DJ's quest to begin with. And they *had* enjoyed a lot of good luck the last few months. Maybe there was something to be done.

DJ swallowed, looked around, and whispered. "If we can make something *air-tight,* zero chance of failure, I'm in."

Francis brightened. "Thank you, young knight. Generations will bless you for this deed."

21

Ho there, Son!

They've begun building the statue of me. They've got it under a sheet in the middle of the plaza, but they've let me see the progress. It's finely made, although I do find it a tad embarrassing.

Enjoy the Library of Artak! You know I'm not much of a reader, but I hope your orc friend finds it riveting. I've heard its halls are a wonder to behold.

How was Blight's Respite? I hope you didn't spend too much time there. There isn't much to enjoy in Fairdell anyway, aside from the oceanside city of Sunsbirth, but I think it's a bit out of your way.

Be safe! You're nearly there! Hope you're home before the Harvest Festival!

-Sir Dashing

Hey, Dad,

Blight's Respite was wild. I used my magic to stop an assassination and the governor gave me some mage robes as a reward. I can't wait to show it to you.

The Library of Artak has been taken over by bandits. But we're going to try to chase them out and return it to the Wordkeepers. I'll let you know how it goes.

The next city is Skyhole, then we'll reach the Temple of the Amulet! It's crazy to think we're almost there! Hopefully the journey back home is faster.

Love you, Dad. I'll write you when we reach Skyhole.
-DJ

As DJ handed the note to the druid, he thought about that last paragraph he wrote. They were almost to the Temple of the Amulet—the objective of their journey. The symbol that would prove he was truly worthy of his knightly position.

The knighting ceremony felt like a lifetime ago. How many months had it been? So much had happened between Beregond and Artak. Broken Lovers Pass, the House of Phillip, the Nether Regions, among so many other things.

The DJ back in Beregond never could have imagined the things he would experience in the coming months. The jeering boys and ignorant townspeople would definitely be surprised to hear them. But then again, maybe they wouldn't care. They never paid him much heed anyway.

DJ imagined the Amulet of the Goddess in his hands. Proof that he was worthy of knightdom. He had imagined it many times before, but for some reason, the current image in his mind felt less... shiny than it did before. What did feel shiny were the people he had met and the places he had seen —the forests, Pebble and Brooks, Kathryn the Kind, shoot, even Sir Percival Buttons.

He noticed that as his experience grew, a hunger inside him shrunk. The realization hit DJ like a hammer, and it caused him to stop in his tracks.

Wait, he thought. *Do I… not care about the Amulet anymore?*

He pushed the thought aside and resumed his journey to a nearby inn. The sun was setting over the mountain, casting a wide shadow over Artak. The cool of night settled on the valley, and with it, the gentle chirping of crickets replaced the shuffling of busy villagers.

Everyone was waiting for him back in the room. They asked DJ if he got his letter written. He said yes. They asked him how Sir Dashing was. He said good. They asked him if everything was okay. He said everything was fine. So they went to work.

For the next hour, they devised a plan. DJ and the gang brought up new ideas and poked holes in them, leading to several moments of frustration and discovery, until finally, they landed on a plan that they felt confident about.

That plan would take time and money, so everyone in the party took jobs around town. Francis worked as a bouncer at one of the seedier taverns. DJ volunteered to shovel manure and feed chickens at a nearby farm. Riley assisted a local blacksmith. And Steve summoned his inner bard to play spoons in the middle of Artak's main crossing. Amazingly, Steve made more money than anyone else.

With each passing day, they earned more than they needed to pay for the nightly room, food, and DJ's necessary baths. And when they could afford it, they gathered supplies: rope, ingredients for potions, and cloth, among other things. Steve turned the room's nightstand into a makeshift alchemy table, combining the ingredients to make potions. The concoctions smelled downright putrid, so they had to open a window to let the room air out.

As they were having supper in the tavern one evening, they were surprised to be approached by a Wordkeeper. The dwarf bowed deeply, almost letting his beard touch the ground. Then he said, "The Grand Wordkeeper wishes to speak with you."

Everyone quickly finished their meal and followed the Wordkeeper to the Temple.

The Grand Wordkeeper was sitting on a stone bench in the courtyard, back straight, hands on his lap. His gray beard was nearly long enough to touch his waist. His thick face and tiny eyes pressed into a smile, and he bowed as his visitors approached.

"Good evening, travelers," he said. "I am Halguut, Grand Wordkeeper of Artak."

Everyone introduced themselves. Then Francis said, "Halguut? Named after the Father of All Dwarves?"

"The very same," Halguut said. "You're well-learned, my orc friend. Peculiar for your kind. Come. Walk with me."

He got up from his bench and the group began to stroll around the edge of the courtyard with him. All around them, other Wordkeepers tended to flowers and shrubs. As the party walked with Halguut, other Wordkeepers stared. DJ caught a few nervous glances and whispers. He wondered if there was a spell that could let him eavesdrop on them.

"We may be better talking inside the Temple, Grand Wordkeeper," Francis suggested as they went. His voice lowered. "We're going to liberate the Library. We've made a plan. But I'd be hesitant to share it out in the open, for fear of listening ears."

Halguut waved his hand. "We cannot enter the Temple at this time. We aren't ready to host you." He smiled. "But I am eager to hear this plan of yours."

Francis shook his head. "This isn't the proper place."

"Very well." Halguut's smile fell into a frown. Whatever grandfatherly warmth he had dissolved to coldness. "My brothers at the gate told you days ago about our feelings regarding the Library."

"I know, Grand Wordkeeper," Francis replied, "but we have—"

"If you have any shred of respect for the Library," Halguut said, "you'll drop this matter immediately. They've threatened to *burn it all* if we retaliate, Francis the Orc. Are you willing to destroy that sacred place of learning from your own recklessness and indignation?"

Francis was taken aback by Halguut's sharpness. He cleared his throat. "The plan will work. There is no cause for alarm. The Library will be returned to you."

"Tell me this plan, then, that you're so certain about."

Francis looked all around. "Grand Wordkeeper, these words aren't safe in the open. You'll simply have to trust us.

But I assure you, the Library will be back in your hands in—"

"And *I* assure that you are making a terrible mistake," Halguut said. He stopped and shook his head. "My foolish friends, I admire your fervor toward the Library, but the risk far outweighs the reward. Let the Nightwolves have their place, no matter how unpleasant it might be."

Francis's eyebrows bent and his hands flexed. "How can you say that? After taking an oath to protect it until your dying breath?"

"*Protecting it* is what I'm trying to do now!" Halguut nearly shouted. He let out a heaving breath to relax himself. "You've convinced me that you're too dangerous to keep here. Leave the village by sunrise. I cannot risk the Library's well-being to a pack of foolhardy adventurers." A pause and a scowl. "I trust that you can see yourself off the premises."

Francis's jaw dangled, then he clamped it, nodded, and squared his shoulders. "I'm sorry, Grand Wordkeeper." He bowed. "Good night to you."

The orc turned and stomped away. His friends followed. DJ looked over his shoulders to see more Wordkeepers whispering to each other and retreating inside the Temple. When they left the courtyard, Riley was the first to speak.

"*Sheesh*, who pissed in Grandpa's oats?" she said. "He knows we're just trying to help."

"He does," Francis growled. "But he's shortsighted. He doesn't want to see the Library destroyed. I understand, but keeping a sacred place like that sealed for profit is… blasphemous."

"So," DJ said timidly, "did you still want to carry out the

plan?"

Francis gave him a look. "Do you?"

Everyone gave their affirmative.

DJ said, "Halguut wants us gone by tomorrow morning, though. So we would have to do it *tonight*. Do you think we're ready?"

"I'm ready," Riley said.

"As am I," Francis replied.

Steve nodded vigorously.

"Steve, are the potions done curing?" DJ asked.

The friar nodded again, twice as fast.

"Then it looks like we have no reason to wait," DJ said. "Steve, say a prayer for us."

Silently, Steve swished his hands and bowed his head. They reached the inn and climbed the stairs to their room. When they entered, they acted quickly. DJ threw on his mage robes. Everyone else packed light, leaving behind anything that could make noise. Daggers instead of swords. No packs. Everything would be left in the room and locked up.

There were two potions curing on the nightstand: a Magic Expansion Potion and a Sleep Potion. Steve and DJ were careful to buy ingredients from the apothecary separately as to not arouse suspicion, and they hoped the smell wasn't pungent enough to waft into the other rooms.

DJ took a sip from the Magic Expansion Potion and passed the rest to Steve. The dark green liquid tasted like pulpy, spoiled tomatoes that made him wince, but between his mage robes and the potion, he felt his magical abilities extended even further. Steve finished off the potion, smacked his lips, and shook his head disgustedly.

Next, DJ held the Sleep Potion—a midnight blue liquid that none of them would taste—and separated it into four small bottles. He handed a bottle to each person. Then everyone made sure they were equipped with several lengths of rope and short measures of cloth.

They looked like a group of bandits ready to commit a burglary, which wasn't far from the truth.

DJ huffed. "Everyone ready?"

Everyone nodded.

"Here we go, then," DJ said. "Riley with me. Francis with Steve. *Invisi-pallyum.*"

Both DJ and Steve cast Evercloak over their respective partners. The team faded into invisibility. DJ felt a little dizzy, but not sick. With the Magic Expansion Potion, the Evercloak spells should last much longer than usual.

The crew filed out of the room and DJ lingered behind to lock the door. He had to feel out the lock and the key to make sure it fit—working with his hands was much harder when he couldn't see them. But DJ locked the door and crept down the hallway with the others.

He bumped into Riley.

"*Hey!*" she whispered.

"Sorry," he returned.

The quiet shuffle of their feet traveled through the inn and across the village. In the moonlight, DJ thought he could see their barely visible boot prints in the dirt. They moved as swiftly as silence would allow. And before long, they were at the Library doors.

Before them, the guards shifted as they looked upon the village. DJ swallowed as he felt their gaze go through him. With his hand, he reached out to the side to feel for one of his friends. Riley found him first. She squeezed his shoulder, and he squeezed hers back. That was the first signal. DJ pulled out the Sleep Potion, uncorked the bottle, and soaked the rag with it.

The guards were just a few steps away. DJ tried to calm his breathing. But he and his friends were operating so close to them, any little sound could alert them. It made his heart thump heavily. He tried not to picture the Library in flames.

"Do you hear something?" one of the guards said.

DJ froze.

"No," another guard replied. "You've had the jitters ever since your girlfriend left you, Reggie."

"Yeah buddy, are you doing okay?" a third guard said. "I've been worried about you."

"I'm *fine*," Reggie said, but a tremble of hurt passed through his lip. "She was a nag anyway, you know, she would —" Reggie gasped then cut himself off with his own sobs.

Under the cover of Reggie's blubbering, DJ put away the empty bottle and readied the rag.

One of the guards patted Reggie's back. "Hey buddy, just let it out. It's okay to feel sad. You're going through a lot."

"Yeah, pal," another guard said. "I'd cry too if I were you. It doesn't make you less of a man."

Reggie kept blubbering, trying to form words. DJ almost felt bad for breaking this beautiful moment.

Almost.

DJ felt Riley squeeze his shoulder—the second signal. He held his breath. Everyone lunged forward and jammed their potion-soggy rags into the guard's mouths. The guards panicked and struggled against the invisible forces, but as soon as the wet rags touched their tongues, the Sleep Potion took effect. Eyes rolled back. Bodies went slack. The guards collapsed into a puddle, breathing peacefully.

Everyone struggled to bind and gag the guards with invisible hands, rope and cloth, but they managed. Francis found the gate key on one of them.

Riley whispered near DJ. "Do you think Reggie deserved it? Or was his ex just the worst?"

"I don't think that matters right now, Riley."

"All right, everyone," Francis said. "We act quickly. Free the books!"

"*Free the books!*" everyone whisper-yelled. Steve covered his own mouth to keep himself quiet.

The gate key levitated in Francis's invisible hand. It unlocked the doors, then the four of them pushed the stone slabs open. What they found inside filled DJ with wonder and awe.

A tall tunnel that stretched for a thousand paces, breaking into rooms and hallways. Vaulted ceilings fifty feet high. Along that ceiling, chandeliers hung made of perfectly cut gems. Great statues were carved from the wall as if they leaped out from the stone—bears, lions, wolves, even dragons. And, of course, rows upon rows of books, complete with rolling ladders reaching to the ceiling.

Now DJ understood why Francis was so eager to visit this

place. But there was no time for gawking. Before them was a dozen Nightwolves, dressed in mismatched armor, carrying weapons of all kinds. DJ felt their penetrating gazes. He swallowed and hoped that his gulp wasn't too loud.

The next phase of the plan had to work, but it all rested on the shoulders of Friar Steve.

"*Nightwolves!*" Steve put a rasp in his voice and shouted to fill the heavens. His voice blasted like a foghorn. "I am the ghost of the First Wordkeeper, Artak! You have desecrated this sacred place, so I have come to exact my revenge!"

The faces of the Nightwolves turned worried. They gathered in knots, trembling and pointing their weapons. As Steve shouted ghostly threats, DJ and the others crept forward, still invisible, potion rags poised.

"What is this trickery?" a Nightwolf cried with a shaky voice. "Show yourself! You are no spirit!"

"*Am I not?*" Steve's voice erupted again. "Stand and tremble, then! But one by one, you shall feel my cold, ghostly hand!"

DJ was upon a Nightwolf. He shoved his invisible rag into their mouth. They tensed, horror-stricken, resisted… and fell asleep. The Nightwolf's chest rose and fell with calm breaths, but to everyone watching, the ghost of Artak had made good on its threat.

A shriek flew from the lips of a Nightwolf. Frightened whispers bounced off the bookcases. Swords and spears quivered in hands white-knuckled with terror.

Riley dropped another Nightwolf. More screams from the others.

"*Flee!*" Steve's voice filled the Library. "Flee for your lives, bitter creatures! Poor, unlearned wretches! Claim your lives *before I do! Fleeee!*"

That did it. The remaining Nightwolves threw down their weapons and made a mad sprint for the entrance. DJ had to throw himself against a bookcase to avoid getting trampled. Their terrified footsteps faded into the night, and the Library was left quiet, except for the gentle snores from those that were knocked asleep.

However, one Nightwolf remained standing. She stayed back, arms folded, scowling and stony-eyed. She had a matching set of iron armor, complete with bracers and scaled boots. Any trace of hair was shaved clean from her head—perfectly bald. And her left eyebrow was pierced.

No one said anything. Not even Steve carried on his charade.

"Very clever," the last Nightwolf said. "They told me I should be expecting someone. Unfortunately for you, I'm not as easily fooled as my men." She sighed defeatedly. "Follow me. We'll talk in my study. But close the doors."

If anyone from the party could see each other, they would have given each other confused stares. They felt their way to each other until they whispered in a huddle.

"Do we follow her?" Riley said.

"Could be a trap," Francis said.

"What does she mean she was expecting us?" DJ asked.

"Very curious indeed!" Steve yelled.

Everyone shushed him.

"She appears to be the last one," Francis said. "Between

the four of us, I believe we can handle her if she tries any-thing. Unless more Nightwolves are waiting for us in her study."

As if hearing their whispers, she called from the distance. "It's only me! I just want to talk. No attempt will be made to harm you. I swear that on the grave of my husband."

After brief deliberation, everyone decided to follow. As they marched down the hallway, they began to materialize. Their invisibility wore off just as they found the door where the Nightwolf turned in.

Inside was a den with a long table, plenty of chairs for reading, and more bookcases. The woman sat comfortably in an armchair with her legs crossed, pouring herself a glass of wine. She looked up as the party entered but didn't move from her chair.

"Evercloak spell?" she asked. "Clever. You two must be powerful mages. I'm Beatrice, leader of the Nightwolves. Have a seat."

Everyone sat across from her. Francis stared daggers, clutching his fists on his lap. Beatrice took a long drink of her wine and pointed at him.

"The orc," she said. "You're the one that wanted to come here so badly, right?"

"What's it to you?" Francis spoke through his teeth.

"Well, *you* aren't going to like what I have to say." Beatrice set down her wine and rubbed her face. "I shouldn't even be telling you this. I made a pact. But that Halguut has been so *insufferable* lately that I'm about to take my crew and get out of here. This isn't worth the trouble."

Francis went from steely resentment to troubled confusion.

"The truth is," she said, "we didn't take over the Library. We were hired. We're mercenaries, not bandits. Halguut and the Wordkeepers saw a chance to capitalize on the Library, so they contacted us. We've been holed up in here ever since, charging people entry and splitting the earnings with the Wordkeepers fifty-fifty."

"That's a lie," Francis said firmly. "Wordkeepers take oaths to protect the Library of Artak. They would never hold it for profit."

"Yet, here we are." Beatrice took another sip of wine. "You know, it seemed like a prime contract at first. But as it turns out, every so often some idealistic do-gooder comes around and tries to *liberate* this place. One of my guys got stabbed last month." She rolled her eyes and took another sip. "They didn't let you in their Temple, did they? The Wordkeepers."

"Nope!" Steve replied.

"That's because they've got things they don't want you to see," Beatrice raised her pierced eyebrow. "Saunas, hot tubs, all sorts of toys. Would raise suspicion, given they're only supposed to subsist on donations and the Goddess's grace." That made her laugh a little. She focused her gaze on Francis. "Look orc, I'm sorry about all this. But the thing about oaths... they get broken. Those white-robed dwarves with sticks up their asses are no more immune to riches than the next sellsword. All it took was one generation who were willing to sell their oaths, and I got stuck cleaning up their messes."

She knocked back the last bit of wine. DJ shot a brief glance toward Francis. The orc's gaze had dropped to the space between his boots. A lifetime of looking up to the Wordkeepers and yearning for the Library, all tarnished by the confession of an exasperated mercenary.

"I'm going to collect my crew." Beatrice stood from her chair. "I'm not even upset. Your plan was clever. As long as none of them are dead, I won't hunt you down. In the meantime," she gestured to the whole room, "take a look around. You've earned it. Leave whenever you're ready."

She gave a little bow and left. As her footsteps faded, everyone turned to Francis. The orc was still curled forward, eyes to the ground, soaking in the devastating truth. He didn't speak or move.

"Francis," DJ said softly. "I'm so sorry."

Riley rubbed Francis's arm. "Come on, let's go look. This place is amazing! And we have it all to ourselves!" She squeezed his big green hand. "Let's make the most of it."

Francis's forced himself to smile, but his eyes had no glimmer. "Yes, very well. Let's go."

There was no way to see the whole library, but they did their best. DJ found scrolls documenting magic techniques that he tried to understand, but the writing was so old he could barely make it out. Were they written in another language? It was hard to tell.

Steve gawked at all the statues and paintings, wandering with his head swiveling about. But Riley stayed firmly by Francis's side. Francis found a considerable section of orcish literature, but it was minuscule compared to the entirety of the Library. Unfortunately, most of it was biographies of clan leaders and warriors. Not many novels or poetry collections. Another disappointment.

When they left, the Nightwolves were trickling back in. The mercenaries scowled and grumbled at the party as they left, but none of them attacked. Probably per Beatrice's orders.

The party noticed Reggie as they walked by, awoken from the Sleep Potion. Riley said, "Sorry about your girlfriend." That made Reggie burst into tears again, and all his friends gathered to console him.

The dirt munched under their feet as they traveled back to the inn. When they passed the Wordkeeper's Temple on the left, Francis stopped. The courtyard was closed, gates locked for the night. He snorted, spat a thick loogie through the gates, and grunted. He didn't speak for the rest of the night.

The party offered Francis the room's one bed, but he didn't take it. So DJ, Riley, and Steve tried to make space for each other. As DJ fell asleep, Francis was lying on his side, reading from *Withered Leafs*.

22

The journey to Skyhole would take nearly two weeks, so they emptied whatever gold they had left to stock up on supplies. They left the village of Artak before the sun cast golden light onto the valley, just like Halguut commanded. As they walked out of the village, they saw the Nightwolves standing guard at the Library doors. Francis said nothing.

For days they ventured northward, skirting the eastern edge of the mighty Camās Gahl Mountains. Francis warned them that it would get much colder the farther north they went, since it was always snowy in the Spine. They would need warmer clothes.

It was that evening that Riley had her first big game kill— a deer that had wandered down from the mountains to drink from a stream. She shrieked with delight and retrieved Francis to help her carry it back to camp. After he helped her dress it, Riley began to treat the hide.

"It's just like treating jackrabbits, just bigger," she said as she scraped off the fat with her knife. Her eyes brightened. "Hey! Maybe if we find enough pelts, we could turn them into winter gear! We won't even have to buy them in town!"

As luck would have it, she downed another one the next day. As luck would *not* have it, they didn't see any more deer for the rest of their journey.

And another stroke of bad luck hit them when they found an unwelcome face standing in the middle of the road. It was the Highway Hag—the same one they encountered between Varis and the Nether Regions. She stood hunched over, rubbing her bony hands together and grinning crooked-jawed at the travelers.

DJ bent his eyebrows and pointed. "You again!"

The Highway Hag cackled. "Hehe! Yes! It is I! Did you get your smoochy-smooch, little boy?" She made a comically loud, sucky kissing sound.

DJ's cheeks turned scarlet and he refused to look at Riley. "Let me guess, you're going to make me play your stupid game again?"

"Yep! *But,*" she said, holding up a wrinkly finger. "You chose *truth* last time. So now, you must choose *dare!* And I'll have you know that I have a *very* lively imagination. Hahaha! *Hahaha!*"

DJ let out something between a growl and a sigh. But before he could respond, Francis stomped up next to him. The great orc towered over the Hag. She stopped rubbing her hands together and looked up at him with large eyes full of worry. Her mole twitched as she blinked.

"Uh—hello," she said nervously.

Francis didn't smile or speak. Instead, he curled his mighty hand into a fist and *bopped* the Hag on the head. Her eyes rolled back and she crumbled into a heap, out cold, her arms and legs in disarray.

Riley's laugh came out like a yelp. Steve said, "Oh my!" DJ let out a relieved sigh.

"I… hope you will forgive me," Francis said to his friends. He hoisted the Hag over his shoulder. "I believe I'm still upset over the Library, and I fear I might have taken it out on this poor creature." He slumped her body against a nearby tree to make her look asleep. "I'll try to exercise a greater deal of restraint."

DJ let out a chuckle. "Fine by me."

A new voice came from the not-so-distant distance. "Fine by all of us, I would say!"

The party turned to see a small knot of people approaching them from the north. They were all Stewards of the Goddess, garbed in warm, furry coats. Clearly, they had just come from Skyhole. The Steward at the front wore a blue sash. DJ remembered seeing a similar one on Father Tuckett back in Beregond.

"That Hag has been terrorizing travelers for years now," the leading Steward said. "I know I should have more kindness in my heart as a Steward, but I do believe you… gave her what was coming." He noticed Steve. "Ah! One of our own. Good afternoon to you, Steward."

Steve bowed so low, his torso went parallel to the ground. "Greetings, fellow Stewards! I am Friar Steve of Beregond! We are traveling to the Temple of the Amulet so Sir DJ can behold the Amulet of the Goddess!"

"All the way from Beregond?" the head Steward marveled. "You have served this crew all across the territory? Sounds like more than the stuff of a mere friar, I say. Fellow travelers, has this Steward rendered his services well?"

For the next thirty seconds, DJ, Riley, and Francis verbally trampled over each other to describe Steve's heroics. The Stewards watched with amusement as Broken Lovers Pass, the House of Phillip, and Varis were described. Through it all, Steve blushed profusely and twiddled his fingers.

Finally, the head Steward gave a smile. "Thank you, all. I'm sorry, I should have properly introduced myself. I'm Father Braten of Blight's Respite. I'll have you know that I'm a close friend of Father Tuckett. After a sacred pilgrimage across the territory and the glowing report from your companions, I believe you are far more worthy of the term *Father* than Friar. Yes, I'll send Father Tuckett my recommendation for your priestly ordination once I reach Blight's Respite. With your permission, of course."

Steve bowed so aggressively his face nearly touched his knees. "I would be forever grateful, Father Braten! May the Goddess bless you with safety and peace!"

"You as well, Friar Steve," Father Braten said. "Oh, and if you're venturing to Skyhole, you'll need these. Please take good care of them. Friar Steve, I look forward to hearing of your ordination."

Father Braten reached into a saddle bag and pulled out three winter cloaks. DJ and the others rained their thanks upon the Stewards, then the Stewards wished them well and continued southward. The Highway Hag still hadn't woken up, but she still snored softly against the tree.

Everyone took a moment to congratulate Steve for his likely promotion. Riley hugged him and DJ and Francis clapped his shoulders. As usual, Steve offered his vocal thanks to the Goddess, but his face couldn't have glowed any brighter.

DJ smiled to himself. *Riley is a ranger. Steve is going to be a priest. Francis saw the Library. All that's left is my point of the quest—the Amulet.* But as he thought it, it didn't bring as much excitement as it should have.

To distract himself, DJ pulled his new coat over his tunic and stroked the fur. It had to have been made from a bear or moose. It was rough and coarse, but he felt significantly warmer.

"Sorry they didn't have one big enough for you, Francis," DJ said.

The orc shrugged. "Orcs are built to live in harsh conditions. The cold may bother me at first, but I'll promptly adjust."

They knew they had reached the Spine when their feet met the snow. Their boots crunched along the frozen earth, marking their path with shallow footprints. DJ kept his hands tucked inside his coat pockets. He looked over his shoulder to see the brown and yellow of Fairdell fade away. Before them lay the bleakest and starkest region in Uh—a great white brushstroke from the Goddess's hand. It took a couple more days before they reached the city of Skyhole.

Tucked in the corner where the Spine and the Camās

Gahl Mountains intersected, Skyhole was marked by a weathered stone wall around its southern and eastern edges. There was no need for the wall at the west and north because there was nothing but sharp mountains to their backs. Guards all along the wall were dressed in furs as they watched the southeast. DJ could tell they were brawnier than other guards he had met previously—probably from a diet of meat and snowyams.

The exterior guards opened the creaky gates that revealed the city's interior. What the party found was an expansive city cursed with cold, but a people that had grown immune to it. Dressed in pelts and wool, they carried themselves as if it were an early summer day. To them, it probably was.

But what caught DJ's attention most was the char-stained houses. Nearly all of them were damaged by fire somehow—patched roofs, mismatched bricks, charred bits on the edges. Whatever fire this city had suffered was clearly extensive.

As they walked through the main concourse, DJ couldn't help but ask a local about it. "Excuse me, what's with all the fire damage? Was there a fire recently?"

The woman laughed. "No one told ya we got dragons in Skyhole?"

DJ's throat went dry.

"Used to be a lot worse than it is now," the local said, shrugging the comment. "All these stains are from years ago, before Devin King became gov'nor. He's the Dragonspeaker, y'know. Dragons like him for some reason. That's why he got elected so eas'ly."

"He must be a magnificent warrior," Francis muttered as

he overheard the conversation.

The woman snorted a laugh. "Go see for yourself! He's open to vis'tors. Stays at the Cloud Tower on the north side of the city."

She pointed to it—a white castle made of a dozen spires, with one particularly wide and tall spire in the middle. DJ thanked the woman, and the crew made their way toward it. They passed several blacksmiths, inns, taverns, and apothecaries. People were friendly enough, greeting them as they walked by. But one man asked them if they made it to the Cloud Tower often, as if it were some kind of joke. DJ ignored him, but Riley called him some choice words before stomping away.

They arrived at the Cloud Tower and asked if they could visit Devin King. One of the guards told them to go right in.

"That's it? Just go in?" Riley asked. "You guys aren't worried about someone attacking your leader or anything?"

DJ frowned. *Probably not the best thing to tell a guard.*

The guard shrugged. "They could try. It's their funeral, though."

"I become more and more curious about this man," Francis wondered out loud.

Riley put her hands on her hips. "If he's so big and mighty, why does he need guards at all?"

"Someone's gotta walk around and tell people to behave themselves. We don't do much else." The guard tapped the armor on his leg. "Arrow to the knee. Put an end to my adventures long ago."

DJ flexed his lower lip and nodded. They pushed the door

open and the crew walked inside.

In the Cloud Tower, they found a roaring fire and a minstrel playing a lute in the corner. A banquet table had been laid out in the middle of the cavernous hall, fully loaded with several types of meats, imported vegetables, snowyams, and sugary rolls. All along the table, burly men in adventure wear dug into their meals like hungry wolves.

Many of the diners' eyes lifted to the uninvited guests, and suddenly, DJ felt very uncomfortable. No one else spoke, so Francis took it upon himself.

"Erm, it seems as though we've intruded," Francis said. "We'll return when you're finished with your meal."

"It's okay!" a friendly voice piped up. "You hungry? Pull up a chair!"

No one could find the source of the voice. DJ craned his neck. "I'm sorry, who… is speaking?"

"It's me! Devin King!"

Amazingly, he was the smallest of the bunch. Flanked by meaty, hairy disciples on either side, the governor of Skyhole was remarkably unremarkable. He waved his hand and even stood a little, like a schoolboy inviting his friends to a lunch table. He was dressed in fine hunting garbs that were disproportionate to his lack of charisma. But the most interesting thing about his outfit was the helm he wore on his head. It was iron with ram's horns jutting out of the sides, with his eyes in just the right spot for a couple of peep holes. But it was just too large for his head, so he had to readjust it often.

This is the fearsome leader of Skyhole? DJ thought.

"The cook just brought everything out, so it's still hot!"

Devin said. "Here, you can sit across from me!"

The party pulled up chairs and filled their plates. The snowyams had tough brown skins but soft purple interior. The texture was almost like a potato, and it was surprisingly bitter. DJ spread a liberal amount of butter on his before he took another bite.

Devin King spoke with his mouth half-full of beef. "So what brings you to the Cloud Tower? You look like pretty experienced adventurers. I might have a job if you're available."

DJ swallowed. "We're passing through Skyhole to get to the Temple of the Amulet. This is our last stop before we arrive."

"Oooh, a pilgrimage!" Devin's eyes widened and he pointed. "I respect that. And honestly, that's nice to hear. I feel like every adventurer comes to Skyhole looking for a dragon to kill, but I've got good relationships with the nearby dragon clans. Can't have anyone screwing that up."

DJ made a mental note not to mention his father. With the eight dragon heads mounted in the dining room back home, a dragon would no doubt do the same thing to him. For once, he was grateful that he looked nothing like Sir Dashing.

"But," Devin continued, "you'll need to hire a reliable guide or buy a clairvoyance crystal if you plan on making it to the Temple. Once you hike north, you'll run into frequent snowstorms—makes it really easy to lose your way. A good guide will cost thousands of gold, and a cheap clairvoyance crystal will run you at least five hundred. I can point you to some decent shops."

"We're short on coin," DJ said, "so we might be open to that job, depending on what it is."

Devin smiled and gave a thumbs up. "Neat! So, okay, um… it actually involves the dragons."

DJ's throat went dry again. Next to him, Steve's face turned white. Riley and Francis stayed quiet.

"It probably won't turn violent," Devin said lightly.

"*Probably?*" Riley repeated.

"They're dragons!" Devin said, throwing up his hands. His helm went askew, so he straightened it out. "They're a noble race, but they can be a little short-tempered. We made a deal years ago with the nearby red dragons. They would get some of our city's livestock twice a year if they agreed to stop laying waste to Skyhole. Pretty reasonable, right? Well, the clan prince, Albyrt, has been a little greedy lately. In the last three months, he's come down on our city twice and pilfered a supply for himself. Several residents identified him, so I need to visit the clan king to talk to him about it."

"A mission of diplomacy!" Steve yelled.

Devin snapped his fingers and pointed. "Yes!"

"But," Francis said, "we could anger the dragon king with the accusation, and he'll burn us to a crisp."

Devin snapped his fingers and pointed again. "Also yes!"

Everyone turned to DJ. He rubbed his arm and swallowed. "How much gold are we talking?"

"Eight hundred each," Devin answered.

Wow, that's a lot, DJ thought. "Are you guys in? It'll give us the funds we need to reach the Temple."

Reluctantly, one by one, everyone agreed.

"Hot dog!" Devin punched the air and had to redo his helm. "I feel a heckuva lot better with you guys coming along! A lot of my guards are ornamental. Not much help in a fight. Which *probably won't happen!*" He said that last part loudly.

Francis leaned toward DJ and spoke quietly. "Let's hope that good luck of ours keeps up."

*

Devin King was gracious enough to let the gang stay in the Cloud Tower. They each had their own bedroom and a communal washroom stocked with fluffy towels and scented soaps. While everyone got settled in and took turns taking baths, DJ went out to find the ravenpost tower.

A couple of lazy guards told him not to lollygag and watch his magic, but he found the ravenpost tower outside the town's center. In the tower, the druids gave him the letter that was waiting for him, then he paid them a gold piece to write his own.

Ho there, Son!

Did you chase out those pesky bandits? You're becoming a world-class adventurer from the sound of things! I'm im-pressed!

The script for the Harvest Festival play was given to me last week. They took some creative liberties, but I approved it nonetheless. Writers are tremendous! I find them charming, personable, intelligent, thoughtful, empathetic, beautiful, magnetic, and most of all, underpaid!

I hope you reached Skyhole safely. The city used to be plagued by dragons, but I sure gave them what-for back in my day! I know at least one of them was from the Rimrod Hills, not far from you!

Be safe, Son!

-Sir Dashing

Hey, Dad,

So the Library of Artak was totally sold out by the Word-keepers. They hired a bunch of mercenaries to take it over and charge people entrance. You should have seen Francis, he was so disappointed. But you were right, the Library was incredible.

Finally reached Skyhole. Not as many dragon attacks here anymore. Their governor is a guy named Devin King who they call the Dragonspeaker, and he's got a good report with the dragons. He's a little strange, though.

We're going to help him on a diplomatic mission then travel to the Temple of the Amulet. Almost there! I'm ready to come back home, though. Sleeping in my own bed sounds like a dream.

Love you, Dad. I'll write again when I've seen the Amulet.

-DJ

By the time DJ returned to the Cloud Tower, the bath was waiting for him. He folded up his underclothes and sank into the water, letting out a relieved *aaahh*. He scrubbed himself clean and let the grimy water run down the drain. Then, since he was last to bathe, he refilled the tub and sat for a while longer. There was something calming and comforting about sitting in warm water. And the gentle silence of the tiled room was a welcome reprieve from the open wilderness.

There he sat, watching the bubbles glide along like lily pads on a pond. And as he sat, he thought.

The Amulet was just one more trip away. They were almost there. Could it be days? Weeks? The thoughts he had back in Artak hadn't gone away. The Amulet didn't appeal to him like it used to. He had experienced too much to care about the opinions of people who didn't even like him.

So that begged the question once again, why was he here? He felt dumb for even wanting to go on this quest. Why should he care about a bunch of farmers and schoolboys comparing him to his father? Sir Dashing never put that pressure on him. It was the pressure of everyone else—people who didn't care whether he was alive or dead.

All this trouble for *them?*

DJ flexed his jaw, drained the tub, and got dressed.

He knocked on his friends' doors and invited them to his room. Curiously, they joined him, rubbing their eyes and following with small steps. They gathered around DJ's bed. He sat on the edge as he addressed everyone.

"Hey guys," he said, "I've been thinking. You know we're really close to the Amulet now."

"Yes!" Steve piped up. "The Goddess has blessed us greatly!"

"Yeah, well," DJ rubbed the back of his neck. "All of you have kind of gotten what you wanted from this quest. Riley's a ranger now. Francis saw the Library. Steve, you're definitely going to become a priest. And to be honest, I don't know if I care so much about the Amulet anymore."

Silence.

Francis's eyes became stone. "That's how you feel, DJ? What would people say if you returned home without completing your quest?"

"To Hundred Hells with them," DJ shrugged. "So much has happened since we left Beregond. The opinion of people back home feels so… I don't know, small now. Does that make sense? I know this is, like, the worst time to have this discussion, but… yeah."

"But we're so close!" Riley whined.

"That's why I wanted to talk to you about it," DJ said. "We don't have to go on this diplomatic mission tomorrow. All of us have gotten what we need from this trip. So if you'd rather just turn around and head back to Beregond, seriously, I'm okay with that."

More silence as the group considered each other. They seemed to be having a silent deliberation with their eyes. As they did, DJ sat back and waited. It didn't take long before they reached a consensus.

"We should keep going," Riley said. "We've already come this far. It would be insane to just turn back."

"I agree with Miss Riley," Francis said. "Our journey is nearing completion. It would be a shame to come this far to turn back prematurely."

DJ turned to the friar. "Steve?"

"The Goddess has led us to *Her* Temple!" he yelped. "She

has granted us safety and success! T'would be rejecting a great gift to turn away!"

DJ teased a grin. "All right then. I guess we'll keep going. Let's get plenty of rest for tomorrow. With any luck, the dragons won't barbecue us all."

23

The journey to the dragon clan would take several days, so Devin King packed appropriate supplies for the journey. Or at least he said he did. There was no caravan or supply cart—just Devin King and his word.

"I've got it all here!" He patted a leather pouch by his side. "It's enchanted so I can carry nearly three hundred pounds of stuff! We've got plenty!"

They left after a long sleep and a hearty breakfast. As Devin marched through town and the crew followed, the townspeople watched. Their steps crunched across frosty dirt and Devin King swung his arms with every stride. DJ noticed a greatsword lashed across his back—it had to weigh half as much as Devin did.

Can he really wield that? DJ wondered. Then he remembered the guards' remarks about Devin. Part of him wanted to see the goofy governor in action, but a larger part hoped it wouldn't be necessary.

They hiked through knee-deep snow all day until Devin noticed a sufficiently large cave to camp in. From out of Devin's enchanted satchel came firewood, a fire sparker, a bedroll, and cheese. Lots of cheese. Everyone was given their own wheel of cheese for supper. Steve dove in without question, but the others traded questioning glances before nibbling on theirs. They tasted fine, but who carries wheels of cheese on their person?

Twice on their journey, they got caught in blizzards. DJ kept his coat wrapped tight against the snowy assault and followed behind Francis as to not lose sight of him. Snow stuck to his eyelashes and lips and made his entire body tremble. But just ahead of Francis, Devin swung his arms and marched as if he hardly noticed the cold. DJ couldn't help but marvel during these moments.

After three days of hiking, they arrived at the mouth of an impressive cave. And in the opening, curled up like a sleeping cat, a red-scaled dragon took deep, rumbling breaths. DJ gulped when he saw it. From end to end it had to be eighty feet, and DJ couldn't look over the top of it even as it slept in the tall snow.

As they approached, the dragon blinked awake. Yellow eyes with black slits focused on them. The dragon stretched and stood to its full height, red scales glistening in the harsh sunlight. Its head rose nearly twenty feet in the air, with a mighty yellow breast and claws that could crush boulders.

DJ shivered as he thought of the heads mounted back home.

"Who approaches?" the dragon rumbled. "Is that you,

Dragonspeaker? Who are the other humans?"

"Hi, Kyndyn," Devin waved. "Yeah, it's me. These are some recent friends I made. Travelers. Sorry to just swing by unannounced, but I need to speak to Byrekoth. It's kind of important."

"Hmm," Kyndyn rumbled again, taking another stretch. "That is bold, Dragonspeaker. But again, that is why my people have taken to you." A pause. "You may go. But make it brief. His patience has been thin lately."

DJ swallowed again as he looked Kyndyn up and down. Devin saluted and strode through the cave's opening. Once they entered, DJ swore under his breath. They had walked into a sprawling cave, nearly filling the entire mountain. Carriage-sized holes marked the mountain's interior, letting snowy sunlight stream inside. The light illuminated piles of gold and jewels that dragons treated like nests. On rocky lips and ledges, more dragons rested, but they lifted their heads when they heard the humans approach. Their golden nests jingled beneath them as they shifted.

The entire cave smelled of soot. In the middle of the expanse, a mound of bones reached dozens of feet high—picked clean of any meat or marrow. Some of the bones were of considerable size. Some weren't. DJ wondered if there were any human bones in there, and the thought made his teeth chatter.

A chorus of deep rumbling sounded as dragons eyed the visitors and whispered to one another. On the opposite side of the cave, a red dragon bigger than all the rest lifted its head. His pile of gold was the largest, and he was flanked by dragons of similar sizes. When the visitors approached, the large dragons got up, stretched, and prowled around the group like tigers, tails swishing, claws stomping along the stone.

Next to the largest dragon was a nearly identical dragon of smaller size—only thirty feet long, with eyes a little too big for its head. But those yellow eyes had a dash of worry in them as Devin King approached. The small dragon sat up stiffly and tucked in its wings, trying to look confident but failing miserably. Curiously, the dragon was missing half of a horn on the right side of its skull.

That's gotta be Albyrt, DJ thought. *And he looks very guilty.*

"Dragonspeaker," the great dragon said, its voice echoing through the cave. "To what do I owe the pleasure?"

"Hi, King Byrekoth!" Devin's tone was unworried. He gave a polite bow. "Oh, you know, just passing through and thought I'd stop by!" A chuckle. "Just kidding. Took us days to get here."

Byrekoth wasn't amused. "I'll thank you to get to the point, human."

"Okay, so listen." Devin rubbed his hands together. "Remember that agreement we made years ago? That we'd give your clan offerings twice per year if you stop laying waste to Skyhole?"

Byrekoth said nothing.

"So the thing is," Devin continued. "I've received reports from my people that a smaller dragon has pillaged some of our livestock twice in the last three months. A small *red* dragon. Looks a heckuva lot like..." Devin motioned to Albyrt.

DJ and the others braced themselves for the retaliation. Their hands found their weapons. DJ tried to still his thumping heart.

King Byrekoth planted his claws and stretched higher. "You accuse my son of breaking our agreement?"

"I'm not saying he did or didn't," Devin raised his hands. "I just have a compelling case that he *might* be involved."

"It's not true, Father!" Albyrt's voice was surprisingly timid for a dragon—like a cat's meow compared to a lion's roar. "I've done nothing! Kill the human!"

"Albyrt, calm yourself," Byrekoth said.

"I would never do anything to displease you, Father!" Albyrt yipped. "I—I just went down to the city to observe the people! The humans are fascinating to me!"

DJ tried not to twist his face. *Wow, Prince Albyrt is a terrible liar.*

"Do you have proof of this crime, Dragonspeaker?" Byrekoth frowned.

"Actually, yes," Devin said brightly. "Gimme a sec."

Devin gathered his enchanted satchel and dove his arm inside. The satchel's mouth came all the way to his armpit. Devin pulled out an extra greatsword, two wheels of cheese, a human skull, and a glowing square box, all while muttering to himself and dropping them on the floor. Byrekoth waited patiently. DJ and the gang shifted on their feet and tried not to become worried.

Meanwhile, the dragons continued to circle—a gang of thick, threatening stomps. One dragon in particular kept drifting close to DJ, sniffing him, studying. DJ tried to tighten his body to keep it from trembling. He bristled every time that dragon got close. On the third pass, the dragon gave a growl that came from deep in its throat. DJ never looked at it but faced stoically forward.

"Ah!" Devin said. "Here it is!"

He held up the fragment of a dragon horn. Dragons gasped all around the cave, followed by hisses and murmurs. Prince Albyrt shriveled as if to hide his face.

"One of my people said he knocked this off the dragon in question!" Devin said, holding the fragment high. "Pretty impressive, if you ask me. It was next to a half-eaten cattle carcass."

Byrekoth turned to Albyrt. "Care to explain yourself?"

With wings still tucked, Albyrt doubled down. "It—it's not true! The Dragonspeaker weaves lies!"

"Mmm, I really don't, though," Devin said.

"Y-you insult my honor as Prince of the Red Dragons!" Albyrt straightened up and tried to look menacing. "For your crime, I challenge you to Dun-Ku-Rah!"

More gasps and murmurs from around the cave. Byrekoth's anger flared. His razor-like teeth bared and his claws dug into the gold beneath him. "Albyrt, you have been caught in your lie! Do not disgrace yourself and our people with such talk!"

Albyrt wasn't listening. "Face me, Dragonspeaker! I, Prince Albyrt of the Red Dragons, will see that you taste death this day!"

The entire cave echoed with dragonly groans as the great

beasts shook their heads.

DJ leaned toward Devin and whispered. "Hey, what's a Dun-Ku-Rah?"

"A duel to the death," Devin said casually. "Dragons only do it to each other when they feel like they've been deeply wronged—insulted beyond reparations. So now I guess I gotta fight Albyrt."

"You're not *worried?* He's still a dragon!"

Devin shook his head. He turned his attention to Albyrt and shrugged. "I accept, Albyrt. Should have just owned up to it. Byrekoth, is this well enough with you?"

DJ had never heard a dragon's sigh before, but it was a pitiful grumble like the march of a hundred sad men. Byrekoth pinched the bridge of his great nose. "Fine. *Fine.* Albyrt, you disappoint me beyond words. Continue with the Dun-Ku-Rah."

All dragons fluttered down from their ledges to gather around the cavern's base. There had to be over a hundred of them—all terrifyingly large, with strong claws, red snouts, and yellow eyes. They formed a circle surrounding the two combatants. DJ and the gang found themselves sandwiched between two dragons who paid them no attention.

Devin strode out to the middle of the circle—near the large pile of bones—and bowed to Albyrt. Albyrt bowed in kind, though there was anger and fear in his young eyes. After they bowed, every dragon in the cave began chanting.

"*Dun-Ku-Rah… Dun-Ku-Rah… Dun-Ku-Rah…*"

The words ascended in volume until it was nearly deafening. Then… it stopped. The echoes faded. The cave became as still as a graveyard.

That's when Albyrt struck. The dragon bent down and leaped into the air, his wings shooting him across the cavern floor, poised to strike Devin. A screech ripped from his jaws. DJ clapped his hands over his ears.

Devin ripped the greatsword from his back and likewise jumped into the air—an impossibly tall jump. Albyrt flew right under him. But in midair, Devin arched his back and made a swing. The tip of his greatsword severed Albyrt's horn, matching the broken one. The severed piece fell to the ground and rolled into the pile of bones.

The dragon dug his claws into the ground, scraping to a stop. His yellow eyes burned. Devin rose to his feet and brandished his weapon. There wasn't a hint of fear on his face.

DJ's jaw dangled. *Goddess Almighty.*

Albyrt leaped forward again but stopped a dozen feet from Devin. Albyrt opened his great jaws, and from the depths of his young dragon belly, spewed a jet of fire. From halfway across the cave floor, DJ and his friends could feel the heat. It was like Flamefist multiplied ten times. Fire danced in the reflection of their astonished eyes.

Albyrt's fire ceased with a hissing cough. Smoke puffed from his snout. In the inferno's wake, Devin emerged from his bearskin cloak, which he draped around himself like a cocoon. Steam arose from the cloak's fur. He brandished his greatsword again, grinning.

It's enchanted, DJ thought. *A fireproof cloak. Smart.*

In response, Devin gave a roar unlike anything DJ had ever heard. It was like the Goddess herself poured thunder from his lips—even making Steve's hollers sound dull in comparison. Every dragon in the cavern retracted fearfully, and a dribble of urine fell from Albyrt's quivering body.

So that's *why they call him Dragonspeaker,* DJ thought.

Prince Albyrt gathered himself. He leaped into the air, ascending with every flap of his wings. Then he dove toward Devin, wings tucked, making a javelin of himself. Devin planted his feet. His eyes flashed.

It was hard to tell what happened. DJ felt like he blinked and missed it. Devin swung his sword and rolled out of the way. And with a mighty, sickening thud, the body of Prince Albyrt flopped to the ground. A streak of crimson blood marked the trail between the prince's neck and severed head. His lifeless eyes were wide and shocked, gazing into nothingness.

Behind DJ, Steve moaned and collapsed onto the floor, passed out. Riley clung to Francis. Francis said nothing.

Devin King got up, stretched, and fixed his crooked helm. His clothing and weapon were smattered with fresh blood, along with his face and neck. He set his sword down and wrung the blood from his fingers and hands.

"Sorry about that," Devin said as if he had forgotten bread at the store.

Byrekoth let out an exasperated sigh. "Of all the sons I've had, he was my most foolish. I will make another—one wiser and more honorable." A pause. "I beg your forgiveness on my son's trespass, Dragonspeaker. I hope it does not tarnish our arrangement."

Devin shrugged. "I'm just glad we got it sorted out."

"If there is nothing else," Byrekoth said, "you and your human friends are free to go. You have my deepest apologies."

DJ replayed the ordeal in his head and sighed. *Thank the Goddess. Hopefully this is the first and last dragon battle I see.*

DJ and the others turned and were about to walk away, but they didn't get the chance.

"Wait. I would like to challenge the human to Dun-Ku-Rah."

DJ couldn't keep the frustration off his face. *Devin just fought one! What did he do to you?*

When he turned around to see the source of the voice, he noticed it was the dragon that kept sniffing him. And the dragon wasn't referring to Devin King. That dragon had its yellow gaze fixed squarely on DJ.

The dragon didn't want to fight Devin. It wanted to fight *him.*

DJ's insides turned cold.

"Grythure," Byrekoth said, "what is the meaning of this?"

"I smell him," Grythure bared his teeth. "The man who killed my father. I smell him on *that boy.*"

DJ's legs turned to jelly. Maybe he was imagining things, but that dragon's face looked a lot like one of the heads mounted back home.

Byrekoth frowned at DJ. "Are you the offspring of the golden-haired demon? The one called Sir Dashing?"

DJ said nothing. How could he? Two terrifying, fully grown dragons had their sights set on him. Even if he wanted to speak, his tight throat wouldn't let him.

"I *know* he is." Grythure prowled toward DJ, never blinking. "That day is etched into my memory. We were feeding on a village in the Rimrod Hills when the golden-haired demon descended. I watched my father fall as that damned human *ran his blade through him!*" The bellowing roar filled the cavern. "And today, I shall have my revenge! *Dun-Ku-Rah!*"

A dragon. A battle with a dragon. One of the very things DJ was trying to *avoid* on this journey. One of the things Sir Dashing told him he wouldn't be ready for. It was here, whether DJ liked it or not. The color drained from his face and he struggled to stand.

In a moment of courage, Riley stepped forward and bowed deeply to the dragons. "Please, don't lay this crime on him!" she pleaded. "Sir DJ is a peaceful knight! He's never killed a dragon and never intends to!"

Francis also found his tongue. "Do not punish him for the sins of his father. Please reconsider, we beg of you."

Steve, unfortunately, was still unconscious.

"I have waited nearly *two decades* for this day!" Grythure commanded. "Stand and fight, boy! Face me as your father faced mine! *Dun-Ku-Rah!*"

Uncomfortably, Devin King put his hands on his hips and slid Byrekoth a look. "Your Highness, this doesn't feel right. Is there any way we can call this off?"

Byrekoth shook his head. "It is one thing for me to intervene in the Dun-Ku-Rah of my foolish son, but Grythure is a fully matured dragon of his own mind. The Dun-Ku-Rah is the human boy's best chance for survival." He faced DJ. "You may fight Grythure and win, young human. But if you reject the challenge and leave this place, Grythure may very well treat you as prey. And you do not wish to be a dragon's prey."

DJ tried to steady his breathing. His heart thrashed in his chest. Byrekoth was right. Beating Grythure was the only way to ensure his survival—his remarkably *slim* chance of survival. But DJ had never dueled anyone or anything before, not really. And this was a *dragon*. A Goddess-damned *dragon!*

But there was no other choice, no matter how he spun it. He had to think of something miraculous, but first, he needed to accept the challenge.

With the shallowest of nods, DJ managed to croak out, "I accept."

Riley immediately fell on him, grabbing his shoulders. "DJ, *don't do this.* It's a *dragon.* Maybe we can get out of here. Do an Evercloak spell or something."

DJ's throat was dry. He shook his head. "It wouldn't be enough."

Riley's eyes welled with tears. "DJ, he'll *kill* you."

"Probably," DJ thought for a second. "Or maybe not? Maybe I'll think of something."

"But if you don't?"

DJ didn't answer that one.

Meanwhile, Francis lifted Steve off the ground and slapped him awake. "Steven! Wake up! DJ has been challenged to Dun-Ku-Rah!"

Blearily, Steve shook the sleep from his eyes. "Huh—wha—?! Sir DJ! I will pray fervently for your safety and strength!"

Grythure was waiting for him in the middle of the circle. "*Face me, boy!* I want to feel your bones break between my teeth!"

With great effort, DJ forced himself forward. Deeper he went toward the center of the circle. Every pair of dragon eyes was on him. And Grythure paced in the middle of the circle like a lion.

As DJ approached, Devin walked in step with him. Devin spoke like a coach consulting an athlete. "So you only have a shortsword? Hm, that might be a problem. Grythure is pretty big, so you won't be able to cut his head off. You could stab him through the heart, but your blade might not reach deep enough. I recommend going for the back of the head." He tapped the back of his skull. "Under their skull is a sensitive spot. If you aim your stab just right, you should be able to get his brain. That's your best bet."

DJ's reply was barely audible. "Thanks."

"Do your best!" Devin clapped him on the back. "I'm pulling for ya!" Then he scurried to the edge of the circle.

The chanting began, whether DJ was ready or not.

"Dun-Ku-Rah… Dun-Ku-Rah… Dun-Ku-Rah…"

DJ didn't pull his sword. He silently thanked himself for wearing his mage robes under his winter cloak. He spread his feet apart, steadying himself. His quivering fingers lifted to the air, and his lips prepared for magetongue. Silently, he prayed that it would be enough.

And for some reason, in this moment, he had a flash of a thought: his father. Sir Dashing. How horrible would it be to never return home? To never see him again? To die in this mountain hundreds of miles from his father's warm embrace?

It couldn't end like this. It couldn't.

"*Dun-Ku-Rah!*"

The chanting stopped. DJ's heart pounded in his ears. Sweat coated his body. The echoes faded into oblivion. And as the silence swallowed them, Grythure crouched down, ready to pounce.

He leaped at DJ. His wings propelled him forward, filling the cavern with a gust of wind as he shot forward like a missile. His jaws stretched open, ready to snap up DJ. Grythure would be upon him in a second.

There was no time to think. DJ's spellcasting was reflexive. He flung his arms and uttered magetongue with blessed precision. He put all his energy into it—his head hurt immediately. The result was a Barrier spell so fast and thick that it turned an opaque royal blue. It was hardly ten feet in diameter.

But it was enough.

Grythure's face smashed into it. Cracks burst along the Barrier like a spiderweb. The crumpling of great dragon teeth crackled though the air. Everyone in the cavern winced at the sound. All that force went directly into Grythure's head, and with it, the great dragon collapsed. Unconscious. His snout and jaw lay mangled and broken. His tongue lolled out of his mouth and his eyelids fluttered.

DJ was so shaken that he could hardly think. The magic headache didn't help either. Dragon body. Still alive. Not for long. Out cold. When he heard his friends shouting from across the cavern, that awoke him to action. *Go! Strike!* With still-trembling hands, he pulled his sword, stumbled up to Grythure's head, and climbed.

Before the dragon awoke, DJ had straddled the back of his neck and pointed his sword into the softness under Grythure's skull. He held the blade in place, shivering.

Strike. Kill it. Win. DJ knew he should, but something stayed his hand. It was the image of the smoldering body at Broken Lovers Pass. The hole it burned in his soul. The feeling he knew he never wanted to have again. In this moment, a portion of that feeling grew fresh, but he didn't stomach the whole thing.

"I can't," he croaked. "Not again."

Grythure stirred awake. DJ knew he had to make this look good, so he gathered himself the best he could and kept his sword pointed into Grythure's neck. He held one of Grythure's horns to steady himself.

"You are *defeated,* Grythure!" DJ proclaimed, trying to fill his voice with fire. "I have bested you in Dun-Ku-Rah! But I shall not be a dragon slayer like my father before me. This is my offering of peace!"

A hush fell upon the dragons, which sprouted into confused whispers. DJ half-expected Grythure to buck him off, but the great dragon didn't budge. He stayed still in defeat, rumbling pitifully.

Byrekoth broke the murmurs with a commanding growl. "It is not our way to spare a life in Dun-Ku-Rah."

DJ frowned. "But I am no dragon, and *I* will not slay him."

To add to that, DJ remembered one of the wizard waffles in his pack. He pulled it out, leaned forward, and lobbed it into Grythure's mouth. The dragon swallowed, and his maw restored to its original form with a landslide of snaps and cracks.

Everyone in the cavern grimaced at the sounds again. Grythure smacked his great lips and lolled his tongue around, feeling his restored teeth. But the great beast still grumbled angrily.

"You have put me in your debt," he growled. "That is a fate worse than death."

DJ held firm and gulped. But still, the dragon didn't throw him off.

"Curious," Byrekoth thought out loud. "To slay a dragon is a great honor for your people. But you refuse. Even when Grythure sought your life. Very curious indeed." A quiet moment. "You seem determined to preserve an enemy's life. However, there must be a consequence for Grythure's defeat."

No one breathed. The entire clan waited with expectant yellow eyes. Byrekoth's great tail swished thoughtfully, then, with an air of resolve, he said, "Grythure, you are hereby banished from the red dragon clan. That is the cost of your defeat in Dun-Ku-Rah. As I have said, so it is done."

DJ hopped off Grythure's neck and tried not to look at the subdued dragon, but couldn't help himself. Grythure bristled with fury, claws trembling, wings retracted in shame. DJ wondered which was worse—being killed or being forever separated from your people.

Then he stole a glance at Francis. It was hard to tell what Francis felt in this moment. But DJ knew one thing for sure —Francis became his truest self in solitude. So he hoped the same could happen for Grythure.

Grythure leaned toward DJ. DJ's hands twitched, almost ready for another spell. The dragon didn't strike but bared his teeth and spoke so closely that DJ could feel the heat on his breath.

"This is not the last you shall see of me," Grythure rumbled. "I pray that the mountains fall upon you and death takes you slowly. Farewell."

Grythure flapped his wings so hard, the wind knocked DJ over. He ascended through the cavern until he disappeared through a hole. Through another hole, DJ watched Grythure fly into the distance. And after everything settled, the dragons all returned to their golden nests. On the cavern's ground, only the humans, orc, and Byrekoth remained.

The dragon king sighed. "A truly shameful day for my people… a son and a warrior, both lost. Please, Dragon-speaker, take your people and go. Your work here is done."

So they went. Some dragons carried the remains of Prince Albyrt onto the bone pile. DJ, Devin King, and the gang readjusted their winter coats and marched out of the cavern, grateful to be gone. The snow once again crunched under their fur-lined boots.

As they went, DJ thought of that fear that he felt right before Grythure struck. In that moment, all he wanted to do was see his father again—to feel the warm safety of his arms and see that glowing smile. In that moment, he would have given that for all the treasure in the world. The return to Beregond couldn't come soon enough.

Another thought came soon after. DJ fought a dragon and won. He actually *won* against a *dragon.* A stifled laugh jumped off his lips. *Dad's never gonna believe this.*

The group passed Kyndyn on the way out. The dragon frowned and nodded as they trudged by. Walking ahead of the group, swinging his arms, Devin looked over his shoulder. His face was bright and cheery, despite being half-smeared with dragon blood. He said, "All things considered, I think that went pretty well!"

24

When they returned to Skyhole, Devin King rewarded everyone with their proper gold. With that gold, the party got supplies for the last leg of their journey. DJ found himself throwing fearful glances at the sky, waiting for Grythure to descend upon him with fiery vengeance, but it didn't happen. Devin assured DJ that the dragons treat honor in highest regard, so Grythure was honor-bound not to kill him. But DJ remembered what Beatrice said about oaths at the Library of Artak, and that made him sweat.

Devin also grossly underestimated the price for a guide to the Temple of the Amulet. The party still had nearly three thousand gold to spend; it wasn't enough to afford the cheapest guide to the Temple. Francis spoke to a creature named Gog'm who was willing to guide them for a few hundred gold, but he was a slippery, hunched little fiend with large eyes and a loincloth. Didn't seem particularly trustworthy.

After the party took care of some necessities (including

DJ's ravenpost, informing Sir Dashing that he bested a dragon), they went to a general store Devin King recommended. The name of the shop was Bragganor's, and it was just off the city's main concourse.

When they entered, they found shelves upon shelves lined with various goods. Weapons, armor, potions, books… looked like Bragganor had a little bit of everything. Bragganor himself stood behind a counter, tall, sour-faced, leaning on his elbows and watching them. He wore fine clothes and had a shrewd look that told DJ he had been in business for a very long time.

"Take a look around," Bragganor said with a gravelly tone. "I'm sure you'll find what you're looking for."

DJ approached the counter and put his hands on it. "We need a clairvoyance crystal attuned to the Temple of the Amulet."

Bragganor laughed in his chest. "You sure you don't want one to the Temple of the Brassiere? Maybe you'll be the first one to return with your life."

"I'd rather not take the chance."

"Got the coin?" Bragganor smirked. "Clairvoyance crystals fetch quite a price."

DJ gave a smirk of his own and patted his pocket.

That seemed to satisfy Bragganor. "Four thousand gold."

Steve, Francis, and Riley stopped browsing the shelves and turned at the sound of that sum. DJ didn't shrink, though. After months of daring escapes and a victorious dragon battle, a little haggling felt like nothing.

"We just visited the red dragons with Devin King," DJ

said. "We've done your city a great service. I think you'd do well to cut that price in half."

Bragganor's hands twitched so hard that his fingernails dug into the counter. Fury flashed across his stony eyes for a moment's fraction. But just as quickly as his rage appeared, it vanished. His face turned soft and he laughed. "A man still has a business to run. But I can't deny the service you've done for our city. I'll do it for three thousand."

That's almost all of our gold, DJ thought. "Twenty-nine hundred. I'm afraid that's the best I can do. If not, I understand. It would be a shame to pass my disappointment to Devin King, though. Your shop came highly recommended."

Riley suppressed a grin. So did Francis. Steve was distracted by a magical dancing frog, so he wasn't listening. Bragganor, however, tried desperately to turn his scowl into a smile. Every word he spoke came through gritted teeth and twitching lips.

"Very well," he said. "Wouldn't want to disappoint our noble governor. Twenty-nine hundred gold, then."

He ducked behind the counter and rummaged for just a moment before emerging with a pink crystal the size of his fist. He held it in front of DJ's face, twisting it and letting the light catch it.

"One clairvoyance crystal attuned to the Temple of the *Amulet,*" Bragganor said. "Give it a rub and it'll show you a pink line leading to the Temple."

DJ counted the gold and dropped it on the counter. Bragganor gave him the crystal, and DJ immediately rubbed it. Before his eyes materialized a bright pink thread that led out the door. DJ thanked Bragganor, and the party left.

As they closed the door, DJ looked over his shoulder. Bragganor glared with slimy disdain, but there was an eerie thread of satisfaction twitching through his lips. DJ frowned at it but didn't think any more of it after he closed the door.

"To barter with such confidence!" Francis said as he shook his head. "The DJ I met back in Beregond never would have had the grit."

DJ half-smiled. "Yeah, you're probably right."

"Come," Francis said. "There must be sights to see in Sky-hole. Tomorrow we embark on the final stretch of our adventure, but today, we celebrate."

Francis was incorrect—there were hardly any sights to see in Skyhole. DJ did find a college of magic in the northeast corner of town. He talked to the administration for a few minutes, but found the professors stuffy, pretentious, and a tad suspicious. When he saw a student struggle with a Flamefist spell, DJ decided he was best studying magic on his own.

Steve found another monastery to offer prayers at. That night, Francis insisted that they find a cozy tavern for dining, and they found one called the Giant's Foot. Inside, a duo of bards kept the diners entertained over a steady hum of chatter, clinking dishes, and sloshing pints. A roaring hearth in the middle of the tavern made it warm enough to shed their coats. The party pulled up a table in the corner and a hostess provided them menus.

They had to be selective with their limited funds, but the party afforded meals with spiced meat, mashed snowyams, steamed vegetables, and red wine. Steve asked for grape cider instead of wine. When the hostess brought them their meals, Francis took his pint and straightened up.

"Young knight," he said, "would it be well with you if I proposed a toast?"

DJ shrugged. "Sure, go ahead."

Francis smiled, then pushed out his chair and stood. "*Hear ye, one and all!* I'd like to propose a toast!"

The steady hum extinguished. Even the bards stopped playing.

DJ's cheeks turned red. *I thought you meant just us, not the whole tavern!* He resisted the urge to slump in his seat.

"To my young friend, Sir DJ of Beregond," Francis said, pointing to him. "For months, we have traveled together, experiencing all kinds of danger and discovery. At first he was fearful, but he has grown into a knight of courage and strength. A warrior, and a scholar. For that, let us drink!" He lifted his pint again. "To Sir DJ of Beregond!"

"*Aye!*" the tavern responded. Everybody knocked back a swig.

Riley stood up, face beaming. "Sir DJ has proved that, even before reaching the age of manhood, he's as brave and noble as any knight in the territory! Another toast to Sir DJ!"

"*Aye!*" The tavern took another combined drink.

DJ's face burned an even brighter shade of red and he caught himself slumping after all.

Friar Steve pushed his chair out and stumbled to his feet. His words were slurred and he had trouble standing. "Sir DJ is blessed by the good, good Goddess! May 'e live with peace and happiness and eternal blessings! Another drink forrr *Sir*

DJ!"

The tavern watched the friar with amusement before they agreed with "*Aye!*" and had another drink. Francis and Riley sat back in their seats. Steve plopped down and nearly fell over.

DJ rubbed his forehead to hide his face. "Please… *never* do that again. But thank you." He took Steve's drink and smelled it. The hostess definitely gave him wine instead of grape juice. The realization was almost as funny as the knowledge that Steve got punch-drunk from a couple of gulps. "How's your grape juice, friar?"

"It tastes funny!" the Steward slurred. "But I like it! Maybeee I'll 'ave another!"

"Maybe just keep it to one tonight," DJ tried not to laugh.

"Sir DJ," Francis said. "I hope you know I meant every word. This journey has been once in a lifetime. I consider you my friend, and I hope that our fellowship will continue for years to come."

"Me too," Riley said, eyes bright. "I'm so glad I ran away from home to do this with you, Deej. It's been amazing."

Steve said, "Mmmee too!" Then he draped his arms around DJ, humming and nuzzling his head into DJ's shoulder.

In this moment, DJ's heart became thick. He had left Beregond with just one friend, but now he had three—not to mention all the friends he made along the way. Gratitude swelled inside him until a lump grew in his throat. He coughed it free.

"Thanks, guys," he said. "I feel the same." He took his pint and lifted it. "To friendship."

Steve released him, and everyone lifted their pints. "To friendship!" They drank.

*

Steve rubbed his temples and moaned as they all got ready the next morning. DJ was amazed that anyone could get hungover from a single pint of wine, but then again, Steve wasn't like anyone else he knew.

Devin King was in the foyer working on a very poor painting of a dragon when the crew came in. The governor waved his paintbrush in the air and wished them the best then went back to work, whistling to himself.

Within the hour, they were on the north end of Skyhole, preparing to enter the treacherous mountains of the Spine. As they went, DJ rubbed the clairvoyance crystal to illuminate their path. The bright pink thread led the way.

For days, they trudged through the knee-high snow. It was hard to tell through the snowstorms and cloud cover, but DJ swore that the crystal was taking them the wrong direction. The Amulet of the Goddess was east from Skyhole, but the crystal seemed to take them west. But the crystal knew better than he did, so he didn't question it.

At night, they found caves and alcoves to camp in. It was tough to find firewood in the snow, and the wet wood made the fires uncomfortably smokey. In the dark, they would often hear wolves howling, so they always made sure to keep the fire glowing, no matter how thick the smoke was.

Along the way, they spotted all sorts of creatures in the distance. Against the sky, they saw dragons flying in small packs. Sometimes they were red, sometimes they were bronze or green. Thankfully, they didn't notice the four of them. And one night, as they were getting ready to make camp, they saw the shadows of giants moving slowly along the mountain top. Riley stared in awe.

"Don't worry," Francis explained, "they won't bother us if we keep our distance. It's not unusual to find orc clans in the Spine, either. We are, after all, the lords of the barren places. But I can't say I've met many cousins from this area."

Days went by of snowy hiking, eating dried food and cooking whatever Riley managed to kill. But finally, one afternoon, they saw it. At the top of a mountain, at its very peak, the Temple of the Amulet stood majestically—an edifice of radiant white pillars and clean stone.

"Behold!" Steve yelped and pointed. "The Temple of the Amulet! Our journey is nearly complete!"

"Our journey is nearly *halfway* complete," Francis corrected. "Don't forget that we still need to venture back to Beregond." He nodded toward the Temple. "I imagine with that distance, it'll take us another day. We're not there yet."

But a day came and went. They found the foot of the mountain with a great set of switchbacks carved into its side. Their legs protested as they ascended. When they reached the top, the Temple stood all the more inspiring. Everything about it—the pillars, the porch, the sloping roof—seemed to reach upward in holiness and power. And the mountaintop's silence only added to the majesty.

But they had a slight problem. The mountain had been severed in two, and a great chasm stretched between their side and the side of the Temple. They all approached the fissure's edge to investigate its depth. It was a nearly endless drop to the bottom. DJ flexed his clammy hands.

There *did* appear to be a way across, however. On the other side of the chasm, a long stone bridge was retracted up. Above it was a statue of a lion with a massive jaw gaping wide. Two more stone lions were standing on the party's side of the chasm, so three in total: one above the retracted bridge on the north side of the chasm and two in front of them on the south side.

DJ examined the lion statue nearest to him. His fingers traced the stone teeth and rubbed the dust that had gathered. Inside the gaping mouth was a small bundle of dry wood where the tongue should have been. DJ furrowed his brows.

Riley put her hands on her hips. "So, we need to get that bridge down if we're going to reach the Temple. Anyone got ideas?"

DJ pointed to the statue. "This statue has dry wood in its mouth. Is it the same with that one? Yeah, I bet they all do. I'm guessing we have to light a fire in all of them. How we're going to get *that* one, though,"—he pointed at the statue above the retracted bridge on the other side of the chasm —"I'm not sure about."

"I shall pray to the Goddess for wisdom!" Steve yelped. He dropped to the ground, crossed his legs, and closed his eyes.

Francis meandered to both statues, inspecting for himself.

But it was between the statues that something stopped him. His attention focused between his boots. He crouched down and rapped his knuckles on the snow. "The texture on the ground is different here," he said. "It's smooth."

With his big green hand, he brushed the snow away to find words etched into an even stone surface. The words were in organized rows like a poem, but DJ couldn't understand any of the letters. He nudged Francis. "Can you read any of this? It's not in commonspeak."

"Fragments," Francis said. "You're correct, Sir DJ, this is oldspeak. The tongue has been mostly lost for thousands of years, but I understand bits and pieces from my studies at the College of Beregond. I found more of it at the Library of Artak."

Riley was over Francis's other shoulder. "What does it say?"

Francis didn't answer. His fingers traced every word, his face riddled with concentration. When he reached the end of the words, he stayed with his elbow on his knee for a long moment, thinking. Then he scratched his chin. "From what I gather, we must light a fire in every lion's mouth simultaneously, then the bridge will drop. But my translation is rough. I may be incorrect."

DJ's eyes darted to the two lion statues before them, then the one across the chasm. Light them all at the same time? How? Two were in front of them, sure, but what about the one across the bottomless fall to certain death?

DJ stared at the distant statue as if to summon an answer. Just across the chasm, the Temple of the Amulet waited for them. He folded his arms under his garbs and thought about how anticlimactic it would be to venture here only to be stopped by a puzzle they couldn't solve.

As he nurtured these thoughts, DJ saw Riley's bow slung across her back. That gave him an idea. Riley turned around and they locked eyes. Yes, they were thinking the same thing. She took the bow off her shoulder and marched up to him. Her eyes flashed with enlightenment.

DJ smiled. "Are you thinking what I'm thinking?"

Riley pulled out an arrow. "I'll wrap an arrowhead with cloth. You light it with your magic—"

"—then Steve and I will use Flamefist on the statues," DJ said. "That could work. As long as Francis's translation is right. Steve, get up! We have an idea!"

The friar's eyes snapped open and he leaped to his feet. "Goddess be praised!"

Riley wrapped the arrow. As she did, DJ rubbed his frozen hands together. Once it was ready, DJ made the backwards S with his fingers and said "*Scintyll.*" Sparks jumped. The arrow's tip caught fire. Riley pulled back and lined up her shot. She grimaced from the heat licking her knuckles.

DJ and Steve got ready by the two statues. They both watched Riley intently. Neither of them said it, but that shot across the chasm would be a difficult one, especially considering the mountain wind. But Riley had been practicing her archery for months. Hopefully it would pay off. Because if it didn't, they were sunk.

Through clenched teeth, Riley let out a pent-up breath and the arrow shot through the air.

The flickering red arrow sailed over the chasm. Everyone held their breath. It arched up, down, and… bullseye. The arrow lodged in the lion's mouth above the retracted bridge.

Together, Steve and DJ shouted "*Mynus-ignys!*" Flames blasted from their fists. Their two lion mouths lit up. All three of the lion mouths had ignited at once.

Everyone backpedaled and congratulated Riley on her tremendous archery. Riley clutched her bow and grinned. They all waited for the bridge to descend, but… it didn't budge. It didn't so much as shudder. They waited a moment longer. Still nothing. Then they all let out a cumulative sigh.

Francis shook his head. "I'm sorry, friends. If only my old-speak were stronger."

But no. The eyes in every lion statue lit up. The bridge trembled. With a loud groan, the bridge unlatched. In a slow, downward swing, it timbered over the chasm until it *slammed* into the opposite side. The mountain shook. They all crouched low to keep steady. But there it was. The path was clear. The stone bridge to the Temple extended across the chasm, waiting for them.

Francis straightened himself. "I redact my apology. You're all very welcome."

They carefully made their way across the bridge. It didn't have rails or ropes, so it was a direct fall to the bottom on either side. DJ tried not to look down. He hadn't realized how uncomfortable he was with heights until this moment. But he kept forward as everyone followed him. And within the minute, the group was on the other side of the chasm.

Before them was the mighty Temple of the Amulet. It just

got even more majestic the closer they got. DJ could make out the carvings etched into the pillars—beautiful curving patterns thousands of years old. The white stone had a glow all its own, as if heavenly hands polished it daily. It showed no signs of fading.

They had arrived. After months of grueling travel, DJ, Francis, Riley, and Steve were finally here.

Behind them, the bridge shuddered and retracted back up to its original position. They all watched it slowly climb as if pulled by invisible cables. It stopped as it stood straight up, and the mountainside rang with a loud *click*.

DJ swallowed. "Well, hopefully that's not a problem later."

"Perhaps, perhaps not!" a familiar voice came. "Things have a way of working out!"

The entire party turned and saw him. The wooden stand. The pointed hat and phony beard. The waffle wizard propped his head in his hands and rested with his elbows on the counter. Next to him was a warm stack of waffles, visibly steaming in the cold. The wizard wasn't wearing any winter clothing, but the weather didn't seem to bother him.

"It's you!" DJ nearly laughed. "What are you doing all the way up here?"

"Conducting business as usual!" the wizard replied brightly. "How's your supply? I have a wonderful new product that *you* would love in particular!"

The wizard reached under the table, pulled out a small chest, and opened the lid. Inside were three spherical pastries that could fit in the palm of DJ's hand. Each was sprinkled with powdered sugar. Steam wafted off them and they smelled delightful. DJ's mouth watered.

Riley studied them. "What are those? They're so small!"

"Magic Waffle Bites!" the wizard said proudly. "No more magic headaches! Once your mind feels weary, just pop one of these Bites and you'll be good as new! Perfect for mages and other magic users." He winked.

"How much?" DJ asked eagerly.

"Fifty gold each!"

DJ's heart sank. He rummaged around in his pack and counted some gold coins in his palm. "All we have is twenty-two gold. That's it. The clairvoyance crystal cost nearly everything we had."

The wizard scratched his head and thought for a moment. "Um… tell you what. You four have been such wonderful customers across… ah, Hundred Hells, just buy one waffle and I'll give you the Bites for free!"

"Whoa, really?" DJ asked with a wide smile.

"Goddess be praised!" Steve yelped.

DJ forked over ten gold and the wizard served up a waffle, followed by the three Magic Waffle Bites. DJ stuffed them into his mage robes and thanked the wizard profusely. But as he did, there was something in the wizard's eye he had never seen before. The jovial disposition was still there, but it felt like a mask for something else.

Worry.

"Well, pleasure seeing you!" the wizard bowed. "But I really must be going! Best of luck to you!"

For just a few seconds, a snowstorm picked up so heavily that it nearly threw everyone off their feet. They could barely see their hands in front of them. But it was gone as quickly as it appeared, and when it lightened up, the wizard and his stand had disappeared.

DJ brushed the fresh snow off his coat. "Best of luck? We're already here, though."

Francis looked the Temple up and down, then turned to DJ. "You're just a few steps away, young knight. The Amulet of the Goddess."

DJ smiled.

The four of them marched to the Temple's edge. Long stairs stretched from the snow to its front porch. Each step was finely carved and pillars around the porch rose fifty feet tall. Above a large set of stone doors, a triangle carved from the wall pointed upward. Behind it, a carving of a sun was shining.

DJ approached the doors, heart pounding. Then he stopped. He took a look at the friends who ventured with him all the way here. Through all sorts of danger, they were there, and he couldn't have been more grateful. They smiled back at him, and it turned his insides warm.

"This is your quest, Sir DJ," Francis said. "You should be the first to enter."

"Yeah, DJ, go!" Riley insisted.

"The Goddess's blessing awaits you!" Steve yipped.

DJ took a steadying breath, put his sweaty palms on the doors, and pushed. They dragged open on resistant hinges, but nonetheless, they opened.

He wasn't sure what the Temple would be like inside, but he wasn't expecting this. It was essentially a ruined indoor courtyard. There were great rocks strewn about, puddles of water, moss growing on rocks and half-destroyed pillars. There was no roof, either—just four ancient walls that opened up to a cloudy sky.

No sign of the Amulet, either. And the Temple was surprisingly warm, even though it had no reason to be.

DJ shed his winter coat as he strolled around, taking everything in. "Weird. Shouldn't there be a pedestal with the Amulet on it? I thought that's what the Stewards told me."

No response. DJ realized he couldn't hear his friends' footsteps.

A frown came to his lips. "Guys?"

He looked behind and his body ran chill. Francis, Riley, and Steve were gone. DJ was alone in the Temple. The hair on his neck stood. When he turned about to face forward again, he nearly jumped out of his skin.

In the middle of the Temple stood a monster unlike anything he had ever seen. It had the head and mane of a lion, the torso and arms of a muscular human, and the legs and talons of an eagle. White feathered wings spread out from its back. In one of its human-like hands, it held a greatsword as long as DJ was tall. DJ only reached up to its waist.

DJ stepped back and planted his feet, looking up, flexing his hands. Fear rocked through him like a tidal wave.

"Human," the beast said. Its voice matched its lion face—a threatening growl.

DJ swallowed before he answered. "Who are you? What have you done to my friends?"

"I am the Harpygriff," it said, "the beast who guards the

Brassiere of the Goddess. And you were the first to enter the Temple. Your friends are of no consequence."

The Brassiere? DJ's blood went cold. He suddenly remembered Bragganor's devious look as he left the shop. *That damned Bragganor sold us the wrong crystal!*

He was at the Temple of the Brassiere. And no one survived the Temple of the Brassiere.

"No," DJ breathed. "Noble Harpygriff, there's been a terrible mistake. I am Sir DJ of Beregond, on a peaceful pilgrimage with my friends. We meant to go to the Temple of the Amulet, not the Temple of the Brassiere."

"Yet you are here," the Harpygriff said.

Swallowing, DJ knelt on the ground. "Please, let us go in peace. We were misled here."

"That is not an option," the Harpygriff said. "I am sworn to confront every living thing that enters this sacred place. You cannot simply leave."

"Please, choose mercy!" DJ tried to sound strong but humble.

"Your groveling will make no difference."

DJ swallowed again, thinking, trying to scrape up a plan. But what? This was the Temple of the Brassiere, and he was at the Harpygriff's utmost mercy. "What would you have me do?" he swallowed.

The Harpygriff tightened the grip on its mighty sword. "Slay me. Prove what no one has before—that you are worthy of beholding the Brassiere of the Goddess."

"I don't want to fight!" DJ said. "We were *misled!* In the name of the Goddess, let us go in peace!"

"*You are not one to swear on Her name!*" the Harpygriff bellowed. "It is *She* who gave me this sacred charge! There is but *one* way out, and it is over my corpse!"

A lump formed in DJ's throat and he felt smaller than he ever had before. The glowing memories of the last few months were now tarnished. He bowed deeper and shook his head. "I can't. I won't."

"Perhaps this shall motivate you," the Harpygriff said.

It swished its sword before DJ, as if pulling back a curtain. There, at the Harpygriff's feet, his three friends appeared. Wide-eyed. Horror-stricken. Still as statues.

"I shall peel the flesh from their bones," the Harpygriff seethed. "Let their screams fill your ears. Is that what I must do? Will that grant you courage to fight, human?"

That lit a fire in DJ. Whatever fear knocked around his trembling body was extinguished, and in its place, a mighty swell of righteous fury crashed through him.

Standing and baring his teeth like a tiger, he proclaimed, "I'll *kill you* if you touch them!"

"Then rise, Knight of Beregond!" the Harpygriff commanded. "Prove this day your worth! Defeat me or embrace death as all have before! *Rise!*"

The Harpygriff lunged.

25

DJ cast Ironflesh right before the first blow fell. The Harpygriff swatted him like a bug, flinging him against a far wall. DJ's mage robes flapped through the air before he slammed into the stone, kicking up a mess of rubble and dust. He fell to the floor and shook the mist from his eyes. A blow that should have killed him only dazed him.

Think fast, but pace yourself, he told himself. *Can't use magic too quickly.*

The Harpygriff stomped toward him, weapon raised. DJ noticed the beast approaching a large puddle. He jumped to his feet. "*Glaci-talum!*"

A three-foot Ice Spike shot up from the puddle and im-paled the Harpygriff's leg. The beast gave a shallow moan of displeasure then snapped its leg free and continued stomping. The sweat thickened on DJ's brow.

"A mage knight!" the Harpygriff mused. "Very few I've

seen of you, very few indeed!"

The Harpygriff lifted a boulder with its free hand and launched it. DJ dove out of the way just as it smashed into the wall behind him, sending out more rock fragments. DJ breathed harder, thinking, desperately forming a plan.

He flipped through the list of spells in his head: Flamefist, Ice Spike, Evercloak—

Evercloak!

DJ cast it. As his body vanished, he darted away. But the Harpygriff's eyes followed him.

"Clever, but not clever enough," the Harpygriff said. "You might be invisible, but your footsteps are *thunderous!*"

The beast swung its sword and DJ had to collapse to dodge it. He felt the massive blade pass inches above his nose. On the ground, lying flat, he tried to still his breathing—to lie totally motionless. But the Harpygriff knew his vicinity, and it was dangerously close.

The Harpygriff used its wings to leap into the air then flapped downward to give a mighty stomp. DJ saw the talons plummeting. His heart rate spiked. He rolled out of the way just in time. The ground cratered under the Harpygriff's legs.

Turning on his back, DJ used one of Steve's signature spells. "*Fulgyr-fylum!*"

With a *bang,* a bolt of blue lightning shot from DJ's pointed finger. It made the Harpygriff buckle, and for a moment, it fell to its knees and shuddered. In that expanse, DJ got up and sprinted away.

His head throbbed. His eyes watered. He needed that Magic Waffle Bite. He fumbled in his pocket for one, but a quick look over his shoulder saw the blurry image of the Harpygriff getting up and spreading its wings.

"*Enough!*" the beast bellowed.

It leaped higher, kicking gusts of wind. It flapped its wings and ascended, becoming a blurry blob against a snowy sky. DJ kept very still, but the Waffle Bite was pinched in his fingers and his head seared with pain. He could barely see the outline of the Harpygriff against the clouds. He couldn't tell what was more dangerous—moving and revealing his location, or staying still with skewed vision.

With methodical slowness, he moved the Bite to his mouth.

Not slow enough. The Harpygriff *cawed* and dove like a spear. DJ pushed the Bite into his cheek. As soon as it passed his lips, his magic was restored.

With a half-full mouth, he spat magetongue and cast Barrier. The transparent blue sheet appeared before him, blocking most of the blow. But the Harpygriff's blade tore through the Barrier like an arrow, and it found its mark deep in DJ's shoulder.

DJ howled and grabbed the wound. Blood oozed between his fingers. Trembling, still chewing his Waffle Bite, he muttered the words for Healing Hand. The skin and muscles stitched up, but it wasn't enough to fully heal it. Blood still sopped around his shoulder.

I never should have left Beregond, he despaired.

The Harpygriff extracted its sword and cut down the Barrier in a blue rain of glass. DJ's shoulder protested, but there was no time to mind the pain. With the Harpygriff so close, he resorted to his very first spell. *"Mynus-ignys!"*

A jet of fire assaulted the Harpygriff. The beast growled and shielded its eyes. While it recoiled, DJ ripped the sword from his sheath and sliced the beast's legs. His strike was true. As he stumbled away, the monster buckled and roared with pain.

DJ sheathed his weapon and cast Ironflesh one more time. His skin and bones hardened. But his mind was starting to weaken again, along with his aching body.

A heartbeat later, the Harpygriff flipped around and grabbed DJ's arm. The monster spun and flung DJ against a wall. Another slam. This time, DJ coughed up blood. And as he fell to the ground, he tried to push himself up but couldn't. The arm the Harpygriff grabbed was a mangled mess of flesh and bone, bloody and useless.

Panic set in. There was no way Healing Hand could repair the shattered arm. And with one arm, he couldn't perform his magic. Breaths came in frenzied bursts. And through stinging, misty eyes, he watched the Harpygriff advance.

Not knowing what else to do, he frantically spoke the words for Healing Hand, but his broken bones only twitched. The more he tried, the more his head hurt, and pitiful whimpers left his bloody lips.

A wash of regret fell over him. This whole quest—this stupid, stupid quest—was all for nothing. It would have been better to stay a nobody back home. Now, death literally approached. His friends would die with him and no one would know their fate.

I'm never seeing Dad again, DJ thought. That's what

made the tears slide down his cheeks.

"Pathetic," the Harpygriff growled.

It grabbed DJ by the throat and lifted him up. DJ sputtered and coughed, clawing at the Harpygriff's hand, but it was no use. The Harpygriff lifted its sword.

"The Brassiere stays protected," the Harpygriff said. "Die now, Knight of Beregond."

The thrust. The sword ripped through bones and flesh. More blood spilled between DJ's teeth.

His last thought before everything went dark was, *I'm sorry, Dad.*

*

DJ felt water lapping by his ears. Then he felt movement in his fingers and toes. He was laying down on something equally firm and soft. The gentle lap of water reached halfway up his prone body—it couldn't be more than a few inches deep.

His eyes stirred and opened. Above him, soft, fluffy clouds drifted through a brilliant blue sky. But there was no harsh sun on his face.

He planted his hands and forced himself to sit up. The water came up to his wrists. But as he sat, the water dripped off his back and didn't linger on his clothes. He was completely dry.

My clothes, DJ thought. He was wearing everything he had just moments before. His purple mage robes were torn and bloodstained around his shoulder and stomach. But the wounds were gone. His body was completely whole.

DJ squatted and stood. That's when he noticed the surface beneath him. Fine sand—like that from the Westfall beaches—with water coming just up to his ankles, but as he looked down, what should have been sand was an inky black expanse dotted with stars.

He turned all around. The blue sky and the night sky stretched to the horizon in every direction—the meeting of two heavens. A blue sky above, a night sky below. And he stood between them.

DJ scratched his dry hair, then let his hand flop to his side. "This is what death is like?"

"*Why do you seek the Brassiere?*"

The voice came from all around him—powerful, authoritative, but not frightening. It could have been a woman's voice, but it was hard to tell.

"*Why do you seek it?*" the Voice asked again.

DJ swallowed. "I don't. I never did."

"*Lies.*"

"It's the truth."

"*Then why were you at its Temple?*"

"My friends and I were misled. My destination was the Temple of the Amulet. I never wanted the Brassiere."

The Voice was silent for a moment. "*Many have sought the Brassiere. All have perished in the pursuit. You have no desire to behold it? To become a legend?*"

"No."

"*A boy untempted by glory? More lies.*"

"Look," DJ said, lifting his hands, "I don't know how to

convince you, but I'm telling you, *I don't care.* I've seen too much in the past few months to care about glory quests. They're stupid."

Another pause from the Voice. "*Explain.*"

DJ took a long breath. "I have a famous dad. Everyone expected me to be like him, but I'm not. I went on this quest to prove to everyone that I'm worthy of being a knight like him, but along the way, I stopped caring what they think. I'm not my dad—I don't slay dragons and save maidens. At first, I hated that. But in the last few months, I learned that I'm actually okay as I am.

"That's why I don't want the Brassiere. I don't even care about the Amulet. I think what I *really* wanted was respect, and I had to find that myself." DJ's tone grew dark. "What sucks is that this whole thing put my best friends in danger. They're probably going to die. *And* I'll never get to see my dad again. He'll probably never know what happened to me." DJ forced down his rising emotions. "I wish I could have at least said goodbye first."

DJ plopped into a sitting position. He stared at the stars that rippled under the water's surface.

The Voice spoke up again. "*With the Brassiere, history would remember you. Not a soul would disrespect you. I can grant you your wish. I can grant you that power.*"

DJ looked up. "Were you listening to me? *I don't care!* Keep your crummy bra! I'd give all of that power and respect in the world for just five minutes with my dad again. And Riley. And Francis. And *Steve.*" DJ's throat started to get tight again.

When the Voice spoke, it was laced with a smile. "*Very good, young knight. Farewell.*"

DJ squinted at the sky. "Farewell? Where am I supposed to g…?"

Sleep fell on him hard and fast. The daylight and starlight faded away. He fell through the water, submerged, but only for a moment's fraction.

When he opened his eyes, he was back at the Temple. His clothes were still damaged from battle, but his body was restored. No broken arm, no throbbing head. He sat with his back against the wall. The Harpygriff towered above him, sword in hand.

DJ gulped, awaiting the final strike again, but the Harpygriff didn't attack. As a matter of fact, it backpedaled.

"At last," the beast marveled. "After thousands of years, She has chosen one worthy. Well done, sir knight. I relent this battle to you."

The beast knelt on one knee, faced the ground, and offered its sword.

DJ didn't move. He just sat there blinking. "Um… what just happened?"

"The Goddess has deemed you worthy," the Harpygriff said, still offering its sword out. "You passed the final test, and with it, you have been restored to life. You may see and handle the Brassiere."

DJ replayed that last sentence in his head to make sure he didn't misunderstand. "The… the Brassiere? Are you serious?"

The Harpygriff nodded.

"But, hey, listen," DJ stammered. "I'm really not that special. I haven't slain monsters or rescued maidens or anything. Why would the Goddess pick *me* to see it?"

"Because you have no thirst for glory," the Harpygriff said. "All who have set foot here yearn to be remembered. To become legends, lauded and envied through the halls of history. The Goddess saw your soul—your pure soul, untethered to your mortal body—and offered you that glory, but you denied it. That is what makes you worthy of the Brassiere."

DJ nodded stiffly, coughed, then stood. "Wow. Okay then. Um… do I *have* to see it? Or is it optional?"

"You must."

"All right," DJ said as he dusted himself off. "Let's do this, I guess. Where is it? You're going to bring my friends back, right?"

"Your friends will remain safe," the Harpygriff said, "but you must first see the Brassiere. They shall return once you've handled it for yourself. Until then, they shall remain hidden."

The Harpygriff pointed to a pedestal that had suddenly appeared in the middle of the Temple. DJ breathed deep and moved toward it, stepping over the broken stone and growing moss.

The Brassiere of Uh. The Artifact that had eluded adventurers since the beginning of time. It stood on a pedestal facing him, cups out, straps placed delicately on hooks, fully displayed in its feminine glory.

DJ swallowed before he picked it up and explored it. He had to admit it was a pretty thing—dark purple with lacey edges, built for comfort and support with a little sass. As he turned it about, he realized this held up the Goddess's gazongas as she crafted the territory. The thought made him blush and he put the Brassiere back, hanging the straps back on their hooks.

"Are you finished, Sir Knight?" the Harpygriff asked.

"Yeah, definitely."

Thought my first time handling a bra would be a little different, he thought as he wiped his hands.

"It is well," the Harpygriff said. "The Brassiere shall return to its resting place, and your friends shall rejoin you."

In a flash of light, Riley, Francis, and Steve all appeared inside the Temple's door, rubbing their eyes as if awakening from a dream. DJ's heart leaped and he sprinted toward them. They were just getting their bearings when DJ hugged them tightly one by one.

"What happened?" Riley asked as DJ let her go. "First we were outside, and then"—she noticed the Harpygriff—"*Hundred Hells!*"

"Language!" Steve cried through DJ's squeeze. "This place is most sacred, Miss Riley!"

"What is…?" Francis pointed awe-stricken at the Harpygriff.

"That's, uh, the Harpygriff," DJ said. "It killed me a few minutes ago. But then I talked to the Goddess—I think—I passed some sort of test—I guess—and she brought me back to life and let me see her Brassiere. So yeah, I'm the only one who's ever seen it, and we got the wrong Temple. This is the Temple of the Brassiere, not the Amulet. That about sums it up."

Everyone stared as if he had goblins crawling out of his

ears.

The Harpygriff bowed. "It is true. The Goddess offered him great power and prestige, and he denied both. Instead, he said he would trade it all to see you three again. And his father."

Riley's eyes grew large and shiny. "Really DJ? You said that?"

DJ nodded sheepishly. Without warning, Francis scooped him up in a back-breaking hug. DJ could barely breathe, but Francis clutched him as if would never have another chance.

"*Thank you*, young knight," he whispered with a shaking voice. "Thank you."

When Francis released him, DJ coughed thickly. Steve put his arm around DJ. The friar smiled wide. "I am most honored to know you, Sir DJ! I'm glad you are my friend!"

DJ put his arm around Friar Steve and squeezed his shoulder. The friar turned a little pink.

Dad's never gonna believe this one either, DJ thought. After fearing that he'd never see Sir Dashing again, the thought of returning home put a lump in DJ's throat.

"Now that your mission is complete," the Harpygriff concluded, "I have been instructed to send you home."

"Send us home?" DJ repeated. "You can do that?"

The Harpygriff nodded.

"Wow," DJ said. "Well… no time like the present, I guess. Are you guys ready?" Everyone gave their affirmative. He turned to the Harpygriff. "I don't know if I should thank you or not. You killed me."

"Trading blows with you was an honor," the Harpygriff

said with a bow. "Perhaps we shall meet again, Knight of Beregond. Until then, I wish you a plentiful bounty of peace and prosperity. Farewell."

Sparkles enveloped the crew. They grew so thick that they couldn't see anything around them. Their feet left the ground. For a short moment, they couldn't breathe. But when the sparkles faded, they were no longer in the Temple of the Goddess.

All around them, they heard the buzzing of busy townspeople. Stone buildings towered over them. A wafting breeze rich with sea salt licked at their weathered clothing. And not far away, a clock tower stretched to the sky. DJ held his hand against the sun and the realization hit him.

They were back in Beregond.

"Well, I'll be…" Francis muttered as he looked all around.

Glee swelled in DJ's chest. There was still one face he needed to see. He said, "I'll be right back!" Then he dug his feet into the cobblestone and peeled away.

Riley called after him, but he didn't listen. DJ sprinted through the plaza, headed for the upper district. As he went, townspeople gave him odd looks. Most ignored him, but others offhandedly asked if that was Sir Dashing's son back from his quest.

When he reached home, DJ ran for the door and slammed it open. There it was—the dining table and the dragon heads. The light streaming in from tall windows. And not far away, Sir Dashing stood with free weights scattered at his feet. The veins bulged on his arms from a fresh workout.

He dropped two dumbbells as soon as DJ barged in. The

old knight's face slackened like he saw the Goddess herself.

"*DJ!*" he cried. "How did you get back so soon? I only read the ravenpost about the dragon yester—"

Sir Dashing didn't get to finish. DJ tackled him with a hug, burying his face in Sir Dashing's chest. The old knight held him tightly, stroking his dark hair. DJ's voice was shaky and tender when he finally brought himself to speak.

"I missed you, Dad," he said.

"I missed you too, my son. Very much." Sir Dashing let the moment hang then sniffed loudly. "Not to ruin the moment, but… you're in desperate need of a bath."

26

While DJ took that bath, Sir Dashing rushed to Master Maeser's mansion to inform the governor of DJ's return. Master Maeser wanted full details on his excursions—there might even be a celebration if the heroics were bold enough. All of the adventurers were expected to attend: DJ, Riley, Francis, and Steve.

DJ fashioned his knightly red cape and lashed his sword around his waist. Underneath, he put on fine clothing of silver silk laced with gold. It felt like a breath of fresh air after wearing rugged travel clothes for months on end. He also did his best to comb his unruly hair, but after so much time abroad, it had nearly gotten a mind of its own.

When DJ and Sir Dashing arrived at Master Maeser's mansion, the other adventurers were waiting for them. Riley wore an emerald green dress and her hair had been brushed. Her father stood over her shoulder—a portly man with a thick face and even thicker hands. He glowered at DJ a little, as if he thought DJ had kidnapped her himself. Francis had his best tunic on. Steve looked mostly the same, but his robes weren't frayed and dusty from travel.

The guards welcomed them and pulled the double doors open. Inside the mansion's great hall, a red carpet led to a throne dais where Master Maeser waited for them. All along the hall's edges, light streamed in from stained glass windows that painted bright colors across the cream stone. Guards stood sentinel all around. As the party marched forward, Master Maeser stood from his seat.

"Travelers!" he said. "Welcome home to the Jewel of Westfall! Please, tell me of your travels. My ears are itching. Sir Dashing, come join me. You should look at your son's face while he unravels his tales."

Sir Dashing joined Master Maeser on the dais and gave DJ a wink. DJ's lips twitched into a smile. He looked over his shoulder at his friends, but they all just gave him supportive nods. He cleared his throat and spun a tapestry of adventure from Vennick to Devin King. He didn't go into excruciating detail but gave just enough to enthrall his audience. They gasped and awed and frowned at all the right moments.

But the last part gave them pause. Once DJ got to the Temple of the Brassiere and the Harpygriff, Master Maeser's smile faded and he drummed his fat fingers on the chair. And all around them, guards whispered to one another.

"…the Harpygriff transported us back here, and that's how we made it home so fast." DJ finished.

Master Maeser nodded curtly. He pinched a speck of dust off his seat, flicked it away, then smacked his lips. "No one in

Uh's history has ever beheld the Brassiere of the Goddess." A stiff pause. "You expect me to believe that you, a boy still shy of manhood, are its sole witness?"

DJ frowned, incensed at his honor being challenged. Sir Dashing scowled at the governor's assertion but didn't speak up. DJ tried to keep the heat out of his voice. "It's the truth, Master Maeser."

"Did any of you see it?" Master Maeser motioned to his friends. "Where were you during the boy's so-called battle?"

The three of them stammered a little, but Francis was the first to speak. "I'm not sure. The memory is unclear… but I remember approaching the Temple's door, there was darkness for a time, then I saw DJ with the Harpygriff."

"That's what I remember, too," Riley said. "But Master Maeser, DJ wouldn't lie. That's not who he is."

"Sir DJ is most honorable, my lord!" Steve yipped. "I have seen it myself—"

"Enough," Master Maeser held up a hand.

"Master," Sir Dashing leaned in and spoke with a smooth voice. "What would my son have to gain by weaving untrue tales? He's already been made a knight."

"Don't let your feelings for the boy cloud your judgment, Sir Dashing," Master Maeser sneered. "His motive is obvious. He's tired of living in your shadow, that one. Had to weave his own tale that put himself above you. I know a tall tale when I hear one and *that*"—he pointed—"is a gigantic tale indeed. Sir Dashing's *son* and the Goddess's Brassiere? *Bah!*" His eyes narrowed on DJ. "I have half a mind to strip you of your title for this lie."

Guards around the room whispered again. DJ's friends stayed still with anger, along with Sir Dashing, waiting for DJ's response. The ire grew inside DJ and his face became hot. Calling him a liar in front of his friends and family was infuriating, but he couldn't care less about his knightly title. That's what drove him to his next words.

"Do it, then!" DJ barked.

The air sucked out of the great hall. Master Maeser watched DJ with a mouth half-open, on the cusp of speaking some strong words, but DJ's response stalled him. No one spoke or so much as breathed. Even Sir Dashing was stunned to silence.

"Yeah, you heard me!" DJ hollered. "Freaking do it! I never deserved the title and you were stupid to give it to me in the first place! Knighting me because you couldn't knight my dad *twice?* Who *does* that?"

Master Maeser's face reddened with anger, but DJ didn't stop.

"I don't care about being a knight," he said, "It doesn't change what I've seen. I just feel stupid that I had to travel all the way across the territory before I learned to *like myself.* A title is just a title. It's not who I am. But I'm not lying, Master Maeser. I saw the Brassiere of the Goddess. So do what you want."

Master Maeser's lip twitched and his fingers tightened on his arm rest. Then he gave a sharp nod. "So be it." He turned to a guard. "See that it is written this day. Sir Dashing Junior is stripped of his knightly title and his no longer recognized as a Knight of Beregond."

Riley, Francis, and Steve raised their voices in protest, but Master Maeser silenced them. DJ didn't budge. He meant every word that he said, and he expected that to be the end of it.

But Sir Dashing had different plans. He stood so swiftly that his golden hair whipped. He stepped off the throne dais to face Master Maeser. His body bristled and his blue eyes became razors.

"Master Maeser," he said, "you believe that I would raise a *liar?*"

The air vanished from the room again. Every guard watched unblinkingly. The governor's countenance changed—like a child who had been caught with their hand in a cookie jar. He swallowed hard through his turkey neck and coughed a little as his face went pale. He sat up and spoke with his hands as if it would soothe Sir Dashing. "Please, Sir Dashing, it's just that, nobody has ever *seen* the Brassiere of the Goddess. He's just a boy still. It's not reasonable that—"

"Answer my question, Maeser," Sir Dashing said. He took a threatening step forward. "With this accusation, you have challenged both his honor and mine. Now answer me this truly. *Do you believe I raised a liar?*"

Master Maeser couldn't answer. His jaw bounced up and down as if trying to form words, but nothing came out. DJ tried not to smile. Sir Dashing had never been put in a position where he had to defend DJ against a major authority, and DJ had always wondered what he would do. This was not disappointing.

"If you strip him of his title," Sir Dashing continued, "strip me of mine as well. If you truly believe I would raise a young man that would weave such fables for false glory, then I'm surely to blame as his father. Make the choice, Maeser. *Both* of us, or *neither* of us."

DJ's eyes widened. The political impact of the demand wasn't lost on him. If DJ stayed a knight, nothing would change for Master Maeser. But if Master Maeser stripped Sir Dashing of his title, there would be an uproar—not just in Beregond, but across the territory. Sir Dashing's fame was too widely known. The decision could tank Master Maeser's public approval and very well put his career in jeopardy. DJ never realized what an effective politician his father could be.

Master Maeser shriveled in his chair, teetering between anger and fear. He felt every pair of eyes on him, expectant and waiting. After a tense moment, he finally conceded. "Fine." He turned to a guard. "Strike my last command. The boy and Sir Dashing will retain their titles as Knights of Beregond." He turned back to Sir Dashing. "But there will be no celebration or feast for the travelers. Until they can prove that they truly reached the Temple of the Brassiere and returned, *I* cannot justify a celebration. That is the best I can do."

DJ tried not to laugh. *The best you can do. Sure.*

Sir Dashing relaxed and stepped off the throne dais. "Thank you for your leniency, Master Maeser. A gentleman and a scholar, as usual. I take it our business here is concluded?"

Master Maeser nodded and pursed his lips.

"Wonderful," Sir Dashing said. "I wish you a good day." He turned on his heels and marched for the exit. He cocked his head. "Come, DJ and friends. The celebratory feast will be at my home instead. We dine immediately."

*

The gang convinced Sir Dashing to push their celebratory feast to the next day so they could rest, and the old knight reluctantly agreed. DJ went to his room to take a nap. The feeling of his feather mattress was a delicious reunion to his road-weathered bones, and he fell asleep within seconds. When he awoke from his nap, it was dark out. Through his bedroom window, a rich black sky was pocked with stars and the clock tower rose above the Beregond skyline.

The clock tower.

He smiled to himself then cast Evercloak and crept through the house. Through the streets he went, unseen, dodging guards that marched with slow feet and loud yawns. He knew they wouldn't care if he was out late, but the thought of invisibly sneaking through town was just too much fun.

DJ reached the clock tower within minutes. He found the secret key then unlocked the door and climbed the stairs. Sure enough, Riley was at the top, feet dangling over the catwalk's edge. In her hand, she clutched an uncorked bottle of wine. She looked out at a brilliant moon.

DJ slowed his pace to a creep, but she looked over her shoulder and smirked.

"I'm a ranger now," she said. "You're going to have to try harder to sneak up on me."

DJ laughed and sat down beside her, letting his feet dangle over the edge. His Evercloak spell faded and he materialized next to her. Riley took a swig of wine and handed it to him. DJ took a long sip.

"Wow," he said. "This is the good stuff. Where did you get it?"

"My dad wanted to celebrate my safe arrival."

"Does that mean he's not mad?"

Riley suppressed a laugh. "Oh, he's pissed. I'm probably grounded for the rest of my life, but he's happy I'm in one piece. He'll have to get used to seeing me go, though. Once I turn sixteen, I'm heading back out there. I already miss hunting and trapping. The forests. The mountains." She turned to DJ. "How are you?"

"I'm good."

"Yeah? You totally deserved a huge celebration. Half of Beregond should be getting drunk in the plaza right now."

DJ grinned and shrugged. "Probably. But I don't mind. People will hear that we visited the Temple of the Brassiere and most of them won't believe it, and I don't blame them. For me, just the adventure was worth it. And the people we met… man, I wish we could have seen them on the way back. Pebble and Brooks are gonna be so mad that we didn't stop by. We should probably write them some ravenpost and explain."

"I'm sure they'll give us hell at the wedding."

Wedding. Love. The thoughts hopped from one thing to another in DJ's head. He felt himself turn pink, and he almost hesitated to ask, but he let courage take hold. "So… you remember what we talked about way back before Blight's

Respite?"

"About being more than friends?"

"Have you thought about it?"

Riley nodded. "I have."

DJ swallowed and braced himself. His stomach fluttered and his face turned hot.

Riley turned to him and said, "I think it's worth a try."

DJ's heart soared. "Wait, *really?*"

"But you have to *promise,*" she said, pointing a finger in his face, "that we'll always be friends. No matter what. This is a test run, but if it doesn't feel right, we *have* to stay friends. Deal?"

DJ nodded vigorously. "Deal." After another nervous swallow, he asked, "So, do we… kiss? Or…?"

Riley blew a raspberry. "No, you idiot. You have to take me on some proper dates first. I'll kiss you whenever I'm ready. But you can hold my hand tonight if you want."

DJ's heart leaped again. "Okay!" He took it, and he immediately felt self-conscious about how sweaty his palm was. Riley didn't say anything, though. She just looked to the night sky. DJ wondered if her heart thumped as hard as his.

Not even a minute passed before they heard footsteps climbing the stairs behind them. DJ and Riley exchanged worried looks. Was it the clock tower manager coming to kick them out? They had never been caught before. But when they turned to see who it was, their faces lit up. It was a seven-foot orc and a sleepy-looking friar.

Riley immediately got up and threw her arms around Francis. Steve waved at DJ, and DJ returned the gesture.

"Francis! Steve!" he said. "How did you know we were up here?"

"You mentioned a time or two that this was your little spot," Francis smiled. "Steven and I took the chance that you two would be up here, and it appears our assumption was correct."

"It is the Goddess that brings us together this night!" Steve yelped.

Together, the four of them sat under the western clock face with their feet dangling off. They watched the sea as a brilliant moon cast shimmering light over the water. The stars couldn't have been brighter. A perfect summer evening.

DJ nudged Steve. "How did the conversation go with Father Tuckett? Should we be calling you *Father* Steve now?"

Steve shook his head with the widest of grins. "My sacred calling has been approved! I shall be ordained a Priest on the morrow! The Goddess above has smiled upon our journey and granted me this gift!"

Everyone congratulated Steve and he radiated with pride. DJ thought of how fulfilling this must be for him—a boy abandoned by his parents, wandering into a monastery and finally achieving a rank of respect after decades of failure. DJ squeezed the friar's shoulder affectionately, and Steve shrugged bashfully.

"And how's the book shop?" Riley asked Francis. "Are you happy to be back?"

"Thrilled," Francis said. "I missed the books and my associates at Klepper's Keep. Carrying that ax each day was straining my back, not to mention sleeping on the ground each night. Additionally," Francis reached into his tunic and pulled out a small scrap of paper. "I came home to *this*."

"What is it?" DJ asked.

"A letter from Gasha."

The others gasped with delight, but Riley gasped the loudest.

"It appears that not long after we left," Francis continued, "a pack of druids came through the Nether Regions and sold a ravenpost bird to her. They trained it to fly to Klepper's Keep, so now she and I can keep a correspondence. I wrote her back immediately."

Riley squealed and clutched Francis's arm. "What does it say? Tell us *everything!*"

"That is between me and her," Francis grinned. "But she sends her regards to the lot of you." He turned his attention to DJ. "Are you well, young knight? I know our journey didn't end as expected."

As DJ looked upon his friends, his insides glowed. Pushing down a smile was impossible. "Yeah. Better than ever, honestly. Things are perfect."

DJ sneaked his hand into Riley's again. Francis and Steve traded smug glances. And together, they stared across a moonlit sea and talked for a good while, recounting recent memories. They murmured and gasped and laughed until tears came out. But with time, sleep gnawed at their eyes, and they all decided to retreat to their homes. DJ gave Riley's hand one last squeeze before he cast Evercloak and sneaked back to the upper district.

Surprisingly, the door was unlocked when he got home.

He frowned but pushed the door open tentatively. Inside, Sir Dashing was waiting at the dining room table with a bottle of wine and two glasses. The eight dragon heads cast tall shadows in the flickering candlelight—one of them looked eerily like Grythure. DJ would ask his father to remove it later. Sir Dashing watched the door with a creased eyebrow, studying, half-smiling.

"An Evercloak spell?" he said, pointing. "I believe I see your faint outline! It's subtle! Ha! Even mages had trouble with me back in my day. You're becoming quite good, though, it's plain to see."

DJ invisibly closed the door then trudged into the dining area and pulled up a chair. He materialized as soon as he sat down. Sir Dashing uncorked the wine bottle.

"Here, have a glass," he said. "It's an excellent year."

"Why are you awake right now?" DJ asked. "You've always told me that adequate rest is best for muscle growth and healthy skin."

Sir Dashing poured the wine in both glasses. "I heard you sneak out and assumed you were spending time with Riley, so I chose not to interrupt you."

DJ smirked. "Nothing gets past the great Sir Dashing."

Sir Dashing lifted his wine glass. DJ lifted his. They clinked together, and the Dashings took a drink.

"By the way," DJ said as he smacked his lips. "Thanks for standing up for me earlier."

"I'll always stand up for you, DJ," Sir Dashing said as if it were obvious. "I meant every word that I said, and I'm very proud of you. The Brassiere of the Goddess! My, oh my..." He swished his wine goblet. "I never thought it would happen in my lifetime, let alone by my own flesh and blood."

"Looks like I might have some of that Sir Dashing greatness in me."

"More than enough, I would say," Sir Dashing smiled. His tone became serious. "Listen, Son. I, uh, learned some things about myself in your absence." He took a sip and cleared his throat as if the wine would wash down rising feelings. "I've had many grand adventures, as you're well aware. And you know I'm not one to show an abundance of emotion." His eyes misted and his voice faltered. "But… I wanted to tell you that among all of my adventures, I'd say my favorite of all has been… raising you. You've become your own man, different from me in so many ways, and I think that's wonderful. I bless the day that you were left at my doorstep. If I could, I would do it all again. No question in my mind."

A lump grew in DJ's throat. He tried to laugh it out. "Wow. The great Sir Dashing, getting all mushy. You should be really embarrassed right now."

Sir Dashing laughed to ease his trembling voice. "I missed you a great deal. This home was empty without you."

DJ smiled. "I missed you too, Dad. You didn't have to take me, but you did." He lifted his glass. "To family."

Sir Dashing's eyes shimmered, he clinked DJ's glass, then took another swig. After a brief pause, he slapped his hand on the table. "But tell me more of your adventures! I need details! What of Pebble and Sir Percival Buttons?"

"Oh gosh, let me tell you," DJ said. "When we first met Buttons, he had Riley captured in a net…"

They talked until the sun came up, then DJ finally went back to bed. As he nestled into the covers and took deep breaths, he wondered how his friends across Uh were doing. The memories attached to each of them felt finer than gold. As he thought of each of one, gratitude grew in him like the rising sun, and he drifted back to sleep.

Thanks for reading! Please leave a review!

If you enjoyed The Legend of Uh, please consider leaving a review on Amazon, Goodreads, Storygraph, or wherever you leave reviews! Independent authors like me depend on positive reviews to spread the word and find more readers. Thank you so much!

Acknowledgments

First, this book is dedicated to my dad. Gary Hall was always the first to read my books and give me story development recommendations. Unfortunately, he passed away before I could even finish the first draft of *The Legend of Uh*. Which is a shame, because he would have loved it. He's the original Sir Dashing. I love him, miss him, and I think of him every day.

Second, this book is dedicated to Adam Anderson, Zach Hauser, and Brando Kersh. These guys are some of my closest friends. *The Legend of Uh* is loosely based on our first D&D campaign. Adam was our DM, Zach played Sir Percival Buttons, Brando played Pebble, and I played Friar Steve. We would adventure late into the night, stuffing our faces with potato chips and soda and laughing our heads off. I promised them that I would write a book based on our quest one day, so this is the fulfillment of that promise. I did take a lot of creative liberties, but they didn't mind. Thanks, guys.

Third, I want to thank my beta readers: Tasia Briggs, Ralene Eller, Darci Maxwell, Daniel Smith, Brady Johnson, Arianna Vincent, Kora Arnett, Spencer Merrell, and Adam Anderson. Their feedback made *The Legend of Uh* a much better book than I could have made on my own.

I also need to thank Leah Taylor for her terrific work editing this manuscript. It's rare to find a top-notch editor who's willing to give a poor indie author a generous price. She provided a thorough edit and asked meaningful questions to make my writing sharper. If you're a fellow writer, I highly recommend Leah's services.

And I'd be out of my mind not to thank the artists involved with Uh's aesthetic. C. Alexander Larson did a phenomenal cover illustration. He made my juvenile mockup shine and tolerated my nitpicky suggestions. You're the man, Al. Joe Spangler has been a friend of mine for years, and he really made the Uh map pop. This wasn't the first time I hired Joe and it probably won't be the last. You rock, Joe.

Last of all, I want to thank you. Thanks for cracking this open and giving it a read. I hope *The Legend of Uh* made you feel all of the things, because that's the reason I tell stories. Please leave a review and share it with a loved one if it made you laugh or smile. I know I laughed and smiled writing it.

ABOUT THE AUTHOR

Photo by Adam Anderson

Aaron N. Hall is the author of the Wevlian Chronicles, the Hammerfist series, *The Legend of Uh*, and multiple collections of stories and poems. When he's not writing (which isn't often), he's doing nonprofit work, lifting heavy things, reading, or sipping a cup of tea. He lives in Utah.

For information on upcoming books, visit **aaronnhall.com**.

OTHER WORKS BY AARON N. HALL

The Wevlian Chronicles
Foreordained
Purged
Awakened

The Hammerfist Series
My Name is Hammerfist
My Name is Hammerfist Vol. 2

Collections
I'm Sorry, Here's a Plasma Rifle: A Collection of Stories, Poems, and Pastry Recipes
Love Letters to a House on Fire: Stories, Poems, and Ransom Notes

www.ingramcontent.com/pod-product-compliance
Lightning Source LLC
Chambersburg PA
CBHW032116310726
48972CB00001B/241